Dear Target Guest,

You're about the read a ⬛⬛⬛⬛⬛⬛⬛⬛⬛ time in my life. Axi and ⬛⬛⬛⬛⬛⬛⬛ based their story on a woman I loved very deeply in my thirties. Last year, my publisher invited me into the office to talk about the power of story, and I shared what happened to Jane.

Here's what I said:

In my thirties, I was very much in love with a woman. Terrific, terrific love story for me. In our early thirties, we were in the post office up on 67th and Broadway when she fell over and had a seizure. We discovered she had a brain tumor and a limited amount of time to live. She went on living for two more years, but the story we told one another is, "Isn't it lucky you didn't die that day in the post office and we have today to be together?" The power of that story took us through those two years, and to this day, it's still one of the most—if not the most—precious times of my life. We all know that we're dying, but we don't really get it. But we did know that Jane was dying, and we really got it, and it made us live every day to the fullest and try to do special things. To this day, it's something that drives me to act rather than just talk about things.

Sincerely,
James Patterson

"Moving... Patterson makes readers care."

— *Winston-Salem Journal*

"An affecting love story awash in tragedy and hope... Patterson again shows us how it is done."   — *Publishers Weekly*

SUNDAYS AT TIFFANY'S

"Entertaining... Readers looking for a romantic escape will enjoy [this book]."   — *Midwest Book Review*

"A love story with an irresistible twist."

— *Woodstock Sentinel-Review* (Canada)

SUZANNE'S DIARY FOR NICHOLAS

"A love story as suspenseful as any thriller... clever, light, and as welcoming as an ocean breeze."   — *People*

"The idea is simply to curl up and enjoy... you haven't guessed how this story ends."   — *New York Times*

"Patterson has hit a home run."   — *Washington Post*

A complete list of books by James Patterson is at the end of this book.
For previews of upcoming books and more information about James Patterson,
please visit JamesPatterson.com, or find him on Facebook or at your app store.

First Love

JAMES PATTERSON
AND EMILY RAYMOND

GRAND CENTRAL
PUBLISHING

NEW YORK   BOSTON

First Love copyright © 2014 by James Patterson
Sam's Letters to Jennifer copyright © 2004 by James Patterson
Excerpt from *Private Vegas* copyright © 2014 by James Patterson
Author's Notes copyright © 2014 by James Patterson
Photographs by Sasha Illingworth

Grand Central Publishing
Hachette Book Group
1290 Avenue of the Americas
New York, NY 10104

www.HachetteBookGroup.com

Printed in the United States of America

RRD-C

Originally published in hardcover by Hachette Book Group
First Target trade edition: November 2014
10 9 8 7 6 5 4 3 2 1

Grand Central Publishing is a division of Hachette Book Group, Inc.
The Grand Central Publishing name and logo are trademarks of Hachette Book Group, Inc.

The Hachette Speakers Bureau provides a wide range of authors for speaking events. To find out more, go to www.hachettespeakersbureau.com or call (866) 376-6591.

The publisher is not responsible for websites (or their content) that are not owned by the publisher.

Library of Congress Cagaloging-in-Publication Data
Patterson, James
 First Love / by James Patterson and Emily Raymond.—First edition.
  pages cm
 ISBN 978-0-316-20704-1
 [1. Runaways—Fiction. 2. Love—Fiction. 3. Automobile travel—Fiction.
4. Cancer—Fiction. 5. Conduct of life—Fiction.] I. Raymond, Emily. II. Title.
PZ7.P27653Fit 2014
[Fic]—dc23   2013006955

ISBN 978-1-4555-8812-1 (Target pbk.)

For Jane—

In the fall of 2010, I turned in the outline for First Love *to my editor, but the story actually began many years before. I was in love with a woman named Jane Blanchard. One morning we were out for a walk in New York City. Seemingly out of nowhere, Jane suffered a violent seizure. She was sick with cancer for nearly two years after that, then died at a young age. Far too young. Janie, I miss your smile. I hope it lives on in this book, this love story that reminds me of our time together (though I don't remember stealing any cars).*

—J.P.

prologue

one

OKAY, I MAY NOT BE PUTTING MYSELF IN the best possible light by admitting this, but let me say right at the start that I was such a straight arrow, such a little do-gooder, that skipping my last two classes that day (AP physics and AP English) made me so insanely, ridiculously jittery that it actually occurred to me this whole crazy plan wasn't going to be worth it.

Looking back on it now, I can't believe I was *this close* to backing out of the most beautiful, funny, painful, and life-changing experience I will ever have.

What an idiot I was.

I was at Ernie's Pharmacy & Soda Fountain, and I had about five hundred butterflies throwing an epic party in my stomach. The toes of my vintage Frye cowboy boots kept knocking against the counter, until Ernie—who's about a million years old and pretty much a total grouch—told me to quit it. Ernie is one Nickelback concert away from complete deafness, though, so I took my boots off and kept knocking away.

I was glad he didn't ask why I was sitting in his ancient shop, drinking a giant coffee (which I needed like I needed a hole in the head), instead of two blocks down the street at Klamath Falls High School, listening to Mr. Fox blather on about the space-time continuum. Because what would I have said?

Well, Ernie—Mr. Holman, I mean—I'm waiting for a boy I could never date, and I'm about to ask him to do something so major that it's going to either save our lives or completely destroy us.

Ernie doesn't care much for teen angst, which is probably why practically no one I know ever comes to his shop—that and the fact that all his candy has dust on it and the Snickers bars are hard enough to use as crowbars.

But I don't mind. And neither does the boy I mentioned. Ernie's is *our* place.

That boy had sent me a note earlier in the day. He'd some-how gotten it inside my locker, even though he doesn't go to my school anymore and we have Navy SEAL–type security guards to protect us against God-knows-what (rioting due to sheer small-town boredom, maybe).

Axi —

So, you got earth-moving news, huh?

I'm shocked you think you can surprise me —

or surprised you think you can shock me.

Or something like that.

You're the word nerd.

Well, anyway, can't wait to hear it.

Ernie's. 1:15.

Yeah, that means <u>cutting class</u>.

No excuses.

— Your favorite "scalawag"

That's Robinson for you. I'd jokingly called him a scalawag once, and he'd never let me forget it. He's almost seventeen years old. My best friend. My partner in crime.

I heard the front door open and could tell he'd arrived by the way Ernie's face perked up like someone had just handed him a present. Robinson has that effect on people: when he walks into the room, it's like the lights get brighter all of a sudden.

He came over and clapped a hand on my shoulder. "Axi, you dope," he said (affectionately, of course). "Never drink Ernie's coffee without a doughnut." He leaned in close and whispered, "That stuff will eat a giant hole in your guts." Then he straddled the stool next to me, his legs lanky and slim in faded Levi's. He was wearing a flannel shirt, even though it was late May and seventy-five degrees outside.

"Hey, Ernie," he called, "did you hear the Timbers fired their coach? And can we get a chocolate cruller?"

Ernie came over, shaking his grizzled head. "Soccer!" he groused. "What Oregon needs is a pro baseball team. That's a real sport." He put the doughnut on an old chipped plate and said, "On the house."

Robinson turned to me, grinning and pointing a thumb at Ernie. "I love this guy."

I could tell the feeling was mutual.

"So," Robinson said, giving me his full attention, "what's this crazy idea of yours? Are you finally going to apply for your learner's permit? Have you decided to drink a whole beer? Are you going to quit doing your homework so religiously?"

He's always getting on me for being a good girl. Robinson thinks—and my dad agrees—that he's such a bad boy because he quit high school, which he found "insufficiently compelling" and "populated by cretins" (*cretins* being a word that I taught him, of course). Personally, I think he has a point there.

"I'm probably going to fail everything but English," I said, and I wasn't exaggerating. My GPA was about to take a nose-dive, because finals were coming up, and with any luck, I wasn't going to be around to take them. A week ago, knowing that would have kept me up at night. But I'd managed to stop caring, because if this plan worked, life as I knew it was about to change.

"Knowing you, that seems highly unlikely," Robinson said. "And so what if you're a little distracted and you—God forbid—get a B plus on something? You're busy writing the Great American Novel—*ow!*"

I'd swatted him on the arm. "Please. Between school and taking care of dear ol' Dad, I haven't had *any* time to write." My dad hit a rough patch a few years ago, and he's been trying to drink his way out of it. Needless to say, the strategy isn't working that well. "Can we focus on the matter at hand?" I asked.

"Which is...?"

"I'm running away," I said.

Robinson's mouth fell open. By the way, unlike yours truly, he never had braces and his teeth are perfect.

"And FYI, you're coming, too," I added.

Two

"DID YOU HEAR THAT, ERNIE?" ROBINSON called. I'd have told him he sounded gobsmacked, but he'd never let me forget that particular vocabulary word, either.

Of course, Ernie hadn't heard anything, not even Robinson's question. So Robinson pushed away the doughnut and stared at me like he'd never seen me before. It's not often I can surprise him, so I was enjoying this.

"Did you ever read that copy of *On the Road* I gave you?" I demanded.

Now Robinson looked sheepish. "I started it…"

I rolled my eyes. I'm forever giving Robinson books and he's forever giving me music, but since he's distractible and my iPod is dead, that's usually about as far as it gets. "Well, Sal— who's really just Jack Kerouac, the author—and his friends go all over the country, and they meet crazy people and dance in dive bars and climb mountains and bet on horse races. We're going to *do* that, Robinson. We're leaving this dump behind and taking an epic road trip. Oregon to New York City—with stops along the way, of course."

Robinson was blinking at me. *Who* are *you?* the blinks were asking.

I sat up straighter on my stool. "First we're going to see the redwoods, because those things are totally mystical. Then we'll hit San Francisco and Los Angeles. East to the Great Sand Dunes in Colorado. Then Detroit—*Motor City*, Robinson, which is so right up your alley. Then, because you're such a speed addict, we'll ride the Millennium Force at Cedar Point. It goes, like, a hundred twenty miles an hour! We'll go to Coney Island. We'll see the Temple of Dendur at the Metropolitan Museum of Art. We'll do anything and everything we want!"

I knew I sounded nuts, so I spread out the crumpled map to show him how I'd figured it all out. "Here's our route," I said. "That purple line is us."

"Us," he repeated. Clearly it was taking him a while to wrap his head around my proposition.

"*Us*. You have to come," I said. "I can't do it without you."

This was true, in more ways than I could admit to him, or even to myself.

Robinson suddenly started laughing, and it went on so long and hard I was afraid it was his way of saying *No way in hell, you totally insane person who looks like Axi but is clearly some sort of maniac.*

"If you don't come, who's going to remind me to have a doughnut with my coffee?" I went on, not ready for him to get a skeptical, sarcastic word in edgewise. "You *know* I have a terrible sense of direction. What if I get lost in LA and the Scientologists find me, and suddenly I believe in Xenu and aliens? What if I get drunk in Las Vegas and marry a stranger? Who's going to poke me in the ribs when I start quoting Shakespeare? Who's going to protect me from all that? You can't let a sixteen-year-old girl go across the country by herself. That would be, like, morally irresponsible—"

Robinson held up a hand, still chuckling. "And I may be a scalawag, but I am not *morally irresponsible*."

Finally, the guy says something! "Does that mean you're coming?" I asked. Holding my breath.

Robinson gazed up at the ceiling. He was torturing me and he knew it. He reached for the plate and took a thoughtful bite of cruller. "Well," he said.

"Well, *what?*" I was kicking the counter again. Hard.

He ran his hand through his hair, which is dark and always a little bit shaggy, even if he's just gotten it cut. Then he turned and looked at me with his sly eyes. "Well," he said, very calmly, "hell yes."

part one

1

IT WAS 4:30 AM WHEN I WOKE UP AND pulled my backpack out from under the bed. I'd spent the last few nights obsessively packing and unpacking and repacking it, making sure I had exactly what I needed and no more: a couple of changes of clothes, Dr. Bronner's castile soap (good for "Shave-Shampoo-Massage-Dental-Soap-Bath," says the label), and a Swiss Army knife that I'd swiped from my dad's desk drawer. A camera. And, of course, my journal, which I carry everywhere.

Oh, and more than fifteen hundred dollars in cash, because I'd been the neighborhood's best babysitter for going on five years now, and I charged accordingly.

Maybe there was a part of me that always knew I was going to split. I mean, why else didn't I blow my money on an iPad and a Vera Wang prom dress, like all the other girls in my class?

I'd had that map of the US on my wall for ages, and I'd stare at it and wonder what Colorado or Utah or Michigan or Tennessee is like.

I can't believe it took me as long as it did to get up the guts to leave. After all, I'd watched my mom do it. Six months after my little sister, Carole Ann, died, Mom wiped her red-rimmed eyes and took off. Went back East where she'd grown up, and as far as I know, never looked back.

Maybe the compulsion to run away is genetic. Mom did it to escape her grief. My dad escapes with alcohol. Now I was doing it...and it felt strangely *right*. At long last. I could almost forgive Mom for splitting.

I slipped on my traveling clothes and sneakers—saying good-bye to my favorite boots—and hoisted my backpack onto my shoulder, cinching the straps tight. I was going to miss this apartment, this town, this *life*, like an ex-con misses his jail cell, which is to say: Not. At. All.

My dad was asleep on the ugly living room couch. It used to have these pretty pink flowers on it, but now they look sort of brownish orange, like even fabric plants could die of neglect in our apartment. I walked right by and slipped out the front door.

My dad gave a small snort in his sleep, but other than that, he never even stirred. In the last few years, he'd gotten pretty used to people leaving. Would it really matter if another member of the Moore family disappeared on him?

Out in the hallway, though, I paused. I thought about him

waking up and shuffling into the kitchen to make coffee. He'd see how clean I'd left it, and he'd be really grateful, and maybe he'd decide to come home from work early and actually cook us a family dinner (or a what's-left-of-the-family dinner). And then he'd wait for me at the table, the way I'd waited so many nights for him, until the food got cold.

Eventually, it would dawn on him: I was gone.

A dull ache spread in my chest. I turned and went back inside.

Dad was on his back, his mouth slightly open as he breathed, his shoes still on. I put out a hand and touched him lightly on the shoulder.

He wasn't a horrible father, after all. He paid the rent and the grocery bill, even if it was me who usually did the shopping. When we talked, which wasn't often, he asked me about school and friends. I always said everything was great, because I loved him enough to lie. He was doing the best he could, even if that best wasn't very good.

I'd written about eight hundred drafts of a good-bye note. The Pleading One: *Please try to understand, Dad, this is just something I have to do.* The Flattering One: *It's your love and concern for me, Dad, that give me the strength to make this journey.* The Literary One: *As the great Irish playwright George Bernard Shaw wrote, "Life isn't about finding yourself. Life is about creating yourself." And I want to go create myself, Dad.* The Pissy One: *Don't worry about me, I'm good at taking care of myself. After all, I've been doing it since Mom left.* In the end, though, none of them seemed right, and I'd thrown them all away.

I bent down closer. I could smell beer and sweat and Old Spice aftershave.

"Oh, Daddy," I whispered.

Maybe there was a tiny part of me that hoped he'd wake up and stop me. A small, weak part that just wanted to be a little girl again, with a family that wasn't sick and broken. But *that* sure wasn't going to happen, was it?

So I leaned in and kissed my father on the cheek. And then I left him for real.

2

Robinson was waiting for me in the back booth of the all-night diner on Klamath Avenue, two blocks from the bus station. Next to him was a backpack that looked like he'd bought it off a train-hopping hobo for a chicken and a nickel, and his face made me think of a watch-dog resting with one eye open. He looked up at me through the steam rising from his coffee.

"I ordered pie," he said.

As if on cue, the waitress delivered a gooey plate of blueberry pie and two forks. "You two are up early," she said. It was still dark. Not even the birds were awake yet.

"We're vampires, actually," Robinson said. "We're just having a snack before bed." He squinted at her name tag and then smiled his big, gorgeous smile at her. "Don't tell on us, okay,

Tiffany? I don't need a stake through my heart. I'm only five hundred years old — *way* too young and charming to die."

She laughed and turned to me. "Your boyfriend's a flirt," she said.

"Oh, he's not my boyfriend," I said quickly.

Robinson's response was almost as quick. "She asked me out, but I turned her down."

I kicked him under the table and he yelped. "He's lying," I told her. "It's the other way around."

"You two are a comedy act," Tiffany said. She wasn't that much older than we were, but she shook her head like we were silly kids. "You should take that show on the road."

Robinson took a big bite of pie. "Believe me, we're gonna," he said.

He shoved the plate toward me, but I shook my head. I couldn't eat. I'd managed to keep a lid on my nerves, but now I felt like jumping out of my skin. When had I ever done anything this crazy, this monumental? I never even broke my curfew.

"Hurry up with that pie," I said. "The bus to Eureka leaves in forty-five minutes."

Robinson stopped chewing and stared at me. "Pardon?"

"The *buuuuus*," I said, drawing it out. "You know, the one we're getting on? So we can get the heck out of here?"

Robinson cracked up, and I considered kicking him again, because it doesn't take a genius to tell the difference between being laughed *with* and laughed *at*. "What's so funny?"

He leaned forward and put his hands on mine. "Axi, Axi, Axi," he said, shaking his head. "This is the trip of a lifetime. We are *not* going to take it on a Greyhound bus."

"What? Who's in charge of this trip, anyway?" I demanded. "And what's so bad about a bus?"

Robinson sighed. "*Everything* is bad about a bus. But I'll give you some specifics so you'll stop looking at me with those big blue eyes. This is *our* trip, Axi, and I don't want to share it with a dude who just got out of prison or an old lady who wants to show me pictures of her grandkids." He pointed a forkful of pie at me. "Plus, the bus is basically a giant petri dish for growing superbacteria, and it takes way too long to get anywhere. Those are your two bonus reasons."

I threw up my hands. "Last I checked, we don't have a private jet, Robinson."

"Who said anything about a plane? We're going to take a car, you dope," he said. He leaned back in the booth and crossed his hands behind his head, totally smooth and nonchalant. "And I do mean *take* one."

3

"WHAT ARE YOU *DOING?*" I HISSED AS Robinson led us down one of the nearby side streets. His legs are about twice as long as mine, so I had to jog to keep up with him.

When we came to an intersection, I grabbed his arm and whirled him around to face me. Eye to eye. Scalawag to Ms. Straitlaced.

"Are you serious about this?" I said. "Tell me you're not serious."

He smiled. "You took care of the route. Let me take care of the ride."

"Robinson—"

He shook off my grip and slung his arm around my shoulder, big brother–style. "Now settle down, GG, and I'll give you a little lesson in vehicle selection."

"A lesson in *what?* And don't call me that." It stands for Good Girl, and it drives me absolutely nuts when he says it.

Robinson pointed to a car just ahead. "Now that, see, is a Jaguar. It's a beautiful machine. But it's an XJ6, and those things have problems with their fuel filters. You can't have your stolen car leaking gas, Axi, because it could catch on fire, and if you don't die a fiery death, well, you're definitely going to jail for grand theft auto."

We walked on a little farther, and he pointed to a green minivan. "The Dodge Grand Caravan is roomy and dependable, but we're adventurers, not soccer moms."

I decided to pretend this was all make-believe. "Okay, what about that one?" I asked.

He followed my finger and looked thoughtful. "Toyota Matrix. Yeah, definitely a good option. But I'm looking for something with a bit more flair."

By now the sun was peeking over the horizon, and the birds were up and chattering to each other. As Robinson and I walked down the leafy streets, I felt the neighborhood stirring. What if some guy stepped outside to grab the newspaper and saw us, two truants, suspiciously inspecting the neighborhood cars?

"Come on, Robinson," I said. "Let's get out of here." I was still hoping we'd make the bus. We had ten minutes left.

"I just want the perfect thing," he said.

At that moment, we saw a flash in the corner of our eyes. It was brown and fast and coming toward us. I gasped and reached out for Robinson.

He laughed and pulled me close. "Whoa, Axi, get a grip. It's only a dog."

My heart was thrumming. "Yeah, I can see that . . . now."

I could also now see it wasn't likely to be an attack dog, either. He was a small thing, with matted, shaggy fur. No collar, no tags. I took a step forward, my hand extended, and the dog flinched. He turned around and went right up to Robinson instead (of course) and licked his hand. Then the darn thing lay down at his feet. Robinson knelt to pet him.

"Robinson," I said, getting impatient, "Greyhound bus or stolen car, the time is now."

He didn't seem to hear me. His long, graceful hands gently tugged on the dog's ears, and the dog rolled onto his side. As Robinson scratched the dog's belly, the animal's leg twitched and his pink tongue lolled out of his little mouth in total canine ecstasy.

"You're such a good boy," Robinson said gently. "Where do you belong?"

Even though the dog couldn't answer, we knew. He was skinny and his fur was clumped with mud. There was a patch of raw bare skin on his back. This dog was no one's dog.

"I wish you could come with us," Robinson said. "But we have a long way to go, and I don't think you'd dig it."

The dog looked at him like he'd dig anything in the world as long as it involved more petting by Robinson. But when you're running away from your life and you can't take anything you don't need, a stray dog falls in the category of Not Necessary.

"Give him a little love, Axi," Robinson urged.

I bent down and dug my fingers into the dog's dirty coat the way I'd seen Robinson do, and when I ran my hand down the dog's chest, I could feel the quick flutter of his heart, the excitement of finding a home, someone to care for him.

Poor thing, I thought. Somehow, I knew exactly what he was feeling. He had no one, and he was stuck here.

But we weren't. Not anymore.

"We're leaving, little buddy. I'm sorry," I said. "We've just got to go."

It was totally weird, but for some reason that good-bye hurt almost as much as the one I'd whispered to my father.

4

WE LEFT THE DOG WITH ONE OF ROBIN-
son's sticks of beef jerky, then headed to the end of the block,
where Robinson pulled up short. "There it is," he whispered,
with real awe in his voice. He grabbed my hand and we hurried
through the intersection.

"There *what* is?" I asked, but of course he didn't answer me.

If things went on like this, we'd have to have a little talk—
because I didn't want a traveling companion who paid attention to 50 percent of whatever came out of my mouth. If I
wanted to be ignored, I could just stay in Klamath Falls with
my idiotic classmates and my alcoholic father.

"There is the answer," Robinson said finally, sighing so big
you'd have thought he just fell in love. He turned to me and
bent down in an exaggerated bow, sweeping his arm out like a

valet at some superfancy restaurant (the kind of place we don't have in K-Falls).

"Alexandra, milady, your chariot awaits," Robinson said with a wild grin. I rolled my eyes at him, like I always do when he does this fake-British shtick with my full name.

And then I rolled my eyes again: my so-called chariot, it turned out, was actually a *motorcycle*. A big black Harley-Davidson with whitewall tires and yards of shining chrome, and two black leather side bags decorated with silver grommets. There were tassels on the handlebars and two cushioned seats. The thing gleamed like it was straight off the showroom floor.

Robinson was beside me, whispering in some foreign language. "Twin Cam Ninety-Six V-Twin," he said, then something about "electronic throttle control and six-speed transmission" and then a bunch of other things I didn't understand.

It was an amazing bike, even I could see that, and I can hardly tell a dirt bike from a Ducati. "Awesome," I said, checking my watch. "But we *really* should keep moving."

That was when I realized Robinson was bending toward the thing with a screwdriver in his hand.

"Are you out of your *mind?*" I hissed.

But Robinson didn't answer me. Again.

He was going to *hot-wire* the thing. *Holy s—*

I ran to the other side of the street and ducked down between two cars. Adrenaline rushed through my veins and I pressed my eyes shut.

There was no way this was happening, I told myself. No way he was going to actually get the thing started, no way this was how our journey would begin.

I had it all planned out, and it looked nothing like this.

Then the roar of an engine split open the quiet morning. I opened my eyes and a second later Robinson's feet appeared, one on either side of the Harley.

We're breaking the law! I should have screamed. But my mind simply couldn't process this change in plans. I couldn't say anything at all. I just thought: *He's running away in cowboy boots! That is so not practical!* And: *Why didn't I bring mine?*

"Stand up, Axi," Robinson yelled. "Get on."

I was rooted to the spot, my chest tight with anxiety. I was going to have a heart attack right here on Cedar Street, in between a pickup and a Volvo with a MY OTHER CAR IS A BROOM bumper sticker. So much for my great escape!

But then Robinson reached down and hauled me up, and the next thing I knew I was sitting behind him on the throbbing machine with the engine revving.

"Put your arms around me," he yelled.

I was so heart-and-soul terrified that I did.

"Now hang on!"

He put the thing in gear and we took off, the engine thundering in my ears. My dad was probably going to wake up on the couch and wonder if he'd just heard the rumble of an early-summer storm.

We shot past the Safeway, past the high school football

field, past the Reel M Inn Tavern, where every Friday night my dad hooked himself up to a Budweiser IV, and past the "Mexican" restaurant (where they put Parmesan cheese on top of their burritos).

Yeah, Klamath Falls. It was the kind of place that looked best in a rearview mirror.

Seeing it flash past me, feeling the rush of the wind in my face, I suddenly didn't care if we woke up the entire stinking town.

Eat my dust! I wanted to shout.

Robinson let out a joyful whoop.

We'd done it. We were free.

5

THIS WASN'T ANYTHING LIKE THE MOPED
I rode once. It wasn't like anything I'd ever felt before. We
weren't even on the highway yet, but already it felt like we
were flying.

Then above the roar of the engine I heard Robinson's voice.
"I don't want a tickle / 'Cause I'd rather ride on my motorsickle!" It
was an old Arlo Guthrie song. I knew the words because my
dad used to sing them to me when I was a little girl.

*"And I don't want to diiiiie / Just want to ride on my motorcy...
cle,"* I joined in, even though I can't carry a tune to save my life.

Robinson leisurely steered us past strip malls on the outskirts of town. He was whistling now (because if you ever want
to blow out your vocal cords, try singing loudly enough to be
heard over a Harley). He was acting like it was no big deal to be
zipping away on a stolen motorcycle.

My God, what in the world did we think we were doing? We were supposed to be on a bus, and instead we were on a stolen motorcycle that cost more than my dad made in two years. Escape was one thing, but robbery took it to another level. Suddenly I couldn't stop picturing the disappointment on my dad's face when he posted my bail, or the headline in the *Klamath Falls Herald and News* — GOOD GIRL GONE BAD — next to an unflattering mug shot that washed out my blue eyes and pale skin.

I tried not to imagine a cop around every bend as we headed south of the Klamath Falls Country Club, where my mom used to go for sloe gin fizzes on Ladies' Poker Night. And I kind of freaked out when we were actually acknowledged by another motorcycle rider, heading into town. As he passed, the biker dropped his arm down, two fingers angling toward the road, and Robinson mirrored the gesture.

"Don't take your hands off the handlebars!" I yelled. "Ever!"

"But it's the Harley wave," Robinson hollered.

"So?"

"So it's rude not to do it back!"

Of course, manners are useless when you're flat on your back in the bottom of a ditch. . . . I didn't say that to Robinson, though, because I had to admit, Robinson was driving the motorcycle like he'd done it a thousand times before. Had he? Didn't a person need a special license to drive a motorcycle? And what about the hot-wiring? It would've taken me that long to figure out how to start the motorcycle with a key. Yeah, we had a few things to talk about, Robinson and me.

Past the Home Depot and Eddie's 90-Days-Same-as-Cash, Robinson yelled something, but the roar of the engine swallowed his voice. I think it was "Are you ready?" I didn't know what he was talking about, but whatever it was, I was probably *not* ready. Then I noticed that the speed limit went up to fifty-five, and Robinson pulled back on the throttle.

This may be obvious, but the thing about being on a motorcycle is that there is nothing between you and the world. (Or between you and the hard pavement.) The wind roars in your face. The sun shines in your eyes like a klieg light. There is no windshield. There are no seat belts. We were going sixty-five now, and the little white needle was rising. I tightened my arms around Robinson's waist.

"What are you doing?" I yelled.

Eighty, and the roar of the wind drowned out the sound of my screaming.

Ninety, and tears were streaming from my eyes. I clung to Robinson for dear life.

One hundred, and I might as well have been on a rocket ship blasting into the stratosphere.

Adrenaline coursed through us like liquid fire. We were charged. Dangerous. The motorcycle shuddered and gained even more speed, and the wind was like a giant's merciless hand trying to push me off the back of the bike.

My life flashed before my eyes — my small, sad life.

Good riddance!

The fear was electrifying. It was terrifying and amazing,

and if I'd thought I was having a heart attack before, I was *definitely* having one now.

And I was totally, dizzyingly, thrillingly loving every second of it.

In those brief moments, I shed my small-town good-girl reputation like an ugly sweater, and I burned it in the flames of the Harley insignia. We were runaways. Outlaws. Me and Robinson. Robinson and me.

And if we died in a fiery crash—well, we'd die happy, wouldn't we?

BUT WHETHER IT WAS LUCK OR FATE OR
Robinson's driving skills, we didn't die. We rode for hours
along twisting back roads, until I felt like I'd molded myself
to Robinson's back. Like I'd become some kind of giant girl-
barnacle he'd need to pry off with that screwdriver of his.

At lunchtime we finally stopped in the town of Mount
Shasta, California. It was tucked into the lower slope of a
mountain, a giant, snow-streaked peak that's supposedly some
kind of cosmic power center.

Yeah, you heard me right.

If you believe local legend, it's home to an ancient race of
superhumans called Lemurians, who live in underground tun-
nels but surface every once in a while, seven feet tall and decked
out in white robes. In other words, Mount Shasta is totally

unlike Klamath Falls, which is the world's capital of monotony and is home to guys with names like Critter and Duke.

Also, UFOs have allegedly landed on Mount Shasta. And that's just the tip of the bizarro iceberg.

Even the smiling attendant at the Shell station was wearing a giant amethyst crystal around his neck and had a chakra diagram on his T-shirt.

Robinson returned the attendant's blissed-out grin, but his didn't come from Mount Shasta's cosmic power rays. It came from the Harley. He struck a pose, one hand on the gas tank, a thumb hooked in his belt loop, and offered me a goofy Hollywood sneer. "Am I James Dean or what? *Rebel Without a Cause?*"

I squinted at him. Though I would never admit it, Robinson kind of looked like he could be a movie star. Sure, he was a little on the skinny side, but that face of his? It belonged on a poster tacked to a tween girl's bedroom wall.

"James Dean died in a car crash. You know, because he was *speeding,*" I said. My legs were trembling so much I could barely stand. The thundering rumble of the engine had burrowed into my bones.

"I only sped once," Robinson countered. "I had to see what this bad boy could do."

"Once was plenty," I shot back, trying to sound stern. I'd loved it, sure. Because *ohmygod* it felt like flying. But I was pretty sure that—like paragliding or jumping out of an airplane—going 110 on the back of a stolen Harley was the sort of thing you only needed to do once.

Robinson walked into the station to pay for the gas and emerged with two Vitaminwaters and a Slim Jim, which, if you ask me, is like eating a pepperoni-flavored garden hose. But Robinson had loved horrible food for as long as I'd known him.

We took a little stroll into the town center. There was a guy wearing a sandwich board that read ARE YOU SAVED? But instead of a picture of Jesus or angels, there was a drawing of a green-skinned alien holding up two fingers in a peace sign. Robinson stopped to talk to him. Of course.

I ducked into a health food store that smelled like patchouli and nutritional yeast and got some vegetables for our dinner. When I came outside, Robinson was reading a flyer that the man had given him.

"We could go on a spirit quest," he said. "Meet our Star Elders."

"No way, Scalawag," I said, snatching the pamphlet from him and tossing it into a recycling bin. "As fascinating as that sounds, I spent months planning this trip, and last I checked, communing with our so-called Star Elders was not on the to-do list."

"Well, neither was stealing a motorcycle, and look how well that turned out."

He looked pretty proud of himself for that comeback.

"Okay, fine," I acknowledged. "It's been great so far. But we can't ride a hot bike across the country. For one thing, we'll get caught. And for another, I don't think my butt can take it."

Robinson laughed. "You actually look kind of annoyed right now. Are you?"

"No," I lied. "But next time, *I* pick the ride."

"Oh, Axi—" he began.

"I don't want this trip to be a huge mistake, okay?" I interrupted. "I'm not interested in jail time."

Robinson leaned over and plucked a swirly glass orb from the sidewalk display in front of the Soul Connections gift shop. He waved it in front of my face. "By everything that is cosmic and weird and awesome, I banish all doubts from your mind." He glanced at the price tag. "Only five ninety-five. A bargain!"

He dashed into the store and a moment later reappeared with the orb nestled in a purple velvet bag. He placed it in my hands. "This is magic," he said. "It will keep you from ever being annoyed at me again."

"Don't count on it," I said drily. But I couldn't help smiling at him. "Thanks. It's really pretty."

"Axi," Robinson said, his voice softer now, "if this trip is a mistake, it's the best one we'll ever make."

And somehow, by the look he gave me then, I knew he was right.

7

BY THE TIME WE STOPPED AT A CAMP-
ground in Humboldt Redwoods State Park, we'd been driving for seven hours. Robinson had stuck to the back roads,
and I wasn't complaining. My fear of getting pulled over by
cops looking for a black Harley with an Oregon plate hadn't
completely disappeared, but I was thinking about it less as
we got farther and farther from home.

The sun was low above the horizon when we pulled into the
park, and it vanished completely as we entered the green can-
opy of trees. Robinson let out a low whistle as the shadows
enveloped us.

Old-growth redwoods. How can I even describe them?
They towered above us darkly, and they felt *alive*. Not alive like
regular trees, but alive like they had souls. Like they were wise,
ancient creatures, watching with only the faintest hint of inter-

est as two road-weary teenagers walked beneath them. The air was cool and slightly damp, and the silence was profound. I felt like we were in church.

"I totally understand the whole Druid thing now," Robinson whispered.

"I think the Druids actually worshipped oak trees," I noted. "They didn't have redwoods in ancient Ireland."

"Smarty-pants," Robinson said, poking me.

I put my hand on a rough, cool trunk. "Majestic tranquillity," I said softly, seeing how the words felt in my mouth. A little too pretentious: I wouldn't be writing that down in my journal. But there were *real* writers who'd seen redwoods like these, and I could steal from them, couldn't I? " 'They are not like any trees we know, they are ambassadors from another time,' " I said.

"Huh?" said Robinson.

"John Steinbeck wrote that in *Travels with Charley*."

He sighed. "Another one of the books you gave me—"

"That you didn't read."

Robinson used to pretend he felt guilty about ignoring the stacks of books I passed to him, but eventually he stopped bothering. "I thought I was supposed to read *East of Eden* first," he said.

"Let me know when you get to it," I said. "I won't hold my breath."

"Well, you can let me know when you listen to that Will Oldham CD I got you."

"I put it on my iPod but, as you know, it's broken," I pointed out. "Your eyeballs work just fine."

We found our campsite then, a small clearing surrounded by a ring of redwoods, with a picnic bench, a fire pit, and a spigot for cold, clear water. I unhooked my tent from the backpack. It was an army-green miracle of engineering: big enough to contain two people and their sleeping bags, it weighed less than a pound and, folded up, fit into a bag the size of a loaf of Wonder Bread. Robinson eyed it, impressed.

"Watch how I set this up," I directed. "Because tomorrow night it's your job."

"I thought it was the woman's job to keep house and the man's job to hunt for food," he said, grinning slyly.

I snorted. "Are you planning to kill an elk with your screwdriver? Good luck."

"I was thinking more along the lines of a squirrel," he said, but even that was ridiculous, because Robinson would never hurt anything. I mean, the guy had to grit his teeth to kill a mosquito.

I unpacked the veggies I'd bought, plus a hunk of aged Gouda and a bag of lavash, the thin flatbread I love and couldn't get in Klamath Falls because apparently it was too *exotic*.

"Well, well, well," Robinson said as he watched me skewer mushrooms and peppers on sticks I'd stripped of their bark. "I guess you'd do all right on *Survivor*."

I rolled my eyes at him. "I paid for this stuff, Robinson. I didn't forage for wild green peppers and cheese. Now, are you going to gather some sticks for the fire or what?"

"You couldn't buy firewood, too?" he asked, but he ambled good-naturedly into the brush to find things to burn.

Soon we had a nice fire going, and we roasted our kebabs over the flickering flames. I stuck slices of cheese between pieces of lavash, wrapped them in foil, and set them near the fire until the cheese melted. When everything was ready, we leaned against a fallen log that was covered with springy green moss, which made a surprisingly comfortable backrest. We didn't have plates, and the vegetables were a bit burned in places, but it was the best dinner I'd ever had. It tasted like freedom.

Robinson complimented my cooking, but within the hour he was raiding my backpack for junk food, claiming to be suffering from vitamin overdose.

"What else do you have in here?" he demanded. "I know you're keeping Fritos or Oreos or something terrible and delicious from me." I watched as he pulled out the map, two feather-light rain ponchos, my Dr. Bronner's, my toothbrush, and my journal.

"Open that on pain of death," I warned.

Finally Robinson held up a chocolate bar, triumphant.

"Half for you, half for me," he said.

"A *quarter* for you and a *quarter* for me," I corrected. "I'm rationing."

Robinson laughed. "You're a planner, I know. You always

have everything figured out. But do you really think there's a shortage of chocolate bars on the West Coast?" He reached out and handed me a small piece of chocolate. When our fingertips touched, I twitched as if I'd been shocked. It surprised both of us.

"You're jittery all of a sudden," he said. "We're safe here, Axi. No one's going to find us." He walked over to the bike and lovingly patted its seat. "Or the hot Harley."

While Robinson fondled his new toy, I tried to calm down, breathing in that "sweeter, rarer, healthier air," as old Walt Whitman would say. Night was coming, bringing darkness and deeper silence. It seemed like in all the world, there were only the two of us.

I'd always told Robinson pretty much everything I thought about, but I couldn't tell him this: I wasn't nervous about being discovered. I was suddenly nervous about something else.

Sleeping arrangements.

INSIDE THE TENT, I UNROLLED OUR SLEEP-
ing bags. There wasn't an inch to spare. We were going to be
thisclose to each other, Robinson and me.

He was still outside the tent, throwing leaves into the fire
and watching them curl and blacken. "Do we need to string up
the packs? You know, to protect them from bears?" he called.

"There aren't any bears around here," I assured him, smooth-
ing out my bag. It was pink camo. Hideously ugly, but it'd been
on sale. "Only elk. Spotted owls. That sort of thing."

Robinson poked his head inside the tent. "Do you know
that for real?" he asked. "Or are you just saying it to make yourself feel better?" He looked me right in the eyes. He knew me
too well.

"I'm, like, sixty percent positive," I admitted. "Or less."

Robinson was unsurprised. "I'm stringing up the packs, then."

He ducked back out and I heard him rustling around. He took a long time, whether because he was new to the demands of camping or because he was sneaking more of the chocolate bar...well, that could be his secret.

When he popped his head in again, he was grinning. There was a tiny spot of melted chocolate in the corner of his mouth. "Cozy in here, isn't it?"

Then he slipped off his boots and climbed all the way inside, and cozy became something of an understatement. I felt weirdly shy. Like suddenly my body was bigger and more awkward—and more *female*—than it had ever been before. I wondered if I smelled like motor oil and BO. I noticed that Robinson smelled like campfire, like soap, like *boy*.

Robinson could have had his pick of girls from our high school. Even after he dropped out (which for everyone else who'd done it was the social kiss of death), all the cheerleaders and the student council girls still wanted to take him to prom. Sometimes I pictured them hanging off his arms, like those little game pieces in Barrel of Monkeys, brightly colored and plastic.

"I'm not interested in them," he'd say. Eventually, I'd gotten up the nerve to ask: who—or what—was he interested in? He'd laughed and slung his arm around my shoulders the way he did sometimes.

"I'm interested in you, GG," he'd said lightly. As if that settled it.

But what did that mean, really? Because as far as I could tell, he wasn't interested in me in *that* way. We'd held hands a few times, like when we were in the movie theater watching *Cabin in the Woods* or *Paranormal Activity*. And once when I'd drunk three-quarters of a beer, I had kissed him, sloppily, good night.

But that was all, folks.

Now we lay side by side, staring at the tent ceiling only three feet above our heads. I listened to the wind in the tops of the trees and the sound of Robinson's breathing, and for the first time considered what traveling together would mean in practical terms. Where was I supposed to change? What if I wanted to sleep in my underwear? What would Robinson think when he saw me in the morning, mussed and sleepy, with tousled hair and flushed cheeks and breath that could kill a small animal?

Not that that was the problem. No, the problem — or, at the very least, the Thing That Mattered — was that we would be sleeping right next to each other. Alone. Not even a stuffed teddy bear between us.

Robinson shifted, trying to make himself comfortable. No doubt he was realizing the same thing I was. I cleared my throat.

"Before you say anything," Robinson said, "here's the deal."

I could almost hear my heart doing a tiny shuffling dance.

"Stealing is — well, it's not a good thing, Axi, but it's not necessarily that bad, either. I mean, we're taking good care of the bike. And this guy's going to get it back."

That dancing ticker of mine slowed. I'd thought we were going to talk about *us*. Honestly, I was already over the stealing. *Regret is a waste of time*, my mom used to say. She'd served up that platitude a lot before she split town. Maybe it made her feel better about leaving.

"And if for some reason he doesn't get it back," Robinson went on, "his insurance covers the loss and he gets a brand-new one."

He made it sound so simple. And maybe it was. In some ways it was simpler than talking about *us*.

Robinson rolled over so he was facing me. His nose, I noticed, was sunburned. His chin was covered in faint dark stubble. I watched his Adam's apple move as he swallowed. Our eyes met, but I quickly looked away.

He reached out and brushed a piece of hair from my forehead. I held my breath.

Suddenly I understood that running away was all the thrill I could stand today. If Robinson touched any other part of me, I might explode into a million pieces.

But he didn't touch me again. He smiled. "Sweet dreams, Axi Moore," he said softly. Then he rolled back over.

Inside I ached a little, but I wasn't sure what for.

9

I STARED INTO THE DARKNESS FOR A long time, feeling the contrast between the cold, hard ground beneath me and the soft warmth of Robinson beside me. Thoughts raced through my mind endlessly: *What if Robinson and I get caught? Or if we chicken out and go back home? Or if we keep on and each night lie side by side, chaste as children? If we kiss? If we whisper the word* love, *or if it remains unsaid forever?*

It would probably only matter to me. I didn't know if it would matter to Robinson. I tentatively put my head on his shoulder, but he didn't move a muscle.

When I finally slept, I dreamed we were on the edge of a cliff, peering down. Dream-Robinson was holding my hand. "Don't worry," he said. "It only looks like a cliff. It's actually a mountain, and the way is up, not down."

Even in dreams, he was an optimist.

By the time Robinson stumbled out of the tent the next morning, looking rumpled and adorable, I'd packed our bags and plotted our route to Bolinas, a tiny town nestled between the California hills and the Pacific Ocean. I wanted to see it mostly because the town is supposed to be a secret. The people who live there are always tearing down the road signs that point to it. But that wasn't going to stop me from discovering what the big deal was about this place.

"Maybe," Robinson said teasingly as he mounted the bike, "buried deep inside the Good Girl, there's the heart of a rebel."

"Haven't I already proven that to you by suggesting this crazy trip?" I climbed up behind him and commanded, "Now, *drive*."

Naturally, we missed our turn the first time, but when we finally got there, we were a little mystified.

"*This* is what they want to keep to themselves?" Robinson asked.

The downtown consisted of two intersecting streets. There was a restaurant called the Coast Café—which, FYI, did not overlook the coast—and an old-fashioned-looking bar. I had to agree: Bolinas didn't seem particularly inspiring.

But the adjacent beach was beautiful. We kicked our shoes off and sat down in the sand, staring at the blue water and feeling the sun on our shoulders. Tanned, half-wild children ran around us, throwing rocks at seagulls. Robinson started digging his toes in the sand, and more than once I caught him looking at me, an unreadable expression on his face.

"So...what are you thinking about?" I finally asked. I hoped he didn't detect the slight edge of apprehension in my question.

"Corn dogs," Robinson answered without missing a beat.

Sometimes I could just kill him.

He could have been thinking about me, about *us*, but instead his mind had settled on wieners encased in corn batter.

We ducked into Smiley's Schooner Saloon, and Robinson walked up to the bar like it was the counter at Ernie's. "Good afternoon, sir," he said. "Two Rainiers, please, and a corn dog."

I swear, if Robinson ever had to pick a last meal, it'd be corn dogs, French fries, and a deep-fried Twinkie.

"ID?" the bartender said.

Robinson fished out his wallet. The bartender's eyes darted from Robinson's fake license to Robinson's face and back again. "Okay...*Ned Dixon*." Then he turned to me.

I shrugged. "I wasn't driving, see, so I left my license back—"

The bartender crossed his meaty arms. "Listen, *kids*, how about you head across the street and get yourself a nice ice-cream cone at the café."

"Actually, I'm lactose intol—" Robinson began, but I interrupted him.

"Oh, *I* get it!" My voice came out surprisingly fierce. "We can fight in Afghanistan, but we can't have a beer and watch the sunset?" My hands gripped the edge of the bar and I leaned forward, hostility coming off me in waves. I had no idea where

49

this was coming from, but it actually felt kind of good to be angry with someone. Someone who didn't matter, someone I would never see again.

I probably would have yelled more, but Robinson dragged me outside. Then he bent over, practically choking with laughter. "Fight in Afghanistan?" he wheezed. "Us?"

"It just came out," I said, still not sure what had just happened. I started to giggle a little, too.

Robinson wiped his eyes. "You don't even like beer."

"It was a matter of principle. A lot of people die in Afghanistan before they're allowed to buy a six-pack."

"A lot of people die every day, Axi. They don't go off on bartenders in secret towns about the unfairness of the drinking laws. I can't wait to see what you come up with next," he said, still laughing at my outburst as he strode ahead of me.

His flip tone made me stop short in the middle of the sidewalk. Yeah, people *do* die every day. Some people, like Carole Ann, die before they even learn to tie their shoes. Others die before they graduate from high school.

Hell, either one of us could die on this crazy trip.

There were so many more important things to do than buy a beer before that happened. I hurried to catch up with Robinson, who was turning the corner to where we'd parked the motorcycle in an empty lot behind the saloon. But now there was a man in a leather jacket and chaps standing right beside it, giving it a long—and much-too-close-for-my-comfort —look.

"Nice bike," the guy said. "Got a cousin in Oregon who has one exactly like it."

My lungs felt like bellows that someone had just squeezed shut. I took a step backward. Should we just run?

But Robinson didn't flinch. "Your cousin has good taste," he said. He glanced at the bike behind Chaps. "You riding a Fat Boy these days? I love those, but my girl here likes a bigger bike." His voice had taken on an easy drawl, like he and Chaps were two dudes who'd see eye to eye over a Harley.

Chaps was still sizing Robinson up: Robinson was taller but about a hundred pounds lighter. Me, I was still thinking about running—and about how Robinson had called me his girl. That sounded… interesting. But did he mean it, or was it just part of his act?

"Happy hour's almost over, y'know," Robinson said.

Chaps gave him one long, last look, then shook his head and went inside.

I was already reaching for paper and pen.

Thanks so much for letting us ride your motorcycle, I wrote. *We took really good care of it. We named it Charley.*

Robinson read over my shoulder. "We did?"

"Just now," I said. "Charley the Harley."

I'm sorry we didn't ask you if we could borrow it, but rest assured that your bike was used only for the forces of good. Sincerely, GG & the Scalawag

I tucked the note into the handlebars. "Come on. Time to find another ride," I said, like I'd been stealing cars my whole life. In all of downtown Bolinas there were only about five cars, though.

"That one," I said, pointing to a silver Pontiac.

Robinson nodded. "Dead boring," he said. "But sensible."

I could feel the tingling beginning in my limbs. Robinson took a quick look around and then got in. I ducked into the passenger side, mentally thanking the owner for leaving the doors unlocked.

From his backpack Robinson removed a small cordless drill and aimed it at the keyhole. I watched as glittering flecks of metal fell onto the seat.

He packed a drill? I thought.

A grizzled surfer was looking right at us. I smiled and waved.

"Hurry up," I hissed at Robinson.

He produced his screwdriver and inserted it into the mangled keyhole. "One more minute."

The adrenaline tingle was growing more intense. Painful, even.

"I had to break the lock pins," Robinson explained.

As if I cared! I just wanted the engine to turn on. I sucked in a deep breath. Any moment we were going to be racing out of town, and everything would return to normal — my *new* normal, that is.

That was when two people came out of the Coast Café — and began heading toward their silver Pontiac. I met the woman's eyes, saw her jaw drop open. The man started running. "Hey," he shouted. *"Hey!"*

His arms flew forward, and he was just inches from us when the engine suddenly roared to life. Robinson slammed the car into reverse and we shot backward into the street. A moment later we were blazing out of town, going fifty in a twenty-five zone.

"I'm going to miss Charley," I said, my heart pounding.

Robinson nodded. "Me too."

"But not Bolinas," I added.

"That was *your* idea," Robinson reminded me with a smirk.

I shrugged and let out a deep sigh of relief. The sun was flashing deep vermilion over the blue ocean, calming me as I watched it slip lower and then vanish before my heart rate had even returned to normal.

Amazing how beauty can be so fleeting.

10

WE DROVE ACROSS THE GOLDEN GATE
Bridge that night, gliding over a dark San Francisco Bay into
the narrow streets of the Presidio. Since the car offered a
solid roof over our heads—and since cops apparently frown
on urban camping—we decided to spend the night in the
Pontiac.

I curled up in the backseat, and Robinson folded himself,
with difficulty, into the front. There was no question of us
touching (or, as the case may be, not touching) with all that
upholstery in the way. A tiny part of me felt relieved, but a
larger part of me longed for the so-cozy-it's-claustrophobic tent.

That was my realization for the night: I was capable of missing Robinson when he was less than two feet away from me.

I was starting to develop a theory about missing things in
general. It had started when we left Charley the Harley behind,

and I hadn't stopped thinking about it the rest of the drive. If I practiced missing small things—like the rumbling ride of a motorcycle, or the faint murmur of my dad talking in his sleep, or now sleeping right next to Robinson—maybe I could get used to missing things. Then, when it came time to miss something really important, maybe I could survive it.

We listened to the radio for a while, Robinson humming along and me keeping my tuneless mouth shut until we drifted off. In the morning, fog rolling in from the bay blurred the streetlights into soft orange halos. I peered over the seat at Robinson's tangled limbs.

"Rise and shine," I sang. He opened one eye and gave me the finger.

Not everyone is a morning person.

"There's someone I want you to meet," I told him.

"Now?" Robinson asked. But I simply handed him his shoes.

There was one book I'd gotten Robinson to read in the last six months. *The Winding Road* was a memoir about growing up as the daughter of an alcoholic father (I could seriously relate) and a beauty-queen mother (ditto) in a small town in southern Oregon. The author, Matthea North, could have been me, which is maybe why I found her story so fascinating. A couple of years ago, I wrote her a fan letter. She wrote me back, and an epistolary friendship—I guess you could call it that—was born.

(*Epistolary:* a word I'm not going to use in front of Robinson.)

55

You must stop by for a visit sometime, Matthea had written. *We'll drink tea and ponder the vagaries of love, the secrets of life, the mysteries of the universe…*

If ever there was a time for that conversation, it was now.

Matthea's house was on Nob Hill, at the top of an impossibly steep street. I rang the bell and we waited nervously on the stoop. Robinson didn't even know what we were doing here, and I refused to tell him. If you ask me, a person doesn't get enough good surprises in life. Birthday, Christmas…that's only two times a year to count on.

But when the front door opened, I was even more surprised than Robinson. Since Matthea North and I had so much in common childhood-wise, I guess I thought she'd look like an older version of me: slender, medium-sized, with the full lips and wide-set eyes of a beauty-queen mother somehow diluted into a slightly less remarkable prettiness.

Matthea looked like Bilbo Baggins. In a Gypsy costume. Under five feet tall, bedecked in scarves and necklaces, she reached up to take my hand. "You must be Axi," she said. Her green eyes, set deep in rosy cheeks, positively twinkled at me.

I swallowed. "Yes!" I said brightly. "Robinson, this is…the one and only Matthea North."

He turned toward her, smiling his wide, gorgeous grin. "Hey, you wrote that book—the one about the town even worse than ours." If he was fazed by her clothes, he didn't look it.

Matthea laughed. Older ladies love Robinson.

We followed her into the darkness of her home, and already

she was chattering about how Mark Twain never said the famous line about how the coldest winter he ever spent was a summer in San Francisco, but he should have, because it was absolutely Arctic today; how birdsong had evolved over decades to compete with the sound of traffic, and weren't those sparrows outside just deafeningly loud; how she'd gotten a bad fortune in her cookie from Lucky Feng's, but did we know that it was the Japanese who'd actually invented the fortune cookie?

She motioned for us to sit on a dusty-looking Victorian couch. "I loved your short story about that old deli, Axi," she said, "the one about that girl and boy who are best friends but maybe something more—"

"Oh, yeah, thanks," I said hurriedly, not wanting to cut her off but needing to.

Robinson cleared his throat. I could practically hear him thinking: *You wrote a story about Ernie's? And us?*

I ignored him. Of course I'd written about him. He was my best friend, wasn't he? The one who knew me like no other. The one I thought about approximately 75 percent of my waking hours, if not more.

"Thanks for letting us come over," I said. "I really wanted Robinson to meet you. I can't get him to finish any book, ever, but he read yours in a night."

"It gave me…insights," Robinson said, looking pointedly at me.

Matthea laughed. "Axi and I share certain background details, don't we? But Axi's much smarter than I was at her age."

"She's ornerier," Robinson said. "That's for sure."

I kicked him in the shins—lightly.

Matthea produced a pitcher of iced tea and a plate of lemon cake, and Robinson helped himself to two slices.

"So, how's the writing going, Axi?" Matthea asked.

"Um, not much at all lately," I admitted, reaching for my own slice of cake. "Please tell me there's some secret to keeping at it. Not giving up. Believing in yourself. That kind of stuff." I tried to keep the desperation out of my voice.

Matthea sighed and began to braid the fringe on her scarf. "My dear, there is no universal secret. There's only the secret each writer discovers for herself. The path forward."

I could feel my shoulders slump. Of course. There's no such thing as a magic bullet. Who doesn't know that?

"Are you aware that European kings used to have their hearts buried separately from their bodies?" Matthea asked.

"Um...no," I said, and I saw Robinson raise his eyebrows with that slight grin I loved. Clearly, he was amused by my weirdo writing mentor.

"It was a way of offering their hearts, literally and figuratively, to their country. Forever." Matthea sighed. "Macabre practice, if you ask me. But I like it as a metaphor. You give your country—which, in this case, is your story—your heart."

"Oh," I said. "Okay." No wonder I hadn't written the Great American Novel yet. My heart was still firmly planted in my chest. Wasn't it?

"Be patient," Matthea said gently. "Keep writing, but keep dreaming, too. Remember that inspiration struck the brilliant mathematician Archimedes when he was in the bathtub."

And inspiration struck the brilliant physicist Richard Feynman when he was in a strip club, I thought. (I may be failing AP physics, but I did learn a thing or two.)

That's pretty much how the rest of the conversation went. We didn't ponder the unpredictability of love or the mysteries of the universe, but since we touched on everything from the mummified hearts of European kings to Einstein's theory that creativity was more important than knowledge, I felt like it was time well spent.

After a fourth piece of lemon cake, though, Robinson excused himself, saying he needed to get a bit of fresh air. I watched his retreating back, feeling a vague sense of unease. My body gave an involuntary shiver, and Matthea looked at me piercingly. We continued our chat, but later, as we were leaving, she put her hand on my shoulder. "Are you all right?" she asked.

For one tiny millisecond, I wanted to tell her everything. The real reason behind what Robinson and I were doing, which I hadn't even wanted to admit to myself this whole time. It didn't actually have anything to do with me escaping my boring life in Klamath Falls. But I couldn't tell her.

"I'm great," I said.

"And your friend?" She squinted toward Robinson, who was leaning against the car, staring down the hill toward the bay. He brought his arms up and almost seemed to hug himself, as if he were cold. Or as if, for a moment, he felt the need to reassure himself about something.

"He's great, too," I insisted. *Why are you lying, Axi?*

Matthea picked a yellow flower from one of the vines around her door and tucked it behind my ear. "Give your story your heart," she repeated.

It sounded reasonable enough. But when I looked at Robinson, I knew I'd already given my heart to something—to someone—else.

11

IF I DIDN'T KNOW IT WAS MEDICALLY
impossible, I'd say that Robinson was born with a wrench in
his hand. Or that as a baby, he sucked on a spark plug instead
of a pacifier.

This gearhead gene was why I was taking him to Torrance,
California, next—because it certainly wasn't my kind of place.
Torrance breeds NASCAR drivers and semiprofessional cage
fighters. (Ugh.) It has a racetrack, a giant rock 'n' roll car show,
and about five hundred stores that sell car parts.

In other words, for a guy like Robinson, it's the Promised
Land. The kind of place he had to—he *deserved* to—experience.

When we pulled into the parking lot of the Cal-Am Speed-
way the following afternoon, Robinson sucked in his breath
and gave me his crooked, perfect grin.

"Axi Moore," he said, "you are greatest person I have ever known."

"You just wait," I said, smiling back.

I steered him away from the glass atrium entrance and toward a side door propped open with a rolled-up copy of *Car and Driver.*

Brad Sewell was waiting for us in the pit. "Alexandra," he said, stepping forward to give me a bear hug. "Long time no see, kiddo."

Robinson clearly wanted to know how this beefy dude with a Dale Earnhardt tattoo and I were acquainted. But I simply said, "Robinson, this is Brad. Brad, this is my friend Robinson."

"Nice to meet ya," Brad said. "Let me walk you through a few things, and then we'll get you in the cockpit."

It was only then that Robinson understood what he was actually here for, and he looked like he might spontaneously combust from excitement.

He turned to me. "It's like *Say Anything,*" he whispered.

We'd watched that old movie a hundred times. One of the best scenes is when the geeky main character takes his reluctant date, one of the Beautiful People, to an art museum after hours. He can do this because he's friends with the museum guard, and because he's hung a painting of the Beautiful Girl in one of the galleries.

Today was my museum moment for Robinson, but better. I'd bribed Brad with a chunk of my savings, and I'd shamelessly pulled the "I knew you when our sisters were in the cancer ward" card.

Brad began talking gibberish to Robinson, something about "initial turn-in" and "apex of the curve" and "neutral throttle on the corner." But Robinson was nodding confidently, and then he was climbing into a flame-resistant Nomex suit, and Brad was fitting him with a radio helmet and snapping him into a five-point harness.

"Any fool can speed on the straightaway; it's the curves that make a racer," Brad said over his shoulder.

"Oh, sure," I said. Like I knew what he was talking about—I couldn't even drive to the grocery store.

Robinson revved the engine and then pulled out of the pit. He didn't go that fast at first, but he must have gotten the hang of it after a while, because the engine got louder and the car became a green blur flashing past us again and again.

"So how's your little sister?" I asked Brad.

"She's in remission. Two years now."

"That's fantastic," I said. Lizzie Sewell had been really nice to Carole Ann. Lizzie, it seems, was one of the lucky ones.

"And what about you?" Brad asked, and I pretended not to hear. Fortunately, just at that moment, the bright green car came screeching to a halt on the track outside the pit, and Robinson opened the door.

"Axi, you have *got* to get in here!" he yelled.

I looked over at Brad. I was hoping he'd tell me that the other seat belt was broken or that he was fresh out of helmets.

"There's a suit over there that'll fit you," he said.

And that's how I found myself in the passenger seat of a

custom Chevy race car, outfitted like Danica Patrick and quivering with excitement.

"On your mark, get set, go!" yelled Robinson, and we peeled out onto the track, zero to sixty in about a millisecond.

The g-force slammed me against the seat, and the stunning, brain-shaking roar of the engine filled my ears. I could feel the noise as much as hear it. It vibrated in my chest and shook me deep in my guts.

I couldn't help it: in joy and terror, I screamed.

I stopped, though, because I couldn't even hear myself. And then I screamed some more.

We came toward the first curve, and I noticed the tall chain-link fence that arced inward over the track. Somehow I understood—even though I was totally incapable of higher thought, of abstract things such as words—that the fence was to keep us from splattering our body parts all over the bleachers in a crash.

The car had thick mesh netting instead of windows, so the wind came rushing in, hot and smelling like asphalt and oil. I couldn't see how fast we were going, and I didn't want to know.

We banked around the curve, the engine squealing.

As we pulled into the straightaway and Robinson hit hard on the throttle, suddenly my vision seemed to narrow. It was like looking through a tunnel. Everything on either side of me blurred and faded, and all that mattered was the airspace in front of us, and how lightning fast we were going to blast through it.

My body was singing with fear and happiness and an incredible feeling of being completely alive in the moment. I was no longer Alexandra Jane Moore—I was a supernova strapped into a bucket seat.

Go, go, go! I thought wildly. Because screaming, after all, was useless.

We took three more sound barrier–shattering laps, and when we finally slowed, I turned to Robinson with wide and no doubt crazy-looking eyes.

"Oh my God," I said, pulling off my helmet and shaking out my sweat-drenched hair. "Oh. My. God."

Robinson cackled madly. Brad came over and said, "Whad-dja think?"

It took Robinson a moment to answer, probably because he had to wait for his brain to stop vibrating. Then he said, "I might have just had the best time of my life."

I started laughing like an idiot, because that was exactly what we'd come for, what I'd wanted to give him.

Carpe diem. Because today, after all, was all we knew we had.

12

"I'M STANDING ON TOM CRUISE," ROB-
inson yelled. "Take my picture!"

"You're on his *star*, Scalawag," I said. But I snapped the
photo anyway: dark-eyed Robinson, handsome as any movie
star, dressed like a hipster lumberjack. Even in Southern California, he couldn't give up the flannel.

We were fresh off the Cal-Am racetrack, still hopped up on
the experience. Hollywood was a hop, skip, and a jump up the
110 from Torrance, so that's where we went next.

Of course we had to go straight to the Walk of Fame. While
Robinson ogled the street performers (buskers, hustlers, and
dudes dressed like Iron Man and Captain Jack Sparrow), I
dashed around taking photos of the names I knew and loved:
Marilyn Monroe, Audrey Hepburn, James Dean . . . and, okay,

Drew Barrymore and Jennifer Aniston, because it's 2013, people, and not all good movies are in black and white.

"This place is nuts," Robinson said, hopping over to Snow White's star. "Look, now I'm on top of a fairy tale."

"'I used to be Snow White, but I drifted,'" I said. Then I cocked a hip and gave my best sultry wink—like Mae West, whose line I'd just stolen.

Then I turned, and together we walked up Highland Avenue, toward the golden Hollywood Hills and the giant, iconic white sign. Our destination: the Hollywood Hotel. Robinson didn't know it, though, because I wanted to keep surprising him. The delight on his face—the way his eyes went wide when he was taken aback—I wanted to keep seeing that for as long as I possibly could.

The fact that we would be alone together in a hotel room had nothing to do with my decision.

(Quit laughing!)

When Robinson saw me striding up to the reservation desk, he said, "Do we have enough money for this?"

I wasn't sure if we did, but it didn't matter. "My back can't take another night in the car, and I am *not* camping out with those shirtless dudes I saw in the park." (If I couldn't tell him the truth, didn't that seem like a good enough reason?)

"I thought that guy with the python looked nice," Robinson joked. "But hey, I'm down with creature comforts. Are we gonna get room service?"

I shook my head. "Nice try," I said. "Spendthrift. Profligate."

"I totally don't know what those words mean," Robinson said, "but I'm not the one who booked us the expensive hotel room."

We rode the mirrored elevator to the fifteenth floor in silence. We didn't meet each other's eyes, either in person or in our reflections. Did Robinson feel shy, the way I suddenly did? I didn't know, because I couldn't look at him.

A minute later, we opened a door onto a spacious cream-colored room, with a giant flat-screen TV, floor-to-ceiling windows, a little seating area, and one giant boat of a bed.

I felt my breath catch in my throat. Robinson and I had slept in a tent, as close together as spoons. And this bed was so stupidly huge that we could be on either side of it and not touch at all. And yet—it felt way more intimate.

I went to the sink to wash the racetrack grit from my face. In the mirror was a girl I hardly recognized. For one thing, she desperately needed a shower. For another, she looked...well, *wild* was the word that came to mind. Certainly she did not resemble a *straight arrow* or a *do-gooder,* which were the kinds of nouns I was used to.

I met her pale blue eyes and smiled faintly at her. *Who are you? What do you want?* I mouthed. But she only offered me that strange smirk.

When I came out of the bathroom, Robinson was already in bed, though it was barely after eight. He was wearing an ancient Bob Dylan T-shirt and pressing buttons on the remote. The TV was on but muted.

"Axi Moore," he said, smiling at me, the blue light from the screen flickering on his handsome face.

"Robinson," I said, barely above a whisper.

"What do you want to do now?" he asked.

I almost cracked up. That was the question to end all questions, wasn't it?

For a moment I stood there, caught between the hallway and the bed, between fear and desire. On the one hand, I wanted to sink into Robinson. Reach my fingers into his hair. Feel his lips on my neck. Hold his smooth skin close against mine.

But then I thought of the dream I'd had among the redwoods—how something could be both perfect and terrifying, both mountain and abyss. *What was the right thing to do?*

"Hey, look," Robinson said suddenly, his voice brightening. "It's *Puss in Boots*."

Just like that, the tension in the air snapped. We loved that movie, even though it's for kids. Robinson insisted—I think seriously—that it was Antonio Banderas's best role.

So the fuzzy orange cat with the big boots and the Spanish accent banished my questions and doubts until another day. I crawled under the covers next to Robinson. The sheets were silky white and smelled like bleach. I took a deep breath, and I scooted right up against his side. Then I tipped my head onto his shoulder.

Robinson seemed to stiffen. I froze, too. My heart sank in my chest, and my eyes closed in shame. Had I read the situation so wrong? I told myself I would count to five and then pull away to the far side of the giant bed.

But then I felt Robinson's body shift. He curved toward me. And he leaned down and kissed the top of my head. Under the covers, his hand found mine. Our fingers intertwined.

That's enough, I thought. *That's all I need.*

For now.

13

OVER BREAKFAST THE NEXT MORNING, Robinson told me he had something to confess.

We were in Starbucks, eating microwaved Artisan Breakfast Sandwiches, which, FYI, have nothing artisanal about them. At the table next to us, a Stormtrooper and an unconvincing Michael Jackson sipped Venti dark roasts before taking up their posts along the Walk of Fame.

"Spill it," I said. I felt a slight fluttering beneath my rib cage. *He's going to say he's sorry, that he should have kissed me last night.*

"I want to see where Bruce Willis lives." Robinson looked up at me from underneath his bangs, his expression only slightly sheepish.

I felt like knocking my head against the table. Why did I keep expecting some profound declaration from him? Sometimes he made me wonder if the human adolescent male was a completely different species from the human adolescent female. (Different as in significantly less evolved.)

But this was his trip as much as mine, and I wanted to be a good sport. So after breakfast, we flagged down the nearest open-top tour van. The guide promised it would give us an *incredible* look at the stars' *jaw-dropping* homes, and a *secret window* onto their *enviable* lives.

I thought it might make me feel like a Peeping Tom, but Robinson had no such worries.

"If you don't want strangers staring at you, don't get famous," he said.

"I guess I should cancel my *American Idol* audition, then." I began to sing "I Will Always Love You"—a tough song for a good singer, and a devastating one for someone like me.

Robinson yelped and covered his ears.

Since we'd bought tickets for the Deluxe Route, we took our time on the tour, getting off one van, wandering around, and then hopping back on the next. We drove along the shopping districts of Melrose and Rodeo Drive; we passed beneath the towering palms of the Sunset Strip; we saw the La Brea Tar Pits and the Petersen Automotive Museum (which included a Hot Wheels Hall of Fame I never thought I'd pull Robinson away from).

It was late in the afternoon when we finally wound our way up into the hills.

"We're getting close, Axi," Robinson said, grinning. "Good ol' Bruce is going to invite us in to dinner."

"Sure," I said snidely. "Then we'll have dessert at Jennifer Aniston's house."

Robinson looked hurt. "Sarcasm doesn't become you, GG." But then his irrepressible smile shone again. "I bet Jen makes a wicked crème brûlée. She probably makes nice coffee, too, which is cool, because I like coffee with fancy desserts." He sounded utterly, completely sincere.

Crazy as it was, I loved this about Robinson: how he was capable of believing in something he didn't *actually* believe in. Does that make sense? He knew what he wanted to be true, what he felt should be true, and for a certain amount of time, by the power of his will (or his humor, or his stupid, boyish hope), it was true.

Believing in believing. Robinson was exceptional at that.

"On the left you will see the house formerly owned by Arnold Schwarzenegger," the tour guide called, interrupting my thoughts about Robinson and, no doubt, Robinson's thoughts about dessert.

Robinson leaned in close to me and whispered Arnold's most famous line: " 'I'll be back.' "

" 'Come with me if you want to live,' " I hissed—an Arnold quote from *Terminator 2.*

"Wait, I've got one—" He slapped his forehead, unable to recall it.

" 'Hasta la vista, baby'?" I asked, smiling smugly.

"Gaah, it was on the tip of my tongue!" Robinson reached out and tickled me in the ribs, which made me squeal.

The tour guide kept talking, but we'd stopped listening. We drove through lush green neighborhoods, peering past iron gates and elaborate landscaping to catch glimpses of enormous mansions. The air smelled like roses...and money.

The driver slowed down around a particularly steep curve and then stopped to let a group of cyclists pass.

I grabbed Robinson's hand. "Let's split."

He turned to me, uncomprehending.

"Over the side," I whispered. And because he still didn't seem to get it, I showed him. I swung a leg over the edge of the open-top van and dropped down to the street.

If the other passengers noticed, they didn't say anything. A second later, Robinson landed beside me, looking utterly baffled. The van started up again and pulled away.

"So what's the brilliant plan now, Axi?" Robinson's hands were on his hips. "We don't know where Bruce Willis lives, and we're probably ten miles from our hotel."

I only smiled. "Follow me," I said. And I led him toward what I'd seen: a FOR SALE sign and a gate left open.

"Oh, duuuude," Robinson whispered, sounding suddenly like a K-Falls cretin. "Really?"

I looked up and down the street. Except for a lone gardener, whose back was to us, it was utterly deserted. We crept up the driveway, then alongside the vacant house to the back gardens. Whoever had lived in this ornate Mediterranean (estimated asking price: a cool five to ten mil) was gone, but the pool was still full, its water glassy and aquamarine blue.

The sun was on its way down and the sky was the color of persimmons. Robinson turned to me. "GG...," he began.

I threw my arms out and spun around. "If *this* hasn't proven to you I'm not a GG anymore," I asked, "what will?"

Robinson didn't say anything, but I already had an idea.

In one fluid motion, I stripped down to my underwear, tossed my clothes in a heap, and dove into the pool. I swam all the way to the bottom before rocketing back up in a cascade of glittering water droplets.

"Come in if you dare," I called to Robinson. *"Scalawag."*

He hesitated for a moment, but Robinson could never back down from a challenge. He took off his shirt, revealing his broad, pale chest, his flat stomach, and the low V of muscle there. I'd never seen that much of his skin before, and the ivory smoothness of it was startling.

Seeing him on the lip of the pool, naked now but for his boxers, I thought of Michelangelo's *David*. Not because Robinson had a perfect *David*-like body (though it was very nice) but because he had that combination of power and vulnerability that Michelangelo had given his sculpture. See, Michelangelo didn't show David triumphant, the way every other sculptor did. He showed David before he fought Goliath — when David believed he was doomed and went into battle anyway.

Robinson reached up to plug his nose, and he no longer looked remotely like a Renaissance hero. "Cannonball," he yelled on the way down. He came up spluttering. "Oh my God, it's cold!"

I laughed. "You mean invigorating," I said. "Revitalizing."

Robinson rolled his eyes at me. "Nerd. I can still call you *word nerd*, can't I?" Then he swam toward me, smiling, and he put his hands on my shoulders. Suddenly I was sure he was going to kiss me. He was so close, and his fingers were on my skin, and there was nothing—*nothing*—but water between us (and some flimsy, soaking-wet clothes).

He moved forward another step, and then he stopped. He opened his mouth like he was going to say something. But then he vanished under the water. The next thing I knew, he was picking me up and tossing me backward into the deep end, and I was squealing, gasping, laughing, and he was saying, "Shhh, shhh, we don't want the cops to come."

We swam as evening fell and distant lights from the inhabited houses flickered on through the trees. I looked over at Robinson, who was floating on his back in the shallow end, and I wondered what it would be like to live in one of these castles.

I'd have everything money could buy, but it wouldn't be the same as having everything I wanted. Not even close.

14

WE WERE LUCKY THAT NIGHT. NOT ONLY did we get away with trespassing, we got a ride home. The gardener from across the street had seen us emerge, wet and shivering, from the gate, and offered to drive us back to town.

"*Estás invadiendo*," he said, smiling. "*¿Si?*"

Robinson nodded. "*Si*," he said. "*Somos traviesos.*" He turned to me. "That means 'we're naughty.'"

I was pressed up against his side in the front seat of the truck, trying to find the warmth of him through our damp layers of clothes. "See? You totally can't call me GG anymore," I said sleepily.

"Maybe BG," he suggested. "For Bad Girl."

My eyelids were so heavy, and then they were closing. "Or MB. Mixed Bag...," I murmured.

And honestly, that was the last thing I remember. I must have fallen asleep in the truck, and Robinson must have carried me up to the room and laid me down on our shared bed. Maybe he fluffed up the pillows for me, and maybe he even kissed me. But if he did, I'll never know.

I woke several hours later to find him staring at me.

"Before we leave, we should actually see a *star*," he said. "Not just a pink symbol on a sidewalk, or the house where one lives."

I burrowed under the covers. "Why can't we just turn on the TV? There're plenty of them there."

"We need to see one in real life," he insisted.

But this isn't real life, the old Axi Moore insisted. *This is a crazy adventure. And as great as it is, it can't last.*

Of course, as both the old and the new Axi well knew, real life didn't necessarily last, either.

I peeked my head out from the blankets, then ducked it back under again. Robinson was at the end of the bed, and he suddenly yanked the covers off me. I tried to grab them, but he was too strong. "Did you bring a nice dress?" he asked, raising one dark eyebrow at me.

I scoffed. "Runaways tend not to pack formal wear."

"Well, put on whatever you've got, because we're hitting the red carpet."

I assumed Robinson was pulling my leg, but I rose and took a quick shower, then put on the Forever 21 wrap dress I'd packed just in case. I put on a little mascara, too, and a dab of lipstick.

His eyes lit up when he saw me emerge from the bathroom. "You clean up good, Axi Moore," he said. Robinson did, too. In a slightly rumpled oxford and a clean pair of jeans, he looked like an ad for Levi's 501s.

He led me down the hall and out to the street, where we hopped into a cab. "Now it's my turn to surprise you," he said. And then he held his hand over my eyes until we pulled up in front of the Hammer Museum. "Ta-da!" he said.

Ahead of us snaked a long line of black limos. There was red carpet laid over the sidewalk, and a bunch of people milling around, and a giant banner that said CHILDREN'S HOSPITAL LOS ANGELES ANNIVERSARY GALA.

I saw the word *hospital* and my stomach suddenly felt like it was full of stones. "What is this?" I asked.

"A benefit," Robinson said brightly. "A party. Major star power, because as you can imagine, no one in Hollywood wants to be accused of not helping sick kids." He climbed from the cab and held out his hand. "Come on, let's go inside."

"*You* are a sick kid, Robinson," I said. "Mentally, I mean. They don't just let randoms crash the red carpet."

"But we're not randoms, as you so ungenerously character- ize us. We are Axi and Robinson, the G-rated Bonnie and Clyde." He lifted me into the sunshine and smiled his dazzling smile. "If we don't belong here, who does?"

79

What could I do but laugh? "I think stealing a Harley ought to at least earn us a PG," I said.

"I'm in complete agreement," Robinson said. Then he held up a finger, signaling me to wait. "As the kids say, BRB."

He walked up to the nearest gatekeeper, a middle-aged woman dressed all in black. I watched as men in suits and women in jewel-colored cocktail dresses filed past her through the doors. The gatekeeper was trying to ignore Robinson, but I knew she wouldn't last. When Robinson turned on the charm ray, few could withstand it.

Sure enough, a moment later, she nodded and beckoned me over. As I approached, she looked at me with...concern, or maybe even pity. I shivered under her gaze. What exactly had Robinson told her? "You two go in over there," she whispered, and pointed toward a side entrance.

And then we were inside, and there were famous people *everywhere.* I saw Matt Damon talking to Mark Wahlberg by a potted fern, and Tina Fey posing in front of a giant stand of paparazzi. Camera flashes popped like fireworks, and in a matter of seconds, I was no longer worrying about what Robinson had said to the gatekeeper. All around us were bona fide superstars, talking and laughing and guzzling free drinks, just like regular people.

"I'm seeing a lot of excellent facial work," Robinson noted. Somehow he'd gotten his hands on a flute of champagne.

"'I love Los Angeles. I love Hollywood. They're beautiful. Everybody's plastic, but I love plastic,'" I said.

"Huh?"

"Andy Warhol said that."

Robinson held out his arm, and I tucked my hand in the crook of it, as if we were on our way to prom. He leaned in close, and I could feel his breath in my hair. "I told you we'd get in, didn't I?"

"And you were right," I said.

"Which makes you...?" He waited, an expectant smile teasing the corner of his mouth.

I sighed. "Wrong."

He laughed and pulled me close. "Axi admits fallibility," he said. "I'm going to treasure this moment forever."

My cheek pressed against his shirt, I smiled up at him. I would, too, I thought, but for a wholly different reason. Just days earlier we were in Klamath Falls, and now we were on the red carpet. What couldn't we do, as long as we were together?

15

THERE IS A LIMIT TO THE SUCCESS OF any partnership — and we discovered ours later that evening, when Robinson decided it was time to teach me to drive.

I said, "Robinson, I can't learn how to drive in a stolen car."

He shrugged. "It's just like any other car. Gas pedal on the right, brake on the left. Four gears forward, one reverse."

He was always so confident. But maybe that was because everything came easily to him: he could hot-wire a Harley, sweet-talk just about anyone, and play whatever musical instrument he was given. His free-throw percentage was ridiculous, and no matter where he was, he could always find true north.

Me, I was not so sure of myself. About anything. "I don't know how I feel about this," I said softly.

Robinson reclined the passenger seat and pretended to close his eyes. "I feel good enough for the both of us. Time for me to relax and enjoy riding shotgun."

I clenched my hands on the steering wheel. *You can do this, Axi,* I told myself. *You've played Grand Prix Legends!* Then came the other voice: *Yeah, and you sucked at it. You always crashed right out of the starting gate.*

"Ready?" Robinson asked.

I nodded, even though I wasn't. Robinson had to lean over and start the car, because I didn't know how to work the screwdriver.

"Okay. So check your mirrors and see if it's clear. Then you're going to step on the brake and shift into drive." He made it sound so easy, like I wasn't behind the wheel of a two-ton death machine.

I must have said this out loud, because Robinson said, "That is a *slight* exaggeration. We're in an empty parking lot, Axi. How much damage can you do?"

"I don't know," I said grimly. "We'll see."

For a second I thought of my physics class, the one I'd skipped the day I met Robinson at Ernie's dusty old counter. *A body at rest will remain at rest unless an outside force acts on it.* That's Newton's First Law. In other words, I was totally safe — until I stepped on the gas.

But I took a deep breath and somehow successfully shifted gears. When the car didn't explode, I forced myself to lightly press the gas pedal. The car moved forward. Slowly. Jerkily. But it moved. "Oh my God, I'm driving," I said.

Robinson grinned. "And the prize for stating the obvious goes to . . . Alexandra Moore!"

"Shut up," I squealed.

Robinson laughed. "Sorry — I couldn't resist. You're normally a much more subtle thinker."

"I hate you," I said, but I was laughing, too.

I was going twenty miles an hour and it felt like flying. I was also quickly nearing the edge of the parking lot. "What do I do now?"

"Why don't you try turning," Robinson suggested. "So we don't, I don't know, go barreling into traffic?"

I slammed my foot on the brake and whirled to face him. Sure, I'd had a good thirty seconds of decent driving, but some things just weren't funny yet. "This is hard for me, you know!" I yelled.

Robinson reached over and put his hand on my arm. It was . . . calming. "Axi," he said gently, "is it really hard for you? Think about it before you answer."

I frowned. It was scary, yes. Unfamiliar. But hard? Well, not really. It was like Robinson said: gas pedal on the right, brake on the left. Four gears forward, one reverse.

All I needed to do was move forward.

It was almost as if Robinson could see the fear leaving my body. He gave my arm a squeeze. "See?" he said. "You get it. You're going to be fine."

And I was fine. I drove around the parking lot for almost an hour while Robinson, the human karaoke machine, sang driving songs: "On the Road Again," "I Get Around," and "Mustang Sally." I practiced turning, accelerating, and even parallel parking.

Finally Robinson said, "I think you're ready for the street."

I said, "I think I'm ready for you to stop singing."

"Deal."

So at the edge of the lot, I looked both ways—and then I pulled into traffic.

"Pedal to the metal, Axi!" Robinson said.

I was giddy, thrilled, scared. I was behind the wheel of a car, in fantastic Los Angeles, with the boy who was possibly the love of my life sitting next to me.

"Whoa, you cut that guy off there," Robinson said.

"I did?"

"Don't drive like you own the road; drive like you own the car."

"That's funny," I said, checking my mirrors and accelerating, "because I don't own it, and neither do you."

"*If I can just get off of this LA freeway/Without getting killed or caught,*" Robinson sang—it was some old country song.

Wasn't he supposed to not sing? "It's not a freeway," I pointed out.

And it was a good thing it wasn't, because what happened next would have been a lot worse.

The other part of Newton's First Law? *A body in motion will remain in motion, unless acted upon by an outside force.*

In this case, the outside force was a parking meter.

I don't know how it happened. One minute everything was fine, and the next minute we were at a dead stop and blood was pouring out of my nose.

16

Dizzy and overwhelmed, I stared out the window with a T-shirt held to my face as Robinson hurried us onto the 10. He'd handed me the shirt as he slid into the driver's seat. We had to leave the scene quickly — there were witnesses.

"You're okay, right?" he asked.

"I think so." My voice came out very small. I wasn't worried about my nose — I was worried about having smashed up a stolen car.

"Don't worry," Robinson assured me. "The LAPD's got way bigger fish to fry."

But his voice sounded sort of shaky. As if maybe he didn't have any idea what he was talking about. And he kept glancing in the rearview mirror, like he was watching for flashing lights.

"I'm sorry," I whispered. But I don't think he heard me.

His eyes darted from road to mirror and back again. "Well, Axi, in the immortal words of Dale Earnhardt Senior, 'You win some, you lose some, you wreck some,'" he said. "Every path has its puddle, you know? Nothing ventured, nothing gained! You can't make an omelet without breaking some eggs. And who wants to live in a world without omelets? Besides chickens, of course. I mean, I'm sure they'd be totally fine with it, ecstatic, really—"

"Robinson, you're babbling," I said.

"What?" He turned to me, his eyes flashing.

I took the shirt away from my face and felt a trickle of blood make its way down my lip. It tasted like salt. "You're babbling," I said. "Are you freaking out?"

His eyes widened. "Who, me? No! I'm not freaking out. Nope, no way! Not me."

"The fellow doth protest too much, methinks," I said, feeling suddenly woozier. Robinson was usually so calm; seeing him flustered definitely didn't make the situation better.

Robinson said, "Huh?"

"A slight modification of a *Hamlet* quote," I said weakly. I realized I was tapping my feet really quickly on the floor— almost like I was trying to run away inside the car.

"Are you speaking English?" he demanded. "Like, even now?"

I clenched my hands. It was my first real moment of doubt. Deep, profound doubt. As in: What were we *doing?* Was this whole trip the worst idea I'd ever had in my life?

I guess I must have said that out loud, too, because

Robinson almost instantly calmed down. He took a long, deep breath, then leaned over and squeezed my knee. "We had a little adventure, and now it's time to be moving on," he said gently. "This trip is a brilliant idea, Axi. The best."

"Are you sure?" I asked. "Are we about to get caught?"

"No," Robinson said, this time sounding certain. "We're fine. Although we're missing a headlight and you have blood on your chin, which looks weird. Like maybe you're a vampire or something. But seriously. We're fine. We're better than fine. We're invincible. What's next on our itinerary?"

I couldn't believe how fast his mood had changed. But if Robinson felt confident again, I would try to, too. Because if I didn't trust him, what was I doing driving across the country with him?

"Well . . . Vegas, actually," I said. Yes, we were in over our heads—I understood that. But maybe things would still work out for us.

Robinson pounded the steering wheel. "Vegas, baby, here we come!"

I could hear the happiness in his voice. Part of me wanted to shake him, and the other part adored him for his unfailing optimism. How many times had I been in the pits of despair, only to have Robinson reach down and haul me up into the sunlight? More than I cared to remember.

"It's all your fault, you know," I said, dabbing at my nose and chin.

He snorted. "I'm not the one who crashed."

"But you're the one who tried to teach me to drive."

"It's a life skill, Axi. I'm not going to be able to chauffeur you around forever." He turned to smile at me then. Maybe it was a trick of the light, but it seemed there was a new glimmer of melancholy behind his smile.

"Yes, you are," I said softly. But Robinson didn't reply.

17

WE DROVE ON THROUGH THE NIGHT.
The dark shapes of the Los Angeles hills gave way to flat
nothingness, and then, after a few hours, an orange glow
blossomed in the sky. It grew steadily brighter, and when the
highway began its gentle slope downward, suddenly a vast
ocean of glittering lights stretched out below us.

"*Oooh, Las Vegas ain't no place for a poor boy like me,*" Robinson sang. Then he turned to me. "That's Gram Parsons," he
said. "Did you listen to that album I gave you?"

I hunched down in my seat, shaking my head minutely.

Robinson laughed. "Doesn't matter. I can sing the whole
damn thing for you."

"And you probably will," I said.

Humming, he drove us down the Strip, which was lit up
like Christmas times a million. It was as bright as day on the

street, even though it was after midnight. We passed signs for the Bellagio, Bally's, the MGM Grand—casinos I knew from *Ocean's Eleven* set in a landscape I knew from Hunter S. Thompson's *Fear and Loathing in Las Vegas*.

"So we have to gamble, right?" Robinson asked.

I nodded, suddenly resolute. "I believe it's required."

I cleaned myself up in a 7-Eleven bathroom while Robinson ate his ten thousandth Slim Jim. Then we went to the Luxor, mostly because it was shaped like a pyramid. It even had a giant Sphinx out front—an absurdity we just couldn't resist.

The moment we stepped inside, we were in yet another world. The sound of pinging slot machines, the smells of air-conditioning and sweat, the flashing lights above the pits: it was total sensory overload.

Robinson put his arm around my shoulders. "You want to win big?" he asked.

"Yeah, we've got twenty bucks to blow."

"Is that what your budget tells you? Well, that's two games of blackjack with a ten-dollar buy-in." He grinned. "That's assuming we don't win, which we will."

"Twenty dollars'll last longer at the slots," I said, because sitting in a semicircle with a bunch of strangers and trying to decide whether to tell the dealer to "hit me" was more than I was up for.

Robinson eyed the blackjack table longingly. He probably thought he could charm the cards into falling the way he wanted them to. Not me. Maybe I wasn't GG anymore, but I'd never be the gambling type. Because it was my babysitting money we were talking about, and I'd wrangled some serious brats to earn it.

Maybe it was just as well that a burly guy in a black vest came up to us as we headed for the slot machines. He wanted to see our IDs.

"Well, you see—" Robinson began.

The guy cut him off. "Save it. If you got an ID, you can play. If you don't, scram."

"Go on," I said to Robinson. "Now you can play a hand of cards. I'll wait outside."

He shook his head. "No way, Axi, we're in this together."

I liked the sound of that a lot. "Okay, what do you want to do now?"

Robinson yawned so deeply I decided not to wait for an answer. I said, "Let's go find a place to sleep."

So we pulled into the nearby parking lot of Treasures, which at first I thought was a gift shop. "Why's it open so late? Who needs a snow globe at two AM?"

Robinson laughed—*at* me, not with me. "It's a strip club, you dope. This is Sin City, remember?"

I was too tired to take offense. I settled down in the back-seat and pulled my sweatshirt over me. Robinson snaked his hand around his seat in the front, and I reached out and took it. Here we were in the car again, three feet of air and eight inches of foam between us. *Why* hadn't I made a move at the hotel?

"Tell me a bedtime story," Robinson said.

"Sing me a bedtime song," I retorted.

"Flip a coin," he said.

I agreed, and he lost. So I fell asleep to Robinson singing, drumming lightly on the dashboard.

> *There was a girl named Axi*
> *who was a runaway.*
> *Instead of taking a taxi*
> *she tried to drive around LA.*
> *She crashed her car and hurt*
> > *her nose*
> *and I don't mean to brag*
> *but who should rescue Axi*
> *but a charming scalawag?*

It was a pretty good lullaby, all in all.

The sound of ringing laughter woke me at 4 AM. A handful of dancers were leaving the club, done with their shift for the night.

One passed by the car and spied me in the backseat. "Hey, girl," she said, leaning in so close I could smell perfume and sweat. "You can't sleep here. They'll tow your car and take you and your friend here to the pound."

Robinson sat up, rubbing his eyes. "Huh?"

"Y'all need to be getting on home," said another. I could hear her smacking her gum. "Wherever that is."

Robinson leaned out the window and smiled at them like they were long-lost friends. "That is excellent advice," he said. "And I thank you for giving it. But unfortunately it is not possible for us to follow it at this time."

The women burst into laughter. One nudged the other with her bony hip. "Look at them! They're as cute as kittens. Chrissy, you take 'em home with you."

The blond one called Chrissy looked us over. She spent an especially long time looking at Robinson. "My car's the white Chevy over there," she said finally. "Y'all follow me out."

SUFFICE IT TO SAY THAT I DID NOT WANT to go. What if Chrissy was an ax murderer?

But Robinson said that for one, the chances of that were very slim; and for two, being killed with an ax was conceivably more appealing than spending another night with the emergency brake poking into his side. So we followed Chrissy toward the old Las Vegas Strip (the place they used to call Glitter Gulch) and into a modest apartment complex.

"Here we go," she said, pointing toward a sagging red couch in the middle of a dingy living room. Neon lights from the signs outside reflected on the bare walls. "You sleep in there, and your boyfriend can have the floor in the kids' room. It's carpeted."

"He's not my boyfriend," I said, out of habit. I could see Robinson getting ready to deliver his line — *She asked me out, but I turned her down* — so I quickly added, "He's not my type."

Chrissy raised one thin, painted eyebrow. "Oh yeah? 'Cause looks to me like he'd be everyone's type."

Robinson, who seemed ready to fall over from exhaustion, made a show of kissing his biceps. He was such a beautiful goof—of *course* he was my type.

"Dork," I said.

"Nerd," he retorted.

Chrissy cackled. "God, you two are seriously the cutest things ever. If you aren't together, I don't know what your problem is."

Then she handed Robinson a pile of blankets and shoved him toward the door of a bedroom. "The kid on the left snores," she said. "Fair warning."

She gave me one last tired, vaguely maternal smile and disappeared into her bedroom. I lay on the soft couch and thought about what she'd said: that if Robinson and I weren't together, she didn't know what was wrong with us.

I didn't know, either. I mean, there was plenty wrong with us. But was that the thing keeping us apart?

I couldn't sleep, thinking about it. About him. Close to dawn, I tiptoed into the room where he was sleeping. He lay on his side, his hand tucked under his cheek. I watched him for a long time, counting his slow breaths and imagining I could hear the strong beat of his heart.

It sounded ridiculous even to me, but I couldn't stand not being near Robinson—especially now that I'd gotten to spend every night with him since we started this totally-insane-but-also-the-best-thing-ever trip. He made me feel the kind of joy I hadn't felt since I was a kid and my family was whole. And he also made me feel…a kind of rush I'd never felt before in my life.

How could I ever go back to being by myself—being without him—now that I knew these feelings were possible?

Before I knew what I was doing, I crept forward and lay down beside him, matching my breathing to his. Whether or not he wanted me the same way I wanted him, we were in this together—that was what Robinson had said. It had never occurred to me before what a complicated word *together* was.

19

I WOKE UP GASPING. THERE WAS A weight on my chest, crushing my heart, squeezing the air from my lungs. *So this is it*, I thought, *this is what it feels like to die.*

Next: *Oh my God, I haven't kissed Robinson yet. Except for that one time, ages ago, when I had that beer, which didn't even count…*

I clawed at the covers, my lungs screaming. My desperate fingers felt something hard and round — a small, bony knee.

There was a shriek, a high giggle, and suddenly the weight was gone. I sat up, dazed and blinking. There was a boy on the floor, gazing up at me with giant green eyes.

"My name is Mason Drew Boseman," he said pertly. "I'm four."

"You must weigh fifty pounds," I gasped, rubbing my sternum, where he'd just been sitting.

Then a small girl wandered in, clutching a dirty stuffed bunny. "That's Lila," Mason said. "She's two and she doesn't know how to use the potty."

"I'm . . . Bonnie," I said, my breath finally returning to normal. "Nice to meet you both."

Mason ducked his head, suddenly shy, like he hadn't just nearly killed me. Lila simply stared, then slowly brought her thumb up to her mouth and began to suck.

"Maybe I'll get up now," I said, untangling myself from the clean but ratty blanket. Still they stared.

I walked into the kitchen, following the smell of coffee. "Morning—" I began to say.

But I stopped. Because Chrissy, who was barefoot and in a silky red nightgown, had Robinson pressed up against the counter—and she was kissing him.

And it looked for all the world like he was kissing her back.

I turned around and stood shaking in the hall. Had I really just seen that? Was there a chance I was still dreaming? Mason looked up at me questioningly.

I counted to twenty, then coughed and tried to make it sound like I was coming down the hall to the kitchen. I heard the shuffling of feet, the screech of chair legs against linoleum.

This time when I rounded the corner, Robinson was at the kitchen table, reading the paper like he was the man of the house. "Morning, sunshine," he said, pushing a mug of steaming coffee toward me. He needed a shave, and there was a smudge of dirt on his cheek.

"He changed my oil, can you believe that?" Chrissy asked me. Her cheeks were flushed.

"That's not a metaphor for something, is it?" I asked, looking pointedly at Robinson.

He chose to ignore the question. "I woke up early. Thought I'd do a friend a favor."

That was Robinson. He never missed an opportunity to help someone out. Apparently, he also never missed a chance to kiss someone — unless that person was me.

Chrissy had hopped up onto the counter, and she was looking at him like she was ready to ask him to move in. She might have two kids, but she was probably only a few years older than we were.

Mason tugged at my leg. "Did you know that dead squirrels can eat you? They have very sharp teeth. Dead squirrels are cool. Also dinosaurs are cool, and Batman, but Spider-Man is better because he got bitten by a spider." Mason began hopping up and down, narrowly missing my foot. "Superman can go into space because he can fly, but not Spider-Man because he needs a web and he can't shoot it in space because there's no buildings up there." His hopping had progressed to a wild bouncing.

Chrissy giggled. "I swear I don't give him coffee."

"He's charming," I said — through gritted teeth.

"I'm not charming. I'm starving!" Mason said.

I took a step forward. "Will you let me cook breakfast?" I asked. "So you can relax?"

Chrissy looked at me in surprise. "Uh...okay."

"You took us in—it's the least I can do." The fact was, I didn't know what to do with my hands, and cooking would calm me down. So I made omelets for everyone, with cheddar cheese and snippets of chives from a pot that Chrissy kept on her windowsill. I thought about undercooking her omelet and putting bits of eggshell in it, but I reminded myself that she wasn't really the wrongdoer. I'd told her Robinson wasn't my boyfriend, so as far as she knew, he was available.

Not that I totally forgave her.

"Wow, I lucked out bringing you two home," Chrissy said, her mouth full of eggs. "This is the best omelet I've ever had."

"I've made a lot of them," I said. "I'm no gourmet or anything."

Robinson pointed his fork at me. "Not true. She can cook anything. She'll make someone a good little wife someday."

"Watch it," I warned.

"It's a compliment," Robinson insisted.

"I didn't take it as one," I said.

"You guys bicker like a brother and sister," Chrissy said, giggling. Then she looked serious again. "Do your parents know where you are?"

I turned back to the stove. "We plead the Fifth."

"We're on vacation," Robinson said.

Chrissy sighed and leaned back in her folding chair. "Okay," she said, "I won't pry. Everyone's entitled to their secrets. But here's a piece of advice: get out of Las Vegas, okay? Because you come here and you just get stuck."

She gazed toward the window then, the one that looked out over the Neon Boneyard, where old signs go to die. Something told me that getting stuck was exactly what had happened to her.

I looked at Robinson, who was dumping sugar into his coffee. We'd never get stuck anywhere, not even if we wanted to. There was an undeniable reason for that — but it was one of our secrets.

20

"I DON'T WANT TO TALK ABOUT IT."

So said Robinson when I asked him what he was doing tonsil-diving with a Las Vegas stripper at nine o'clock in the morning. (As if it would have been just fine later in the day.)

"Well, I want to talk about it," I said. I had dragged him and our few belongings outside as soon as breakfast was over, trying to avoid giving Chrissy a chance to ask us to stay.

Robinson looked at me for a moment, his expression unreadable, and then he turned and walked away. He wound through the cars parked near the Neon Museum, shaking his head and seemingly talking to himself.

I felt so helpless. Was I crazy? Had I imagined the romantic tension between us? What if Robinson had never wanted anything from me but my friendship? If that turned out to be true,

then it was too bad Chrissy wasn't actually an ax murderer—
because I was going to die a long, slow death of humiliation.

I wiped a bead of sweat from my lip. It was 10 AM and already
hot. I sat down on the toe of a giant metal high-heeled shoe,
which used to be part of the sign for the Silver Slipper Saloon.

I *hated* Las Vegas.

"What are you doing?" I finally called to Robinson.

He didn't answer—he was still pacing. I wasn't about to
follow him up and down the street, so I stared at all the dead
signs. There was one that said WEDDING CHAPEL and another
right next to it that said SIN.

I thought about all the people who had come to Vegas looking for love or money, and what a minuscule percentage of
them must have actually found it.

Robinson appeared at my side, and even though he was
finally saying something, it wasn't anything I was interested in.
I'd listen when he explained the kitchen kissing. In the meantime, I'd keep looking at the signs: GOLDEN NUGGET, JOE'S
LONGHORN CASINO...

Then Robinson grabbed my arm and turned me toward
him. He said, "The thing about a Boxster is, it eats tires. Especially if you dump your clutch. But since we aren't in this for
long-term ownership..."

I scrutinized the shoe's peeling paint. "I don't know what
you're talking about."

Robinson sighed, exasperated. "I'm talking about a Porsche,

Axi, because we're taking one." He pointed to a low black shape a hundred yards off. "It's an older model, so it won't have a tracking system. Hard to steal cars that send out little beacons to the LVPD, you know?"

Finally I looked at him. "We have a car already."

"I'm sick of it," Robinson said. "We need a better one." He kicked at the tip of the shoe.

"I don't want to steal another car," I said.

"Oh, my beloved Aximoron—*you* don't have to," he said. He flashed me his beautiful grin, then bounded away.

I clenched my fists and stared up at the white desert sky. Robinson was crazy—*He kisses some girl and then calls me his beloved? What gives?*

There was a screech of tires as Robinson pulled up in front of me. "Get in," he ordered.

If I didn't, would he drive off without me? Honestly, he looked like he might. It was times like these when Robinson seemed like the bad boy my father always claimed he was.

I barely had my seat belt on before Robinson gunned the engine and peeled out into the street. He was going sixty-five before I even blinked.

"That's what I meant by dumping the clutch," he said calmly. "In case you wondered."

I stared out the window, refusing to look at him. "I didn't," I said.

We were heading out of town, leaving the glittering lights and broken promises of Las Vegas behind us. Quickly.

"Slow down," I told him.

Robinson only laughed. "Speed never killed anyone! It's suddenly becoming stationary . . . that's what gets you."

I crossed my arms. "Yeah, if a thousand other things don't get you first," I huffed.

But it was Robinson's turn to ignore me. He began to whistle Bruce Springsteen's "Born to Run," and he kept on doing it, over and over, until I was ready to beg him to stop.

Then he saw the flashing lights coming up behind us, and suddenly I didn't have to.

21

OBJECTS IN MIRROR ARE CLOSER THAN THEY *appear.* That's what your car's side mirror will tell you, but I am here to say that the minute you can make out that the object you see is a police car, it is already way too close.

"Robinson," I hissed, panic rising in my voice.

"Maybe they're not after us," he said. "I was only going… hmm, twenty miles over the speed limit. Heck, it's practically a crime to go any slower around here. This is Las Vegas, baby— everything's legal but good behavior."

I could tell by the sound of his voice that Robinson didn't believe this but wanted me to. He didn't want me to be afraid. He never had, for as long as I'd known him.

"Pull over to the right-hand shoulder." The amplified, crackling voice came through a megaphone mounted on the side of the police car.

Robinson glanced down at the speedometer as if checking to see how high the numbers went. Like he was wondering if he should try to outrun the guy.

"Don't even think about it," I warned. "Do what the policeman says."

"You don't sound much like Bonnie," he said reproachfully.

"For God's sake, this isn't a movie. This is life! *Pull over!*"

I was reaching for the wheel to yank it to the right when Robinson slowed, flicked on his turn signal as polite as you please, and eased onto the right shoulder.

"See? I can follow directions," Robinson said. He tried to keep his tone light.

But it didn't matter now. I put my face in my hands. We were caught. I saw the headlines, the court-appointed lawyer, the hideous orange jumpsuit they'd make me wear. Was I old enough to be tried as an adult?

"It's going to be okay," Robinson said quietly.

Liar, I thought.

The officer approached Robinson's window. From my angle I could see only his belt and the soft, round stomach above it. "License and registration," he said gruffly.

Not even a "please."

"Sir," Robinson began, "is there a problem?"

The officer's hand shot out. "License and registration," he said again.

Robinson smiled ingratiatingly. "I believe I was going the speed of traffic—perhaps it was a trifle fast—"

"License and registration."

Robinson turned to me, his eyes wide. "He seems to have a somewhat limited vocabulary," he whispered, and to my horror, I almost burst into giddy laughter.

I covered my mouth as Robinson made a show of rooting around in the glove compartment. "It's in here somewhere," he said.

The cop began tapping impatiently on the roof of the car. Then he leaned in and looked at both of us carefully. He had small, mean eyes and an angry mouth. "Not many kids got a car this nice," he said. "You'd think their folks'd teach 'em how to drive it. But spoiled little rich kids—they don't listen to their parents much, do they?"

It was the first time in my life anyone had ever mistaken me for rich.

"I liked him better when he didn't talk," I whispered to Robinson.

Robinson pulled out the registration and handed it over. The cop inspected it. "License," he said.

"Sir, this is all a mistake," Robinson said. "I'm very sorry for speeding. If you'll just let us go with a warning, I promise I'll never do it again."

The cop barked out a laugh. "I heard that one before. There's a sucker born every minute, son, but you're not looking at one." He stared philosophically down the highway and then turned back to us. "See, these rich kids," he went on, his eyes narrow and cold, "if their folks can't teach 'em things, the law has to. The law just loves to give lessons."

Robinson was so used to charming people. I'd seen him talk his way out of detentions, and into a Hollywood party, and everything in between. So now he looked as though he couldn't believe what he was hearing. But he nodded. "Of course, sir. I understand. I'm going to have to get out, though. I keep my wallet under my seat, and I can't reach it from in here. May I step out, sir?"

The cop backed away. Robinson reached over and grabbed my hand. Hard. "Bonnie," he whispered.

"What?" I asked. But he was already out of the car, and I could still feel the pressure of his fingers on my skin.

I saw it all through the window. At first Robinson kept his hands in the air, to show the cop he meant no harm. But the next thing I knew, there was a flash of movement, a grunt, and then a holler of rage.

Robinson yelled, "Get out, Bonnie, I need you!"

Without thinking, I obeyed. And that was when I saw the love of my life—car thief, trespasser, and kisser of strippers— pointing a gun in a young cop's face.

I nearly fell to my knees. I reached out to the hood of the Porsche to steady myself. The metal of the gun glinted in the desert sunlight. *This can't be happening*, I thought. *This is definitely a dream or a scene from a movie—or a hallucination or something.*

Robinson half-turned to look at me and, I swear to God, *winked*.

My jaw dropped. If I'd thought he was a little crazy before, now I was sure he'd gone utterly insane. Then I saw that tiny smile flicker at the corner of his mouth. That smile I knew better than my own. It said to me: *This is all a game, Axi. No one's going to get hurt.*

I took a step toward them, and I prayed that he was right.

"I'm really sorry that I have to do this," Robinson said, turning back to the cop, "but you gave me no choice."

The cop's face was red and glistening. He was silent, full of brutal but impotent rage. He seemed to have lost the power of speech altogether.

I looked up and down the road, watching for traffic. Never had I been gladder that Robinson stuck to the back routes.

"Bonnie," Robinson said, "you take his cuffs and put them on him."

Fumblingly, I did as I was told. When I snapped the metal around his wrist, the cop flinched. "I'm so sorry," I blurted. "Are they too tight? I don't want them to be too tight, but I don't exactly know how to work them."

The cop merely turned redder in the face.

Robinson was jittery, like he might jump out of his flannel. Even on a back road, someone could drive by at any moment. "Again, I'm really sorry about this, sir. It's just that we're on a mission. We have to keep moving. It's a life-or-death situation."

The red-faced cop cleared his throat like he was going to say something. But then his mouth contorted and opened, and he spit. A whitish glob of mucus landed right on the tip of Robinson's cowboy boot.

"Well, that was rude," Robinson said, sounding shocked.

As if the cop should be more polite. I wondered if Robinson had somehow hit his head in our fender bender and the blow had knocked his conscience out of whack.

"You kids have no idea the trouble you're going to be in," the cop suddenly bellowed. His anger and his scarlet face frightened me. I could hardly look at him.

Maybe it wasn't the cop who was the problem—maybe it was us. The teen outlaws.

Maybe I was kind of terrified of who we'd so quickly become. We'd just threatened a police officer with his own gun and locked him up with his own handcuffs!

How had our trip gotten so out of control after I had mapped it out to perfection?

And why...didn't I care anymore?

I suddenly felt exhilarated. Unstoppable. This was the moment to make a real choice about the rest of my life, no matter how afraid I was to do it.

I steeled myself and dragged my eyes up to meet the cop's. "We're not going to get caught," I said.

I said it softly but firmly. It was a promise. A prayer. A wish.

22

ROBINSON TOOK A STEP BACK FROM THE cop, using the gun to point toward the door of the police car. "Bonnie," he said to me, "you're going to need to drive the cruiser." He turned to the cop. "I haven't taught her how to drive a stick yet," he explained.

By now I was nearly numb with shock, but I climbed into the driver's seat of the black-and-white. Gas pedal, turn signal, ignition. Everything looked to be in pretty much the same place. Meanwhile Robinson was gently shoving the cop into the back. Thank goodness for the glass between us, because, even cuffed, that guy petrified me. If looks could kill, Robinson and I would have been goners.

"You gonna be all right?" Robinson asked me, poking his head in the front window.

I put both hands on the wheel, one at ten and one at two. I

tried to seem like I wasn't having a small heart attack. "Well, there aren't any parking meters to hit."

He gave me a crooked smile. Maybe it was totally inappropriate, but I needed it.

"Awesome, you're good to go, then. Now follow me," he said. He got into the Porsche, drove a little way, then took a dirt road off to the left. We followed it for a couple of miles, passing nothing but dirt and scrubby sage.

I refused to look into the rearview mirror because I could practically feel the death glare the police officer was giving me. I was so on edge from the last fifteen minutes that I knew if I met his eyes I was going to freak out completely, crash, and end up killing us both. I was gripping the steering wheel so tightly that my fingers were turning white.

When Robinson stopped, I braked too hard and scrambled out of the car, barely remembering to put it in park.

"Whoa," Robinson said, catching me by the elbow as I stumbled toward him. "Everything okay? He's all locked up in back?"

"No, I let him out," I snapped, yanking my arm away. *Breathe*, Axi. "Sorry. Nerves."

"Let's get out of here."

"But—" I glanced at the police car. The cop was sitting motionless in the back, but I thought I could hear him cursing.

"Someone will find him, don't worry," Robinson said, pointing into the distance at what looked like tract houses — or a mirage. Everything was flat all around us. The desert was so empty. There wasn't even a cactus.

Robinson took my arm again and led me toward the Porsche. When we were strapped in, he gunned the engine, and we shot out of there in a great cloud of dust that billowed up so high it hid our crime completely.

"We've got to ditch the Porsche," Robinson said as he pulled onto the main road. For some reason he was heading back into town.

Suddenly I began to shake. My legs jumped and twitched and even my teeth were chattering. Had we just done what I thought we did? "Robinson —" I said.

"What?" He looked at me, concerned.

"I can't steal a car right now. My nerves can't take it."

"No problem," Robinson answered. "We can go back to Axi's Plan A."

"I don't even remember what that *is*," I moaned.

"The bus, of course — petri dish for superbacteria. Because I don't know about you, darlin', but I'm just itching for some kind of dreadful infection." Then Robinson grinned maniacally.

"Tell me — honestly. Have you lost. Your. Mind?"

As usual, Robinson ignored my question and instead pulled into a bus station on the edge of the city. "There it is! Our ticket to bacterial meningitis."

We got our backpacks and left the Porsche in a fire lane. I just wanted to be gone. I didn't have time to write a thank-you note to the owner, but it was probably just as well. Now that we were bona fide criminals, we should try to leave fewer clues behind.

Inside the station, it was dark and cool and grimy. All my adrenaline-fueled courage had faded, and I wanted to curl up in a ball in the corner. "Where do we go? We were supposed to see the Great Sand Dunes next," I whispered.

Robinson scanned the departure board. "Interesting," he said. "Because these famous dunes of sand happen to be near Alamosa, Colorado, correct?"

I frowned in confusion. "How did you know that?"

"My dear, that bus leaves in moments. See?" Robinson pointed. "The luck of the traveler is with us." He was already walking toward the ticket booth, one hand reaching for his wallet.

Could it really be that simple? "I thought it was luck of the Irish," I called weakly.

He turned around and shrugged. "Who cares? We've got our ride. But for your information, my grandma was an Irish rose from County Cork."

I looked at him in surprise, because Robinson never, ever talked about his family. "Okay, but what about the cop?" I asked, hurrying up to him. "We can't just leave him. We have to call someone."

"I thought you weren't GG anymore," Robinson said.

I couldn't tell if he was joking or not. "Just because I want to make sure someone doesn't die of heatstroke?" I found an old pay phone and fished in my pockets for change. I told the woman who answered that I'd been out riding my horse when I'd come upon a cop car in the middle of nowhere. I made myself sound young and stupid, but I gave all the necessary details.

She wanted to know my name. "Carole Ann," I said.

"You did a good thing, Carole Ann," she said.

Lady, if only you knew.

23

THERE'S AN OLD SAYING ABOUT HOW only the guilty sleep well in jail. The innocent man stays awake all night, freaking out, while the guilty one sleeps like a baby. He figures he's finally where he belongs and he might as well get some shut-eye.

Robinson and I weren't in jail, of course—we were on a Greyhound. But it was uncomfortable and smelly and confined, the way I imagined jail to be. And we hadn't been on the bus more than five minutes before Robinson leaned over, put his head on my lap, and fell asleep.

Guilty, I thought. *We're both so guilty.*

For a while I stared out the window, watching the flat, dry land go by. I still couldn't believe the way things had turned. A few hours ago, Robinson making out with someone else was just about the worst of my problems. Now? Try felony assault, grand theft auto, and who knew what else.

Back in the moment, of course, what we'd done made perfect sense. We'd *had* to do it. A stolen Porsche, a hijacked gun, and suddenly cuffing and abandoning a cop seemed like a fine idea because, hey, it would keep us out of juvie.

For now, I thought darkly.

Reality came down on me with a crushing weight. What in the world had we done? This was supposed to be a road trip—a lark—and it was turning into a crime spree. What would we do next? Steal a kid's lunch money? Rob a bank?

In the seat ahead of us an old lady was knitting. I could hear her needles sliding and clicking. Every once in a while she'd turn around and smile at me. At first I smiled back, but then I started to get nervous. Was it possible she knew something? Could she read the guilt on my face? Did the Nevada police employ undercover agents old enough to collect Social Security?

I shook Robinson awake. He sat up, rubbing his eyes, and gave me a grumpy look.

"We can never do anything like that again," I said quietly. "Ever."

Robinson ran his hand through his tousled hair and sighed. "I know, Axi. Do you think I wanted it to happen like that? You know that's not me. But we couldn't let him stop us." His dark eyes, with their heavy lashes, searched my face. He wanted to be sure I knew he'd done the only thing he could. "I don't want this to end," he said. "Not yet. Do you?"

I shook my head. I wanted to go on like this with him forever, except I wanted more kissing and less crime. "What if we'd—" I began, but Robinson held up a hand.

"There's no point in what-ifs. What's done is done."

"You sound like my mother," I said. "Who, I have lately realized, was usually full of BS."

Robinson grinned, then faced forward and said hi to the old lady, who'd turned to look at us again. "It was total insanity, I admit that," he whispered to me when she turned back around. "But it's over, okay, Axi? Everything is going to be fine. In the words of Irving Berlin, one of the greatest songwriters of all time, from here on out, there's nothing but blue skies."

Maybe I'm an idiot—actually, I'm definitely an idiot—but hearing him say that made me feel better.

Robinson reached out and brushed a piece of hair from my cheek. "I never want anything bad to happen to you, Axi," he said quietly. "And while I have not yet been in one, I suspect that jail is bad."

"You think it's worse than a pediatric cancer ward?" I blurted.

Robinson seemed to pale. Then he laid his head on my lap again. "I promise," he said, "we'll never do something like that again."

"Pinkie swear," I said, holding out my little finger.

We shook on it.

"And Axi?" He looked up at me from below, his eyes wide and deep enough to drown in.

"What?"

"I'm sorry about Chrissy. Honestly, she came on to me. It took me by surprise. And I didn't want to be rude."

I sighed. Robinson was the only guy in the world who could deliver that line and actually have me believe it. "Yeah, I know how much you dislike rudeness," I said.

"I do," Robinson said, closing his eyes. His voice grew sleepy again. "Rudeness is so...rude..."

I smiled. And then I rested my head against the greasy bus window and fell asleep.

24

WE GOT OFF AT THE ALAMOSA STOP AND stuck out our thumbs, trying to look wholesome and innocent. When that didn't work, Robinson told me it was time for me to show some leg.

"*You* show it," I countered. "You're the one who always charms everyone." (Also? I hadn't shaved since we left home.)

"Except that cop," he said ruefully.

Eventually, a nice old man in an El Camino pulled up. We told him we were headed to the Great Sand Dunes National Park, and he nodded approvingly and drove us right up to the visitors' center. He wouldn't even take ten bucks for gas.

Instead, he slipped me a twenty as I was pulling my backpack from underneath the seat. "Go out for dinner tonight," he urged. "Y'all need some meat on your bones." For a moment he gazed wistfully at the sand dunes, gleaming golden at the base of blue, snow-capped mountains. "If my Meg was alive, I'd call her up and tell her to put a roast in the oven." His eyes seemed to film over. Then he snapped back to the present. "Take care of yourselves, all right?" And then he drove away.

I tried to shake off the strange, sad feeling his good-bye had given me. I looked over at Robinson, who was waving at me from the edge of a creek that cut along the base of the dunes.

"It's like someone picked up a piece of the Sahara and put it down in Colorado," he said when I approached.

"It's amazing," I said, snapping a picture that I knew wouldn't do it justice. "Why do people end up in towns like K-Falls when there are places like this in the world?"

"That's an excellent question," Robinson said. He flung his arms out wide, as if he could hug the whole huge vista. "We should probably never go back." He looked pretty pleased by that idea.

We began walking up a ridge to the top of the dunes. It was tough going—the sand was loose, and our feet sank deep into it. I could hear Robinson breathing hard behind me. As we neared the top, the wind picked up the sand and flung it, stinging, against us.

"It's like full-body exfoliation," Robinson said, wiping the grit from his face. "There are people who pay good money for this."

"The glass is always half-full for you, isn't it?" I asked. I would have smiled, but I'd have gotten sand in my teeth. Optimism was one of his best qualities.

Stinging sand aside, we arrived in a spot that was breathtakingly beautiful. On nearby dunes we saw some people hiking up and others sliding back down on what looked like snowboards. Their delighted shouts carried through the air, which was already shimmering with heat.

Robinson began to strum an imaginary guitar: *"Even castles made of sand…"* Then he looked at me somewhat sheepishly. "Jimi Hendrix."

"I know," I told him. "My dad has that album." I squinted into the distance. Beyond the dunes, the prairie was full of yellow wildflowers. I held my camera at arm's length and took a picture of us squinting and grinning, on top of the world.

We might have hiked back down then, but I turned and saw an old plastic sled half-buried in the sand. I pointed, and Robinson's eyes lit up. "Are you thinking what I'm thinking?" I asked, but I knew he was, so I didn't wait for an answer.

I climbed onto the front of the sled, and Robinson stood behind me, his hands on my back. He began to run, pushing me, and then he leapt in. He wrapped his arms around my waist and buried his head in my hair as we raced down the slope. The wind whipped the sand into my face, but I didn't care—I screamed with delight.

At the bottom of the dune, we lay on the sand, breathless.

"Wow," Robinson said.

"Who needs snow?" I yelled, flinging up my arms. "Want to go again?"

Of course he did.

We spent a giddy, thrilling hour hiking up and then racing down, after which we were so hot and tired we could barely move.

"I'm dying of thirst," Robinson said, collapsing at my feet. "Also I think my nose is fried."

" 'What makes the desert beautiful is that somewhere it hides a well,' " I said.

"Huh?" Robinson asked, rubbing his nose.

"It's a line from *The Little Prince*."

"You and your books," he said teasingly.

"It wouldn't kill you to read one."

He raised a dark eyebrow. "You never know. It might," he said, and smiled. "So where's that well, then?"

I tossed him a water bottle from my backpack, but it arced wide. He scrambled to get it, then opened the lid and drained the liquid in about two seconds.

"You're lucky I've got another one for myself," I chided. "Otherwise that would've been very greedy. Very scalawag-ish."

He snorted. "I know you, Axi. Of course you have extra water. Now I'm going to close my eyes. Wake me in ten." Then he put a shirt over his face and fell asleep, just like that, at the bottom of a sand dune.

We washed off the grit in cold, clear Medano Creek, and we set up our tent at a nearby campground. After dinner — canned chili heated over the fire — we stored our food and packs in the metal bearproof box on the edge of the campsite.

Night came suddenly, as if someone had blown out the sun like a candle. And then the stars burst from the sky, more than I'd ever seen in my life. I stared up, dazzled, and by this point almost too spent to speak.

Robinson looked up, too. "There's something I wanted to say to you that I never got a chance to," he said.

I knew not to get my hopes up by now. "What's that?" I asked.

"You throw like a girl."

"You are such a jerk," I said, laughing. I picked up the rinsed-out chili can and took aim. "I'll show you throwing like a girl!"

"I'm kidding. Those are the last lines from the movie *Sahara*," he said. "Since we spent the day in the desert and all."

I put the can back down. I was too exhausted to throw, anyway. Instead, I took a deep drink of water. And I looked at the long, lean shape of Robinson through the darkness, thinking that there were many different kinds of thirst.

25

WE STOLE A PICKUP JUST AFTER DAWN,
as the sun was rising golden over the mountains.

Isn't it crazy, how matter-of-factly I can say that?

*Well, Your Honor, we ate breakfast, and then we stole a truck.
Granola bars and a Chevy, sir, if specifics matter to the court.*

If I ever meet that judge, I'm sure he'll ask me, "Did you
two think you were invincible?" And I'll look him right in the
eyes. "No, sir," I'll tell him. "In fact, I thought the opposite."

The engine of our borrowed truck was loud and rattling,
and the radio played only AM stations. "This thing needs a
new muffler," Robinson said, frowning. "The exhaust manifold
could be cracked, too."

"Awesome, a broken getaway car," I said. "And wow, are we
listening to *Elvis* right now?"

"*Love me tender, love me true,*" Robinson sang. Then he stopped abruptly. "It's not like I had time to give it a checkup before I stole it." Was it just me, or did that sound a little…huffy? "Anyway, variety is the spice of life, and we can trade up at the next stop. Would you care to tell the chauffeur where that is, Ms. Moore?"

I shrugged. The next stop I'd planned was Detroit, fourteen hundred miles away. "I don't know. The world's biggest ball of stamps? Carhenge? The Hobo Museum?" We were driving northeast, toward Nebraska, heading into what residents of the East and West Coasts liked to call flyover country.

"Carhenge?" Robinson asked, sounding interested. "I bet that's like Stonehenge, but with cars."

"Wow, ten thousand points for you," I said. He gave me a hurt look. "I'm sorry," I mumbled.

I was irritable because I'd been awake most of the night. And it wasn't the claustrophobic tent or the hard ground; it was Robinson. What was I supposed to do about him? About us? We'd been through so much together—and our journey had started well before the trip began. Wasn't it time for me to tell him how I felt (even if I wasn't exactly sure how to describe it)?

I spent a long time thinking about what I'd say, and revising my lines, but in the end I was about as successful as I'd been with my good-bye note to Dad. As in: Not. At. All.

Sample: *Robinson, I think I loved you from the first moment I saw you.* (But I was high on painkillers that day, so I loved everyone.) *When I look at you, I see a better version of myself.* (Wait—so I want to kiss myself?) *I don't know what I'd do without you in my life.* (Um…not steal cars?)

It was stupidly, infuriatingly impossible. No wonder I hadn't written anything decent in ages — I couldn't even figure out how to tell a boy that I loved him. That whenever I looked into his eyes, I felt like I was drowning and being saved, all at the same time. That if I had to choose between dying tomorrow or spending the rest of my life without him, I would seriously consider picking imminent death.

I was afraid of what I felt. But was that the only reason it was so hard to admit it to him? Or was I afraid that he didn't feel the same? Yes, I was definitely afraid of that.

Now, as we drove in silence through the wide-open morning, I wanted so much to slide over to his side of the bench seat. I wanted to put my hand on his leg and feel the answering tremor go through him. I wanted to say, *Pull over and kiss me.*

I took a deep breath. I couldn't sneak over toward him, inch by cowardly inch. I was just going to have to go for it. *All or nothing, Axi. Now is the time.*

I closed my eyes, offering a prayer to the gods of young love, Cupid or Aphrodite or Justin Bieber: *Don't let this be a terrible mistake.*

When I opened my eyes again, I saw that the truck was drifting to the right.

"Robinson?" I said, my voice rising as we veered toward the shoulder.

He didn't answer, and I looked over. His face was so pale it looked almost blue. He began to cough — a terrible, racking, wet sound that came from deep within him.

He looked at me and his eyes were full of fear.

And suddenly he was vomiting.

Blood.

"Stop the truck!" I screamed, reaching for the wheel.

We were already on the shoulder, and Robinson somehow managed to hit the brake while still gagging. Cars whizzed past us, shaking the cab with their speed.

"Oh my God, Robinson!" I cried, moving toward him. I was holding out my hands as if I could catch the blood — as if I could stop it from coming out of him and then put it back inside, where it belonged.

The air swam in front of my eyes. I was crying.

After a horrible, endless moment, Robinson stopped coughing. He wiped his red-streaked mouth with the sleeve of his flannel shirt.

"It's not that much, really," he said weakly, looking at his shirt. "I'm okay now."

But I knew this if I knew anything: *Robinson is not okay.*

Then again, it was possible that I wasn't, either.

part Two

26

AND SO NOW, UNDER A COLORADO SKY so blue it hurt my eyes, we arrived at the terrible truth. You can plot your escape, you can ditch your life and your family, and you can race down a two-lane highway in a stolen car. But there are things you can never outrun.

Things like cancer. Because that comes along for the ride.

I managed to get us to a hospital forty-five minutes up the road in La Junta. Robinson lay with his head in my lap, and I ached to run my fingers through his hair and tell him every-thing would be all right. But because the truck didn't have power steering, I needed both hands on the wheel.

And I wasn't sure that everything *would* be all right, not at all.

The small hospital waiting room was freezing cold, lit with the kind of harsh fluorescent light that makes people look as damp and gray as fish. Robinson shivered and leaned against me. There was a bloom of dark blood on his T-shirt. He buttoned his flannel self-consciously. "Otherwise I look like I've been stabbed," he explained.

"I'm not sure that's a bad thing," I said. There were four other people in the waiting room, and by the looks on their faces, they'd been there awhile.

Robinson shook his head. "I just need to sit down," he said in a raspy voice.

The woman at the desk glanced at me warily as I approached. Maybe she saw the fear in my eyes—or maybe she thought I was homeless or on drugs. I could see my pale reflection in the corner of a mirror, and I couldn't exactly blame her.

"Can I help you?" she asked. Her name tag read DEBBIE.

"My friend is sick," I said, pointing to Robinson, who was huddled on a plastic chair in the corner. The scene in the truck played over and over in my mind. It was nightmarish.

"The doctor has been paged," Debbie said. She inspected my face, frowning lightly. "Do you need to see him, too?"

"I'm absolutely fine," I said stiffly, even though I felt like I might collapse from exhaustion.

I rejoined Robinson, and we sat in the corner for what felt like hours. Eventually, an old man with his arm in a cast leaned over and put his good hand on my knee.

"It's a Saturday morning, hon," he offered. "Most of the doctors and whatnot are fishing."

I bit my lip, hard. We had no doctor. And when we got one,

I knew what it would mean: blood workups, fine-needle aspiration biopsies, positron-emission tomography scans.... The thought of going through this again made me want to run and hide.

"Welcome to small-town America, Axi," Robinson said, "where the bowling alley and the Elks lodge have larger staffs than the hospital."

"Don't worry, the doctor is coming," I said. "Hey, in the meantime, we can watch TV. I know you haven't been getting your daily dose lately."

Robinson nodded. "If only you had a Slim Jim and a box of Oreos, everything would be perfect."

I tried to wipe a spot of blood from his collar. "You really have to eat better."

"I know," Robinson said. "I'm in the ER because of too many Slim Jims and not enough TV." He looked at me slyly.

Oh, if only that were true, I thought. For just a moment I clung to a wild hope that the doctor would give him a spoonful of extra-strength Maalox, and then we could be on our way to the Gateway Arch in St. Louis, or the world's largest ball of twine. But I'd seen his blood, the way it was dark, almost coffee-colored. I knew that meant it came from his gastro-intestinal tract — where the cancer had been.

Where maybe it still was.

"Why do they have to pick the Home Shopping Network?" Robinson asked.

I looked up. A lady with long red nails was selling figurines, smiling at the camera with glossy lips and blindingly white teeth. "Come on. Don't tell me you don't love that jade elephant," I teased.

Why were we talking about crap made in China? About junk food? The elephant we needed to talk about was the one in the room: Robinson's *blood*, his *illness*, which wasn't a matter of nutrition.

On the other hand, ignoring that truth was exactly how we'd gotten as far as we had. We didn't sit around and mope. We took charge; we took *off*. We laughed and we drove too fast and we stuck our heads out the window and gave cancer the finger. Because we understood that a person could be dead long before he or she actually died. And no matter what the future held for us, we didn't ever want to be that kind of people.

Robinson blinked drowsily. "I do kind of like the elephant. I think jade's supposed to be good luck. We could probably use a little of that."

His voice was thick with sleep. His eyes closed, and he leaned his head on my shoulder. I squeezed his fingers, still wrapped in mine. Just like he'd said, we were in this together.

"Everything's going to be fine," I whispered. But Robinson had fallen asleep already, and he couldn't hear me lie.

27

THE BITTER IRONY OF MY LIFE WAS THAT two years after my sister, Carole Ann, died in a pediatric oncology ward in Portland, Oregon, I became a patient in the same wing. I recognized all the nurses, who'd shaken their heads in disbelief. "Both Moore babies?" they'd whispered. *"Both?"*

If God or fate or karma has decided you're going to get cancer, though, you cross your fingers for a kind like mine. Hodgkin's lymphoma is not uncommon, which means that doctors know a lot about it, and by now they're pretty good at curing it. That's the glass half-full.

"Yeah, the glass half-full...of shit," Robinson used to say. I'd met him for the first time in that place, and every time he'd curse, I'd sort of punch him in the arm, because I didn't like it. But I did like *him*, which made being there a little bit easier.

Don't get me wrong. Even a highly curable cancer is no walk in the park. Yes, the hospital walls were painted pretty colors, the nurses wore Winnie-the-Pooh scrubs, and some of the older kids pretended the ward was a boarding school complete with uniforms of thin blue gowns, fuzzy slippers, and bald heads covered in colorful scarves. But being there and being sick totally sucked.

Until the day I met Robinson. Until the day he found me.

If life were a movie, we'd have had what they call a "meet cute." Sort of like this: I'd knock into Robinson while carrying a giant stack of magazines I'd borrowed from the waiting room. And all those good, trashy weeklies like *Us*, *People*, and *Life & Style* would slide everywhere on the floor. I'd make a joke about studying for my pop culture quiz, and he'd laugh as he helped me pick up the mess. By the time the magazines were back in my arms, we'd have realized we were totally hot for each other, and hilarity and romance would ensue for the next ninety minutes.

In real life, it went like this: in a narcotic haze from a bad reaction to a chemo treatment, I was staring at the TV, convinced that Barney the purple dinosaur was speaking directly to me. When I failed to decipher his message, I fell asleep, waking later to see a beautiful dark-haired boy sitting next to my bed. I knew then that I had died, because unless I had been transported to heaven, there was no way a guy that hot would be smiling at me.

But I wasn't dead. It was Robinson, and he was real. He said to me, "You look like shit. I feel like shit. Let's be friends."

And just like that, we were. That's how magnetic Robinson

was: he could tell you that you looked terrible, and you'd still adore him.

Robinson was sicker than I was, but he didn't act like it. He had a rare kind of non-Hodgkin's lymphoma called Burkitt's. The *non* means it's worse.

"Burkitt was the doctor who discovered the cancer in equatorial Africa," Robinson informed me. "It's a lot more common there." He sounded almost proud of his strange and exotic cancer. Then he grinned. "Burkitt also had this whole elaborate theory about the right posture for taking a crap. He said if you squatted—you know, like a baseball catcher—you'd never get colon cancer. Seriously, you can't make this stuff up."

I looked up Burkitt's immediately. For patients with Robinson's numbers (his cancer was Stage IV) the survival rate was 50 percent.

There were kids on the ward who'd only have to have a foot amputated or a mysterious lump removed, and then they'd live to be a hundred. Why Robinson? Why this disease? But Robinson was philosophical. He said, "Fifty percent? I've seen worse."

We all had.

A 50 percent chance of surviving was a flip of a coin. So the night after I learned what the odds for him were, I sat up in my adjustable hospital bed, held a penny tight in my palm, and squeezed my eyes shut. "Heads, he lives," I said. I didn't even whisper what tails meant. I threw the penny into the air, and when I caught it, I had to breathe deeply for a long time before I could look.

It was heads.

I can't tell you how much weight I put on that coin toss. I believed in it with every single cell of my body. *Our luck would not run out.* That's what I told myself.

But they were only words. My mom could predict rain by the dull ache in her knee. My childhood dog, Sadie, could sense the mailman when he was still two blocks away. In this weird, quiet way, they knew what was coming.

And now, so did I.

Now, in the cold, cold waiting room, Robinson leaned against me. I could feel his breath. I imagined I could see the faint, precious pulse of his heartbeat, fluttering beneath the skin. He was so beautiful, so alive.

But for how long? I didn't need a doctor to tell me what I already knew. Robinson — my better self, my heart, my life — was very possibly dying.

Our luck would not run out? *Please*, Axi. Everything runs out eventually. *Everything.*

EVENTUALLY, ROBINSON WAS ADMITTED to the La Junta hospital, and a nurse took us to a private room. She helped him into a bed, and I hopped up on the empty one beside him.

"Are you going to write this down?" Robinson wondered aloud. "In your journal?"

"I only write down the good parts of our adventures," I said.

Robinson snorted. "You can't write a book without a conflict."

I said, "Who said anything about a book? This is my journal. It's a pink notebook I got at Walgreens for two ninety-nine."

Robinson shrugged. "You never know…"

For some reason, this made me laugh. "Sure, I'll write a book," I told him, "as long as you promise to actually read it."

He held up his little finger. "Pinkie swear."

But before I could lean toward him, a voice boomed from the doorway. "So — just what do we have here?" We looked up to see a bearded giant wearing a lab coat and staring at us.

He introduced himself as Dr. Ellsworth, and he hadn't even asked Robinson's last name before he launched into a list of questions. Did Robinson use drugs? Alcohol? Had he traveled internationally recently? Had he ever had an ulcer? Was he allergic to any foods? Had he eaten any spinach during last month's *E. coli* outbreak?

Robinson shuddered at the thought of spinach. He answered no to everything.

I was still amazed by the doctor's size. He could have been a circus strongman, but now he was bending over Robinson's chest, listening to his heart and lungs.

He was frowning.

He palpated Robinson's stomach, and Robinson inhaled sharply, wincing. I had to look away then. I couldn't bear to see him in pain.

After several minutes, Dr. Ellsworth spoke. "I'm going to send you to get a CT scan and an X-ray. There are…abnormalities."

Just because I was expecting to hear something like this didn't mean it didn't knock the wind out of me. I drew in a wobbly breath as Robinson said, "Actually, if it's all the same to you, Doctor, I'd rather not have those things."

"You might be a very ill young man," the doctor said.

Robinson watched him, blinking his dark eyes. "Might," he

allowed. "But let's just leave it at that. No news is good news, right? In the meantime, I do think I have a touch of the flu or something." He offered the best rakish grin he could muster, which, considering the situation, was pretty impressive.

"You have walking pneumonia," Dr. Ellsworth said. "And pleurisy is likely. I can tell you that right now."

"Please let that be all he has," I whispered. I suddenly thought of the orb Robinson had bought me in Mount Shasta, and I reached for it at the bottom of my backpack. I ran my fingers over its smooth surface. It was both a worry stone and a good-luck charm.

The doctor turned to me. "And you?" he asked. "Are you in need of any medical care you'd like to refuse?"

I shook my head. "I'm just here for moral support," I said.

Dr. Ellsworth walked over to the side of the bed I was borrowing and touched my neck. His fingers were cool. "I see the scar right here," he said. "It's from a radiation burn, isn't it?"

I moved away from his touch, saying nothing. I wasn't a patient here, and I didn't have to answer. It didn't matter what I'd had. I was clear. In remission.

Although, as my dad's friend Critter used to say, *Just because it's sunny today don't mean the shitstorm ain't comin'.*

Dr. Ellsworth crossed his arms over his massive chest. "What's going on with you two?" he asked. "Where did you come from?"

Robinson and I looked at each other. He shook his head almost imperceptibly.

I spoke for us. "We can't say at the moment."

Dr. Ellsworth gave us both sharp looks. "This is not a game. It is my belief that this young man here has a mass in his abdomen. A tumor. Do you comprehend the seriousness of that?"

Robinson tried to sit up. "Hey, Axi. What's the difference between a doctor and a lawyer?"

I knew this joke—it was one of Robinson's standards. And I was only half-surprised he was trotting it out now. Playing along, I said, "I don't know. What?"

"A lawyer will rob you; a doctor will rob you and kill you, too."

Dr. Ellsworth made a sound in his throat—a choked-back laugh? A grunt of annoyance? "I'm trying to help," he said.

"Then bring in a TV," Robinson quipped. "Preferably one with cable."

The truth was, Robinson and I had a routine down. We'd perfected it in the halls of the Portland cancer ward. The nurses loved us. We were the Abbott and Costello of cancer. "Hey, Robinson," I said. "What do you call a person who keeps getting lymphoma over and over again?"

"I don't know—what?" But he was already laughing.

"A lymphomaniac!" I cried.

Robinson whooped and pretended to slap his thigh. "Oooh, that was a good one," he said.

Dr. Ellsworth sighed. "If there were a drug to prevent gallows humor, I'd prescribe it for both of you." But I could tell that he thought we were just a tiny bit funny.

He stepped toward the door. "I'm going to give you some intravenous antibiotics, and I'm going to encourage you to think very hard about those tests I mentioned."

"I don't like tests," Robinson said. "I always fail them."

"Where are your parents, young man?"

I glanced at Robinson. That was a question whose answer I didn't know, either.

Robinson turned away. "I'm a legal adult," he said. "Do you want to check my ID?"

Dr. Ellsworth gave Robinson one more long look, then shook his head and left the room.

Robinson closed his eyes. "I'm just going to take a little nap," he said. "If you can stand to be without my company for a while."

I got up and pulled the thin blanket over him. I didn't want him to leave me, not even for a minute. "I think I can manage," I said softly.

He said, "You should close your eyes, too."

"I'm not tired," I said, lying again. But I knew I couldn't sleep, anyway; I needed to watch him. To make sure he didn't start coughing again. To make sure the blood stayed inside him, where it was supposed to be. To watch his chest rise and fall, rise and fall.

I sat down by his bedside. I hoped the antibiotics would work their invisible cellular magic, and quickly. And I wished that what Robinson needed was only—to use his terminology —a little tune-up. Because we weren't going to stick around to get six weeks of chemo in La Junta. That wasn't in the plan.

A few minutes later, I looked up to see that Dr. Ellsworth had returned. "We're moving you to a different room," he said. "I don't want you too far from a ventilator. Or the nurses' station."

Robinson looked over at me and offered a faint, sleepy smile. "Precautionary, of course," he said.

"Of course," I repeated. "You just have a touch of whatever's been going around." Like cancer was contagious, the way doctors once thought it was. Like it was no more serious than the common cold.

I didn't dare look at Dr. Ellsworth. He was going to add *crazy* to Robinson's list of diagnoses, I could already tell. And that was just fine with me.

Because as far as I knew, nobody ever died of crazy.

29

IN THE EVENING THEY SEDATED ROBIN-son, because his breathing had become labored and painful. That, apparently, was the pleurisy. Or maybe it was the pneumonia. I didn't want to know. When they said things like "peritoneal fluid analysis" and "low platelet count," I put my fingers in my ears.

Alone, I read every magazine I could find: *Golf Digest*, *Sport Fishing*, and *Fit Pregnancy*. None held any useful information for me, but considering I'm a golf hater, a vegetarian, and a virgin, that was not exactly surprising.

Then I wandered the corridors, noticing again how much one hospital resembles another. They sound the same (the beeps of heart monitors, the hiss of oxygen machines, the murmuring tones of visitors). They serve the same food (syrupy, too-sweet grape juice; soggy dinner rolls; and pink, plastic-looking ham).

They even smell the same (odors of disinfectant, recycled air, and bodies and what comes out of them—a mix I can only describe as *lavatorial*).

As terrible as La Junta General was, a tiny part of me relaxed a little. Unlike the rest of our cross-country journey, the hospital ward was known territory. A place I could navigate. And I guess I was glad to have a roof over my head again.

But as Robinson would be the first to point out, you can't be Bonnie and Clyde in a hospital. You're in a different movie altogether.

"Pace much?" one of the nurses asked with a friendly smile when I walked by the station for the twentieth time.

I smiled. "Sorry. Just stretching my legs."

"No worries, keep at it," she said. "Exercise does a body good."

She looked like she could stand to get a little exercise herself, but she was busy playing FreeCell on her computer. Slow night in the ER, I guess.

I turned down a new hallway and came upon a set of heavy double doors. Pushing them open, I found myself in the foyer of a small chapel.

It was utterly unlike the rest of the sterile white hospital. The front wall was a deep red. There was a plain wooden altar with LED candles flickering alongside it. There was no statue of Jesus on the cross, though—no Mary or Ganesh or Buddha or L. Ron Hubbard, either, or whoever it was people prayed to around here. There was just that red — the red of valentines, of blood. Faint classical music came from invisible speakers.

I sat down on a bench. My parents had taken me to church about three times before they lost interest in shushing Carole Ann and me every other second. Now I was the only one in the room, so I didn't quite know what to do with myself. I put my face in my hands. Anyone who poked a head in would think I was praying.

I thought of Carole Ann and Robinson — and myself, too. How we'd all been affected by forces that felt terrifying and supernatural but were actually just terrifying and basic. Cancer is abnormal cells dividing without control and invading other tissues. It's that simple. But it was still always a mystery: *Why in the hell is my body trying to kill me?*

Before I went into remission, I hated my body for betraying me. And considering that I was being treated for cancer at the same time I was suddenly growing breasts and having to shave my legs and stick giant pads in the crotch of my underwear — well, it felt like my body was adding insult to injury.

Having Robinson with me on that journey meant everything. We were able to laugh at how weak we were. We had contests over who had the worst mouth sores (chemo causes them; they're awful). We goaded each other to eat food when food was the last thing we wanted.

We'd saved each other, Robinson and me. Or at least, he had saved me.

But why me? Why was I doing so well when Robinson was so sick? When Carole Ann was dead?

What I know about sickness—beyond the fear, the uncertainty, and the nightmarish drudgery of it—is that it builds a wall between the sick and the well. Back in the pediatric oncology ward, Robinson and I had been on the same side of that wall. Now I couldn't bear the idea of any wall between us. I wanted to experience what he was experiencing. I wanted to be with him. For everything.

In a way, I felt like my body was betraying me again—but this time, it was killing me by keeping me well. I knew that wasn't rational. It wasn't like I wanted to get cancer again... right?

I stared at the flickering lights for a long time. When no priest or angel or epiphany from above came to answer my question, I decided to go back to Robinson.

He was getting the intravenous antibiotics for his chest infection. They'd given him morphine, too, because otherwise the medicine hurt too much going in.

Robinson turned toward me and smiled. His eyelids were heavy, his skin pale. "Have I ever told you how beautiful you are?" he asked.

I straightened the edge of his blanket. "That's the morphine talking," I said.

But still I blushed. And I hoped and prayed that it was really him talking.

30

I WAS STANDING ON THE EDGE OF THE cliff again, and dream-Robinson was beside me, holding my hand. I knew he was supposed to tell me something that would reassure me, but he was so silent he could have been a ghost.

I took a step forward, about to plummet into the depths—

I woke with a start.

In the darkness, there was soft rock playing from the radio at the nurses' station, a kind of music that Robinson liked to claim was as deadly as cancer. The nurses always had a good laugh at that one.

I was about to close my eyes and roll back over when I saw the shape at the side of my bed. *Robinson*. He moved forward and touched my shoulder. Even in the darkness, I could see that he had his clothes on—not a hospital gown. "Axi?"

I pushed myself up.

"It's time to leave," he said softly.

He placed my backpack at the foot of my bed and held out his hand to help me up. His fingers were warm and reassuring, as if I were the sick one. Robinson was always so careful with me. I remembered walking the long halls of the Portland hospital with him, the two of us so weak we shuffled like octogenarians.

"Octo-what?" he'd said.

"Octogenarians. People in their eighties."

He'd laughed. "Oh, I don't have to worry about living that long."

I'd stopped in my tracks. What about that coin toss? Didn't that mean anything? "What are you talking about?" I'd demanded.

Robinson grinned. "Axi, I'm going to be a rock star—I'll wear out my body by sixty-five," he explained. "Too many decibels. Too much rock 'n' roll. You can read about me in books someday. I'll be the guy slayed by music. *I knew that dude*, you'll say. *He was cool.*"

Now, in the middle of the night, in the middle of nowhere, I touched Robinson's shoulder. "Are you sure you're okay?"

Faintly, I could see him smile. "I think I've seen enough of La Junta," he said. "We'd better be moving on."

31

I DIDN'T BOTHER ASKING HIM TO LOOK away while I changed into ever-so-slightly-less-grimy clothes. For one, it was dark, and for two, what secrets did I still have from him?

Besides the fact that I loved him, obviously. But maybe it was time to let go of that secret, too, if only I could be brave enough.

Robinson had moved over to the window, his face dimly lit by the orange glow of the parking lot lights. When I was dressed in my jeans and a rumpled sweater, I went to stand beside him.

"Did you know that Cancer is the dimmest constellation of the zodiac?" he asked.

When I shook my head, he pointed to the dark sky. "It's over there. And it doesn't look anything like a crab."

"I didn't know you were such an astronomer."

Out of the corner of my eye I could see his grin. "Axi, I have facets you can't even imagine."

I felt almost dizzy when he said that. Is it possible that you can love someone more than you love life itself, and yet you're still never going to know for sure everything he's thinking? I wanted—I needed—to see every facet of Robinson that I could, for as long as I could.

"And the crazy thing?" Robinson went on. "Every star that you see out there is bigger and brighter than the sun. They only look small because they're farther away." He was still gazing out the window as if a message were written for him in the sky.

The message is right here, Robinson, I wanted to say. *Look at me, and I'll tell you.*

Still, though, I was mute. I tentatively moved closer to his side and clumsily knocked into him with my hip. For a moment I worried the bump I'd given him was too hard. How fragile was he? But when he didn't seem to notice, I wondered if I should try it again. I wondered if I should grab his hand. I wondered if I should tackle him, throw him to the floor, and kiss every inch of his frail, beautiful body.

I scooted closer to him again, and this time it felt like it registered. He was suddenly more aware of me. He stayed very still as energy seemed to ripple in the air between us. I held my breath, and I think he was holding his, too.

Now is the time, Axi, I thought. *Carpe diem.*

I reached across him to his far hand and turned him toward me. "I have something to tell you," I whispered.

"I'm all ears," he whispered back.

He waited silently, giving my eyes time to search his face: his high forehead, his deep-set eyes, his full mouth.

I opened my lips, but nothing came out. I was the writer, the reader—and now, when I truly needed to say the things I'd been wanting to say for what seemed like forever, words were utterly failing me.

"It's okay," Robinson said softly.

What's okay? I could have asked. *Nothing is okay! We're in a hospital because you could be dying! How many more chances will I have to chicken out before you're suddenly gone?*

If I couldn't say anything, I had to do something. Right this second. Or I might never get to feel the sensation of his lips touching my lips.

I couldn't live without that.

And that was all it took. I wrapped my arms around his neck and brushed my face so close to his that his unshaven chin tickled my skin. And then—I kissed him.

When our lips met, in a rush of warmth and softness, electricity flooded my body. I was sure that I began to glow. That I was full of starlight.

Finally. This was what I'd been aching for. And from the way Robinson's breath instantly melted into mine...I felt for all the world like he'd been aching for it, too.

Why on earth had we waited so long?

Robinson's arms tightened around my waist, and his hands found their way into my hair. A tiny moan escaped from his throat, and he kissed me full-strength, like he'd never been sick and never would be again...like he was more alive than ever.

And so was I.

After a minute, or an hour, we pulled apart, breathless. My cheeks were burning, and my whole body felt like it was vibrating. Like it was singing.

At first Robinson's eyes looked so solemn that my breath caught in my throat. Then, like a light blinking on in the darkness, came the smile that I craved, that crooked grin full of life.

"I love you, Axi Moore," he whispered. "What else can I say?"

I shook my head and smiled, my eyes glistening. I was still so overwhelmed that I couldn't say a word.

If this was what life was like without words—a life of *doing*, not just talking—I just might be willing to give them up forever.

32

IT WAS TIME TO GO. WE HURRIED OUT into the darkness, Robinson's arm wrapped around my shoulders. It was like a hug — as if now that we'd finally really touched, we couldn't bear to let go of each other — but it was also him using me to hold himself up.

I was still glowing. I felt brighter than any of the stars.

Kissing Robinson was like coming to the end of the desert and finding a spring. It was sunshine after years of winter. It was Christmas in June. It was — oh, give me a break, why bother with dumb poetic phrases?

What I felt was joy.

Joy that totally swept away the anxiety of breaking out of a hospital against medical advice. My list of rebellious feats was growing longer by the second.

At the edge of the parking lot, Robinson leaned down and gave me another deep kiss. Then he pulled away, smiling. "Suddenly I feel like I can do anything," he said.

I felt exactly the same way. Everything would be fine. Or even better than fine. Magical. "Just tell me that *anything* doesn't include taking a different car," I said, pressing my hand against his scratchy cheek. "This is excitement enough."

Robinson kissed me again, his lips soft but urgent. At this rate, we'd never leave the parking lot—and maybe I didn't even care, as long as this kept happening.

"I'd never ditch Chuck the Truck," Robinson said after a while. "He needs to see Detroit."

I laughed giddily—clearly the making out was messing with my head a little. "Chuck the Truck?"

"Yes, ma'am," Robinson said. "Second cousin to Charley the Harley."

He laughed at his own joke and climbed into the truck. He started the engine, revving it a few times to warm it up. Then, for some reason, he scooted over into the passenger seat, where I was about to sit.

I quit my giggling. "Um, Robinson?" I said, eyeing the empty space behind the steering wheel.

He leaned back against the headrest. "Yeah, I know I said I felt like I could do anything...but I think it's probably better if you drive right now."

I noticed that his voice had become raspy again, and he

had his hand over his chest, as if he were having trouble breathing.

"Then we should turn around and go back to the hospital!" I insisted. "Detroit will still be there in a couple of days."

Robinson shook his head. "No way, Axi. I'm done with that place."

"But what if it's not done with you?"

He patted the seat. "Come here, Axi. Sit beside me."

I went around to the other side and clambered onto the truck's high bench seat. Robinson put his arm around my shoulders, and I buried my face in his flannel shirt. It smelled like the hospital, but underneath that, like him. Like soap and pine and *boy*.

Of course I wanted to leave. I wanted to be alone with Robinson again. I wanted more of what we'd started in the hospital. A *lot* more.

But was this a mistake?

When Robinson spoke again, his voice seemed stronger. It also seemed like he'd been reading my thoughts. "Who cares if leaving here is a mistake? I'd make this mistake again, a million times," he insisted. "We're together. That's what matters. I want to take this trip with you. That's all I want. That's all I need. I'm not going to be irradiated or scanned or biopsied or whatever it is they want to do to me."

I spoke into his shirt because I didn't want to move away from him, not even a single millimeter. "But what if it's a death sentence? To refuse treatment now?" I whispered.

Robinson scoffed. "A hospital is a death sentence. You can cut your finger, get a staph infection, and the next thing you know, you're checking out the grass from underneath. Leaving now, Axi, is choosing life."

I could hear the quick beating of his heart. "But what if it's a shorter life?"

He shrugged. "Well, as Kurt Cobain said, 'It's better to burn out than to fade away.' Although, actually, he was quoting a Neil Young song."

I sat up suddenly. What in the world was I going to do with this infuriating person? "May I remind you that Cobain used it in his *suicide note?*"

"Well, you have to admit he had a point, GG," Robinson said mildly.

I closed my eyes and breathed in deeply, calming myself. Robinson's hand reached out, and his fingers slipped between mine, trying to reassure me.

What if doing what you wanted and doing what was right seemed like two entirely different things? What if by living the life you chose, you somehow doomed yourself—or worse, someone you loved?

After a minute, I opened my eyes. We couldn't know the future or how long it would last. We could only choose to be happy and alive right now.

"Okay, okay, you win, Robinson," I said. "But only on these conditions." I held up two fingers. "One: do not call me

GG, remember? Two: you are not allowed to die. Do you hear me?"

Robinson grinned and saluted me. "Yes, ma'am," he said. "Agreed. Ten-four. Et cetera."

We shook on it, as if it were just that simple.

And then I gritted my teeth and started driving.

33

ROBINSON FELL ASLEEP ALMOST IMMEDI-
ately. This was fine with me, because I needed complete and
total focus on my new assignment: piloting a speeding death-
and-dismemberment trap across the country.

Because, FYI, car crashes kill way more kids than cancer
does. Those crosses you see on the side of the highway, the little white ones hung with fading silk flowers? They're for people my age. ("People who were texting," my dad liked to
remind me—because he never wanted to blame Budweiser for
anything.)

I managed not to become a highway statistic in those early
hours, but there were occasional...problems. For instance, I
pulled into a Texaco for gas but didn't know how to operate the
pump, and Robinson was sleeping so deeply I couldn't wake
him. After I begged some nice old man to help me fill my tank,

I got back on the highway going in the wrong direction. For thirty miles.

After I turned around, I tried playing the radio softly. It barely worked, so I turned it off and had only my thoughts to keep me company:

I never knew how damn big *the United States is.*

Where's the nearest Starbucks?

How come my dad hasn't found me yet?

The miles ticked by, monotonous but nerve-racking. Eventually, I just started talking out loud to keep myself company.

"Don't take this the wrong way," I said, though I knew Robinson was still in dreamland, "but I don't think I ever believed we'd make it this far. Like, wouldn't my dad call the cops when he woke up and found me gone? Or even just call Critter? That guy's a human bloodhound."

Critter had even found the diamond that had fallen out of my mom's engagement ring—in a river. Not that having the diamond back encouraged her to stick around.

"Obviously, I'm not saying I want to be caught. I want to keep going. But I guess I wonder if we've just been really lucky so far? Or is there a certain amount of…disinterest on my dad's part concerning the location of his remaining daughter?"

I took a sip of cold truck-stop coffee. It felt good to talk about it, even if—or especially because—Robinson wasn't listening.

"And then there's you," I said to Robinson's sleeping silhouette. "Where are your parents? Aren't they worried about you? Do they have any idea where you are?"

When I met Robinson on the cancer ward, he'd brushed off all talk of his family. No sad-eyed father sat with him while he got his chemo; no weeping mother held his hand while he was bombarded with radioactive particles.

He was, for all that the rest of us could see, 100 percent alone.

On the other hand, no one was more popular. Robinson could turn a Domino's delivery guy into his new BFF in five minutes. Once I heard two of the nurses talking about how they wanted to adopt him. And of course he could've had his pick of girls, on or off the ward. He was magnetic.

Out of everyone, he'd chosen me. I was his family.

When we were discharged, Robinson followed me to Klamath Falls. "We need to stick together, Axi," he'd said. "Plus, I have an uncle there. Says I can live in his basement."

I didn't question it—all I cared about was not saying good-bye.

I realized now how much he'd left behind in the course of his life: his parents, his uncle, the doctors who wanted to treat him. It was as if he'd run from everyone but me.

"Am I enough, Robinson?" I heard myself ask. "Can I really be everything you need?"

He shifted in his sleep, stretching out his long legs. But he didn't wake up to answer that critical question.

"I wonder," I went on, "if it's possible to go so far that I'll stop being afraid of us not ever coming back." I chewed on my lip for a while, then drank some more bitter coffee. "I thought

I'd figured out the risks. I thought I had everything planned out. But I hadn't counted on you getting sick."

I sneaked another glance at him. His eyelashes made a dark curve against his pale cheek, and his left hand twitched, moving in a dream.

There was another thing I hadn't counted on. And that was falling in love, as fast and irrevocably as you would fall off a cliff, and realizing that loving someone might mean to simultaneously want to slug them and hold them and possibly have to watch them die. . . . I hadn't counted on that.

I reached over and touched his cheek. "I love you," I whispered. "Please stay with me."

In his sleep, Robinson turned and sighed.

34

ROBINSON AND I STOOD, OUR FINGERS intertwined, and stared at the ruins: crumbling buildings, burned-out houses, litter-strewn sidewalks, and the empty hulk of an old Ford factory.

"Welcome to Detroit," Robinson said happily. He was feeling much better today, and I was hoping our location had nothing to do with it. "Motor City. Motown. I could have been stuck growing up here if my parents hadn't left."

"It was probably a little nicer back when they were growing up here, huh?" I said, all the while hoping it wasn't symbolic that the first place Robinson and I visited together as a couple (because that's what we were now, right?) was in total shambles.

With the tip of his boot, Robinson sent an empty can of Red Bull arcing into the summer air. "Yeah, probably it was."

I took a picture of a mildewed sofa with a bunch of pigeons

perched on it. To our left, a tree was growing out the side of a building.

"I guess it could be beautiful, in a way, if you were into romantic decay or steampunk or something," I said. "Or maybe we should imagine it like the Parthenon in Greece. A bunch of grand old ruins."

Robinson nodded thoughtfully. "That old Ford factory is where my grandma and grandpa met and fell in love," he said. "On the assembly line." He gestured off vaguely in another direction. "And down that way was the Chrysler plant where my mom and dad did the same thing."

I bent down and plucked a dandelion from a crack in the pavement. "So I guess this used to be a pretty romantic place then," I said.

Robinson was quiet, gazing out on the desolation. Thinking, maybe, about his family, wherever they were. So it took me completely by surprise when he whirled me toward him. He held me close for a moment, his arms tightening around me. And then he bent down and kissed me, long and deep, until I felt that familiar softening inside, my legs going wobbly. Like maybe if he didn't keep holding me up, I might dissolve.

When he pulled away, he smiled. "What do you mean *used to be?*"

I kept my arms around his waist. I wanted to be as close to him as possible, for as long as possible. "I stand corrected," I said, looking up at him, backlit by the sun, so the ends of his dark hair looked like they were on fire. "Two generations of your family fell in love here. That's pretty amazing." Thinking: *Now three.*

He nodded, but he didn't elaborate. His eyes had that faraway look in them again.

"I guess you come by your car obsession naturally, then," I continued. I wanted him to keep talking, because he was always so tight-lipped about his family that I knew almost nothing about them.

"My dad always said his first baby was his 1967 Mustang," Robinson offered.

"So you grew up here?" I asked.

Robinson began to whistle that Sufjan Stevens song about Detroit.

I jabbed him in the ribs. "Seriously, you're not going to answer? You tell me you love me, but you don't want to tell me where you were freaking born?" I was laughing, but I was a little offended, too.

When Robinson looked down at me again, his face was clouded. "I'm just not…in close touch with my parents these days. It makes me sad to think about them. So I try not to."

Seeing as how he'd had enough hardship lately, I decided not to press the issue. "Just give me a natal city."

Robinson smiled. "You and your fancy words. *Natal.* World, I ask you: Who says *natal* besides Alexandra Jane Moore?"

I jabbed him in the ribs again. There wasn't anyone but pigeons to answer him.

"No, I wasn't born here," Robinson said finally. "Chrysler moved the plant before I was born. My parents went to North

Carolina, and that's where I showed up. My dad worked for a steel company for a while, and then he opened up his own auto repair shop." Robinson began to whistle some other song I didn't recognize, ending our conversation.

I sighed. "At this rate, it'll take me fifty years to learn about your childhood."

He reached out and touched my cheek with his fingertips. "Oh, Axi-face, who cares about the past? We have now."

"Axi-face?" I repeated. I took his hand and brought his fingers to my lips. Smiling, I kissed them on their tips, one after the other.

He nodded. "It's new. You like it?"

"I'll get back to you on that." The truth was, I'd like any pet name he came up with. But I wasn't going to admit it.

For a while we just stood there, being quiet with each other, our fingers touching lightly. We watched birds circling overhead, and the clouds shifting. It struck me then that the earth could be covered in trash and wreckage, but you could always find something that seemed clean and perfect. Maybe that was a metaphor for something.

After a while I leaned in to give Robinson a gentle kiss. He took my face in his hands. "So," he said, "can I buy you dinner or what?"

I smiled. "Does that make it a date?"

Grinning back, he shrugged. "Depends. Am I going to get past first base?"

"Pig," I said, laughing.

"Pig!" he repeated. "Speaking of which, let's go eat some."

35

WE PLAYED MOTOWN IN THE CAR—
Diana Ross, Stevie Wonder—as we drove downtown. Robinson hummed and tapped his fingers on the dash, following
the drumbeats and adding little flourishes of his own.

We found a restaurant full of Christmas lights and orange-
velvet banquettes, its walls hung with funky instruments and
dozens of black-and-white pictures of Detroit in its old-timey
heyday. Someone was playing the piano in the corner, loudly,
and the place was packed.

"It's like a speakeasy crossed with a TGI Fridays," I said as
we sat down.

"Or, like, if Liberace were a gangster and this was his living
room."

"Or it's the hangout of a pimp who likes jazz and antiques,"
I said.

Robinson grinned. "It's awesome."

We found a table in the corner, and the waiter came by and set two small glasses full of clear liquid on the table. "Hungarian moonshine," he said, by way of greeting. "It's Ed's birthday." He seemed to think we should know who Ed was. "I'll be back to take your order in a minute."

Robinson and I looked at the glasses and then at each other. "Should we?" I asked.

He pretended to look disappointed. "I have so many fake IDs. I really wanted the chance to use another one."

We held up our glasses and clinked them together. "*Sláinte*," I said.

"*Slan-cha?*" Robinson said, frowning. "I've heard that before...what does it mean?"

I shrugged. "Dunno. It's just some old Irish toast." But of course I knew exactly what it meant. It meant "health." Because didn't that matter more than just about anything these days?

We knocked our glasses back, and the liquid burned down my throat, making me shudder. "Is that what radiator fluid tastes like?"

Robinson was sloshing it around in his mouth. Then he swallowed. "This is more like rubbing alcohol, I'd say."

I could feel it in my stomach now, warming me. Was it possible that I felt looser, almost light-headed already? "Funny how a tiny little shot makes me feel so rebellious, when I'm already a car thief."

"I believe your term was *borrower*," Robinson noted.

"Because that's going to go over really well with the judge," I said. *"Oh, you were only borrowing that Porsche? No problem, then!"*

"You guys aren't from around here, are you?"

Robinson and I both looked up, startled. Guilty people are jumpy people, I guess. But it was only our waiter, who looked like he'd had a shot or two of the moonshine himself.

"No, sir," Robinson said, polite as can be.

The waiter pointed a finger at us. "Well, when you go back home, tell your friends how the Big D is doing just fine. I know you went and saw the closed-up factories; everybody does. But don't remember just the dead stuff. Remember this." He waved his arm around the happy, noisy room. "Remember the music and the moonshine. Is that a deal?"

Robinson and I nodded in tandem, and the waiter nodded back, satisfied. "Be back in a minute for that order."

When he left again, Robinson reached for my hand. "He's right. You have to remember the good stuff, Axi."

There was something about the way he said it that made a chill crawl up my spine. Like he was talking about much more than just Detroit. But I smiled and shook his hand anyway. "It's a deal. Scout's honor," I said. "Pinkie swear. Blah blah blah."

Robinson smiled. "You really are beautiful, you know that?" he said.

I looked down at the tabletop, but he reached out and tucked a finger under my chin, tipping my face up so I had to look right into his dark eyes.

First Love

"I mean it. Someone should tell you that every single day of your life. And right now, it gets to be me."

"It's always going to be you," I whispered.

He smiled again. "Get over here."

I went around to his side of the booth—and I sat down in his lap. It surprised both of us.

"Axi," he said, his voice soft and throaty. He ran a fingertip along my collarbone. "I never took you for the PDA type."

I shivered under his touch and pressed my forehead to his. When I spoke, our lips were tantalizingly close. "I'm learning how to live dangerously," I said.

He moved a fraction of an inch closer, so his lips almost brushed mine. "And what do you think of it?" he whispered.

I could almost taste him, and I held out for another long, delicious moment before finally pressing my mouth against his. Pushing my fingers into the tangle of his hair. We kissed, and warmth flooded my body.

"I like it," I whispered. "A lot."

I was nearly dizzy. *So this is what being intoxicated feels like.* But it wasn't from the shot I'd taken.

I am here to say that moonshine has nothing on love—and lust.

36

"THE BLUE STREAK, THE MEAN STREAK, and the Millennium Force," Robinson said. "I want to go on all of them. You only get to go on the Mean Streak, Axi."

He was pretending to be mad at me because I'd told him he couldn't have a Slim Jim until he'd eaten a banana. *Who are you, my mother?* he'd asked. I told him I couldn't watch him eat things made from mechanically separated chicken, aka *slimy pink meat paste*, anymore. Then he'd accused me of being a snotty vegetarian, and I had tackled and tickled him in the cab of the truck until he pleaded for mercy.

Now we were inside the gates at Cedar Point, the roller-coaster capital of the world, nestled away in Sandusky, Ohio. Robinson, the daredevil, and me, the one who gets queasy on swings.

"I feel like the Junior Gemini might be more my speed," I said.

Robinson snorted. "Axi, you've done things lately that were a lot scarier than a roller coaster." He cocked a finger at me, miming a gun.

"Don't remind me," I said.

"So. Shall we?" he asked, and held out his arm.

How could I refuse him? My scalawag, my partner in crime, my heart. He seemed like he was in perfect health. Was he? I didn't know, but now was the time to enjoy it.

We stood in the first line for an hour at least, surrounded by tired parents, their hyperactive eight-year-olds and sullen thirteen-year-olds, and a handful of sunburned retirees apparently willing to risk a heart attack to pull four g's on a single plummet.

Robinson saw me picking nervously at the hem of my T-shirt. "I'm telling you, this is going to be awesome," he said. "You're going to love it."

He reached out and stroked my hair, and then his fingers moved down to my neck, kneading gently, reassuringly.

I almost moaned in pleasure. "Whatever you say..." Suddenly I wasn't thinking about the ride at all anymore. I was thinking about his hands. "Just keep doing that."

He laughed, rubbing my shoulders now, his body long and warm against my back. "Is this all it takes?" he asked. "A little back rub and tough Axi Moore turns into a quivering pile of acquiescence?"

"Ooh, that's a big word for you," I teased, trying to reclaim some measure of my sass. It wasn't easy.

"Maybe a good vocabulary is contagious," he said.

"Mmmmmmm."

"Although it seems like you might be losing yours."

"Mmmmm, lower..."

Robinson pulled me against him then, wrapping his arms around me from behind. "Maybe we shouldn't get too carried away," he said into my ear.

I sighed. "I guess..."

"But you're not afraid anymore, are you?"

I shook my head firmly. I wasn't.

Of course, my heart *did* begin pounding as soon as we climbed into the rear car of the Millennium Force, but I told myself it was because of excitement, not fear. I told myself that compared to all the things we'd done that were authentically dangerous, like stealing cars and riding motorcycles and breaking into people's pools, this was a walk in the park.

When we rose slowly up the hill, the tracks amazingly smooth beneath us, I grabbed Robinson's hand. Ahead of us people were already screaming. My knuckles went white around Robinson's fingers.

"Here it comes," he said.

When it seemed that the car could climb no higher into the faultless summer sky, we came to the top, paused for one silent, anticipatory second—and then plunged down. *Downdowndowndowndown.*

I screamed more loudly than I ever would have thought possible, and beside me Robinson let out a wild whoop of joy. We raced and looped above the park, the wind making my eyes water and the car whipping me back and forth. I never stopped screaming, not for one single instant. And Robinson, he just laughed and laughed, letting my fingernails dig half-moons into his skin.

When we finally slowed down on the last approach and pulled under the awning to stop, I turned to Robinson, an enormous smile on my face. "Wow," I declared. "I want to do that again."

He gave me a triumphant look. "I knew you'd like it. I know you better than you know yourself." Then he reached up. "Give me a little help here, will you?"

I bent down and grabbed his hand, felt the weight of his palm in mine. "Thanks," he said. He brushed my bangs out of the way, and then his lips against my forehead were soft and sweet.

Holding hands loosely, we walked out onto the concourse, which was lined with flowers, streaming with people, and fragrant with the smells of fried food and sunscreen.

"Let's get cotton candy," I said.

"And sodas as big as our torsos," Robinson added.

"And nachos and licorice ropes," I cried, beginning to skip.

Robinson laughed as I tugged him along behind me. "I think the roller coaster knocked a screw loose. Don't you want some kale or something?"

"Tomorrow! Today we're going to act like normal teenagers!"

Because today I actually felt like one. As if nothing made Robinson and me different from anyone else our age—not sickness, crime, or anything. We were carefree. Lucky. Immortal.

"Have I ever told you I love you?" Robinson asked, catching up to me.

"Yes, but tell me again," I said, stopping to press myself against him.

"I love you," he said.

"I love you back," I said.

And then we kissed on the midway as crowds of people streamed around us and the roller coaster cars corkscrewed overhead.

37

"So," Robinson said, "onward to the Big Apple?" We were finally heading for the truck, so exhausted it felt like we ought to take turns carrying each other.

"No one calls it the Big Apple, you know," I said. "That's a tourist thing."

"And we're not tourists?" he asked, lifting one dark eyebrow.

"No, we're *adventurers*," I said. "Explorers."

Robinson handed me the souvenir key chain he'd bought at the last gift shop before the exit. It was a tiny model of the Millennium Force, tucked inside a snow globe. "Since you're a driver now and all," he said, grinning crookedly.

"Of course, I don't have any keys," I pointed out.

"Hey, if you don't want it, I can hook it to my screwdriver or my cordless drill."

But of course I wanted it. It was a present from the boy I loved. "I'm going to get you something, too, you know," I said, giving the snow globe a little shake.

Robinson demanded to know what it was, but I shook my head and mimed zipping my lips. "It's a surprise."

As I climbed into the driver's seat of the truck, I caught Robinson eyeing a sporty black BMW parked next to us. "Don't even think about it," I said. "I can't drive a stick."

"I'll teach you that next," he said. "And then, ATVs."

"Then dirt bikes," I said. "Why not?" Because everything was going to be just fine from now on. Maybe we really did have all the time in the world.

With Robinson as my navigator, I got us onto I-80. We had a long drive ahead of us, and the back roads just weren't going to cut it. I wanted something lined with Starbucks.

"Doesn't time move slower the faster you go?" Robinson asked, staring out at flat green fields and signs for Pacific Pride truck stops.

I thought back to my physics class, which felt like it was about a million years ago (so what does that say about time?). "It's only a matter of nanoseconds or something. Time moves slower the closer you are to the earth, too."

"That gives me an excellent reason not to go mountain climbing."

"As if you needed one," I said.

"True. Somehow the thought of plunging hundreds of feet to my death never appealed to me." He toyed with the key chain, watching the snow sift down over the tiny roller coaster. "Do you ever think about what happens after?" he asked suddenly.

"After what?" I asked, moving into the passing lane.

"After we earn our wings," he said. He looked at me, waiting for a reaction. I kept my eyes on the road. "Don't joke," I said.

Robinson crossed his arms over his chest. "I'm not joking. I'm asking."

"After we 'earn our wings' . . ."

"Don't you remember? Nurse Sophie used to say that all the time. She was totally sincere."

I pressed harder on the gas pedal. I was actually going the speed limit now. "Because she believed that when you die, you become an angel," I said. "Whereas you think we just take a dirt nap."

Robinson snickered. "Sorry. That dirt nap thing always gets me."

"It's not funny," I said.

But the truth was, we'd joked about death constantly back in the ward. All of us had, because somehow it made us less afraid. *Oh, I'm sooo tired*, someone would say, *I think I'll go sleep with the fishes*. Someone else would pipe up: *Lately I've been thinking about buying a pine condo*. Or: *Yeah, I'm planning on going into the fertilizer business*.

It was flipping Death the bird. And it made awful things like chemotherapy-induced nausea and hair loss just slightly less awful. But I thought—or hoped—that Robinson and I had left that sort of thing behind us. That such humor was no longer...medically relevant.

"I don't know, Robinson," I said, gripping the steering wheel. "I want to think there's something on the other side, but where's the evidence? No one sends you a postcard from the afterlife."

"Which is totally rude of them," he replied.

"I know, right?" I raised my fist. "Do you hear that, Carole Ann? *Rude.*"

Robinson reached over and put his hand on my knee. "Don't worry," he said. "I'll write you."

I felt like I'd been punched in the gut.

And I wanted to laugh, to show that I knew he was joking. But I wasn't entirely sure he was.

38

WE CROSSED THE WIDE EXPANSE OF Pennsylvania while Robinson slept. In the dark it looked like any other state, and I shot through it at seventy-five.

In East Orange, New Jersey, at midmorning, I sent Robinson into a Pathmark to buy groceries ("healthy stuff," I'd said, fully expecting him to try to pass off Froot Loops as actual fruit) while I went across the street to a place called All That Glitters Is Gold.

Thanks to my dad, I knew my way around a pawnshop. Which was how, for fifty bucks and the pearl-and-gold bracelet that had been my mother's, I bought Robinson an acoustic guitar.

"Where'd you go?" Robinson asked when I pulled up outside the Pathmark. He set the bag of groceries in the backseat, and I was shocked to see an actual banana in it.

"Just a quick errand," I said, trying not to smile at the thought of the guitar hidden under the tent behind the backseat. "Did you honestly buy fruit and vegetables?"

He leaned over and kissed my neck. "Tell me where you went," he said, his lips ticklish on my skin.

I drew in my breath. "No." Every time he touched me, I felt my whole body begin to hum and shiver.

"Tell me," he said again, moving from my neck to my earlobe, his mouth light and teasing.

"Robinson," I whispered. I'd tell him anything, I'd give up every secret I'd ever had, if he kept doing that.

I pulled him toward me, my mouth finding his. Before I knew it, my fingers were on the buttons of his shirt. I managed to get the top two undone, but then suddenly he moved away from me. He backed up against the car door, rebuttoning his shirt quickly.

I sat up straight, blinking. Confused. Didn't he want it, too?

"What?" I asked. "Why—"

"Security guards," Robinson said, nodding toward the burly guys walking up and down the rows of the parking lot.

There were three of them—two only a stone's throw away. But they could have been sitting in the backseat and I wouldn't have noticed while Robinson was filling up all my senses.

"We should probably go," he said. "We can, um, do some more of that later."

My cheeks were pink with embarrassment. "Okay," I said. As if I didn't want to shout, *Hell yes, we will!*

Robinson smiled. "But you know what? I think I want to drive."

I was so relieved that he was feeling good, so thrilled at the way I could kiss him now whenever I wanted — security guards notwithstanding — that I, small-town girl Axi Moore, didn't freak out at *all* when the New York skyline became visible along the turnpike, with its hills and valleys of silvery skyscrapers. I didn't care that we sat in traffic outside the Holland Tunnel for forty-five minutes, or that Robinson got lost on the way across town to the East Village.

He was driving. He was happy and strong. That made everything okay.

39

TOGETHER, ALONG WITH A CRUSH OF
tourists, we walked down St. Marks Place, trying on cheap
sunglasses at the outdoor booths and browsing a two-story
store called Trash and Vaudeville, where Robinson posed for
a picture in a silver pleather biker jacket and I tried on a
bright blue wig. We stopped in to St. Mark's Bookshop, and I
got a copy of Whitman's *Leaves of Grass* and a book of Dylan
Thomas poems.

"Poetry?" Robinson said, looking aghast.

"Just read one," I said.

Robinson opened the Whitman to a random page and
cleared his throat. " 'A child said, What is the grass? fetching it
to me with full hands; / How could I answer the child? . . . I do
not know what it is any more than he. / I guess it must be the
flag of my disposition, out of hopeful green stuff woven.' " He

looked at me, intrigued. "Okay," he said, "I like that well enough. 'Hopeful green stuff woven.'"

I laughed. "I've got something you'll like better, though." I took his hand and led him down the street to the car.

"Is it my surprise?" he asked excitedly.

"Look under the tent," I said.

When Robinson pulled out the guitar, his whole face lit up. He hefted the weight of it in his hands and plucked a string experimentally.

"Axi, how—"

"Let's go play it," I said. I didn't want to have to tell him that I'd given up my mother's bracelet—the last thing I had of hers—to buy it. And that I wasn't the least bit sorry.

Hand in hand, we walked over to Tompkins Square Park and found a bench beneath a ring of ginkgo trees. Robinson strummed for a moment, finding the chords. They seemed familiar to me, but I didn't recognize the tune until he began to sing.

"*Moving forward using all my breath*," Robinson sang. The song was "I Melt with You."

I haven't talked about Robinson's voice, and this is partly because I can't explain it. It's clear and rough at the same time; it's intimate but also demands an audience. It's usually soft, but somehow you hear it not just with your ears but with your whole body. And with your heart most of all.

People who were walking by began to stop to listen as he sang. Robinson didn't seem to notice them gradually gathering around him, though. His eyes were on his boot, tapping on the cobblestones. Every once in a while, he looked at me, right into my eyes, singing: *"I'll stop the world and melt with you..."*

Soon there was a big circle of people, young, old, and in between. Most of them were parents, with kids carrying stuffed bunnies or pockmarked Nerf footballs or—the older ones—iPhones. And these parents all knew the song, because it was the one they'd danced to twenty years earlier, when they were in high school and in love for the first time.

At first a few of them just mouthed the words, but then, quietly, they began to sing. Then others joined in, too, and they lost their hard, blank city faces and smiled, and in another minute it was a damn *sing-along*. I swear to God, there were people with tears in their eyes, because that's how beautiful Robinson is when he plays.

When the song ended, there was silence. For a moment I felt like the entire city went quiet and took one long, sweet breath. Like everyone, everywhere, was thinking about life, and how it is the happiest and saddest thing, the most wonderful and the most terrible and the most precious.

Then the silence broke. A woman in a bright yellow dress began to clap, and then, just the way the singing had grown, so did the clapping, until the applause was really loud. There was another woman blowing her nose, and a man staring up at the sky and blinking really hard and fast—but most people were just smiling.

An old man stepped forward and placed his cap on the ground. "You forgot to pass the hat," he said.

Robinson looked up, startled. "Pardon?" he said. He was still in the world of the song. He didn't realize there was anyone but him and me.

The old man looked a little like Ernie. He turned back to the crowd and called, "Cough it up for the young performer, all right?"

Robinson and I watched as almost every person stepped forward with quarters and dollars. I saw a woman give her daughter some money, and the girl tiptoed up and put a twenty into the hat. She was about Carole Ann's age when she died, the age she'd be forever. Her hair was even red, like my sister's.

"Thank you," I whispered.

Then it was all over, and the people left. Robinson and I were alone again. The hat was full of money.

Robinson was smiling at me. "We're rich," he said, and he pulled me onto his lap.

And truly, then, it felt like we were.

40

WE DECIDED TO SPLURGE ON A HOSTEL that night. It sounded like a better idea than sleeping on a park bench, though we would've had plenty of interesting company had we gone that route.

The Grand Street Hostel was on the edge of Little Italy, where it bleeds into Chinatown, and it looked decent enough from the outside. There were a couple of backpacker types smoking out front, and the guy at the desk was friendly in a stoned sort of way.

But Robinson and I quickly learned that the difference between a hostel and a hotel goes way, *way* beyond the minor distinction in spelling. When the *s* is added, you subtract things like privacy, comfort, and in this case, ceilings. The hostel was a maze of tiny, thin-walled cells, sloppily constructed inside an enormous hangarlike room.

"It's a bit more prison-y than I might have expected," Robinson said.

"No kidding," I agreed, stepping over a lone boot in the hall. "I feel like we should have gotten fingerprinted."

Luckily, we had our own room, with two single beds pushed right up against each other, and about six inches of floor space on either side.

"Well, the sheets look clean, at least," Robinson said brightly. Then he gave me a quick kiss and headed down the hall to the bathroom.

I sat on the corner of the bed and looked up at the non-ceiling. I could hear one end of an unpleasant cell phone conversation from a nearby room. *It's not my fault you got kicked out*, someone said. *Everyone's hated you for years.*

I hummed a little, trying to give this person some privacy. The song was "Tangled Up in Blue," but you wouldn't know it, since I can't carry a tune. I can't play an instrument, either. "It's okay," Robinson used to assure me. "You'll make me a great roadie someday."

I hummed faster and plucked at the corner of the sheet. I realized I was nervous, but also excited. Robinson and I hadn't been alone in a room together since LA, when we ever-so-chastely watched *Puss in Boots*. What would happen tonight, I wondered. How *un*chaste would we be?

This was another thing I definitely hadn't planned for. It was a road I'd just have to feel my way along.

No pun intended.

When Robinson came in from the bathroom, his hair was wet and he smelled like Ivory. His shirt hung loosely on his shoulders, and he was wearing blue plaid boxers.

He placed his folded jeans on top of his backpack. The bed sighed as he sat down.

"Hi," I half-whispered.

"Hi back," he said softly. "Well. What do you want to do now?"

I knew the answer to that question, even if it kind of…scared me a little. I took a deep breath, willing myself to be brave.

I slipped my shirt over my head.

Robinson sucked in his breath. And then he gently swept the long waves of my hair away from the back of my neck and kissed me there. I shivered, goose bumps rising on my arms.

I could feel his breath, the impossible softness of his lips. I tilted my head back, and he ran a finger down my neck, stopping in the hollow of my clavicle for a moment before tracing each of my collarbones. He kissed along my shoulders, tickling me with the tiniest scratches of his unshaven chin.

We fell back against the bed, and above me, Robinson shrugged off his flannel. Then he bent his dark head down, and we were nothing but lips and tongues and teeth until we had to stop to catch our breath.

Then we lay there, our eyes locked in the half-light. Robinson was looking at me the way you'd look at something you'd lost a million years ago and never thought you'd find.

I gazed back at him in wonder, realizing how much of him there was still to discover: the scar on the inside of his palm, the blue veins in his wrist, the triangle of freckles on his chest, just to the left of his breastbone. These small, secret places. I wanted to know all of them.

But I didn't know how far things would go tonight. I wanted to be slow — and I wanted to go fast.

Robinson cleared his throat. "Do you — ?" he began.

"I don't have any protection, if that's what you were going to ask." My voice came out too loud, and I shrank back against him in embarrassment.

He made a noise — a grunt? A half-laugh?

"I don't want to have kids," I blurted.

Then he really did laugh. "Whoa, Axi. Moving a little fast, are we?"

I pulled the blanket up over my face. This was all so new to me. Could I help it if I was doing it wrong?

But still, there was something I wanted him to know. I forced myself to keep talking, though part of me was ready to die of humiliation. "I didn't think we were about to make a baby, Robinson. I meant it as a philosophical thing. Between the Moore family cancer genes and, like, global warming, any kid of mine would be doomed. She'd be born with blue eyes and a ticking time bomb inside her, just like the rest of my family. Talk about getting dealt a shitty hand of cards." I tried not to sound as bitter as I felt.

Robinson was slowly stroking my fingers. "The blue eyes are so nice, though," he said quietly.

I smiled and placed my hand on his smooth chest. His arm was tucked under my neck, and as we lay there, it felt like we were extensions of each other. Like our bodies and our hearts had to be together to make one whole, perfect person.

41

THE NEXT MORNING WE WOKE UP IN that same position—through some miracle, Robinson's arm hadn't fallen asleep during the night. We got coffee and big, pillowy bagels from the corner deli. We asked for them toasted and dripping with butter—Robinson's favorite. Then we took the subway up to the Metropolitan Museum of Art.

When a panhandler made his way through the subway car, dressed as if it were winter instead of June, Robinson reached into his pocket and produced a crumpled five.

The panhandler bowed as he accepted it. "Money and a beautiful woman. You have everything, sir."

"Well, actually, now *you* have my money," Robinson pointed out.

The panhandler considered this fact for a moment. "But who needs money when you have her?"

"My thoughts exactly," Robinson said. He put his arm around me like I belonged to him.

When we got to the Met, we wandered among the huge, high-ceilinged rooms, ogling famous works we'd only seen in tiny reproductions: Monet's *Rouen Cathedral*, Van Gogh's *Cypresses*, Georgia O'Keeffe's *Black Iris*, and Jackson Pollock's *Autumn Rhythm*.

And although I was staring at masterpieces, what I kept seeing was Robinson the night before, shirtless, lying next to me. It made it hard to concentrate. Sometimes, when he looked at me in a certain way, I wondered if he was having the same experience. "A pretty girl who naked is / is worth a million statues." The poet e. e. cummings wrote that. (Not that I'd been totally naked. Just... partially.)

Robinson stopped in front of *Madame X*, a portrait of a beautiful woman by John Singer Sargent, and shook his head in wonder. "We sure don't have art like this in Klamath Falls," he said.

"We don't even have *falls* in Klamath Falls," I replied.

I'd thought that maybe a part of me would miss my hometown. Crappy as it was, it was still mine. But I missed nothing—because everything that truly mattered to me was either already gone or right here next to me in the museum, holding my hand.

When we ended up in front of the Egyptian tomb—the one where Holden Caulfield almost has a breakdown in *The Catcher in the Rye*—Robinson bent to wipe a scuff from the toe of his boot.

"I'll try not to take this as a sign," he said.

"A sign of what?" I asked sharply.

"Doom," Robinson answered. "Isn't stumbling across a pharaoh's tomb worse than, like, a black cat crossing your path? You know, King Tut's curse and all those stories…"

I slid my hand into the back pocket of his jeans. "No, Scalawag, don't be silly. We were randomly walking. We could have just as easily ended up in the café or something."

"Which reminds me—"

"—that you're hungry."

"Exactly." He stood up a little straighter, and I could see the way he shook off his moment of worry. "Do you know what else I want?"

"No," I said, but the word caught in my throat, because I did know, of course. I just wanted to make him show me the answer.

Robinson backed me up against the wall and pressed his lips to mine. My arms circled his waist and I arched myself against him. This was what *I* was hungry for…

A group of kids in Camp Treetop T-shirts filed into the room, so we ducked into the tomb to make out in secret. We hardly even cared when a few giggling kids spied us and called some of their friends over.

But we pulled apart and, exchanging some giggles ourselves, quickly made our exit.

42

OUR FINAL NEW YORK DESTINATION: Nathan's Famous. It was all the way out on Coney Island— which is not actually an island but is so far away from Manhattan on the lurching, sluggish F train that it felt like an entirely different world.

When we finally got there, the beach was as wide and flat as a parking lot, the waves small and distant. There were a lot of people, and some of them were actually swimming, which no one in Oregon did without a wet suit. The Pacific is *cold*.

Though Robinson seemed drained, we strolled along the boardwalk past bumper cars and an arcade popping with digital gunfire. People were flying kites and skateboarding and jogging and hawking cheap souvenirs, like huge foam sunglasses and T-shirts that said KEEP CONEY ISLAND FREAKY.

"You want to ride the Cylone?" I asked, pointing to the roller coaster in the distance. "Or the Wonder Wheel?"

Robinson shook his head. "Let's just get the hot dogs."

Because he seemed so tired all of a sudden, I suggested, ever so delicately, the idea of going back to the hostel. But Robinson wouldn't hear of it.

"I need my daily dose of nitrates," he said. "Plus, we're tourists, and it's our job to be touristy."

So we turned up Surf Avenue, where the enormous green sign for Nathan's loomed above the street. There was a big outdoor seating area, with seagulls perched near the plastic tables waiting for scraps. The air smelled like the sea and beer and grease. Not that appetizing, in my opinion, but Robinson's whole demeanor had changed. He looked like a kid on Christmas morning.

"How many should I get?" he asked.

"I don't know," I said, scanning the menu. "Two?" I was going to have to order the Caesar salad, since this wasn't exactly the place to get a tofu dog.

Robinson scoffed at two. "Sonya 'the Black Widow' Thomas ate more than forty. Says right there on the sign."

"But that was a hot dog–eating *contest*," I said. "This is just a meal."

Robinson considered the statement. "True. I'll settle for . . . four. One with chili, one with sauerkraut, and two plain."

"You're taking your life in your hands," I said disapprovingly.

"Only my gastrointestinal tract," Robinson countered, and I grimaced.

Instead of eating with the rest of the crowd, we took our food back to the beach and sat on the warm, gritty sand. It was littered with cigarette butts and half-buried beer cans. But still! The ocean was a gorgeous blue-green, and the weather was perfect, and we were together.

"Can you believe that two weeks ago we were on a beach in California?" Robinson asked.

"Crazy," I said, taking a stab at a limp piece of lettuce. "We've done so much."

Robinson waggled his eyebrows at me. "Not enough, if you know what I mean."

"Pervert," I said, nudging him with my bare toe.

He bit into his second—or was it third?—hot dog and nudged me back.

I decided to abandon my wilted, greasy salad and lay back in the sand, watching the kites swoop and dive above me. I must have fallen asleep for a little while, because when I woke, Robinson wasn't next to me anymore.

I looked around for a moment, and when I didn't see him, I got up and began walking toward the boardwalk. Maybe he'd gone off to find the Headless Woman or Insectavora, the tattooed fire-eater. Maybe he was buying me a Coney Island shot glass to go with my Cedar Point snow globe.

But he wasn't doing either of those things. Instead, I found him leaning against a fence, shaking.

And vomiting.

I reached out to touch his shoulder, but he waved me away. I took a step back. "You need to see a doctor, Robinson," I pleaded.

After a moment he looked up, his face pale and his eyes red and watering. "Before you go all drama on me," he said, "it was the hot dogs. Not the you-know-what."

"And how do you know that?" I asked.

"I'm *fine* now. And actually, this is totally awesome," he said, wiping his face and trying to smile at me. "I could so beat that Black Widow lady—I'll just eat and barf, eat and barf, and that way I can consume an unlimited number of hot dogs."

I sighed. "You are sick, Robinson. In a lot of ways."

"But you love me," he said, reaching for my hands.

"I do," I said. *So much.*

Robinson fell asleep on the train home, and I practically had to carry him up to our cell in the hostel. He seemed feverish, but I told myself it was just sunburn. Windburn. Whatever it needed to be, as long as it wasn't another infection.

I sat for a long time, listening to the sounds of the city all around us, but mostly just watching him sleep. Were his cheeks less full? His eyes deeper, more sunken? It could be happening so slowly, so subtly, that I hadn't been able to see it . . .

I lay down beside Robinson and curled my body around his, remembering how I'd refused to tell him a bedtime story back in Las Vegas. I pressed my cheek against his beating heart and vowed I would never say no to him again.

43

"WE HAVE TO GO TO PHILLY," ROBINSON announced.

"We do?"

He nodded. "I'm not saying this trip is a bucket list or anything, but it is extremely important that I eat a Philly cheesesteak."

I handed our room key to the stoned front-desk clerk, and we stepped into the sunshine. "Tell me you're joking," I said, thinking, *He can't keep a hot dog down, so why on earth is he talking about cheesesteaks?*

Robinson shook his head. "Today I want to do everything, Axi. Every silly thing I can think of."

I put my hand on his waist, slipped my fingers under the edge of his shirt to feel his skin. I could feel him shiver at my touch. "As opposed to yesterday, or the day before, when you were a good boy and did only what others told you to do?"

He laughed and wrapped his arms around me. "Okay, you have a point."

I didn't want to spoil the mood, but I had to say what I was thinking. "We've had a lot of fun, and we can definitely keep on having it. But I think you should see a doctor, just to be sure."

Robinson shook his head again, this time more emphatically. "No can do, Aximoron. Places to go, people to see…"

I looked at him carefully, weighing his stubbornness against mine. If I fought hard now, maybe I could get him to go. Just a minor checkup, I'd say, a quick ear to the lungs and heart, maybe a *tiny* little X-ray and reading of his LDH levels. I'd sit in the waiting room, staring at stale magazines and waiting for good news.

Because maybe it would work out. Who was to say it couldn't?

On the other hand, if Robinson went to the hospital, he would resent me for it. Intensely, and possibly eternally.

Whose trip is it, Axi? I asked myself. *Yours? Or his?* Because in the end, someone had to make the call.

"It's less than two hours away," Robinson said, interrupting my thoughts. "It's not like I'm asking you to drive me to Daytona."

"You're not going to do that next, are you?"

"No, ma'am. Scout's honor."

I sighed. "Fine," I said. "You win."

He smiled his beautiful smile. "I love it when you roll your eyes like that," he said. "It's adorable."

"Oh, stop."

"And when you sort of wrinkle up your nose, like you smell something funny, but it's really that you're trying to decide whether to laugh or be annoyed."

"Oh, *really*. What else do you love about me?" I was annoyed, but it was at myself rather than at Robinson. Or not annoyed, exactly—more like...scared.

We were at the car now, and I was climbing into the driver's seat. "Let's hear it," I said. I pulled into the street and pointed us toward the Holland Tunnel. You'd almost think I had a license to drive.

"Well, everything," Robinson said. "But specifically? The list is kind of long."

"You are such a flatterer," I said.

Robinson didn't say anything for a while after that. In fact, we were on the other side of the river before he spoke, and I thought he'd fallen asleep.

"I love how you touch the tip of your nose when you're thinking hard about something," he said, turning to fix his gaze on me. "I love how you tuck your hair behind your ears but it always slips right back down immediately. I love your eyes and your perfect lips. I love that your nail polish, when you bother to wear it, is always chipped. I love how you use fancy words that I have to look up at home. I love the tiny little crescent moon of a birthmark on the tip of your left pinkie. I love the way—"

I didn't need to hear any more. I needed to kiss him. So I pulled over to the side of the road, and there, with the New York City skyline behind us, I did.

"It's going to take a lot longer to get to Philly this way," Robinson said, talking and kissing and smiling all at once.

"We have time," I said. "We have so much time."

44

"So, Scalawag, do you want to go to Pat's King of Steaks or Geno's?" I asked, poking Robinson awake—gently, of course. We'd made it to Philly in under two hours, and now I was parked between the two cheesesteak institutions, which stood a block away from each other like captains of opposing teams.

Robinson yawned and stretched. "You know," he said, frowning slightly, "I'm not actually that hungry right now." For a moment he placed his hand over his stomach—a strange kind of gesture for him. "What I'd like is a nice warm drink."

I looked at him sharply. It was eighty degrees out, and I was sweating against the truck seat. "You're not cold, are you?"

Being cold meant that Robinson might have a fever, and if he had a fever, that meant he might have an infection, and if he had an infection, then he needed to get to a hospital. Stat. Because infections in what doctors like to call an immuno-compromised person—a person like Robinson, who'd had high-dose chemo, radiation therapy, and a stem cell transplant—could be deadly.

I reached toward his forehead to feel it, but he brushed my hand away. "No!" he said, a little too loudly. "I just thought some tea sounded nice. Then we go get the cheesesteak."

He got out of the truck and started walking. I stayed where I was, staring at him through the windshield, feeling both mad and worried. What was I supposed to do? Drag him to the ER so they could take his temperature? He wouldn't let me.

So I got out and caught up to him—easily, because he was walking at an old man's pace. Like every step took concentration and effort.

"A little caffeine and I'll be good to go," he said, pointing to a coffee shop at the end of the block.

Please be right about that, I thought. I took his hand.

In the café we found a window table and sank into the worn but comfortable seats. Then a salesman type burst in and commandeered the table next to us, talking on his cell phone and at the same time waving the waitress over, as if it were a matter of life and death that he got served before we did. "...QR codes are going to increase the conversion rate of your sales funnel—" he was saying. When the waitress walked by he shouted, "Large Earl Grey with soy milk on the side and raw sugar, *two lumps*."

James Patterson

Robinson glared at him for a moment. "This is the City of Brotherly Love, jerk," he muttered. Then he rested his head on the table. "Man. I don't know why I'm so tired."

I wanted to scream, *Because you have cancer?*

Instead, I reached out and ran my fingers through his thick, dark hair. I'd almost forgotten what he looked like without it. It took a while to grow back after the chemo, but when it did, he grew it longer.

"That feels good," he said, his voice muffled.

I took a deep breath, steeling myself for what I had to say. "Robinson, we need to get you back to a hospital—actually, *our* hospital. I'll use my credit card and we'll fly home. We can be there in ten hours."

"I don't like planes," Robinson said to the tabletop.

"You have to see Dr. Suzuki. Now. She'll know what to do."

"Every time I hear her name, I think about violin lessons. Have you heard of the Suzuki method of teaching music?"

"*Don't* change the subject."

Robinson lifted his head from the table. His tired eyes met mine. "You say she'll know what to do. But what if there's nothing to be done?"

"There's always something to be done," I said, my voice rising. I didn't like this new fatalistic tone of his at all.

"You've planned everything so perfectly, Axi. Please don't get all freaked out now."

I reached for his hands and gripped them hard. "But when does it end, Robinson? We can't run like this forever."

210

"We're not going to," he assured me. "We just have one more stop to make. It's the last one."

"One last stop?" I asked. "Where's that? Please don't say you want to go to New Orleans to eat jambalaya or something."

He laughed and squeezed my fingers. "No. My stomach is no longer dictating our travels. But it's...well, it's a couple of states away."

"A couple of *states?*" I repeated. I doubted Chuck the Truck would make it that far.

Next to us the salesman had begun shouting. "No, Ed, the goal is to *shorten* the amount of time it takes the *probable purchaser* to become a *product owner!*"

Both Robinson and I glared at him now. He'd taken a table that could have seated six, and he was treating it like his desk. Scattered across it were his iPad, a BlackBerry, a leather binder, a copy of the *Philadelphia Inquirer*, car keys...

His car keys.

It was then that I had an idea that would have shocked the old Axi Moore to the depths of her soul. Good thing she no longer existed.

"Axi?" Robinson said, waving a hand in front of my face. "Aren't you going to get on my case for not telling you where I want to go?"

"Yes," I said distractedly. "Later." I was staring at the salesman. *Get up*, I thought. *Get up.*

"The numbers don't add up, Ed," he yelled.

And then, as if what I'd just imagined were totally meant to be, the salesman stood. Still yammering into his Bluetooth, he made his way toward the bathrooms.

I got up and threw a five on the table. "Meet me at the southeast corner of the block," I said, and I was out the door before Robinson had even opened his mouth to ask me why.

Outside, I half-jogged down the street, clicking the automatic lock button on the key chain and watching for the answering flicker of headlights. Would it be the blue Acura? The silver Toyota? I had such a mighty sense of purpose that I hardly noticed the racing of my heart. I was taking care of Robinson. If he needed to go somewhere, I was going to see to it that his journey took place in a reliable vehicle.

I'd crossed onto the next block and was nearing the third without a single chirp of a car. My pulse quickened and my head began to hurt.

I was stealing a car.

In broad daylight.

Fear began to trump my sense of purpose. I started jogging faster. *Where are you? Flash your lights*, I whispered, like I had magical powers or something. Or phenomenal luck. It didn't matter which.

Finally, when I was about to give up, I heard the beep of a horn answering its remote key. I turned toward the sound and gasped. It was a midnight-blue Mustang GT. A convertible.

I started cackling like a crazy person. Robinson was going to freak out.

Easy as pie, I opened the driver's-side door and jumped in.

The seats were tan leather, and the inside sparkled like that salesman spit-shined it every morning. He was going to seriously miss his ride. A wave of remorse came over me, but I shook it off.

The Mustang practically leapt into the street. I pulled up to our truck and quickly tossed our bags in at the same time I called to Robinson, who was leaning against a telephone pole as if standing up on his own were too much work. "Hurry, the bus is leaving."

He walked toward me and his eyes widened. "Wha—"

"Just get in."

It took him another second to wrap his head around the directive. But then he slid in next to me, and I gunned the engine.

And we were gone.

"How—what—I don't—" Robinson stuttered. "Am I—"

"Keys, Clyde," I said, feigning complete nonchalance. "They're *so* much easier than a cordless drill."

"I just don't—" He couldn't even finish a sentence.

"I borrowed them from the loud guy in the coffee shop."

Robinson's eyes widened even further as he looked around the car. He ran his hand over the dashboard. "Four-point-six-liter V-8 with three-fifteen horsepower and three hundred twenty-five pound-feet of torque. Pure American-made muscle. This thing is a beast, Axi." He turned to beam at me. "Just when I thought I could not possibly love you more."

He began to laugh—a strong laugh like I hadn't heard in days. "Seriously, *thank God*," he finally said, gasping for breath. "For a minute, I really, truly thought I'd died and gone to heaven."

45

ROBINSON TOLD ME TO DRIVE SOUTH, SO I did. For once, no questions asked. I'd do anything he asked me, and I had to admit, the Mustang was a major step up from the truck. It had power steering, air-conditioning, and, according to Robinson, "an aftermarket Bose speaker system that costs more than a new Kia." It just ate up the miles.

He was staring sleepily out the window now, watching the world go by the way I used to do. "Have you noticed," he said once, "how this entire country is, like, in patterns? It goes city, then suburban sprawl, then farmland. And then city, suburban sprawl, farmland again..."

"And you're never more than fifty miles from a McDonald's," I joked.

"That's a relief," he answered.

Later that evening, after speeding through Delaware, Maryland, and half of Virginia, I pulled into a rest stop in the middle of the Blue Ridge Mountains. In the humid twilight, I spread out our sleeping bags near the border of trees. I didn't bother with the tent, because I didn't want to draw any attention our way. According to the strange logic of the interstate rest area system, *sleeping* is fine, but camping isn't. And although camping at a rest area would be pretty low on my list of crimes and misdemeanors, I saw no reason to be awakened by a cop tapping his flashlight on our tent pole.

I held out the Slim Jim I'd bought for Robinson at the last gas station, but he shook his head. "That Filet-O-Fish we had for dinner is sitting in my stomach like a ball of lead," he groaned. "I think I'm going to have to sleep it off."

"I told you to order the salad," I said. "It was good."

He snorted. "Getting a salad at McDonald's is like going into Car Toys and coming out with a pencil sharpener." He slipped into the sleeping bag, not bothering to remove anything but the belt from his jeans.

"Well, I feel just fine," I said a bit huffily.

"Well, *you* don't have cancer," he snapped.

I sucked in my breath sharply and held it. In the silence that followed, I heard the crickets chirping and the rushing waves of cars passing by on the highway. If I closed my eyes, I could almost imagine it was the sound of the ocean.

I felt Robinson reaching for my hand. "I'm sorry," he whispered. "I shouldn't have said that."

I turned to him, tears now wetting my cheeks. "What, we

should just pretend that everything's all right? We should just believe what we want to believe? Is that what we should do, Robinson?"

He was quiet for a moment, his brow furrowed in concentration. "I don't know what we should do," he said softly. "Wake up and drive some more tomorrow. Try to laugh. Love each other. I mean, what else is there?"

"I'm scared," I whispered.

"There's nothing to be afraid of, Axi." He brought my hand up to his lips and kissed it, right in the center of my palm.

"Again, is that what we *want* to believe? I just feel like we're stumbling forward now, hoping for the best. I mean, where are we going? And where is the road map? The metaphorical one, I mean — the directions. LEGO sets come with directions. Temporary tattoos come with directions. Once I saw an entire Web page dedicated to telling you how to order coffee from Starbucks!"

"Really?"

"Yes! Step one is 'Decide what you want to order before your turn in line.' I'm like, oh, really? Wow! Thank you so much! I never would have thought of that."

Robinson was laughing now. I was glad I'd cheered him up, but I wasn't feeling any better. "Where are the directions for the big things? Because I want them," I cried. "What are the instructions for, I don't know, *life?*"

Robinson's laugh slowly faded. "Axi, if we had directions, it wouldn't be life. It would be an assignment. Grunt work. Not knowing is a major part of the deal."

I knew he was right, but I didn't like it. Sighing, I scooted as close to him as possible, but the zippers of our sleeping bags kept us apart.

" 'As far as the laws of mathematics refer to reality, they are not certain; and as far as they are certain, they do not refer to reality,' " I said.

"Huh?" said Robinson.

"Einstein," I said. "Mr. Fox had that written at the top of his chalkboard."

"I like it," Robinson said.

"Well, I want certainty," I said.

I felt like Robinson and I were caught between two different worlds. There was the world we'd been living in—a world of freedom, beauty, and, *okay*, yes, utterly wonderful and terrible irresponsibility—and then there was the darker, sadder world that I sensed we were about to enter. I wanted to know how to navigate it.

Robinson tilted his head closer to mine. "You can put it on your Christmas list."

I turned away. "Don't patronize me. I don't even know where we're driving to."

Robinson rolled over and stared up at the sky. It was a deep, velvety blue, and little pinpricks of stars were appearing, more and more every minute. "Here is certainty," he said. "I love you,

Axi Moore. And I will never not love you, for the rest of my life."

The tears came again, and I didn't bother to wipe them away. "I love you, too," I whispered. "For the rest of my life."

We kissed, wrapping our arms around each other and holding on tight. And then, exhausted, we said good night and closed our eyes to sleep.

Lying there in the summer night, it was almost as if I could feel the earth moving beneath us, turning on its axis. And as I listened to the crickets singing to each other, I wondered if the rest of my life and the rest of Robinson's life meant two entirely different lengths of time.

How do you know anything for sure? I thought. But I knew the answer to that already. *You don't.*

Finally I fell asleep. In the middle of the night, Robinson and I rolled toward each other, our arms crossing. The night seemed to hold us, too, in a big, soft, dark embrace.

Robinson's voice was low and groggy. "Maybe we should get married," he said.

I couldn't speak; my heart was too full. Full of joy and surprise—and futility, too, because they don't let you do that at sixteen. I put my head on his chest, wishing I could melt into him entirely. The best I could do was match my breathing to his long, steady breaths. In a moment, I realized that he was asleep again.

It was possible he hadn't even been truly awake in the first place.

46

IN THE EARLY AFTERNOON, SOMEWHERE in North Carolina, we took an exit off the highway and ended up in a park, near the shore of a small lake.

"Let's stop for a little while," Robinson said. "I like this spot."

Ringed by trees and rolling hills, the lake was calm, reflecting the blue sky back at itself. I rolled down the window and breathed in the smell of clean, piney air. "It's pretty here," I agreed.

We climbed out of the Mustang and walked toward the edge of the shimmering water. Robinson bent down, selected a flat stone, and then skipped it across the surface—one, two, three times.

He snorted. "Terrible. I used to be able to do twelve."

I stood beside him and snaked my arm around his waist. It

felt so good to be off the road—to feel my muscles loosening, my gas-pedal foot slowly uncramping. "Maybe we should rent a paddleboat or something. Take a break. Drive some more later."

It was like he hadn't even heard me. "I used to love coming here," he said.

"What?"

His eyes swept over the lake, but he seemed to be seeing some other thing. Or some other time. "We used to build these crazy rafts and tow them over in wagons. Then we'd see how many kids we could pile on them before they'd sink. We'd get in trouble because you need a permit for a boat. And we'd always argue that we weren't on a boat—we were on a raft made by nine-year-olds out of packing crates and big pieces of Styrofoam."

"Wait a second," I said, dropping my arm from his waist and taking a step back. "Are you talking about *this* lake?"

"Of course," Robinson said. "I was born three miles away."

Before I could stop myself, I shoved him, and he stumbled a little. "I'm so sorry," I said, grabbing his hand. "But wait. You brought me...home?"

"I wanted you to meet my parents," Robinson said, as if this were the simplest, least surprising thing in the world.

I was totally gobsmacked. I didn't even know where we were, really, and now I was about to meet Robinson's parents, who until now had been about as real to me as a couple of unicorns.

"Welcome to Asheville, North Carolina," Robinson said, gesturing to the trees and paths and joggers around us. "Formerly Tuberculosis Central, and now known as the Paris of the South, or, to the writers of *Rolling Stone*, the New Freak Capital of the US."

I shook my head in disbelief. I didn't know whether to kiss him or kick him. "You wait until now to tell me?"

He smiled. "A guy ought to surprise his girl once in a while," he said. "It's romantic that way. Now let's go see the sights, such as they are."

And for the next hour, he showed me around his hometown. I saw the shop where he bought his first guitar; the elm tree that he broke his arm falling out of; the elementary school where he'd started a rock 'n' roll club ("It got huge, even though some super-ancient dudes protested, saying rock 'n' roll was 'the devil's music,'" Robinson said proudly).

Nothing was particularly special—and yet everything was extraordinary because it was a part of Robinson's previously classified childhood. I wanted to stop at every corner, peer in every window. I wanted to stop strangers and ask them to tell me a story about Robinson. He'd opened the door to his past, and I wanted to walk right through it.

Robinson touched my arm, directing my attention toward a drugstore sandwiched between a café and a crystal shop. "Look," he said. "There's even a place like Ernie's. But the coffee's even worse—it's like battery acid. I swear it once ate a hole in my jeans." He shook his head at the memory. "Of course, it could have been actual battery acid that did that. I certainly spent enough time in my dad's shop."

"His shop?" I asked.

"He owns a car repair shop. Robinson's Repairs."

"Wow, he named it after you?"

Robinson shrugged noncommittally. "Sort of."

"What do you mean, sort of? Who else would it be — the Swiss Family Robinson? Jackie Robinson? Robinson Crusoe? Smokey Rob —"

"Hey, see that?" he interrupted. "That's the streetlight that my brother ran his custom-built Cheemer into."

"Cheemer?" I said. "I don't know what a Cheemer is." Clearly the shop-naming conversation wasn't going anywhere.

"A Chevrolet with a BMW engine," Robinson explained. "You know, Chevy plus Beemer? Jay Leno has one."

"Oh," I said, wishing these names meant anything to me. "So it's like an automotive mash-up."

He laughed. "Exactly. It's the car version of that Eazy-E and Johnny Cash thing, 'Folsom Prison Gangstaz.' *I got beat for the street, Ta pump in ya jeep* —"

"You should probably stop," I said. "That guy over there is looking at you funny."

"Like I care," Robinson replied, but he stopped anyway. He seemed tired again. "Drive that way, why don't you?" He pointed vaguely to the east, and that was how I saw the Biltmore House, an enormous Gilded Age chateau built by a Vanderbilt whose name Robinson couldn't recall. It looked like a fairy-tale castle — a place where Cinderella would live happily ever after with her prince.

Where was my happily-ever-after, I wanted to know. Why did that silly girl get one when my chances were so slim?

Without even thinking, I pulled onto the shoulder of the road. I looked over at Robinson as if I were about to ask him these questions.

"Oh, this is perfect," he said. "This is a very special place."

I looked around. We were stopped in the middle of a bunch of trees. "What's so great about it?"

Robinson unbuckled my seat belt and pulled me toward him. He brought his mouth close to mine and whispered, "It's where I did *this*."

And then he kissed me, so long and sweet and tender that I almost cried — because here we were, together, and maybe this was finally the end of the road.

47

THE HOUSE WAS A THREE-STORY VICTO-
rian with a high, round turret, stained-glass windows, and
an enormous porch. The front steps bowed in the middle,
and the paint was beginning to fade and peel. But it was pic-
turesque that way — a little bit of shabby chic.

There were rosebushes everywhere, blossoming in all different colors: snow-white, yellow tipped with sunset orange, the
soft pink of a ballet slipper. The roses climbed a trellis on the
porch and spilled over the railings, filling the air with their glorious perfume.

I climbed the steps after Robinson, cold with nerves. He
gave me a quick squeeze and then rang the doorbell.

For a moment, nothing happened. I heard a voice and barking inside, and then a woman who I assumed was Robinson's
mother appeared in the doorway. When she saw who had rung,

she opened her mouth as if to shout, but instead she fell to the floor—she just sort of crumpled in the hall, like a marionette whose strings had been cut.

Robinson yelped, "Mom!" And he went to help her up, but before he got to her, a man who had to be Robinson's dad appeared in the hall. He saw Robinson, and for a second he just gaped at him.

They were acting like they'd seen a ghost.

Awkward! I thought—and they had yet to even notice me, the other unannounced visitor.

Of course, if I showed up at my apartment after vanishing the way I had, my dad would probably assume I was some booze-induced hallucination and slam the door in my face.

Robinson's dad slowly bent down to pick up his wife. It was like they were in some kind of slow motion. When they both were finally vertical again, their shock started giving way to a kind of joy I couldn't remember seeing in my father since I was a little girl. Robinson's mom grabbed her son and squeezed him *hard*. "Oh my God!" she cried. "You're here! I missed you so much!"

Robinson's dad was wiping his eyes, trying to keep it together. He reached out and grasped Robinson's shoulder. "Oscar," he said, his voice full of wonder and relief, "you came back."

Robinson was blinking hard and fast and maybe sniffling a little bit. And I was crying, too, at the sight of their reunion, and at the same time thinking, *Oscar? Who's Oscar?*

The barking began again, and a small brown dog came waddling up as fast as her short legs would carry her. "Leafy!" Robinson cried.

She was as fat as a sausage, and her whole body wagged while her tail stayed still. Robinson got down on the floor, and she proceeded to attack him in an ecstasy of yipping and licking. "Sit, girl," he said, laughing, and she obeyed him for about five milliseconds before launching herself at him again. "I love you, too," he said, rubbing her long brown ears.

Then a tall man who looked almost exactly like an older, burlier Robinson came into the hallway and said, "What's all the ruckus?"

When he saw Robinson, he rushed forward. He looked like he was going to tackle Robinson, and without thinking I jumped in and shot my arm out, as if I—all five feet five inches and 120 pounds of me—could block his charge.

The man stopped short and said, "Wow, hot bodyguard, man."

I flushed as Robinson and his brother hugged and slapped each other on the back.

Then Robinson stepped away and put his arm protectively around my shoulders. "Everyone," he said, "this is Axi." He looked down at me and smiled. "My partner in crime." And then in front of everyone, he kissed me—a little less chastely than I might have expected.

"Well, well," said his mother, sniffling and trying to smile at me, too. "Axi, I'm glad to meet you." And then instead of shaking my hand, she pulled me close into her rose-smelling neck, and I realized how long it had been since a mother—any mother—had held me. "Oh, I'm sorry, dear," she said, patting the damp spot she'd made on my shirt. She laughed, embarrassed. "I'm a bit overwhelmed."

Robinson made the rest of the introductions. "That's my brother, Jonathan. He's twenty, but he's probably still living here, because he's a bum like that." The affection was obvious in Robinson's voice.

Jonathan pretended to take offense. "I've got my own place," he said. "I'm just over here borrowing Dad's tools."

"And waiting to see what your mother will make for dinner," his father added.

"Maybe," Jonathan allowed.

Robinson said, "And this is my dad, Joe, and my mom, Louise, but everyone calls her Lou."

"And what about you?" I whispered. "Oscar?"

He gave a slightly embarrassed shrug. "You can see why I go by Robinson," he said. Then he pulled me close to him again. "I promise," he whispered, "that's the last of my secrets."

48

AFTER A DELICIOUS DINNER OF LASAGNA, garlic bread, and salad, during which there were more tears and more fits of laughter than I could count, Robinson took my hand and led me to the back of the house.

"I wasn't allowed to have girls in my room," he said, "but I'm going to assume my parents are over that by now." He pushed on a rather rickety door, but instead of opening into a bedroom, it led to a porch, with windows on all three sides. The painted wooden floor was scuffed and pitched; there was a wicker love seat along one wall and a double bed shoved against another. Guitars and amps were arranged in the corners, alongside neat stacks of CDs.

"This is your bedroom?" I asked, thinking of my dark closet of a room back home.

"It's the old sleeping porch. This place was once a boarding-house for TB patients," Robinson said. "People with tuberculosis were supposed to sleep in fresh air, so there are rooms like this all over Asheville."

"I love it," I said, running my finger along the windowsill.

Robinson sank down onto the bed. "I slept on the floor out here for two weeks," he said. "Staking my claim. Finally, they said it could be mine."

I sat down next to him. The sheets were clean and the pillows freshly plumped; either someone had sneaked in to make the bed, or Robinson's mother had kept up his room as if he'd only gone out for a walk. "Your parents are amazing. Why weren't you with them — all along?" I asked.

Robinson frowned. "We went to Portland because of the experimental immunotherapy program with Dr. Suzuki. She's the best there is, right? But my parents were living in this terrible motel and going to the hospital every day, and it was just awful. It was too hard on them. I said, 'Please go home. This isn't what I want. I don't want you to see me go through this.'"

"And they just *left?*" I don't know why it shocked me as it did, considering the way my own mother split town.

"They didn't want to, believe me. But I made them. I said if things got really bad, obviously they could come back. But things didn't get really bad — they got better. The immunotherapy was helping, and I got discharged from the hospital."

"The same day as me," I said, smiling at the memory of that perfect morning.

"Right. And I'd planned to come back here, but then there was the problem of you."

"The *problem?*" I asked.

He smiled. "The problem of having a giant crush on you and you not knowing it," he said. "But conveniently, my uncle had just moved close to your hometown. You were going to K-Falls, and I decided to follow you. I wanted to be with you."

I flushed. "I'm glad you did. But still—I can't believe they let you do it."

"I told them I'd come back here in the fall. Do senior year at my old school. They understood—I wanted to pretend like I was normal, at a school where no one knew I had cancer. I was just a kid who got to study somewhere else for a while." He smiled. "A semester abroad, in bucolic K-Falls."

I snorted. "You'd better look up *bucolic* in the dictionary."

"I don't have to, because I have you," Robinson said, rolling his eyes.

"Oh, right," I said, nudging him with my foot. But his story still didn't entirely make sense to me. "Why wouldn't you ever talk about your family? Why were they such a huge secret?"

Robinson sighed. "I didn't like talking about them because I felt so guilty. I knew it was selfish of me to be away from them. But I wanted to see things, Axi. I wanted to have a bigger life." He reached up and twisted a strand of my hair around his fingers. "I wanted to fall in love."

I nodded. It wasn't totally insane, I guess. "But you, like, wrote them and stuff?"

"Of course," he said. "They knew I was okay."

"But what about this trip? How'd you explain that?"

He smiled. "I told them school was out—"

"Even though you weren't in school anymore," I interrupted.

"Well, they didn't know that. And they weren't going to check the calendar and see that there were three more weeks of classes I should have been in. I told them I was going to Camp Motorsport. It's a summer camp for gearheads." He paused thoughtfully. "It sounded pretty cool, actually..."

I rolled my eyes. "You're crazy."

"But you love me."

I leaned over and kissed him on the side of his soft mouth. "I do."

A blast of music came from the garage, where Robinson had said Jonathan was fixing up an old Buick into a custom racer.

"Did you know we'd come here, then?" I asked.

Robinson shook his head. "I thought we'd go back to Oregon first. But then..."

He didn't finish the sentence, but I could fill it in. He'd started feeling sick. And he'd wanted to go home.

I understood that. I'd want to run to my mom, too, if I had one who was any use to me. If I knew what *state* she was living in.

I looked out the window then, and I saw all these floating lights. They were yellowish green, flashing on and off. "What are those?" I asked.

Robinson gaped at me. "Haven't you ever seen a firefly before? A lightning bug?"

"A what? No! We don't have them in Oregon."

Robinson sat up and peered out at the lawn. "I had no idea you were so deprived. They're the best bugs in the world because they can light their butts up. It's how they find mates."

"They're beautiful," I said.

Robinson reached up and brushed the hair from my face. "Not like you."

"Don't be corny."

"I'm not. I'm dead serious." He paused. "Dying serious, I should say."

"No, you should *not* say that."

Robinson sighed. "Oh, Axi, I'm tired," he said. "Tell me a bedtime story."

"Sing me a bedtime lullaby," I said with a smile. "Like in Vegas." I had every intention of giving in this time, but not that easily.

"Story," he insisted.

"Song."

"I'll flip a coin," he said.

"No! Don't!" I yelped.

He looked at me strangely. "Why not?"

"Just don't."

"Okay, fine. Then you have to tell the story."

We lay back on the bed. I took a deep breath and began. A fairy-tale beginning. "Once upon a time, there was a girl and a boy."

"So far so good," Robinson said. He rolled over so that his face was in my neck. "The girl was always bossing the boy around," he said, his lips brushing my skin. "She kept telling him to eat better."

"The girl had only the boy's best interests at heart," I retorted.

"Mmmm," said Robinson. Already his voice was thick with sleep.

"She wanted to take care of him," I whispered. "And to be taken care of by him."

I paused, listening to the music coming from the garage. It was Bob Dylan, I thought, but I didn't know the song.

"She knew how lucky they were," I went on, "because they had found each other. She understood that sometimes people had to search for years to find what they wanted. Whereas some—the charmed few—just stumble upon it. Like children on a beach. Some come home with only rocks and broken shells, while others unearth a perfect sand dollar, fragile but beautiful."

Robinson sighed. By now he was sleeping.

"And the girl understood something else—and maybe the boy did, too. Love was magical and infinite. But luck, in the end, was not."

Out in the garage, Jonathan turned up the music, and Dylan's nasal, sandpapery voice finally reached me clearly. *"The future for me is already a thing of the past. You were my first love and you will be my last."*

I clenched my fists against my sides. I looked out the window for a star to wish on, but clouds had come in the evening. The only lights were those of the fireflies, turning on and off, on and off.

49

ROBINSON'S PARENTS WELCOMED ME LIKE a family member — and they said nothing about me spending the night in their son's room. Joe, who was a history buff, told me all about the Asheville tuberculosis sanitariums the next morning. (Even F. Scott Fitzgerald, my ninth-grade literary crush, had spent time in one.) Jonathan walked me around the car he was working on, explaining various things about its engine that I didn't understand and promising to take me for a ride as soon as he got new tires. Lou bought tempeh bacon when Robinson mentioned I didn't eat meat, and one afternoon she braided my hair.

"I always wanted a daughter," she said wistfully. "Those boys and their cars. I love them to the moon, but it's horsepower this and carburetor that, and I always thought to myself, *Who's going to help me prune the roses?*"

"I don't have much experience with gardening," I admitted. Dad and I had had a spider plant in our apartment, but it was probably all dried up by then.

"You'd like it," Lou said. "You're a careful person, I can see that."

Used to be, anyway, I thought.

"It's like the Little Prince says," she went on. " 'You become responsible, forever, for what you have tamed. You are responsible for your rose.' You can't tame a stock car, Axi. It's not the same thing."

I smiled. "I've quoted that book to your son."

"Oscar—I mean Robinson, I guess—could never be persuaded to read it."

And then we walked outside, into the soft summer air, and she showed me how to deadhead the roses so they'd bloom all the way until late fall. When we came back, we had armfuls of blossoms, enough to put in every room.

The point is, life with Robinson's family would have been perfect if only Robinson hadn't been getting sicker, minute by minute. It was as if being back home allowed him to finally stop pretending he was all right. And had there been any doubt about his prognosis—or any denial of what it meant—a visit from his childhood specialist had wiped that away.

"I recommend you call hospice," the doctor had said. Meaning: all you can do now is keep him comfortable. *Until.*

Word spread quickly around town, and visitors began to arrive, bringing casseroles and cookies and boxes of Kleenex.

There was a procession of friends, neighbors, classmates, and soccer coaches who had known and loved Robinson.

Robinson held court on the old sofa in the living room, pale and covered with blankets, even though the rest of us were in short sleeves and dabbing at our sweating upper lips. His spirits were high, though he tired easily. And though he was in pain, he rarely hit the button on his morphine IV—he said it made his head feel like a hot-air balloon.

Everyone had stories to tell, like the time Robinson won the Soap Box Derby race, then just kept going for another half-mile because he'd neglected to give his car a set of brakes. About how he'd "borrowed" the high school's mascot costume to perform a gut-busting bump-and-grind during halftime at the homecoming game. One neighbor told me that Robinson mowed and raked her lawn for her but always refused payment, and a pimply twelve-year-old told me that when he was eight, Robinson had saved him from drowning in Beaver Lake.

It was as if I were seeing Robinson's life flash before my eyes, in the words and stories of the people who loved him.

When he felt good enough, Robinson entertained his guests with tales of life "out West," which he made sound way better than it actually was.

"If Klamath Falls has a boom in tourism, it'll be because of you," I told him one evening. "And they'll all come home disappointed."

"K-Falls has its charms," he said.

"Oh yeah? Name one."

"Her name is Axi Moore," he said. "Sheesh, that was easy. Oh, and Wubba's BBQ Express has that great pulled pork sandwich."

See what I mean? Spirits high.

During the days, I passed around snacks and reheated bowls of pasta or soup in the microwave. Even though we in the house weren't hungry, everyone else was. It was like a dinner party that never ended.

Lou moved through the house as if in a dream, or a nightmare. Joe looked pale and scared. Jonathan, on Robinson's orders, hung a sign on the wall that said NO CRYING ALLOWED — not that anyone was capable of following that particular order. Even fat Leafy whined and barked, as if she had stories about Robinson, too.

"She used to be an agility champ," Joe said once, shaking his head. "Can you believe it?"

"Now she's an eating champ," Jonathan added, tossing her a cracker.

I bent down and rubbed Leafy's feathery ears, and she responded with a warm lick of my hand. I had a sudden pang of longing for my old dog. Or maybe it was a longing for the healthy, loving family I'd never really had. It was hard to tell.

50

"CLOSE YOUR EYES," ROBINSON SAID. HE was reaching into the drawer by the side of his bed. I pretended to squint, then opened my eyes wide as he pulled out a pocketknife with a gleaming silver blade.

"When a knife's around, I like to pay attention," I said. "Sort of as a matter of policy."

He laughed, then coughed. "I'm not going to point it at you," he said. "Only this." He gestured toward the sleeping porch's wainscoting.

"What are you going to do?"

"It's a surprise," he said. "You'll see. Just close your eyes."

I watched him dig the tip into the wood, and then I did as he asked. I don't know how much time passed, but I must have fallen asleep, because the next thing I knew, Robinson was nudging me awake. "Look," he said.

First Love

Carved into the wall of the porch was a message: B&C4EVER.

"Bonnie and Clyde," he said. He was smiling at me, his perfect, crooked grin. "That's us."

"Forever," I said.

We lay back down, and Robinson wrapped his arms around me. I traced the veins of his wrist, their delicate blue lines showing through his skin like a road map, and I thought of the map in my backpack, the one we'd marked with every stop: LA. The redwoods. Detroit. I thought, too, of my bag of souvenirs. Magical objects—a snow globe, a glass orb—that in certain lights looked exactly like junk.

"I miss you already," Robinson said softly.

"I'm here," I whispered back. "I'll always be here."

"But I won't," he said.

In my chest swelled an ache unfathomably deep and dark. And I said nothing, because I knew he was right. I kissed his face, his lips—and then somehow, we slept.

But in the middle of the night, we woke up, and without words we turned toward each other. Robinson's hands reached for me, and his mouth pressed itself against my neck. I brought his face up to mine, hungry to taste his lips. We kissed, and I heard a low moan—mine. I realized I was trembling.

Robinson smiled, lightly tracing the lines of my brow, my nose, my mouth. "Don't be nervous," he whispered.

How could I not be nervous? I knew what was going to happen. The air was charged with it. We were going to kiss until we were breathless, and then...and *then*...

239

I moved closer to him, running my hand along his hip and down his thigh. I felt him shiver as I brushed my fingers along the smoothness of his stomach.

He caught my hand and held it. "I love you," he said.

"I love you back," I whispered. And then I slid my fingers out of his so I could touch him again.

We kissed for what seemed like hours — sometimes tenderly, sometimes almost desperately. Sometimes we stopped and just looked at each other. As if we were memorizing our bodies and memorizing this moment. I felt like I was made of nothing but longing.

Then Robinson pulled away, and I watched as he slipped his shirt over his head. His white skin seemed to glow in the half-light. He looked at me questioningly, and then he reached for the buttons on my blouse. He was whispering my name.

"Do you want to —" he asked.

"*Yes*," I said.

We wriggled out of the rest of our clothes, and then I wrapped my arms around his back. I guided him toward me. I wanted to pull him into my body — as if we could become one person; as if, finally, I could protect him.

Robinson was breathing hard and we were kissing. I touched him everywhere, even as I felt myself dissolving. He was whispering words into my mouth, but I couldn't concentrate on what they were, because something inside me was unfurling. I was no longer Axi Moore. I was me and I was him; I was the night and the stars. The two of us lay on that bed and shuddered with desire.

Afterward, he slept right against me, and I stared at our initials in the flickering candlelight. B&C4EVER.

And somehow I knew it was true. We would be together forever.

51

I OPENED MY EYES TO THE SOUND OF birds making a loud and unmelodious racket in the big oaks in the backyard. I snuggled closer to Robinson, glad they hadn't woken him up, too. Leafy, who'd taken to standing guard outside his room at night, came in when she heard the rustling of blankets, and sat at the foot of the bed. She immediately began whining, because she knew I couldn't resist those big brown eyes of hers. In the four days we'd been here, I'd already fed her almost an entire box of treats.

"Hush, Leafy," I said. "Be patient."

She wagged her tail and whined more loudly, and when I didn't immediately go in search of the Milk-Bones, she began to bark.

"Quiet," I whispered. "Robinson's asleep."

But behind me there was no movement, despite the noise,

First Love

and a terrible, panicky feeling came over me. I turned to look at Robinson's chest, and I saw that it wasn't rising or falling. *He wasn't breathing.* And suddenly I was backing out of the bed, my hands clutched to my face.

Leafy began yapping even more loudly — a treat was coming any minute now, she was sure of it — and I didn't bother to shush her because it didn't matter. *Nothing* mattered. I dug my nails into my cheeks, and the tears came out fast and hot. I was gasping for breath, and I couldn't say his name, even though I wanted to scream it out.

Robinson, come back! I'm not ready! I'm completely, totally not ready!

Leafy's barks took on a tone of wild confusion. I grabbed her by the collar and buried my face in her warm neck, and I thought, *Oh my God, how am I going to tell Lou? How am I going to do anything ever again?*

I had a mouthful of Leafy's hair and she was still barking, but more softly now, dissolving into a pitiful whimper.

It was done. It was over.

And I'd been asleep.

52

A HAND CAME DOWN AND TOUCHED MY shoulder, and I jumped like I'd been burned. I looked up through tear-blurred eyes.

Robinson's face, seeming to float above the bed like a ghost's. And then his familiar low voice. He said, "Axi? Are you okay?"

I nearly fell over. It was him. He was alive. "Do I look okay?" I yelled. I crawled back up onto the bed and gripped his hands as if he'd rescued me from drowning. Never in my life had I been more relieved. "Tell me: *do I look okay?*"

"Your eyes are sort of red," he said, his voice groggy but teasing. "Are you allergic to Leafy or something?"

"I'm going to kill you," I gasped. I let go of his hands and lay down next to him in the bed, pressing myself against his side and trying to calm my breathing. I'd been so close to losing him.

"Oh, you probably won't have to bother," Robinson said. "Something's already on that job. But don't worry. I'm still around to torture you."

"Never stop," I said.

"I'll do my best." Robinson patted the edge of bed, and Leafy hopped up, too, though it was obviously not easy for her. I watched him pet her soft head and ears. He yawned and then moved around in the bed, restless and uncomfortable as he woke up to his sickness and the pain it caused him.

I ran my finger along the side of his cheek. "Do you want anything?" I asked.

He didn't answer me. His eyes closed, and I thought he was falling back to sleep. He'd been sleeping so much lately. As his breathing became more regular, I slowly eased out of the bed and went to the door, ready to check on his parents. Then he said softly, "Yes."

"What?"

"I want more time," he said. His lashes were dark against his pale skin.

I bit my lip and felt the sting of tears again. "Okay," I whispered. "Coming right up."

When I was in the hallway, he called me back.

"Axi," he said, half-sitting up again. "Listen, okay? First thing: Leafy does not need another treat, no matter how much she thinks she does. So leave the Milk-Bones in the pantry. Second thing: there's a hole in your shirt, and you should get my mom to sew it. Third thing: like that dumb Mason Jennings song says, there are so many ways to die."

I held up a hand. "Whoa, Robinson—"

He ignored me. "It doesn't matter what the end looks like—what matters is that it came. Bam, you're done. But life, Axi? There are degrees of life. You can live it well or half-asleep. You can go sledding down a sand dune, or you can spend your life in front of the TV. And I don't mean to sound like a stupid after-school special, but you have to keep living the way we did these last weeks. Risk, Axi. That's the secret. Risk everything."

I nodded, trying not to cry again. "Okay. But I might not keep stealing cars."

"That's all right," he said.

"What am I going to do—?" I asked. I couldn't say the final two words of the sentence: *without you.*

Robinson smiled. "You should probably try to not fail physics. And you should keep writing."

I thought of my journal, the sloppy, haphazard notes in it and all the pages to be filled. At least I'd taken some pictures on our trip. "I'll write the good parts."

"No, you have to write the good and the bad." Robinson picked at the edge of the blanket. His eyes were so huge and serious. "You can write all about me, and I'll live forever that way."

What could I say? I sank down onto a chair and put my head in my hands.

"You know, yours was the only book I ever wanted to read. So just write it, Axi. You can do it. You can do anything. I mean, look at you. You're not GG anymore—you're so much bigger than her."

I laughed bitterly. "I don't miss her."

"I loved her," Robinson said. "And I loved the sick girl you were when I met you, and I loved the good student and the bad driver. I loved the car thief, the hitchhiker, the quoter of novels I haven't read, and the hater of Slim Jims…Axi Moore, I've loved every you there ever was."

I walked over to the bed and laid my head on his chest. "I'll always be your girl," I whispered.

"I know," he said.

I watched the way our fingers intertwined, and I thought, *What are hands made for but this? For holding. For holding* on.

53

THE DAYS BLURRED INTO ONE ANOTHER as Robinson began to dream more and speak less. Time had lost meaning for him, but I was overcome by a sense of waiting. Something was coming, something that would be dreadful darkness and that would also be relief.

We stayed with him in shifts: Lou in the mornings, Joe in the afternoons, Jonathan in the evenings, and me at night. I read to him from Lou's books: Steinbeck, Whitman, Fitzgerald, Hemingway. She read him *The Little Prince*.

One night, in the middle of my watch, I slipped outside into the warm darkness. The crickets were going crazy, and the lightning bugs were like tiny lanterns flashing a kind of insect Morse code.

Through the window, Robinson looked small and frail

under the covers, like a little kid in his childhood bed. Like he ought to be clutching a teddy bear.

I picked a star and wished as hard as I could that somehow I could protect him from what was on the horizon.

We're in this together, Robinson used to say. I remembered the first time he'd ever said it to me, at dinnertime in the cancer ward when we'd been handed a tray of brown slop and green peas. "We're in this together," Robinson had declared. "Axi, we can do this." He'd lifted his fork high in the air, like a sword. "We can eat this...this...whatever it is!"

It was a joke back then; now it was real. We were in this together for just a little bit longer, because what was coming next, Robinson was going to have to go through alone. I would have traded my life for his, but there was no one to offer this to. No one who could make the exchange. No star that would grant my wish.

At three o'clock that morning, I was dozing, my hand on his, when suddenly he was awake.

"The motorcycle," he said, his voice haunted and urgent. "Does it have gas?"

I was instantly at attention. "Yes," I said.

"I think the head gasket's blown—it's seeping oil."

"Your brother's looking into it," I said. Whatever world Robinson was in now, I would play along. "He says not to worry, he'll take care of it. It's going to be up and running right away."

"What about the clutch cable? It's worn."

"He'll fix that, too."

Then Robinson looked at me for a long time. At some point, he seemed to come back to himself. "Axi," he whispered.

"Hi," I whispered back.

He gazed around the room at the Bob Dylan poster, the leaning guitars, all the things he'd left behind when he went away to the hospital. His fingers fluttered, and I reached out to grab them.

I knew what was coming. What I should say.

There was a stone in my throat, but I swallowed hard. "It's okay," I said. "It's okay to go." The final stop.

He brought my hand up to his lips and kissed it, right in the center of my palm. Then he closed my fingers around it, as if the kiss were something I could hold on to forever.

I climbed into bed with him. He shifted, sighing. "Axi," he said.

"I'm right here."

I held his head in my arms. I pressed my mouth to his cheek. *We are in this together.*

"Axi," he said again.

I told him I loved him. He loved me, too, he said—always. And I heard him say my name again. He whispered it over and over until it didn't sound like my name at all anymore. It was only sound, only rhythm. Almost like a song.

"Axi." He sighed. "Axi."

And then, finally, he was silent.

Outside, the song of the crickets seemed to crescendo. I reached into my pocket for the lucky penny I had flipped so long ago in the cancer ward, hoping that it somehow meant Robinson would make it. I'd kept that penny with me every single day after it showed me heads, that he would always be with me.

Now I held it tight, and then I flipped it high into the air and watched it land. But on what, it didn't matter. There was no question anymore, no wish—only the answer, and the emptiness it brings.

epilogue

54

IN BUCOLIC KLAMATH FALLS, EARLY FALL is bright and dry. The leaves are already turning brown, letting themselves be blown from their branches into sad little piles on unmown lawns.

My dad is down in the courtyard, searching for the watch he dropped on his way home from the bar last night. He's been looking for half an hour already. (If you ask me, I think Critter found it and took it straight to Jack's Pawn.) Dad keeps looking up at me, sitting here on the apartment's tiny balcony, like he thinks that any minute I might vanish into thin air.

I'm not going anywhere. My first community service session isn't until tomorrow afternoon. See, when I got back home, the first thing I did was walk to the police station and turn myself in.

Yup. Once a GG, always a GG.

I think I knew from the moment we stole the Harley that I was going to have to make amends for our journey. It was the right thing to do. And even though Robinson's eyes are likely rolling out of his head right now, I think he might have been smiling down on me, too, when the judge handed me my sentence. Grand theft auto is a felony and usually lands people in jail, but miraculously I was only charged with a misdemeanor and was banned from getting a driver's license until I turn twenty-one, and I'm basically going to do community service until my arms fall off.

It's completely worth it to me. After all, the people who "lent" us their cars gave Robinson and me an incredible gift, and I'll gladly pick up trash for the rest of my life if I have to. In fact, I'm thinking about volunteering for the police department, too.

"Axi," my dad calls up, "shouldn't you be heading to school soon?"

"I'll be down in a minute," I reply. *Ugh.* I'd forgotten about my mandatory physics tutoring session, which starts in an hour. Turns out you can't pass a class when you ditch the last three weeks of it and stop being able to understand the supposedly important laws of physics.

Those laws don't explain why Robinson had to die. They don't explain how I'll keep going without him. So I'm pretty sure I don't care that much about understanding how "the entropy of any isolated system not in thermal equilibrium almost always increases."

But then, like a contrarian voice from the heavens, something from class pops right into my mind: *a body in motion tends to stay in motion; a body at rest tends to stay at rest.* That's the definition of *inertia*, a word that would have made Robinson roll his eyes.

I am in motion. I will stay in motion. Maybe one of those magical forces of the physical universe will kick in and keep me going, no matter how much pain I feel.

Or not.

I wrap my arms around myself, inhaling the scent of Robinson that lingers on his flannel shirt, which I'm wearing. And my tears well up and start to spill out all over again. I'm just really, really tired.

"Hey, Axi, check this out!" my dad calls. I lean over the balcony and he points to a part of the withering rosebush in the yard—one solitary flower still miraculously in bloom. I smile weakly. I was hoping he'd finally found his watch.

"You okay?" he asks.

I shrug. I mean, how am I supposed to answer that question? I saw Dr. Suzuki last week, and my cancer is still in remission. My five-year survival rate? Almost 93 percent.

So technically, yes, I'm okay. *Technically.*

But as I sit here letting the sun warm my face, I know that there's a part of me that's missing. It's as if the doctors had sliced something essential out. A vital part that I was sure I needed to keep me breathing. Not just existing. Even now, sometimes I think I hear Robinson's laughter, and for a moment

257

my heart lifts. But when I turn my head to look, it's never him. It's the wind, or the call of a bird, or a hallucination of my own mad dream.

I think it was love at first sight for both of us; it just took us a little while to figure it out. That was understandable, considering we were being stuck with needles, shot through with radioactive particles, possibly poisoned by the horrific substances the hospital tried to pass off as food, and then, when we got discharged, running away and stealing cars together.

So we had other things on our minds.

Of course, sometimes I think maybe we *did* know our feelings right away, but we couldn't admit them to ourselves. Like we secretly thought, *Okay, cancer is scary, but love is* terrifying.

And it is. But it's also exhilarating and bewildering and miraculous.

Right before Robinson and I left on our trip, I'd written a paper on the French essayist Michel de Montaigne. ("Ooooh, *faaaahncy,*" Robinson had teased.) "The greatest thing in the world is to know how to belong to oneself," Montaigne wrote. And while Montaigne was a very smart man, I'm sure, in this particular instance he's full of shit.

The greatest thing in the world is to know how to belong to someone else. The way Robinson and I belonged to each other. We held on as tight as we could, as long as we could. It wasn't enough.

And yet it has to be.

At night when the stars come out, I look up and remember Robinson at the window of the hospital in La Junta, me standing so close to him that it took my breath away. I think about what I didn't say then, which is this: the stars we see aren't even real stars. We see the light that they gave off millions of years ago but that is only now reaching our eyes. We don't see a star as much as a memory.

"Remember the me before this," a pale, sick Robinson said to me. "Remember the me with the guitar."

And since memory is all I have now—unless you count a glass orb, a key chain, a shirt, and a penny that once was lucky—I tried to do what he asked.

"Write about us," Robinson urged. "Tell our story."

And I did it; I told our story. You hold it in your hands.

I just wish I could have done it better. How can you, through my plain and simple words, possibly experience the joy I felt when Robinson jumped into that Los Angeles pool, sledded on the golden sand of the Great Dunes, or kissed me in an ancient temple? How can you understand what Robinson meant to me? His laugh was like a peal of bells. He really did consider Slim Jims to be their own food group. When he played the guitar and sang, whether it was in the cancer ward or in Tompkins Square Park, everyone stopped to listen. He was magic.

"Axi!" my dad shouts from below. "I found it!" He's holding up his Timex and grinning like it's a winning lottery ticket.

"Good for you!" I call down. As if he's the kid and I'm the mom.

I feel like I owe my dad, running off the way I did. He almost drank himself to death, worrying and missing me. I'm trying to make up for the fact that I barely got back in time to save him.

I only wish I could have saved Robinson, too.

But I know Robinson didn't want me to be broken after his death. He wanted me whole, well, and writing. About us.

"Make sure to throw in a lot of words I wouldn't understand," he'd said—using the last bits of his energy to tease me. "And a lot of fancy metaphors and stuff."

I just nodded. I'd do anything he wanted.

Loving Robinson made everything seem brighter and more beautiful. And if life has faded a little since he's been gone, it's still a lot more vivid than it used to be. Now the sun dazzles. That vermilion rose flings its perfume into the air. And the breeze soothes me, if I let it.

Most days I think of him and smile, even if I have to cry my eyes out first. He never stopped believing he was lucky. Maybe not lucky enough to survive, but lucky simply to have lived.

He was my light, my heart, my beautiful scalawag. And I was—I *am*—his GG.

OSCAR JAMES ROBINSON

JUNE 21, 1996–JULY 6, 2013

Missing me one place, search another.
I stop somewhere waiting for you.

— *Walt Whitman*

Two memorable love stories entwined in one
novel of hope and heartache.

Please turn the page
for the complete novel

Sam's Letters to Jennifer.

Just Like Always

SAM AND I are sitting on a mostly deserted beach on Lake Michigan a little north of the Drake Hotel in Chicago. The Drake is filled with treasured memories for both of us, and we had dinner at our favorite table there earlier. I need to be with Sam tonight, because it's one year since, well, everything happened that shouldn't have happened — it's one year since Danny died.

"This is the spot where I met Danny, Sam. In May, six years ago," I say.

Sam is a good listener who holds eye contact beautifully and is almost always interested in what I have to say, even when I'm being a bore, like now. We've been best friends since I was two, maybe even before that. Just about everybody calls us "the cutest couple," which is a little too saccharine for both of our tastes. But it happens to be true.

"Sam, it was freezing that night Danny and I met, and I had a terrible cold. To make it worse, I had been locked out of our apartment by my old boyfriend Chris, that awful beast."

"That despicable brute, that creep," Sam contributes. "I never liked Chris. Can you tell?"

"So this nice guy, Danny, comes jogging by and he asks if I'm all right. I'm coughing and crying and a total mess. And I say, 'Do I look like I'm all right? Mind your own blanking business. You're not going to pick me up, if that's what you're thinking. Scram!'" I snorted a laugh Sam's way.

"That's where I got my nickname, 'Scram.' Anyway, Danny came back on the second half of his run. He said he could hear me coughing for two miles down the beach. He brought me coffee, Sam. He ran up the beach with a hot cup of coffee for a complete stranger."

"Yes, but a beautiful stranger, you have to admit."

I stopped talking, and Sam hugged me and said, "You've been through so much. It's awful and it's unfair. I wish I could wave a magic wand and make it all better for you."

I pulled out a folded, wrinkled envelope from the pocket of my jeans. "Danny left this for me. In Hawaii. One year ago today."

"Go ahead, Jennifer. Let it out. I want to hear everything tonight."

I opened the letter and began to read. I was already starting to choke up.

Dear, wonderful, gorgeous Jennifer . . .

You're the writer, not me, but I had to try to put down some of my feelings about your incredible news. I always thought that you couldn't possibly make me any happier, but I was wrong.

Jen, I'm flying so high right now I can't believe what I'm feeling. I am, without a doubt, the luckiest man in the world. I married the best woman, and now I'm going to have the best baby with her. How could I not be a pretty good dad, with all that going for me? I will be. I promise.

I love you even more today than I did yesterday, and you wouldn't believe how much I loved you yesterday.

I love you, and our little "peanut." . . . Danny.

Tears started to roll down my cheeks. "I'm such a big baby," I said. "I'm pathetic."

"No, you're one of the strongest women I know. You've lost so much, and you're still fighting."

"Yeah, but I'm losing the battle. I'm losing. I'm losing real bad, Sam."

Then Sam pulled me close and hugged me, and for the moment at least, it was all better — just like always.

PART ONE

The Letters

One

MY TWO-BEDROOM apartment was in a pre-war building in Wrigleyville. Danny and I had loved everything about it — the city views, proximity to the real Chicago, the way we'd furnished the place. I was spending more and more time there, "holed up," my good friends said. They also said I was "married to my job," "a basket case," "a hopeless workaholic," "the new spinster," and "romantically challenged" — to name just a few of their more memorable jibes. All of them, unfortunately, were true, and I could have added some others to the list.

I was trying not to think about what had happened, but it was hard. For several months after Danny's death I kept having this terrible, obsessive thought: *I can't breathe without you, Danny.*

Even after a year and a half I had to force myself

not to think of the accident, and everything that happened after it.

I had finally begun to date — Teddy, a tall-drink-of-water editorial writer from the *Trib;* sportsaholic Mike, whom I met at a Cubs game; Corey, a blind date from the tenth circle of hell. I hated dating, but I needed to move on, right? I had a lot of good friends — couples, single women, a few guys who were just buddies. Really. Honest. I was doing okay, I told everybody, which was mostly crap, and my good friends knew it.

My best friends in the world, Kylie and Danny Borislow, were there for me again and again; I loved Kylie and Danny and I owe them so much.

So, anyhow, my deadline for that day's incredible, awe-inspiring column in the *Tribune* was three hours away and I was in a jam. I'd already tossed three ideas into the recycle bin and was staring at a blank screen again. The really tricky thing about writing a "witty" newspaper column is that between Mark Twain, Oscar Wilde, and Dorothy Parker, everything worth saying has already been said, and said better than I could ever say it.

So I pushed myself up from the sofa, put some Ella Fitzgerald on the Bose, and dialed up the air conditioner to high cool. I took a sip of coffee from my Uncommon Ground take-out cup. Found it sooo-ooo good. There is always hope in small things.

Then I paced around the living room in my writer's outfit du jour: one of Danny's Michigan U. jogging suits and my lucky red writing socks. I was dragging on a Newport Light, the latest in a string of bad habits I'd picked up lately. Mike Royko once said that you're only as good as your last column, and that's the truth that dogs me. That and my anorexic twenty-nine-year-old editor, Debbie, a former London tabloid reporter who wears Versace everything and Prada everything else with her Morgenthal Frederics glasses.

The point is, I really care about the column. I work hard to be original, make the words sing on occasion, and get the work in on time, without fail.

So I hadn't answered the phone that had been ringing on and off for hours. I *had* cursed at it a couple of times, though.

It's hard to be fresh three times a week, fifty weeks a year, but, of course, that's the job the *Trib* pays me to do. And in my case, the job is also pretty much my life.

Funny, then, how many readers write to say that my life is so glamorous, they'd like to swap places — wait, was that an idea?

The sudden crash behind my head was Sox, my

year-old mostly tabby cat, knocking *The Devil in the White City* down from a bookshelf. That startled Euphoria, who'd been snoozing on the very typewriter F. Scott Fitzgerald supposedly wrote *Tender Is the Night* on. Or something like that. Maybe Zelda wrote *Save Me the Last Waltz* on it?

And when the phone rang again, I grabbed it.

When I realized who was on the line, a shock ran through me. I called up an old picture of John Farley, a family friend from Lake Geneva in Wisconsin. The minister's voice cracked when he said hello and I had the strange sensation that he was crying.

"It's Sam," he said.

Two

I GRIPPED the phone receiver tightly with both hands. "What's wrong?"

I heard him suck in a breath before he spoke again. "Ah, there's no good way to tell you this, Jennifer. Your grandmother has taken a fall," he told me. "It's not good."

"Oh, no!" I said, and sent my thoughts out to Lake Geneva, a resort community about an hour and a half north of Chicago. Lake Geneva was where I'd spent most of the summers of my childhood, some of the best times of my life.

"She was all alone in the house, so no one knows for sure what happened," he continued. "Just that she's in a coma. Can you come up to the lake, Jennifer?"

The news was a jolt. I'd just spoken to Sam two days before. We'd joked about my love life and she'd threatened to send me a box of anatomically approximate gingerbread men. Sam is a comedian, always has been.

It took me all of five minutes to change my clothes and throw a few things into a duffel bag. It took me a little longer than that to catch and cage Euphoria and Sox for an unexpected journey.

Then I was gunning the old Jag up Addison Street, heading toward I-94 North. The '96 Jaguar Vanden Plas is a midnight blue sedan that was our pride and joy, Danny's and mine. It's a handsome thing with a quirky detail; the car has dual gas tanks.

I was trying to think about everything *but* Sam. My grandmother was the only one I had left now, the only family.

Sam was my best friend after my mother died when I was twelve. Her own marriage to Grandpa Charles made me and everyone else want whatever it was that they had. My grandfather wasn't the easiest guy to get to know, but once you broke through to him, he was great. Danny and I had toasted and roasted them at their fiftieth-anniversary gala at the Drake. Two hundred friends stood to applaud when my seventy-one-year-old grandfather dipped Sam low and kissed her passionately on the dance floor.

When Grandpa Charles retired from his legal practice, he and Sam stayed at Lake Geneva more than in Chicago. After a while, they didn't get so many visitors. Even fewer came after my grandfather died four years ago and she moved to the lake full-time. When that happened, people said that Sam would die soon, too.

But she didn't. She'd been doing fine — until now.

At about 8:15 I got on Route 50 West and took it to 12, a local two-laner that skirts Lake Geneva — the BPOE, "best place on earth." After three miles, I turned off 12 onto Route NN. Lakeland Medical Center was just a couple of minutes away and I tried to prepare myself.

"We're close, Sam," I whispered.

Three

~

REALLY BAD THINGS *happen in threes,* I was thinking as I arrived at the Lakeland Medical Center. Then I tried to banish the thought from my mind. *Don't go there, Jennifer.*

I got out of the car and started uphill to the main entrance. I remembered that many years before, I had been there to have a fishing hook removed from just above my eyebrow. I was seven at the time, and it was Sam who brought me.

Once I was inside, I tried to get my bearings, taking in the horseshoe-shaped ICU with patients' rooms on three sides. The head nurse, a thin, forty-ish woman with pink-framed glasses, pointed out my grandmother's room. "We're so glad you're here," she said. "I enjoy your column, by the way. We all do."

"Thank you," I said, and smiled. "You're very kind. That's nice to hear."

I walked quickly down the corridor to Sam's room. I slid the door open and entered. "Oh, Sam," I whispered the second I saw her. "What happened to you?"

It was so awful to see the tubes in her arms and the banks of beeping medical equipment. But at least Sam was alive. Though she looked diminished and gray, and as fragile as a dream.

"It's Jennifer," I whispered. "I'm here now. I'm right here." I took her hand in mine. "I know you can hear me. I'll do the talking for now. I'm going to keep talking until you open your eyes."

After a few minutes, I heard the door slide open behind me. I turned to see the Reverend John Farley. His thick white hair was askew, his smile tremulous. He was still a handsome man, though stooped now. "Hello, Jennifer," he whispered, and welcomed me with a warm hug.

We walked out into the hallway and suddenly I was remembering how close he had been to my grandparents.

"It's so good to see you. What have you heard about Sam?" I asked.

He shook his head. "Well, she hasn't opened her

eyes, and that's not a good sign, Jennifer. I'm sure Dr. Weisberg will have more to tell you tomorrow. I've been here most of the day, ever since I heard."

Then he handed me a key. "This is for you. Your grandmother's house."

He hugged me again, whispering that he had to get some sleep before he wound up there as a patient. Then he left and I slipped back into Sam's room. I still couldn't believe this had happened.

She had always been so strong, almost never sick, always the one who took care of everybody else — especially me. I sat for a long while just listening to her breathe, looking at her beautiful face, remembering all the times I'd come to Lake Geneva. Sam had always reminded me a little of Katharine Hepburn, and we'd seen all her movies together, though she vehemently denied there was any resemblance.

I felt so scared. How could I lose Sam now? It seemed as if I had just lost Danny. Tears began to stream down my cheeks again. "Shit," I whispered under my breath.

I waited until I got back some control and then I moved close to her. I kissed both of her cheeks and stared at her face. I kept expecting Sam's eyes to open, for her to speak. But she didn't. Oh, why was this happening?

"I'm going back to the house. Pancakes for breakfast," I whispered. "I'll see you in the morning. You hear me? I'll *see* you in the morning. First thing, bright and early."

One of my tears fell onto Sam's cheek, but it just trickled down her face.

"Good night, Sam," I said.

Four

I HAVE LITTLE or no memory of the drive from Lakeland Medical to Knollwood Road on Lake Geneva. I was just suddenly *there* at my grandmother's house, and it felt incredibly familiar and safe.

A century of parked cars had worn away the grass under an ancient oak in the side yard, and that's where I brought the Jag to a stop. I shut off the ignition and just sat for a minute or two, hoping to gather myself before I went inside.

To my left, the lawn flowed downhill to the shore-line. I could see the long white dock jutting out onto the moonlit and glassy surface of Lake Geneva. The water was a mirror for the star-pricked sky.

To my right was the old white clapboard lake house, porches all around, rising up to two asymmetrical stories of added-on dormered rooms. My grandparents' home sweet home. I knew every curve and angle of the house and the view from every porch and window.

I released my seat belt and stepped out of the car into the humid summer air. And that was when the fragrance of the casa blanca lilies hit me. They were Sam's and my favorites — the prize of the garden, where we had spent many a night sitting on the stone bench, smelling the flowers, gazing up at the sky.

It was here that she'd tell me stories about Lake Geneva — how it freezes east to west, how when they were digging ground for the golf course at Geneva National they unearthed a cemetery.

Sam had stories about everything, and no one told them the way she could. *This* was where I became a writer. Right here at this house, and Sam was my inspiration.

I was suddenly overwhelmed. Tears I'd been holding in broke free. I dropped down to my knees on the hardpan parking area. I whispered Sam's name. I had the terrible thought that she might not ever come back to this house. I couldn't stand it.

I had always thought of myself as strong — and now this. Somebody was trying to break me. Well, it wasn't going to happen.

I don't know how long I stayed there in the parking area. Eventually I stood, opened the trunk, shouldered my duffel bag, and started inside with the cats. They were vocalizing from their cages and I was about to liberate them when I saw a light go on in a house a hundred yards or so down the shoreline. A second later the light winked out.

I got the feeling that somebody was watching me. But who knew I was there?

Not even Sam.

Five

~

SAM'S HOUSE was my favorite place in the world, the sanest, and always the safest — until tonight anyway.

Now everything seemed off-kilter. The kitchen was dark, so I threw on the light switch. Then I put down the cats and opened their cage doors.

The girls sprang forward like little racehorses out of the gate. Sox is three-quarters alley cat, one-quarter loudmouth Siamese. Euphoria is an all-white longhair with green eyes and a smoochy nature. My hands were still shaking from stress as I fed the two of them.

Then I walked from room to room, and it all looked exactly the same.

An old burnished hardwood floor secured with square-headed nails. A chaotic mass of houseplants crowding the bay window in the dining room. An

astonishing view of the lake. Books spread everywhere. *Bel Canto.* Queen Noor's memoir. *A Short
History of Nearly Everything.*

And the artifacts that Sam and I loved: antique
ice tongs from the days when blocks of ice were
shipped by horse teams to Milwaukee and Chicago;
old snowshoes; paintings of the round pink crab
apple trees along the lake and of the old train depot.

I heaved a big sigh. This really was home to me,
more than anywhere else, especially now that Danny
was gone from our apartment in Chicago.

I took my duffel bag upstairs to "my room," with
its views down onto the lake.

I was about to drop the bag on the vanity table
when I saw that it was already occupied.

What is this?

There were a dozen banded packets of envelopes, probably a hundred envelopes in all, maybe
more. Each was numbered and addressed to me.

My heart started thudding as I guessed about
the letters. For years, I had been asking Sam to tell
me her story. I wanted to hear it, and record it
for my own children to hear. And now here it was.
Had she known what was going to happen to her?
Had she been feeling sick?

I didn't bother to undress. I just slid into the soft

folds of bedcovers and took a stack of the letters into my lap.

I stared at my name written in blue-inked script. Sam's familiar handwriting. Then I turned over the first envelope and carefully peeled open the flap.

The letter inside was written on beautiful white linen paper.

I took a deep breath, and noticed I was trembling as I began to read.

Six

Dear Jennifer,

You've just left after our most recent "girls" weekend together and my heart is full of you. Actually, I decided to write this when we were saying good-bye at the car. It just came to me.

I was looking into your eyes and I was struck by a feeling so hard that it physically hurt. I thought about how close we are, always have been, and how it would be a shame, almost a betrayal of our friendship, if I didn't tell you some things about my life.

So I've made a decision, Jen, to tell you secrets that I've never told anyone before.

Some are good; a few you might find, well, I guess *shocking* is the word I'm looking for.

I'm in your room right now, looking out at our lake, drinking a mug of that heady spearmint tea we both like, and it makes me happy to think of you reading my letters a few at a time, just the way I'm writing them. I can see your face as I write this, Jennifer. I can see your lovely smile.

Right now, I'm thinking about love: the hot, crazy kind that turns your chest into a bell and your heart into a clapper. But also the more enduring kind that comes from knowing someone else deeply and letting yourself be known. What you had with Danny.

I guess I believe in both kinds of love, both kinds at the same time and with the same person.

By now you're probably wondering why I'm going on about love. You're twirling your hair around your finger, aren't you?

Aren't you, Jennifer?

I want, I *need,* to talk to you about your grandfather and me, sweetheart. So here goes.

The truth is, I never really loved Charles.

Seven

Jennifer,

Now that I've written that difficult sentence, and you had to read it . . .

Please take a good look at the old black-and-white photo I've clipped to this letter. It was taken the day the direction of my life changed forever.

I remember it was a humid morning in July. I know it was humid because my hair had sprung into those stupid Shirley Temple curls that I just hated at the time. See the apothecary jars inside the plate-glass window behind me? I'm standing in front of Dad's pharmacy, squinting in the sun. My dress is blue and a little faded. Note my hands-on-hips stance and the self-possessed grin. That's who I was. Confident. A little forward. Naive. Full of

potential to be anything I wanted to be. Or so
I believed.

Here's what I was thinking at that very
moment.

My mother had died some years before and
I was managing the store that summer. But the
next year I was going to leave Lake Geneva,
go to the University of Chicago, and eventually become a doctor. That's right, I planned to
be an obstetrician. And I was proud of myself
for working hard to make it come true.

After this picture was taken, I followed my
father back into the dimly lit and narrow store.
I swept the wooden floor with Dust Down
compound and set the daily newspapers out
on the radiator near the door.

I was sponging down the marble counter
at the soda fountain when the door opened
and slammed shut with a sharp bang.

It would be accurate to say that my whole
life changed right there, with that bang!

I looked up, scowling, and my eyes locked
with those of a most handsome young man.
I noticed everything about him in a flash: that
he was limping, and I wondered why; that
he was dressed in expensive clothes, which
probably meant he was a lakeshore person,

a summer visitor; that he looked at me hard —
bang — like a shot to the heart.

We continued to make twenty-twenty eye
contact as he slowly walked to the soda fountain, then sat down on one of the swivel stools.
On closer look, he wasn't conventionally
handsome. His nose was a little too wide and
his ears stuck out some. But he had jet-black
hair and dark blue eyes and a nice mouth.
That's exactly what I thought. I remember it
to this day.

I took his lunch order. Then I forced myself
to turn my back and I made him an egg salad
sandwich, no onions, extra mayo on the side.

I put coffee on to perk, feeling his eyes on
me. I could almost feel steam coming off the
back of my neck.

I had lots of things to do that morning.
Cartons of Listerine, Ipana, Burma-Shave all
needed unpacking, and my father had asked
me to help him measure out prescriptions.

But I was stuck there at the soda fountain
because that boy wouldn't leave. And to be
completely honest, I didn't want him to.

He finally pushed back his plate and asked
for another "cuppa joe," which made me
laugh.

"You're beautiful, you know that?" he said as I poured more coffee into his cup. "I think we've met. Maybe in a dream I had? Or maybe I just want to know you so badly that I'll say anything right now."

"I'm Samantha," I managed to say. "We've never met."

He gave me a brilliant smile. "Hi, Samantha. I'm Charles," he said, and extended a hand for me to shake. "Will you do a soldier a big favor? Have dinner with me tonight."

Who could say no to that?

Eight

~

Jen,

Charles and I had dinner that night at the posh and wonderful Lake Geneva Inn, where you and I still have two- and three-hour lunches. I'd never been inside the place before and I was dazzled by the grandeur, the lights, the *class*. (Remember, I was all of eighteen.) Candles winked, glasses clinked, silent waiters served lavish dishes, and the wine kept coming — champagne, too.

Charles seemed so much older than his twenty-one years, and I was fascinated by everything he said and everything he *didn't* say that night. After much urging by me, he finally told me about the bullet he'd taken in Sicily, and he hinted at a deeper hurt that he said he'd tell me about someday.

I found this promise of future intimacy by Charles irresistible.

At eighteen, I was very impressionable. I was a small-town girl, and being with Charles opened me to a much larger world, one that intrigued me. How could it not?

You have to understand that life felt very precious during the war, Jen. Gail Snyder's brother had been killed at Pearl Harbor, my uncle Harmon had been wounded, and nearly every boy I knew was fighting overseas. (I say "boy" because that's what most of them were, and that's what war has always meant to me — a place where boys are sent to die.) It seemed a miracle that Charles had come home and that we had met that summer.

We went out every night for a month and a half, and he usually stopped by for lunch as well. I got my spunk back and began to have more fun than I'd ever had before. Charles talked easily about all the countries in Europe he'd seen and cracked me up by singing popular American songs with a French accent. He was moody occasionally, but it mostly seemed a dream come true. He was so handsome and quick-witted, and a war hero.

Then one moonlit night on the lake, Charles whispered that he loved me and always would: he was so certain of it that he convinced me. When he proposed marriage nine weeks after our first date, I almost bounded over the moon. I shrieked, and he took that to mean yes. Then Charles kissed me tenderly and slid a large emerald-cut diamond on my ring finger. Oh, I was the happiest girl in the world.

We were married on a late September day, the sun shining brightly one moment, disappearing behind woolly gray clouds the next. The changing light was like a curtain falling between acts of a play, and the wedding, too, felt like a dazzling Broadway production. I was mad for Charles. Nothing felt completely real, but it was wonderful.

The ceremony was held at the Lake Geneva Country Club. We weren't members and my dad couldn't pay for a wedding like that, but the Stanfords could and did, so we deferred most decisions to my in-laws-to-be.

But my dad *had* interceded with Mrs. Sine in town, who made the most beautiful white silk dress. It was high-necked with dozens of buttons down the back and more buttons from the sleeves to the wrists, and a long, full skirt that bunched around my feet.

You know it well, Jen, because you wore it when you married Danny.

I can still see it. The country club, all our guests, Charles with his slicked-back jet-black hair, his ramrod-straight posture. My dad handed me off to the handsome groom. An Illinois Supreme Court judge officiated. I shyly whispered my wedding vows, meaning them with all my heart.

Charles and I exchanged rings, and then he lifted my veil to kiss me. There were cheers and applause, and everyone spilled out of the main country club building and onto the sprawling lawn. Billowy white tents had been set up near the edge of the lake. The best catered food money could buy was served and a top band from Chicago played Benny Goodman and Glenn Miller.

Half the guests had polished manners and wore clothes that had been designed in Chicago and New York; my friends and family wore their Sunday best and stared down at their shoes a little too often. But the champagne worked its magic. We danced and danced on the lawn, and huge flocks of migrating geese winged across the sky. My friends fluttered around me as the sun set and they told me that I was the envy of them all. I understood what they meant, and I had to agree.

It was just perfect, Jennifer.

Or so I believed for that one glorious night, my wedding night on our beautiful Lake Geneva.

Nine

~

I READ only a couple of the letters, as I'd been told. Then I fell asleep in my clothes, no doubt dreaming of Sam, past and present. I awoke with the vaguest feeling of dread, as if I'd been shaken out of an awful nightmare, a fantasy not of my choosing.

It took a moment to place the apple green walls and the fluffy mohair throw over my legs, but then I got it. I was at Sam's house. I was supposed to be safe and protected here, happy too. I always had been in the past.

There was a weight on my chest — Sox in deep slumber.

I had just dislodged the cat when a high-pitched, almost bloodcurdling scream came through the thin panes of the bedroom window. Was someone being murdered outside? Of course not — but what was that awful noise?

I bounded over to the window, parted the curtain, and peered out into the front yard. It was early morning.

I couldn't see too much out the window, mostly shadows and wisps of mist coming off the lake. A row of shingled houses stretched south. Then I saw and heard a man yelling with the exuberance of a ten-year-old. He charged across the lawn of a house maybe a hundred yards down the shoreline.

The running man cleared the lawn quickly and nimbly, negotiated the length of rickety-looking dock painted white, and, without breaking stride, performed a shallow dive into the lake.

What a neat dive it was. And what an odd scene for so early in the morning.

I watched for a minute or so as he stroked a smooth freestyle before disappearing into the mist. He was a good swimmer — graceful, strong. That made me think of Danny. He'd been a great swimmer, too.

I turned away. I was awake now, so I pulled off the day before's clothes and tugged on clean jeans and a blue Cubs sweatshirt from the top of my duffel bag. I picked up Sam's letters, which had fallen to the floor. I remembered "I never really loved Charles." I couldn't deal with that one yet. I had loved my grandfather. How was it possible that Sam hadn't?

I went downstairs to the homey, golden oak kitchen where so many summer mornings had started. I fixed coffee and called the hospital to check on Sam, and to make sure her doctor could see me later that morning. Sam was holding stable. She still hadn't opened her eyes, though.

I slammed around the familiar kitchen, making breakfast for myself: Grape-Nuts, orange juice, a "cuppa joe," whole wheat toast with sweet butter. I fed the cats — and peeked to see if the swimmer had returned. He hadn't. Maybe I'd made him up.

While I sipped the last of my coffee, I watched Lake Geneva. God, it was beautiful. The early fog had lifted some. *And what is this?* The swimmer was hoisting himself up on his dock and was sluicing water off his body with the edge of his hands. I noticed something I hadn't seen before. He was naked.

Well, he had a decent body, whoever he was. Obviously, *he* liked it, too. Typical male narcissism, not to mention thoughtlessness. "Jerk," I mumbled.

Maybe ten minutes later, the Jag was purring softly under the oak. I set a big bunch of freshly picked flowers next to me on the passenger seat. I hit the road to see Sam. She had some questions to answer.

Ten

~

I SHAVED a couple of minutes off the usual
fifteen-minute run to the hospital. Once I was there,
I found my way to the ICU. Visitors were already
gathering at the nurses' station, but I caught the attention of one of the physicians. Dr. Mark Ormson
apologized but told me that I should wait. Sam's
doctor was examining her right now.

There was a coffee machine in the waiting room
around the corner. I pressed quarters into it and
was thinking that I needed to see Sam but that I
didn't need any more coffee.

Out of the corner of my eye, I saw a man of about
seventy-five, tanned, with a well-trimmed beard.
He waved, then rose from one of the linked plastic
chairs and walked toward me. It was Shep Martin,
Sam's lawyer and a neighbor on the lake.

We sat down, and when he started talking about

Sam, it was obvious that Shep was as surprised and shook up about her condition as everybody else seemed to be.

"I've adored Sam for forty years," he told me. "You know, I met her right here at the hospital." Shep then told me a story that sent shivers racing up and down my back and neck.

"One night, this was about forty years ago, Jennifer, I was out of town when I learned that my father had been in a car crash. I got to the hospital the next morning — only to find a woman I'd never met before sitting beside my critically injured father. The woman was holding his hand. I didn't know what to say.

"Fortunately, Sam spoke first. She explained that she had been visiting a friend the previous night. Your grandfather was out of town. She was passing my father's room when a nurse came out. The nurse mistook Sam for my sister, Adele. She gripped her by the wrist and brought her to my father's bedside, saying, 'Your father is asking for you.'

"My dad was semiconscious or worse. He never realized that Sam was a stranger, and she never set him straight. Sam stayed the entire night with my father — just because he needed someone."

As Shep finished his story, I heard someone call my name, and it startled me some.

I turned and saw a doctor standing in the entrance to the waiting room. It was Max Weisberg, blond and clean-shaven, wearing green scrubs and holding a chart in front of him. Max is a few years older than I am, but I've known him since we were kids on the lake.

His expression was distressingly grave as he walked toward me and extended his hand. "Jennifer, I'm glad you're here," he said. "You can go in and see your grandmother now."

Eleven

~

ON THE WAY to Sam's room, Max Weisberg answered most of my pressing questions, but then he told me to go inside with her. I still had the freshly cut flowers in my arms as I walked up close to Sam's bed and bent down low so that maybe she could smell them.

"Hi, it's Jennifer. I'm here to pester you again. I'm going to keep coming until you *tell* me not to," I began.

"*Everybody* in town is asking about you. They want you to get well immediately, if not sooner. We really miss you, Sam. I'm speaking for the whole town, by the way. . . . But more than anybody else, I miss you."

I found a nice place for the flowers on the windowsill near the bed. "I got your letters," I said. "How could I miss them?" I reached over and touched Sam's cheek, then kissed it.

"Thank you — for sharing the letters with me. I promise I won't read them in one gulp, though I want to."

I stared at Sam's face. I thought I knew everything about her, but obviously I didn't. She was still so pretty — real down-to-earth beauty. My eyes started to tear again, and I felt a pain in the center of my chest. I couldn't speak for a moment. I loved her so much. She and Danny were my best friends, the only ones I ever really let inside. And now this had to happen.

"Let me tell *you* a story," I finally said. "This goes back to when I was four or five. We would drive over to the lake from Madison half a dozen times every summer. Those times at the lake *were* the summer for me.

"Do you remember, Sam? When we used to leave, every single visit, you would stand on the porch and call out, 'Bye, I love you guys.'

"And I would lean out the car window and call back, 'Bye, Grandma, I love you, too! Bye, Grandma, I love you!' What you didn't know is that I would keep repeating it all the way home — 'Bye, Grandma, I love you. Bye, I love you.' I *do* love you, Sam. Do you hear me? I love you so much. And I refuse to say *bye*."

Twelve

~

I HATED to leave Sam but I'd made a lunch date that I wanted to keep. I drove out of the hospital parking lot and was soon cruising down the main street in town.

Lake Geneva is like a toy village, only life-size, and I've seldom met anyone, except the worst cynic, who didn't love it. The wide and busy street is lined with pretty good restaurants and nice shops selling antiques, and the shining lake glitters magnificently as a backdrop.

I stopped at the light and watched people drift in laughing clumps along the sidewalk, overlapping my memories of recent summers I'd spent doing the same with Danny. *Oh, Danny, Danny, I wish you were here.*

I parked in front of what used to be my great-granddad's pharmacy and entered the cool interior.

John Farley was waiting for me at a booth with red leather seats in the back of the store. He looked dashing with his thick white hair, and was wearing a striped blue and yellow rugby shirt and khakis.

He rose when he saw me. "You look like hell," he said, beaming.

"That means a lot, coming from an expert on hell," I said, smiling for the first time all day. While many clergy seem to have gotten life's lessons from books, John was as in touch with reality as a good Chicago shrink. We ordered grilled cheese sandwiches and chocolate shakes from a teenage girl who had no idea I was seeing the fountain through an old sepia-colored filter, remembering Sam's description of meeting my grandfather there.

"What kind of man was my grandfather?" I asked John after our lunch arrived.

"He was a fine lawyer, crooked golfer, good family man. He was what you would call a man's man," he said.

"Charles and Sam met right here," I said. "Not ten feet from where we're sitting."

John must have seen something sad cross my face. He reached out and took my hands in his. "When I think about your grandfather, what jumps out at me is that he couldn't stand to get his clothes dirty, Jennifer, but he was always out in the yard raking or moving rocks around for your grandma. Or stacking firewood or tinkering with her car.

"Meanwhile, she took care of him. Cooked what he liked to eat. Kept his spirits up. In their own way, they were devoted to each other."

I nodded, and wondered if he was telling me the whole story. "And what about Sam? What kind of woman was she?"

John Farley had the most dazzling smile. "Your grandmother is the strongest person I know. I'm sure she's going to get through this, Jennifer. Don't ever count Sam out."

Thirteen

THAT AFTERNOON I was back at Sam's house, and I was trying not to let what had happened get me down. I was thinking about making one of Sam's famous "wacky cakes" and then eating it all by myself. The huge oak tree out front cast a soft shade over the front yard. Just like always. A couple strolled along the footpath that encircled the lake; sailboats blew across the water, pulled by their colorful sails.

A rosy-cheeked older man sat out in a wheelchair at the water's edge, tossing a green tennis ball for a brown terrier mutt. The dog brought the ball back every single time. The man finally saw me, and as people on the lake do, he waved.

I waved back, then went inside. I returned to the front porch with a big glass of lemonade and a packet of Sam's letters.

I had so many questions about Sam and my
grandfather now. *I never really loved Charles.* Was
that true? Was it possible? What other secrets did the
letters hold?

I settled into a wicker rocker, untied the packet,
and gave the string to Sox, who took it off into the
bushes to kill.

Then, with a breeze riffling my hair, I began to
read the story of who my grandmother really was.

The first few letters were notes about Sam's garden, her feelings about a provocative column I wrote
on the post office disaster in Chicago, some thoughts
on President Clinton, whom Sam both adored and
was terribly disappointed in.

Then I picked up the thread of her life story —
and Sam dropped another bombshell on my head.
Geez, I had hardly recovered from the last one.

Fourteen

～

Jennifer,

This could be the worst of the letters that I'll write.

Charles and I honeymooned in Miami, as you know. We stayed at the Fountainebleau, a wonderful old hotel on Collins Avenue, right on the beach. But Charles was unhappy the whole time we were there. He complained that the hotel staff was too servile, the food too rich, the sand too sandy. To put it mildly, he found fault with everything.

And he especially found fault with me.

On our third night there, right after dinner, we were on the small terrace outside our room, listening to the ocean pound against the jetties. Charles had had several drinks.

I was trying to make conversation. "I enjoyed

meeting that couple from North Carolina. We had some good laughs, didn't we?"

His face darkened with a storm that seemed to come out of nowhere. He looked me straight in the eye. "If you ever stand up against me, if you ever cross me in any way, if you ever become a bore or a simpleton, I will leave you and without a dime." Then he raised his right hand and slapped me across the face. Quite hard. Bone-jarring. I think it was the first time I had ever been hit in my life.

Then Charles thundered inside, leaving me devastated on the terrace. I sat outside for a long time, listening to the surf of the Atlantic Ocean, or maybe it was the blood pounding in my ears. I wanted to throw up, to run home, but how could I?

Jennifer, I was crushed and terribly confused. Do you understand? I'd left my home, all my friends, so that I could be with Charles. Things were very different back then, especially for small-town girls. A woman didn't get divorced, not even if she was struck.

I grew up that first night of our honeymoon; I saw our future together and felt there was little I could do to change it. But I did do one thing. Before we left Miami, I told Charles that if he ever hit me again, I would leave him on the spot and damn the consequences. Everybody would know what a bastard and bully he was.

After the honeymoon, Charles and I moved to a large apartment in Chicago. It still wasn't very good between us, though. Once he'd passed the bar, your grandfather joined the family firm. Soon I gave birth to your mother, then to your aunt Val. But, Jennifer, I lived for the summers, when I always returned to Lake Geneva.

But I dreaded the weekends, when Charles would come up from Chicago. He brought his moods with him, though he rarely raised his hand to me. He was selfish and enjoyed putting me down in front of the children and friends of ours. But he did provide for us, and he eventually did make good on the promise he'd made to tell me the dark secret in his past. What Charles would never tell me were the secrets in his present, the girlfriends he had in Chicago and elsewhere.

I'm sorry to have to tell you this, but you wanted to hear my story.

Fifteen

Sweetheart,

Let me tell you some other things about your grandfather so you can understand how he came to be the man that he was. The husband, even the grandfather.

Picture Charles telling me about what he called "sins of the father," events that shaped his life — and mine. It was three years after we were married. Your mother was in her crib in the next room, and she was such a good little sleeper. Charles and I were in bed, and cars whooshed by in the rain, lighting our faces with headlights as they passed our window in the Chicago apartment.

It was on this dreary night that Charles finally told me about the transforming event of his life. It had happened when he was just sixteen, and it is an incredible story.

Charles's parents had thrown a party in their imposing home for their older son, Peter, who had just graduated from prep school. It was after dinner and the guests had moved to the library for coffee. Peter was opening his gifts and Charles made a careless remark to his father that his older brother always seemed to get the best of everything.

Arthur Stanford just snapped. He turned on Charles, called him an ingrate. He then said that it was time for Charles to know the truth. "You're not even our son. You're adopted!" his father yelled at him. Just like that, in front of everyone in the family. The party stopped, and in the brittle silence that followed, Charles ran upstairs to his room. His father was right behind him. When they reached the top landing, Charles screamed, "It isn't true! I know it isn't true!"

Arthur Stanford had calmed some by now. "Believe me, Charles, I'm not your father. I'm your *uncle*," he said. "Your father is my brother Ben. He got a girl pregnant, a little nobody from nowhere."

"You're l-l-lying," Charles stammered piti-
fully.

"Go and ask your father then," Arthur said.
"It's time you knew him anyway. The last I
heard, he was working at the Murray Tap. It's
a gin mill in Milwaukee." Then Arthur Stanford
lowered his voice. "Caroline and I took you
in. We've tried to love you, Charlie. We do our
best."

That night, when he was just sixteen, Charles
went to the Wabash and Adams Street train
station. He bought a dollar ticket and caught
the North Shore Line to Milwaukee.

Inside our bedroom, Jennifer, passing headlights lit Charles's face and I could see his eyes
lit up in terrible pain. My heart went out to
him. If I couldn't completely forgive him for
everything, at least I understood what had happened to make him so angry, and occasionally
cruel.

Charles continued his story, and some of
the words were so vivid that I can remember
them to this day.

He told me that the train ride ended two
hours later. His uncle's phrase "a little nobody
from nowhere" kept playing like a bad song in
his head. He walked out onto Michigan Street

at midnight. Two huge Milwaukee breweries were nearby, and the smothering smell of beer lay heavy in the air.

He asked directions, then walked east, until he found Murray Avenue. He almost passed the place he was looking for.

There was no sign out front, only a dirty window to the left of the door lit by a Miller High Life sign. Charles pulled on the creaking door and entered a barroom that was darker than the night outside. There was a long bar and a thick layer of smoke hovering over it.

Men who worked at the breweries and smelled like stale malt looked up at him. No one said anything or seemed to care that he was there.

When his eyes adjusted to the gloom, Charles climbed onto a covered stool. He sat in the shadows, taking in every detail: the dice cups on the bar — a few working men gambling for drinks — a sign that said

HOUSE SPECIALTY, PANTHER PISS.

Mostly he looked at the bartender, a rough-looking man with a scarred face but unmistakable Stanford features: the aristocratic, slightly crooked nose, the stuck-out ears. Charles told me, "The love I felt for him was almost painful."

As he watched, he saw his father short-change a customer and tell vulgar jokes about women, which made Charles's face go red.

Finally his father wiped down the bar with a greasy rag, leaned into Charles's face, and sneered. "Get the hell out of here, kid. Take a hike before I kick your ass across the river."

Charles opened his mouth, but nothing came out. The terrifying moment dragged on. His face burned, but Charles couldn't speak.

"A pansy," his father said to loud laughter. "Kid's a pansy. Now get the hell out of here!"

Shaking with emotion, Charles slid off the stool and left the bar. He never introduced himself to his father, never said a word. Not then, not ever.

I asked Charles, "How could you leave without talking to your father?" His voice got very flat, as if it hurt him to answer. He said that when he looked into his father's face, he saw Arthur's eyes — the same cold lack of feeling. And he knew that his own father had never loved him, and never would.

"I found him so easily," Charles said. "Why hadn't he ever found me?"

That night I took your grandfather in my arms, Jennifer. I understood that I was his only friend, whatever that meant to him. But as I pressed his head to my chest and smoothed his hair, I knew something else. I knew why Charles had married me. I was a little nobody from nowhere. Our marriage had been an act of defiance, Charles's way of putting his thumb in the Stanford family eye.

I was twenty-two years old, but I felt that my life was over.

Sixteen

I WAS REELING from Sam's sad story about my grandfather. As much as I had adored him, something about it rang true. Though she'd asked me to read the letters slowly, I wanted to know more. How could she have stayed with Charles all those years?

I was sitting in the kitchen and had just opened the flap of the next envelope when I was startled by a movement out of the corner of my eye and the sound of footfalls on the grass outside.

A man rounded the side of the house. The odd thing was, I thought I knew him but I didn't know from where. I went out onto the porch to see what he wanted.

His hair was light brown, with a soft tousled wave and a fiercely independent lock that sprang forward. He had very blue eyes.

"Hi," he said.

"Hi." Tentatively.

He was probably close to forty, wearing khaki shorts, a Notre Dame T-shirt, and the strangest old-man sandals.

Then it clicked. The last time I'd seen him, he wasn't wearing any clothes. This was the war-whooping swimmer.

"Jennifer?" he asked, and that threw me some. I was wondering how he knew my name when he put his hand on the banister and began to board Sam's front porch.

"Whoa," I said. "Do I know you?"

"Hey, I'm sorry. I'm Brendan Keller. I'm staying with my uncle Shep, four houses down. He said he ran into you at the hospital. *Brendan Keller?* You don't remember me, do you?"

I shook my head no. Then I nodded yes. It was all coming back. Brendan Keller and my cousin Eric had been a big part of my early summers at Lake Geneva. They were the brothers I never had. I'd followed them everywhere for a summer or two. They'd called me Scout, after the little girl in *To Kill a Mockingbird*.

I didn't remember having seen Brendan Keller since I was a little girl, though. I put out a hand. "Hey, long time."

The two of us wound up sitting on Sam's porch, talking over a couple of iced teas. Mostly we reminisced about Lake Geneva "back in the day." He knew my newspaper column, and I managed to get out of him that he was a doctor now.

"Eric and I called you Scout. You were very advanced for a ten-year-old. I think you'd actually read *To Kill a Mockingbird*."

I laughed and cast my eyes down, embarrassed by something I couldn't quite get a handle on. He followed my gaze. "You're looking at my shoes."

"No, I —"

A slow smile spread across his face.

"I borrowed them from my uncle. Listen, speaking of Shep. He says the Lions Club is having a lobster boil over in Fontana. You're invited if you'd like."

I shook my head, almost a reflex. "No. I'm sorry. Tonight's not good. I'm writing my column. I'm way behind."

"If I change my shoes? I have really nice loafers. Sneakers? I could go barefoot."

I smiled. "I can't," I said. "Sorry. I have a deadline. Honestly."

Brendan stood up and set down his tea. "Okay. Well, I'm just down the road. I hope I'll see you around. *Brendan Keller.*"

"Scout." I smiled.

We mumbled good-byes and I waved as he walked back in the direction of his uncle's house. My former contemplative mood was blown. I put Sam's letters aside and went into the house.

I did some work that afternoon, and once or twice I thought about the lobster boil going on in Fontana without me. Eventually I made a salad for dinner, wondering why I'd been so hell-bent on eating alone.

But I knew why. Danny.

And our little "peanut."

Seventeen

~

THAT NIGHT I had the dream about Danny again, the one I hate more than anything, the dream where I am Danny but I'm also myself watching him.

It's always the same.

Danny is surfing on the north shore of Oahu, at one of the most beautiful beaches anywhere. The waves there are some of the biggest in the world one day, and then the ocean can be as flat as glass the next.

The bad part is that Danny is alone this day. He's supposed to be on vacation with me, but at the last minute I have to stay in Chicago to work on a big story for the *Tribune*. It's my choice to stay behind.

So there he is, waiting for his wave. And then he's up. The trouble is, the wave crests a lot faster than he expccts. Suddenly he's slammed down on the seafloor some twenty feet below. Danny can't tell which way is up, which is down. He remembers a basic rule: one hand up, one hand down; feel for the bottom, feel for the air.

Then he's smashed to the ocean floor again, and he can't believe the strength of the wave. His ears are pounding and water's being rammed up his nose. His body is wrenched and twisted. His legs feel numb. Has he broken something? There's a terrible burning sensation in his lungs.

Then Danny lets go of everything . . . except for me and the baby. . . . He calls out: *Jennifer! Jennifer, help me! . . . Please help me, Jennifer!*

I woke up from the dream in my old room in Sam's house. I was in a cold sweat and my heart was racing. How could I put the past behind me when Danny was always in my dreams? I was late meeting him in Hawaii — everything that happened was my fault. Everything.

Eighteen

~

I LAY IN BED for a few minutes until I heard someone yelling outside. I finally perked myself up and parted the curtains of my bedroom window.

There he was, but at least he was wearing a bathing suit this morning. I watched him do a perfect racing dive from the dock into the lake. "Grow up," I muttered, then wondered when I had become such a grump.

I showered, dressed in yesterday's jeans and a *Tribune* softball T-shirt, clipped my hair into an upside-down ponytail. I walked outside into the fragrant summer morning. I needed to be outside and away from my nightmares.

There are about twelve hundred identical white docks around the twenty-six-mile circumference of Lake Geneva. Each dock is eight feet wide, thirty or so feet long, and nearly every house on the shore seems to have one. In November the docks are taken out of the lake for the winter; then come spring, they're painted and placed back in the water.

I took my coffee mug down to the end of Sam's dock, where I could watch the mallards and the swooping seagulls fishing for breakfast. Wisconsin is crazy for fish, mostly perch, some cod, and trout. This is the birthplace of the Republican party, but also the fiscally responsible Democrat William Proxmire, he of the Golden Fleece award given to government agencies that waste taxpayers' money. Interesting state.

Out on the lake, I could see Brendan Keller doing that strong freestyle I'd noticed the morning before. As I watched, he started swimming toward me. He got bigger in frame, closer, then he came right up to the edge of Sam's dock and hauled himself up.

He shook himself off like a dog.

"*Hey!*" I said.

"You ought to get into a bathing suit and come for a swim, Scout. The water is unbelievable. That is not an exaggeration."

"Can't," I said, sounding a little like a poop even to myself. "Previous engagements."

"Working?" He smiled as he sluiced water off his body with the edges of his hands, as I'd seen him do before.

"I'm on my way to see Sam," I said. "I was just thinking about doing a column on government waste. Life of the mind, y'know."

"You eaten?"

"Drinking my breakfast this morning," I said, lifting my mug.

"You can do better than that," he said. "Now, don't give me any trouble. I make five-star blueberry pancakes. Really fast. Trust me, okay?"

Trust him? I opened and closed my mouth, but I was tired of sputtering. And I didn't want to argue right then, or even have a discussion.

So I did what he asked. I trusted him to make five-star blueberry pancakes.

Really fast.

Nineteen

~

EVEN AS I WAS walking down the shoreline with
Brendan, I was asking myself what I was doing. But
what was the harm? And to be honest, I was hungry
and five-star blueberry pancakes sounded pretty
good.

Shep Martin's place was new but homey. The
kitchen had tall windows and skylights, spanking-
clean marble counters, hardwood floors. Acoustic
jazz was playing (someone great singing "Stagger
Lee"). And the pancakes *were* excellent. Not gummy,
not burned, not dry. They were *jusssssst* right.

Unfortunately, it was turning out to be a little
awkward between Brendan and me. He said that
he'd gone onto the *Trib* website to re-read some
of my old columns. He'd been touched by my kid-
napped child story, and my survey "Who would

you rather be stranded with on a desert island —
your spouse or your cat?" made him laugh out loud.

I nodded pleasantly but didn't really give much
of a response. It was starting to feel a little uncomfortable for me. I didn't want to be there any longer,
but I didn't know how to make a graceful exit.

As we finished the pancakes, Brendan told me
that he was a radiologist and that he lived in South
Bend, Indiana. I said that was great — a one-word
answer.

He shook his head, seemed puzzled. "I don't
usually talk about myself," he said. "I guess all this
fresh air is working on me. I'm taking a sabbatical.
You can sit in the dark looking at X-rays for only so
long before you want to go off screaming in search
of some sunlight."

I really had stayed longer than I'd meant to. I had
planned to eat and run. Finally I thanked Brendan
for breakfast, then headed back to Sam's. It was all I
could do not to run.

I walked east a hundred yards along the path at
the edge of the lake, until I reached the foot of
Sam's long front lawn.

The girls greeted me with little meows, and we
climbed uphill toward the house, taking the path
beside my grandmother's perennial border. Sam did
so many things well, didn't she? Except maybe find

the right husband. And God only knew what else was coming in the letters.

She had planted a lavish three hundred feet of flowering plants that ran the length of the property from the lake almost to the road. The border was already at its summer peak. Antique pink and red shrub roses exulted; irises fluttered like flights of bluebirds on their stems.

Then I noticed that someone else was in the garden, a man, and I found myself grinning. "Hey, *you,*" I called.

Twenty

≈

"HENRY! It's so good to see you," I said to the tall, wiry man who was taking gardening tools out of a pickup truck. His hair was a snowy semicircle around a balding pate, his bright eyes sparkled, and he moved with more agility than you'd expect from a man in his mid-seventies.

"Jennifer, I was hoping I'd see you," he said. "I missed you at the hospital by a couple of minutes yesterday. You look beautiful, sweetheart." Then Henry gave me a big kiss and a hug that might have left a permanent impression.

I told him what I knew from that morning's call to the hospital — that Sam was the same. Henry nodded and I saw the pain in his eyes. I was remembering all the times I'd seen him and Sam putting the garden through its paces.

Henry Bullock had trained at Wisley in England

and was Lake Geneva's resident master gardener. Sam was an obsessive amateur. But Henry always bragged that "Sam has a great eye. She's a great partner."

"I almost died myself when I found her on the kitchen floor," he told me, shaking his head as if he didn't want the memory in there.

"You found her?" I asked in surprise.

"I did," he answered, touching a handkerchief to his eyes. "I wish Sam could see her border this morning."

My God, his pain brought back mine. I hugged him again, and we murmured assurances to each other that Sam would be home soon. Henry had always seemed like a part of our family.

Moments later, a machine chatter made our conversation just about impossible. Joseph, one of Henry's sons, had started up the mower in the front yard. I said good-bye, then mounted the porch steps.

My watch read twenty to nine, and I figured I had time to read a couple more letters before I went to see Sam.

Twenty-one

Dear Jennifer,

I want to ramble on a little about the importance of second, and even third, chances. I was helping out in the library one day when a bookmark fell from the pages of a novel. Actually, it was a handwritten note, a quote attributed to a Father Alfred D'Souza. D'Souza had written: "For a long time it had seemed to me that life was about to begin — real life. But there was always some obstacle in the way, something to be got through first, some unfinished business, time still to be served, a debt to be paid. Then life would begin. At last it dawned on me that these obstacles were my life."

Jennifer, that's how I felt as my life creaked

forward. I know that I always put up a cheer-
ful front, but that's how I felt inside.

More than twenty years had passed since
I'd sworn I'd give myself a second chance
and still I hadn't done it. I'd raised two wonderful daughters. I'd made about ten thousand dinners, thirty thousand beds, Brownie
trooped and PTA'd and lawyer-wived my heart
out. But I was resigned to my marriage with
Charles, and you know what? I no longer
believed that a second chance was really
possible.

That little quote moved me.

And maybe it prepared me for one of the
most important moments in my life.

I was only forty-three, but I had been married for nearly twenty-six years. My children
had grown, and I felt that my spirit was drying
up like a bug in a web in the corner of a dusty
room. Jennifer, I had never really been in love.
Isn't that something?

Three weeks after reading that note at the
library, I met someone. I won't tell his real
name, Jennifer. Not even to you.

I called him Doc.

Twenty-two

~

Jennifer dear,

If this blows your mind a little, and it should, imagine how it blew mine. KA-BOOM! Rockets to the moon!

Let me tell you how it happened. Actually, Doc and I had known each other for years, but the night I began to really know him was at an endless dinner for the Red Cross at the Hotel Como. We happened to be seated at the same table, and once we began to talk that night, we never wanted to stop. I can't even put it into words, but soon I was glowing. I was feeling something again, too. I think the electricity between us straightened my curls right to the ends. I could have talked to him all night, right into the morning. We even made a joke about doing just that.

Of course Charles never noticed a thing.

I remember exactly what Doc was wearing that night: a beige linen suit, with a blue oxford shirt, and a hand-painted blue tie. He was slender and tall, with thick blond hair streaked with silver, easily the most handsome man in the room (in my eyes, anyway). Over dinner, he told me about the stars, in particular about a comet that was about to cross our patch of the universe and wouldn't appear again for two hundred years. He knew about all sorts of things, and he was passionate about life, which I loved and had been missing for years.

We had many common interests, but electricity aside, I felt comfortable with him. Immediately. He liked to listen, and for some reason I felt I could trust him to accept who I really was. Jen, for that night anyway, I felt that I was home. For the first time in twenty-five years I almost felt like myself again. Can you imagine what that's like? Actually, I hope that you can't.

I should tell you why you've never heard of Doc until now. It isn't his real name, but it suited him perfectly (because he looks *nothing* like a Doc), and I loved calling him a name that was just ours. It was one of our "secrets" — one of many, as it turns out.

We saw each other several times that summer, accidentally and accidentally on purpose, and I think we were a little in love before we knew enough to admit it. I think I fell for him first, but he wasn't far behind, and he fell as hard and as far as I did.

Jennifer, I know how terribly sad you still are about Danny. I understand as much as anyone can. And no one can tell you how long to grieve. I just want to tell you this one important thing. Don't shut out love for good. I couldn't feel this more strongly, my sweet, sweet, smart, smart girl. It's why I'm writing these letters to you.

Please don't shut out love — it's the best thing about life.

Now, stop reading right here. Think about what I'm telling you. These letters aren't just about my life, Jen; they're about yours.

PART TWO

Young Love

Twenty-three

~

I WAS SETTLING into the quite wonderful ebb and flow of life on Lake Geneva, and I was loving it even more than I thought I would.

Sam's friends were there for me at every turn. I could have eaten at somebody's home every night if I'd wanted to. In many ways, I was on summer vacation. Except that, of course, Sam was sick, and I didn't know if she would get better.

Early one afternoon I sat in her kitchen, an old-fashioned black phone cord connecting my laptop to the Internet. My e-mail in-box was crammed with notes from readers, many of whom said they missed me and hoped I was okay.

I absolutely love this connection to my readers. It's one of the best things about my job. Actually, keeping my job depends on it. If readers react to me emotionally, they buy the *Trib*. So an hour ago my editor and I agreed that I'd write from Lake Geneva for now; 750 words per column, three columns a week, just like always. Only completely different.

I opened my word-processing program and was fooling around with a couple of ideas, but my thoughts kept drifting to Sam. And I thought about my mom, who should've been there but wasn't. My mom, who shouldn't have died but had. And I thought about Danny, of course. He was always on my mind, or not far from it. And then I stopped thinking about the past. I just had to.

A light tapping on the back screen door broke into my thoughts. I went to the door and discovered Brendan Keller standing there. I hadn't seen him in a couple of days and was surprised to see him now.

He smiled and asked, "Can you come out and play?"

Twenty-four

⁓

"OKAY," I said, probably surprising both of us. Then, before either of us could change our mind, I stepped outside. I wasn't in the mood to write, anyway — or rather, to stare at a blank computer screen.

"Double-chocolate thick shake," Brendan said, and I immediately knew what he had in mind.

"Daddy Maxwell's," I said, and smiled.

Daddy Maxwell's Arctic Circle Diner is a white stucco, igloo-shaped local eatery at the highest level of low cuisine. It has blue-striped awnings, and what it lacks in class, it makes up for in really good food. Just two miles from Knollwood Road, it took all of three minutes to get there.

Nothing seemed to have changed since we were kids and Maxwell's was the place to be seen. We took a table by a window and turned our attention to Marie, Daddy Maxwell's latest perky waitress. She took our order, then disappeared into the kitchen.

Less than ten minutes later, I was staring over my veggie burger at Brendan's plate. He'd ordered the special of the day. Plus a chocolate thick shake. The special was a scrumptious-looking southern omelette made of three eggs wrapped around grilled onions, "dirty" fried potatoes, and extra cheddar cheese.

"You're a *doctor,*" I said.

"You only go around once." Brendan grinned. "Show some guts, Jennifer. Give it a try. The omelette *and* the shake."

I laughed, reached my fork over to his plate, and lifted a bite of steaming omelette to my mouth. Then I had another bite.

And a sip of the chocolate thick shake.

Then Brendan ordered me my own omelette and shake.

"You're too thin, anyway," he said, which was one of the more endearing remarks I'd heard recently.

We lingered over the meal, and then coffee. I was surprised that I was kind of enjoying myself. We were filling each other in on our headlines of the past twenty five years. I told him a few details about Danny, but he already knew. Brendan told

me that he'd been divorced for a year and a half—
his ex-wife had been having an affair with a partner
in her law firm. "Figures, that ma belle Michelle
would get involved at the office," he said. "Workaholic that she was — is, whatever."

I nodded, then had a guilty thought about how
Danny had called me a workaholic, and he'd been
right. I felt a curtain of sadness drop. Brendan noticed, and he touched my hand. I told him I was
okay. Reflexively, I pulled my hand away. So maybe
I wasn't okay.

"I have to get back," I said.

"Sure," said Brendan. "Let's go."

Once we were in the car, I told Brendan that I
had another deadline and would probably be
working half the night.

"I get it," he said, and smiled. "Buzz off."

"No, no, nothing like that," I said. "It's just, well,
buzz off." Which got a laugh out of him.

We said good-bye in the parking area of Sam's
yard, and I immediately went for a twenty-minute
run through the twisty streets around Knollwood. I
still weigh the same 130 pounds I did in college and
I wanted to keep it that way, even though Brendan
said I was too thin.

I thought a little about him as I ran. He was pretty
funny. And definitely smart. He also listened when I

talked, and most men don't. But there had to be secrets, issues, *baggage*. What was he really doing there at the lake? Still recovering from his divorce? The truth was that he was too good-looking and charming and nice to be up there by himself.

When I got back to the house, I stood under the showerhead, letting the hot water beat down on my overactive mind. Then I dressed in shorts and a tank top, made iced tea, and took a few of Sam's letters out to the back porch.

I sat cross-legged on the floorboards, and as sunshine pinned me to the spot, I opened another envelope that had my name neatly inscribed on it.

Twenty-five

Dear Jen,

When you were a little girl, and so adorably cute and sweet that you could give me a tooth-ache, you used to cry so hard when the summer was over. Every summer. Until I hit upon a plan to make it all better for you.

On the last day of summer, I would give you a big Hellmann's mayonnaise jar and send you down to the shore to "bring the beach home" with you to Madison.

I knew you'd remember and treasure those smooth, fist-size gray-and-black stones you found when walking barefoot in the shallows. And the pale rounded pebbles that had washed up to the shoreline. And, of course, there was the sand and the cold, clear water of Lake

Geneva. It was fascinating to watch you try to fit your whole summer into a mayo jar.

It took several tries over one long morning in late August — "Grandma Sam, is it full yet?" — but you finally figured out that the way to fit in the best of your haul was to put the big rocks into the jar first. After that, the pebbles and snail shells would sift down into the spaces between the rocks.

When the jar looked filled to the brim, you could still get in a few lids of sand.

And finally, when there didn't seem to be room for another thing, you dunked your jar in the lake and topped off your "beach" with water. Smart girl!

And I told you, Jenny, that living life was like putting the beach into a jar. The point wasn't to fit everything in; it was to attend to the most important things first — the big, beautiful rocks — the most valuable people and experiences — and fit the lesser things in around them.

Otherwise, the best things might get left out.

I've been thinking about big rocks and how much my priorities have changed over the years. What used to be most important to me was pleasing other people; your grandfather

and my mother-in-law, to name two. Going
to dinner parties and having a house clean
enough to stand up to a Sir Charles military
inspection, to name two more.

Now that I please myself, my priorities are
better. The people I love. My health. Getting
the most I can out of every day. The actor
Danny Kaye used to say, "Life is a great big
canvas. Throw all the paint you can at it." I
like that thought. More important, I try to live
by it as much as I can.

I get up really early most mornings so I can
watch the sun rise. I put flower buds in a lot
of little bottles around the house so I can see
the blossoms open everywhere. I feed whole
peanuts to the blue jays because they love
having their food gift-wrapped, and I never
tire of watching them try to fit more than one
peanut into their bills at a time. I read good,
hard books, and if I can't sleep, I might throw
a few logs onto the fire and watch *Law and
Order* reruns.

And here's something I love to do. Once a
month I make a huge bowl of pasta and red
sauce and invite my friends who live alone
to a potluck supper. They like the company
over a home-cooked meal. We laugh hard and

often, and they don't gossip about me too much in the car on the way home!

And in case you're wondering, Doc always comes to the potluck supper. The others just don't know that he's Doc.

Twenty-six

Dear Jen,

Here's a good laugh for us to share.

I've just come back from an afternoon in town and realized that the hem of my skirt was caught up in the waistband of my panty hose for the whole trip. I'd been to the grocery store, the hardware store, Daddy Maxwell's — with my tail feathers blowing in the breeze the whole day. No one said a word. *What a hoot!* So here's a thought that I like very much, Jen, and it took me a while to get it right. If you're going to look back on something and laugh about it, you might as well laugh about it now.

Things are almost never as bad as they first seem. Loosen up, girlfriend! You're very funny in your columns in the *Chicago Tribune*. But it seems to me that you could giggle a little more in real life. I read somewhere that the act of laughing releases some nice chemical into your brain. You feel good, and it's free!

Twenty-seven

〜

I LAUGHED at Sam's letter, and then I *wasn't* laughing. Tears were rolling down my cheeks. I missed her so much, I almost couldn't stand it. Visiting her twice a day at the hospital wasn't enough. Reading her letters made me want to hear the sound of her voice, even if it was just one more time. I needed to talk to Sam about some things.

Like, who was Doc? Did I know him? Was he still alive, and if he was, wouldn't he be visiting Sam at the hospital? Had I seen him there?

I remembered trying to stuff Lake Geneva into a mayo jar when I was five or so. But that Sam not only remembered but found it so meaningful had cracked me up, and choked me up, too.

I walked down to the lake and toed up a beautiful black stone with a few rough edges. I brought it back and put it on the growing pile of Sam's mail on the coffee table.

Right next to my laptop, which was humming softly, waiting for me to start writing.

You have a day job, Jennifer.

The first thing I did was to dump the column I'd started that morning. I had a new idea, but for a long while I didn't know where to start.

Finally I wrote:

> *The last time I saw my Grandma Sam at her house on Lake Geneva, we were saying good-bye at the end of a beautiful Labor Day weekend.*
>
> *Sam looked healthy and happy, but as she hugged me, I got the feeling that something was on her mind and maybe she didn't know how to tell me. The moment passed, and I didn't ask her about it.*
>
> *I got into the car and honked a little salute as I reached the end of her driveway. How could I have known that the next time I'd see my grandmother, she would be in a coma and that maybe she would never be able to talk to me again.*

As I chiseled my column, the day disappeared into night. At one in the morning, I was still writing and rewriting about how lucky I was that Sam had put her thoughts down for me to read. How many of my readers were so lucky? How many of us know the true stories of our parents and grandparents? How many of us share the stories of our lives with our own children? What a loss to the children if we don't. What are we but our stories?

Writing the column was like unraveling a sweater. I tugged on a thought and the words came free in a smooth, untangled line. I completely overshot the 750-word limit on my first draft and had to cut and rewrite and cut again.

When the piece was as good as I could make it, I ended it by inviting my readers to tell me stories about their loved ones. I was already anticipating the mail I'd get, the stories I'd be privileged to read, the family secrets that would be shared with me.

At 2:00 in the morning, just before I went blind from staring into the computer screen, I pressed the SEND button. A microsecond later, my story was in Debbie's electronic mailbox at the *Trib*.

Then I went to bed and cried into my pillow. I wasn't sad, not at all. It was just so beautiful to have an intense feeling and the right words at the same time.

What are we but our stories?

Twenty-eight

I WOKE UP excited and kind of happy. My column was written — it was about as good as I could do — and I had the day off. Yippee!

My blue swimsuit was still inside the duffel bag, where I'd packed it back in Chicago. I put on the one-piece with the scooped neckline and quickly did a few chores. Then I did something completely unexpected. I went looking for Brendan.

His uncle's house was sparkling in the morning sun, the light glinting off all that glass. Behind the house, the lake was calm and glistening.

I knocked on the kitchen door, but there was no answer. I finally cupped my hands and peered between them through the window.

I felt a little disappointed, I guess, because Brendan wasn't around, and I wanted to play.

Then I saw him through the living-room window, and when I looked more closely, I was floored. Brendan was on his knees in the middle of the rug, his hands folded in front of him.

He was praying.

Twenty-nine

~

TOTALLY EMBARRASSED, I turned away and walked off the porch and across the lawn unnoticed. Suddenly the kitchen door whined open and slammed closed behind me. I looked around to see Brendan coming toward me. *Oh no. Busted.*

"Hey, Jen. I thought I heard somebody knock. You up for a swim?" he called.

"Umm, sure," I said.

He flashed me a grin — a beauty, nothing self-conscious about it. Then he yelled a goofy challenge about rotten eggs and sprinted toward the lake.

So I did the most instinctive thing — I took off behind him. I raced down the lawn and then thirty feet of white-painted dock, and when I got to the end of it, I cannonballed into the water. Just do it, right?

I smacked bottom first into the lake, came back up, and started stroking behind Brendan, who was headed toward a channel marker about fifty or sixty yards out. I raced to win. But Brendan was a very good swimmer, and to his credit, he beat my pants off.

He grinned. "So who's a rotten egg, you rotten egg!"

The two of us hung on to the buoy bobbing in the wake of a particularly noisy motorboat zipping around the lake. I squinted through wet eyelashes at Brendan. I'm a pretty good swimmer, but the recent smoking hadn't helped my time, and Brendan's freestyle was awesome.

"You could have let me win," I said. "Or get a little closer."

He shrugged. "Winning is overrated in this country. It was a great swim, though."

"I think you're right," I said. "And mornings at the lake are underrated." The temperature of the water was just about perfect, and the sun was warm on my face and shoulders.

"I'm starting to *really* remember you now, Scout. You were stuck-up and totally impressed with yourself."

No kidding? I must've had him fooled back in the

day. "Still am," I told him, splashing water in his face. "Hey," I said, grinning up into his eyes. "I think I've got an idea."

Brendan looked momentarily confused. "For another column?"

Thirty

~

"DO YOU WANT to go sailing?" I asked.

"*You? Sailing?* Aren't you swamped with work?"

"Actually, I just wrote one of my better pieces in a while."

"Champagne!" Brendan cried.

"One step at a time."

Now here's what I was beginning to discover about Brendan. He'd grown up to be a really nice person — interesting, fun, and not self-involved, as far as I could tell. Not only did he encourage me to talk about Sam as much as I needed to, he was thoughtful in other ways. For instance, he made the sandwiches for our impromptu outing and brought me a long-billed cap to wear so that I wouldn't get burned. Pretty sweet, actually.

Right off, I could tell that the years Brendan had spent landlocked in Indiana hadn't compromised his skill as a sailor. He rigged his uncle's scow in ten minutes flat and got the boat away from the dock on the first try.

Scows are top-heavy, flat-bottomed sailboats, fast and unstable, as I well knew from all the summers I'd spent racing up and down the seven-mile-long lake in my grandfather's sixteen-footer. Brendan manned the mainsail while I dropped the centerboard into the well and took charge of the jib, our movements meshing as if we'd been sailing together for a while.

It was such a tremendous day to be out on the water. A cooling breeze gusted under a hazy sun, and the air was a perfect seventy-five degrees.

Brendan commented on the beautiful, historic homes lining the lakeshore. He hadn't seen them for so long, he felt as though he were seeing them for the first time. The pleasant thoughts were cut off abruptly by the roar of a Jet Ski as a pair of teenagers rode circles around us, swamping our boat. I reached for the jib line, and Brendan scrambled to the high side — but it was too late.

The boat capsized, dumping the two of us into the drink.

"You okay?" I heard as I sputtered to the surface.

"Fine. You?"

"Yep. Don't worry. I got the little bastard's plate number."

I laughed as Brendan righted the scow and helped me back in. Soon we were sailing again, soaking wet but otherwise okay. The rest of the afternoon was a very nice blur. We sailed through the Narrows, passing the Lake Geneva Country Club and Black Point, an eccentric-looking, thirteen-bedroom summer "cottage" built at the end of the nineteenth century. When our faces were stiff from sun and wind, we sailed back to Knollwood Road — to change our clothes.

Brendan had asked me out to dinner.

And I had accepted.

Thirty-one

I HAD JUST the right dress hanging in my closet: a simple black shift that set off my sun-pinked skin. *This isn't a date,* I told myself as I put on makeup, but not too much. *It's a reunion. A chat between old friends.*

"Wow. Look at you!" Brendan said as he arrived to pick me up for . . . whatever it was supposed to be.

"And look at you!" I said. He had on pressed jeans and a blue cashmere sweater, loafers, no socks, and he was tan.

"Your very own beach bum," he said, and winked.

"You look great."

"It's the loafers," he quipped.

We had dinner on the dockside terrace of the French Country Inn, with a candle sputtering on the table between us and the lake bumping up against the pilings. We were still catching up over braised breast of duckling and wild rice when Brendan said a few words about his folks and asked about mine. I told him that neither of my parents was still alive. "It's just Sam and me," I said.

"I'm sorry about your folks. And everything else that's happened to you."

"It's okay. Anyway, here we are on the lake again."

By the time coffee was served, we had moved on to lighter subjects. We joked and laughed and were still so in sync, it surprised me a lot. I had expected dead spots in the conversation, but there hadn't been many. When they happened, it was mostly me being too guarded.

Then the dinner was over and it was time to go home. That's when I realized, or maybe admitted to myself, that I *was* on a date. The best date I'd had in quite a while, actually.

Thirty-two

IT CERTAINLY hadn't been planned that way, but Brendan and I had been together nearly the whole day. And now there was an awkward moment at the front door. We were standing close enough that I could smell the cologne he used. *I need to stop this nonsense right now,* I told myself. *For both of our sakes.*

I caught my breath as that notion flashed through my mind. Then I put the brakes on any fantasy that could lead to the kind of trouble I couldn't handle. I stepped back away from Brendan.

"Well, I'd ask you in for coffee," I said, "but I should start writing my column for tomorrow."

"Okay," Brendan said. But then he sat down on the porch steps, and he showed no sign of leaving.

"Come swimming with me, or just sit out here and shoot the breeze for a little while more. Anything you want. Just don't work tonight. You don't need to work. Come on, Jenny. Loosen up."

The words *Jenny, loosen up* stung a little. But I was also struck by the choice of words. Sam had said almost the same thing in one of her letters.

"Okay," I said. "But you can't ever call me 'Jenny.' Danny called me Jenny."

"I'm sorry. So talk to me, Scout. You've hardly talked about him at all."

"Sometime I will. Maybe. But not tonight," I said. "I'll talk about Danny when I'm ready." Danny and other things.

He seemed confused, or troubled.

I settled down on the porch steps beside Brendan. "What?" I asked.

"Oh, it's nothing. I just wanted to tell somebody that I quit my job," Brendan finally said, pulling on his lower lip. "I quit today."

My head rocked back a little. "You quit your job? Why? What happened, Brendan?"

"Nothing too dramatic. I've been looking at shadows on sheets of plastic for too long. I was thinking it's time to get a few priorities straight," he said. Then he gave me a dead-on look that grabbed and held me.

I glanced away reflexively. The moonlight cast a pale glow over the lake. Peepers and crickets chirped in the bushes. We were sitting very close to each other. Too close.

"I really have to go in," I said. I stood up from the porch steps. "Thanks for the day. It was fun."

Brendan stood, too. He was physically imposing, and he *was* handsome. He leaned in and kissed my forehead, which was oddly nice. Then he gave me his best smile. "Good night, Jennifer. I had a good time, too."

Soon I was in my bed, the same one I'd slept in for years at the lake. A cup of spearmint tea was on the night table. I stared at the ceiling, and some strange, conflicting thoughts swirled in my head. *Brendan and I had a nice night,* I thought. *And that's the end of it. Why? Because it is, that's why.*

I opened another letter from Sam.

Thirty-three

~

Jennifer,

Nothing much worth writing about happened between Doc and me at first. Almost no touching, not even a lingering look in town. It was complicated. His wife had died a few years before, but I was certainly married, and with children, though they were grown. Doc still had children at home. There was one remarkable moment that first summer, and it became a touchstone for us.

One night when your grandfather was having dinner after golf with his pals at Medinah outside Chicago (or so Charles told me), Doc used some connections to get us into the Yerkes Observatory. Yerkes was strictly a scientific observatory back then, home to the largest refracting telescope in the world and not open to the public. At night, no one would be there.

So imagine the two of us sneaking across the parklike lawns, briefly holding hands, approaching the Yerkes complex of buildings with the three huge domes silhouetted against the summer night sky. Then we climbed the wide steps and entered the most beautiful marble halls I have ever seen.

Doc had a flashlight and we followed the beam up the back staircase until we reached a door that opened into the largest of the domes. I was stunned by how large it was inside, like a sports stadium in the round. A telescope in the center pointed up through a slit in the dome to the cobalt sky beyond.

"Watch this, Samantha. You won't believe it," he said. "Ready?"

"I think so." I wasn't really sure.

He pulled a lever, and the floor we were standing on — at least seventy feet across — began to lift us upward. Suddenly we could actually look into the fixed eyepiece of the telescope.

It was Friday, the beginning of the weekend, and I knew that Charles would be driving up from Chicago soon. Still, Doc and I dared

to stay in the cavernous dome for over an
hour. The stars were dazzling, as if the universe was putting on a display just for us.
He talked about the fact that what we were
watching in the sky had actually happened
hundreds of years before, and then Doc
admitted how long he'd secretly wished to be
alone with me like this.

"I wished for it, too," I confessed. Wished,
prayed, fantasized, almost every day since the
Red Cross dinner.

We kissed under all those billions of
twinkling stars. Then we kissed again, longer
and harder. But that was it. There we stood,
two people falling in love but separated by
my marriage, our families, but especially his
children, who were still at home with Doc.

He eventually drove me to the corner of
Knollwood Road — and *didn't* kiss me when
I got out of the car, though, God, I wanted
him to. I entered the house and found that
Charles was sleeping. I had hoped I wasn't
going to have to make up a story, but I
shouldn't have worried.

I undressed quietly, and when I was under
the sheets, I looked into Charles's face. To
my surprise, I didn't feel any guilt about my

adventure with Doc that night — but I did have an interesting thought. I wondered if Charles would notice anything different about me in the morning. *Would he notice that while he slept, I'd become happy?*

Thirty-four

WHEN I ANSWERED the phone by my bed, it was barely 6:40 A.M. and I got a surprise that I wasn't prepared for. Brendan spoke into my ear. "Wake up, Jennifer. The lake is calling."

I wasn't sure what I was doing, but I began to smile and then I put my bathing suit on. I felt like a kid again, and it was good. I felt free.

Outside, I joined Brendan in a jog that turned into a full run to the lake. Finally both of us were screaming his semimaniacal war whoop, which actually made all the sense in the world. The water was freezing, fricking cold at that hour.

"It's not even seven," I sputtered as I did a stiff, chilly breaststroke beside him.

"Perfect time for a swim. I have a new mantra: 'Live every day from the crack of dawn until I can't keep my eyes open a second longer.'"

Okay. Who can fault a philosophy like that, especially since his spirit *was* contagious. We swam over to Sam's dock and hauled ourselves up. He shook off some water, then rolled onto his back. I did the same, and lying next to each other, we stared up at the morning sky. It *was* perfect, actually.

"Takes you back," I said.

"Or maybe forward," he mumbled under his breath.

I was aware that my right side from shoulder to ankle was touching Brendan's left side. The pressure made my body tingle, but I didn't move.

When he turned his face toward me, I avoided his eyes. So he put his hand on my waist and pulled me even closer. I wasn't expecting it, but the heat that flashed through my body almost melted my swimsuit.

And then Brendan kissed me on the lips. A good, long kiss, a really nice one.

And I kissed him back.

And neither of us said a word, which was exactly the right thing to do.

Thirty-five

～

FROM THE MORNING of the kiss, Brendan and I spent more and more of our time together. To be perfectly honest, I knew exactly what this was — a sweet, fleeting summer romance. And so did he, I was sure. We hadn't even "done anything," as the popular saying goes.

Brendan and I launched most mornings with a swim; then we took turns making breakfast, sometimes including his uncle Shep in the ritual. And we visited Sam every day before noon; then I would go again, usually about seven. I always talked to Sam, sometimes for hours at a time. I told her what was going on in my life and asked questions about her letters.

On one particular day, I waited outside Sam's room while Dr. Brendan Keller and Dr. Max Weisberg conferred. When they found me in the hallway,

Brendan had a serious expression on his face. He saw me looking, though, and brushed the look aside.

I'll admit I'd been hoping for a little good news. Maybe I thought that because I was reading Sam's letters and hearing her voice and seeing her so vividly in my mind, she would get better, she had to get better. But now I thought, *She isn't going to get better. I can see it in their eyes. They just don't want to tell me.*

"She's a strong lady," Brendan said, and put his hand over my arm. "She's hanging in there pretty well, Jen. Maybe there's a reason for that."

When we left the hospital, Brendan tried to cheer me up. I liked that he was sensitive to my needs, and I also sensed what a good doctor he must be. Why had he quit his job, though?

He said, "How'd you like to go on a road trip? It'll be fun."

Well, it *was* a glorious day for a drive. So with the CD player blasting James Taylor's and Aretha's and Ella Fitzgerald's greatest hits, we took a route that skirted Chicago, bringing us into South Bend, Indiana, just before noon.

I was in for a real treat, Brendan said, winking. A friend of his was one of the coaches for the Fighting

Irish, and we had been invited to watch the Notre Dame team scrimmage down on the practice field. We sat cross-legged in the short grass while a couple of dozen top-notch bruisers ran their plays. Watching football on television has never moved me, but the sport has a whole different feeling up close. The speed of the action at ground level was incredible, and so was the sharp crack of contact as helmets and shoulder pads collided.

Watching the Blue and Gold was a surprisingly nice way to spend an afternoon, probably because it was Brendan's team. It was also fun to see where he lived, though he stopped short of showing me his old house, or even the apartment where he'd moved after his divorce. "It's a complete, off-limits disaster area; I'd be too embarrassed," he said. So we headed back to Lake Geneva without seeing his place. A little strange, I thought, but no big deal.

The day after our Notre Dame adventure, I had a surprise for Brendan. I took him to the Yerkes Observatory. I kept seeing parallels between him and me and Sam and Doc, so I had to go there. It was daytime and there was a crowd ringing the perimeter of the big dome, but it was still a magical place.

The whole time I kept thinking about what it had meant to Sam and Doc. And I wondered, Who is

Doc, anyway? The next time I talked to Sam, she was going to give up her secret, so help me.

On another morning I arranged for Brendan and me to catch a ride on the mail boat, a double-decker ferry that scoots along the shoreline, delivering mail to the lakefront homes. That same afternoon we saw a couple of silly blockbusters at the little theater in town, one right after the other. We had another habit, too. Last thing at night, after I came back from seeing Sam, we took a long walk on the path that circles the lake.

Being with Brendan definitely felt like an old-fashioned summer romance — fast, irresistible, and probably a little dumb, but even if it was, we both seemed to feel the same way about it. I had the sense that Brendan needed it, too, and also that he was holding back, careful that this didn't get too serious.

I even called him on it while we were delivering mail on Hank Mischuk's ferry.

But Brendan just laughed. "I'm an open book, Scout. You're the mystery woman."

Then one day the strangest thing happened. I didn't turn in my column! It was the first time I'd ever done it, or rather *not* done it. I apologized to Debbie and promised to make up for it, but inside I was exultant. Something was changing, wasn't it?

Maybe I was living every day "from the crack of dawn until I closed my eyes."

That morning I told Sam everything at the hospital, and even though she never said a word, I felt I knew what she wanted me to do next. It was what Sam would have done herself.

Thirty-six

~

LATE THAT AFTERNOON Brendan and I sat together at the tip of Sam's dock. I was wiggling my toes in the water. Brendan was, too.

It was time for me to tell some of my secrets to him. I wanted to do it. I was ready.

"It happened off a beach in Oahu." I spoke in a soft, low voice. "Danny liked bright lights and big cities, so if it had been up to him, we would've taken our vacation in Paris, or maybe London. We decided on Hawaii because *I* wanted to go there."

I sighed, then caught my breath. "At the last minute I got involved in a terrible kidnapping story. So Danny went on ahead of me. A couple of days later I was finally on my way from Chicago," I said. "Late that afternoon, he went out for a run — alone, of course."

Brendan was watching me intently as I managed

to get the words out somehow. "You don't have to do this, Jennifer," he finally said.

"Yeah, I do. I have to do this. I need to get it out and I want to, Brendan. I want to tell you. I don't want to be a mystery woman anymore."

Brendan nodded, and he took my hand. Something had happened between the two of us in the past couple of weeks; I had come to trust Brendan more than I could have ever imagined. He was my friend. No, he was more than that.

"It was a beautiful evening on the north shore of Oahu, a place called Kahuku. I've read all the weather reports. Danny took off his T-shirt and ran down into the surf, which was high, but he was an athlete, a good swimmer. He loved to push the envelope as much as he could. That was one of his favorite sayings, 'Let's go for it, Jenny!' He was always teasing me to go for it."

I felt tears slipping down my cheeks, and I really didn't want to cry. Not in front of Brendan. "He was a good, caring person . . . and there were so many things he still wanted to do —" My voice faltered badly. I didn't know if I could finish what I'd started. "I loved him so much. . . . I *see* every minute of what happened in Hawaii. This horrible and recurring nightmare that I have. For the past year and a half, I've *watched* Danny die over and over again.

He calls out to me. With his last breath, he calls my name."

I stopped to collect myself. I realized that I was squeezing Brendan's hand very tight.

"It was *my* fault, Brendan. If I had gone to Hawaii when I was supposed to, Danny would be alive today."

Brendan held my hand. "It's okay, it's okay," he whispered, his voice soft and gentle.

"There's more to it," I said so low that I could barely hear myself. "When I got back to Chicago, I couldn't stop crying and thinking about what had happened. Sam came and stayed with me. She took the best care of me, Brendan."

I couldn't talk for a minute. But I had come this far, hadn't I?

"I was in my bathroom. I felt this sharp pain, and then I was doubled over on the bathroom floor. I screamed and Sam came running. She knew immediately that I had miscarried. She held me and cried with me. I lost the baby. I lost our baby, Brendan. I was pregnant, and I lost our little 'peanut.'"

Thirty-seven

BRENDAN HELD ME for a long time on the dock. Then I had to say good night to Sam, so I drove over to the medical center about 8:30. Brendan offered to come, but I told him I was all right. I brought Sam roses from her garden.

"Sam, wake up. Look," I said, "you have to see your roses. And I need to talk to you."

But she didn't respond in any way. She couldn't even hear me, could she?

I placed the flowers in a crockery jug on the windowsill and fluffed them until they looked just right.

Then I turned back to Sam. "You're missing everything. A lot is happening, Sam."

She looked pinched and faded, not good. I'd never been more worried about losing her. Every time I saw Sam I was scared it could be the last.

I pulled a chair up close to the bed. "I've got a secret to tell you," I said. "Sam, there's someone I like at the lake. I'm trying hard not to like him too much. But he's so sweet; he's smart in a good way. He's even kind of a hunk. I know, I know, you never get all three of those qualities in the same man."

I gave Sam a moment to take in the news. "I'll call him Brendan. Ha, ha. Because that's his name. I could also call him *Doc*. He's a doctor.

"You remember how I used to follow Brendan Keller around when I was a little kid? Well, he's all grown up. I trust him completely, Sam. I told him about Danny, and the baby. I don't know how much he likes me. I mean, he definitely likes me, but he's holding back a little. I guess we both are. Confused yet? I am."

I finally stopped babbling and took one of Sam's hands and held it. I played that game where you think something and you pretend somebody else can hear your thoughts.

I need you to meet Brendan, Sam. Can you do that for me? Just this once.

Thirty-eight

~

"YOU KNOW that this is completely unreal, this life on the lake that we're living this summer," Brendan said, and smiled. We were driving home from dinner at the Lake Geneva Inn the next night. It was pouring rain, sheeting the stuff. I almost told Brendan to pull over to the side of the road.

"It was your idea — every moment from sunup until I can't keep my eyes open any longer. Those were *your* words," I said.

When we got to Sam's, the two of us raced across her puddled yard to the protective wing of the front porch. I yanked open the door.

"Stay here. I'll get towels," I said, and walked inside first.

I was halfway to the linen closet when a table lamp flickered out — I smelled something burning. Uh-oh.

I shoved the armchair away from the wall with my hip and saw a limp white rag lying in the corner.

It was Euphoria.

Something was wrong with Euphoria.

I called, "Brendan, come quick," and then he was right there beside me. He lifted my cat and gently laid her down again in the center of the carpet. What I saw made me sick. The fur around Euphoria's mouth was singed and bloody. And then I realized that she wasn't breathing.

"Oh, God, what's happened to her?"

"Looks like she bit into an electric cord," Brendan said. He placed two fingers high up against the inside fold of her left hind leg.

"She's in arrest, Jennifer. Poor thing's got no pulse."

I'd loved that little girl since I rescued her from the pound right after Danny's death. Euphoria wasn't just a cat to me. I loved her dearly. I clutched at Brendan's arm.

"Please! Can you help her?"

He took a deep breath.

"Okay, listen to me. When I say so, press right *here*. Five times." Then Brendan turned Euphoria onto her side. She made no movement on her own, no sound.

Now he opened her jaws and bent to fit his mouth to hers. Then he blew a little breath into her lungs.

Phh.

"Do it now," he told me. "Press, Jennifer."

I pressed on the left side of Euphoria's rib cage, massaging her heart, praying with mine. Then Brendan signaled me to stop. My heart was racing, thundering.

He bent over her and breathed into her mouth a second time. *Phh.* Then he had me press again. He was working very hard. Being a doctor right before my eyes.

Then I got to see a miracle happen. I *felt* Euphoria come back to life under my hands. She quivered and coughed. Then she opened her beautiful green eyes and looked up at me. Her eyes were filled with love. She was breathing on her own.

She finally wobbled to her feet and said, "Yow."

I grabbed her up in one arm and kissed her. I threw my other arm around Brendan's neck and kissed him. I hugged him hard, almost crushing Euphoria between us. "You saved my baby," I whispered.

Brendan sat back on his heels, a look of complete satisfaction on his face. Then he said a very cool thing.

"You gotta know I love you, Jennifer. I just gave the kiss of life to a cat."

I stared into his eyes with amazement — Brendan had just said *I love you*.

Thirty-nine

~

IT WAS OCCURRING to me lately that the summer was going too quickly. It was the "magic hour" again — our favorite time to be out on Sam's dock. Brendan and I were sitting side by side, dangling our feet, leaning into each other. I noticed that he was staring out across the lake, lost in his thoughts, wherever it was that they took him.

"You okay?" I asked. I knew that he was, of course. How could he not be?

"I . . . uh . . . ," he said. And then Brendan didn't say anything.

"*You're* at a loss for words? I can't believe it. I *don't* believe it. You . . . uh . . . what?" I kidded.

But he didn't joke back for once. What was this? Was it time for Brendan to share a few secrets, too? Did he trust me enough?

"I have to tell you something, Jennifer," he said.

I turned my shoulder so that it wasn't touching his anymore. I could see his face better now. Brendan was averting his eyes.

"You're not going to tell me that you're still married?" I asked, and didn't like those words as they came out of my mouth.

He looked at me. "I'm divorced, Jennifer. That's not it. . . . The problem is that when we met a couple of weeks ago, I had no idea that any of this was going to happen. Who could have? I had no idea there was somebody like you out there."

"What a shame, buddy," I said. "I feel pretty bad for you."

But Brendan didn't laugh. If anything, he looked worried. Not like himself. Now I got it. He was falling for me. "But . . ."

I had a feeling that I wasn't going to like *but*. I was so sure of it that my body went cold.

"But *what?*" I asked.

Forty

~

HE DIDN'T ANSWER my question right away, and my insides continued to churn. Whatever was happening, it wasn't good. Brendan wouldn't, or couldn't, look me in the eye, and he'd never been like that before.

"Brendan, what is it?"

He sighed. "This is going to be hard. I think I'm going to have to back into it."

"Okay," I said. "Just tell me what's going on."

He held out his wrist. "Have I ever shown you this, Jennifer?"

It was a handsome Rolex watch. Of course I'd noticed it before, but he hadn't said anything about the watch.

"Kind of fancy for you," I said.

"It was a gift from a friend who used to live next door to me in Indiana. His name was John Kearney.

Patterson*

John was a professor at Notre Dame. Very, very nice guy. Four kids, all girls. We used to go to football games together, play tennis once a week. When he was fifty-one, he went to his doctor about a little cough and came back with an X-ray showing a large spot on his lung," Brendan said.

"He showed it to me. When I saw the film, I got John into the Mayo Clinic, where I had interned. I found him a top surgeon. Oncologist. Jennifer, six months later, John weighed a hundred and ten pounds. He couldn't eat and couldn't get out of bed. He was in constant pain and he wasn't getting any better."

Brendan looked into my eyes. I was touched by the depth of his sadness. I had been there myself; maybe I was still there.

"I was going to take John in for another radiation treatment, but he flat out refused. He said, 'Please stop this, Brendan. I love you and I know you mean well. But I've had a good life. I have four beautiful daughters. I don't want to be like this. Please let me go.'

"I apologized and I hugged him, and then both of us cried. I knew John was right. I couldn't change what I'd already done, but the way I viewed the aggressive measures that doctors sometimes take, because we *can,* changed forever.

396

"When he died, John left me his watch," Brendan said. "What it means to me is 'quality time,' making the best of it. So when I read my own CAT scan at the beginning of the summer, I decided to do what's best for me. I'm sorry about this. I can't tell you how sorry. I don't like melodrama very much, especially when it's happening to me. I'm dying, Jennifer."

Forty-one

I MAY HAVE blacked out for a second or two. I heard Brendan say "my own CAT scan" but I'm not completely sure I grasped what came after that. Then he said, and I heard this very clearly, "There's nothing that can be done for me. Believe me, I've examined every possibility."

I felt this incredible core of pain at the center of my chest, or maybe where my heart *used* to be. I was dizzy and nauseous and I couldn't really believe what I knew I'd just heard. Everything around me on the dock seemed fuzzy and unreal. The water I had my feet in, my own body, Brendan's hand resting on mine. Suddenly I reached out and held him as tightly as I could. I kissed his cheek, the side of his forehead. I felt so incredibly sad, and empty.

"Tell me what's wrong," I finally said.

"Well, it's called glioblastoma multiforme, Jennifer. Big name for a bad cancer that I have right *here*." He pointed his finger to the back and side of his head, just behind his left ear. He explained that he'd looked at his own case over and over, consulted experts from as far away as London, and kept arriving at the same unfortunate conclusion.

"The only treatment for this form of cancer is experimental, extremely radical," he told me. "Surgery is a nightmare. The risk of paralysis is phenomenal. They probably can't get all of the cells, anyway. The cancer usually keeps coming back, even with radiation and chemo."

Tears were rolling down my face, and I felt hollow. "This isn't true," I whispered.

"I didn't know how to tell you, Jennifer. I still don't." He pulled me into his arms, and I let Brendan hold me. When he spoke again, his voice was low and measured. "I'm so, so sorry, Jennifer." He was soothing *me*. "I'm sorry."

"Oh, Brendan," I whispered. "How can this be happening?"

"A little quality time. That's all I wanted," he said in the softest whisper. "That's why I decided to have a last summer up here. And then I found you again, Scout."

Forty-two

~

BRENDAN AND I hadn't even been to bed together, and now maybe I understood why. It was
one of the few things that I did understand at that
point.

"I don't want to be alone tonight," I said against
his cheek. "Is that okay?"

Then Brendan gave me that incandescent grin of
his. "I didn't want to be alone for the past thirty-
four nights."

"But who's counting?"

"I am," he said.

I took Brendan's hand and kissed it. "You *were*."

It seemed that we got from the dock to the bedroom without even touching the ground. We held
on to each other inside the doorway, swaying together on the threshold. We kissed for a long moment, and I finally admitted to myself that I really

loved Brendan's kisses. Then we fumbled with our clothes and fell onto the bed in my room.

"I guess my sob story worked," he cracked.

"Shhhhh. No jokes."

He couldn't resist, though. "Scout? Is it you?" he asked, and both of us started laughing again. Actually, I loved laughing with him, loved that he could make me laugh.

I put my hands in Brendan's thick hair and kissed him over and over. I loved the sensation of his skin rubbing against mine. I loved his smell. I touched the soft curls on his chest, then ran my hands down the length of his body. I was taking him all in, learning about him. I wanted to consume Brendan, and in every way that I could, I did. I couldn't deny my feelings anymore. I didn't want to.

Brendan tenderly kissed my breasts, the hollow of my throat, my mouth, my eyelids; then he did it all over again. I was completely lost. He was so gentle and good. He murmured my name, his hands gliding over my body. He had a wonderful touch, and it gave me goose bumps.

"You're beautiful without your clothes on, even more beautiful than I imagined," he said. It was very nice to hear, just the right thing. I doubt that he knew how much I needed to hear that. I hadn't been to bed with anybody in over a year and a half.

"So are you," I said.

"I'm beautiful?"

"Yep, you are."

We didn't hold anything back; there was no shyness, not too many first-time nerves. It was as if this had always been meant to happen. Maybe that was even true. After a while we rested in each other's arms, whispering. I couldn't stop staring into Brendan's incredible eyes.

All of my fear was gone, all of the uncertainty and doubt. Finally, we lay on our sides, facing each other, snuggled in so tight that there was no space between us. My legs were hooked around his waist, his knees tucked into mine.

That's how we slept.

When I woke up, I was still in Brendan's arms. I had to admit I liked it there.

"Scout?" he whispered, and I punched him in the arm.

"See, you're still a tomboy."

"How can you say that — after last night?"

"Right. A tom*girl*. Definitely a *girl*. No, you're a beautiful woman, Jennifer. You make me so happy."

I hugged him tightly, and just then "the crack of dawn" sliced through the part in the curtains.

Almost on cue, Brendan's eyes widened, and there was that amazing smile of his.

"We're off!" he said.

How could I possibly say no?

Not wearing any swimsuits, we ran like little kids out into the yard. A flock of startled ducks flew up through the mist that was rising off the lake as we thundered down the dock. The planks clanked and clunked beneath our bare feet.

We screamed as we dove into the crystal-clear lake.

As if everything was right with the world, instead of terribly, terribly wrong.

Forty-three

~

I VISITED SAM that morning and I had to tell her everything. In the past Sam would have said, "You're bubbling over. Slow down, Jennifer." But I couldn't slow down; there wasn't time. Still, we talked — well, I talked — for over an hour.

"Sam, I don't feel guilty anymore, and I don't much want to examine why. Maybe it's because Brendan is sick. I have to try and do something. What do you think, Grandmother? I need your help. You've been resting long enough." But Sam had nothing to say to me, and it was terribly sad and frustrating. All my life, she had always been there.

Later in the morning I had a meeting with Max Weisberg. I needed a second opinion, and not about Sam. I wanted to talk to Max about Brendan.

I followed the charming aromas of burned macaroni and coffee to the hospital coffee shop, a cafeteria-style room with Formica tables and a commanding view of the parking lot. I filled a paper cup with sugar and coffee, then turned to see Dr. Max sitting at one of the tables near the window.

I'd met with Max so many times in the past couple of weeks, he'd almost lost his power to intimidate. Actually, he looked really young, sitting across from me in his scrubs. His brush-cut blond hair was standing at attention as he polished off dry rye toast and black coffee.

"Yum," I said.

"Eat your heart out. What's up?"

I summed up what Brendan told me the night before, that he had a serious brain tumor, with a very poor prognosis, and that he'd elected to have a great summer and not to pursue any radical treatment program.

When I was finished, Max said, "When are you going to stop smoking?"

"Max. Don't. Please. Besides, I basically quit. Until yesterday."

"I mean it." He sighed. "Look, I'm not going to lie to you. GBM is a horror. Brendan is absolutely right about that. The surgery *is* dangerous; the treatment fails as often as it works. Brendan knows all of this."

"Max, can anything be done? Is there any chance he could come through this with a decent quality of life?"

"*If* he survived the experimental surgery, if he survived the treatment, he'd have a thirty percent chance of living for two to five years. But, Jennifer, he could go through the surgery and be completely paralyzed. Brendan would be able to think but not speak or do anything for himself. Believe it or not, I'm understating the risk."

I didn't want to start crying in front of Max, but sometimes he had the bedside manner of a stun gun.

"I don't know what to do," I said. "I'm going a little crazy here. Can you tell?"

"Sorry," said Dr. Max. "My specialty is neurology."

I glared at him, tears started down my cheeks, and to my amazement, his cold demeanor melted.

"I'm sorry. That was bad," he said. "Even for me."

He put his head in his hands and his elbows on the table. "Let me say this in a better way, Jen. It sounds to me like Brendan has decided to make good use of whatever time he has left. He's chosen to have a beautiful summer with you. He's lucky to spend a summer with you, and I'm quite certain he knows it. In other words, I think he's making a very intelligent choice. I really am sorry." Then Max actually took my hands in his. "You don't deserve this, Jennifer. And neither does Brendan."

Forty-four

I TURNED OVER a lot of things that Dr. Max Weisberg had said as I drove toward Sam's house. I parked the car under the oak, kicked off my loafers, and walked to Shep's dock. Brendan was out on the lake, swimming. He looked so vital — not sick, certainly not terminally ill. My stomach started to churn.

He saw me and waved. Then he called, "Come in, the water's perfect. *You* look perfect."

"No, you come," I said, patting the dock beside me. "Sit by me. I'm saving a spot. The *dock* is perfect."

Brendan swam my way. He pulled himself up in one smooth motion. Then he put his arm around me and we kissed.

"Not right now," he said after the kiss.

"Not right now, what?" I asked.

"Let's not talk about it right now, Jen," he said. He looked me in the eye, squinting on account of the sun. "It would be a waste of such a beautiful day. We have time to get into the serious stuff."

Fine. So I made lunch and served it on Sam's wide front porch: chicken salad with white grapes on eight-grain, chips, iced tea. Below us, sunlight skipped across the lake and the fragrance of Sam's roses saturated the air. Henry was working in the garden; he seemed to be there all the time.

It *was* a perfect day, wasn't it? The right guy, the right girl, only the timing was wrong. I couldn't help it, I felt as though I was going to break down and cry all through lunch, but I held it inside. Maybe Brendan was used to the idea of his dying, but I wasn't.

He was waterproofing Shep's deck and the job was only half done, so after lunch Brendan went back to work. I was clearing the table when I found a note folded under my plate. It read:

JENNIFER,
YOU ARE FORMALLY INVITED TO
DINNER AT THE GUESTHOUSE.
7:00 P.M. MORE OR LESS.
COME AS SWEET AS YOU ARE.
BRENDAN

Forty-five

〜

A CHORUS of peepers and crickets accompanied me as I walked across the lawn at dusk and headed west along the shore path. It was such a gorgeous night, with clear skies and a cooling breeze. I wore black pants and a halter topped with a black cardigan, and I carried sandals. I wanted to look nice for Brendan and I thought that I looked passable. I am no beauty queen, but I dress up okay.

There was a small guesthouse in a clearing by the lake with an attached bluestone patio. I saw steaks marinating and a bottle of red and Brendan stirring coals in the barbecue, raising sparks into the sky.

He kissed me, and he *was* a good kisser. His kisses lingered on the lips. "Special occasion," he said, handing me a glass of wine. "My birthday."

"Ohhh, Brendan. Jeez Louise. Why didn't you tell

me?" I know that I turned the brightest shade of red, and I felt just terrible.

"I didn't want any fuss," he said, and shrugged. "It's not a big birthday. Doesn't have any zeros in it."

I did the math. He was forty-one. *Only forty one.* I clinked my glass against his and said, "Happy, happy birthday!" I held back all the coulda-woulda stuff.

"I love it that you're here," he said. "It *is* a happy birthday."

The fireflies traced cursive neon letters in the night air as I tossed the salad and Brendan put the steaks on the grill. There was a CD player in the guesthouse, and soon Eva Cassidy was remembering the night as only she can. Brendan asked me to dance. I took his hand and immediately felt the blood rush to my head. He wrapped me in his arms and shuffled with me barefoot on the grass. Simple as this was, I loved it. Eva was followed by Sting on Brendan's personalized CD.

He was a good dancer, very coordinated, even barefoot in the grass. He could lead, or follow, and he was so light on his feet that I felt as if I were blending into him. The two of us floated over the lawn, cheek to cheek. It was so nice — glorious, actually. The two of us fit together.

"The steaks are burning," I whispered as Toni Braxton started in on "Unbreak My Heart."

"Doesn't matter," said Brendan.

"You're an incredible Prince Charming, you know. Handsome, witty, sensitive for a football fan."

He smiled at me. "What a nice birthday thought."

"After we eat," I said, "I have a really nice present for you. I've been thinking about it all afternoon."

"So you must have known it was my birthday."

"I'm improvising," I said, and smiled.

So we ate first and drank some delicious wine from somewhere in Washington State. *Two* bottles. We danced to Jill Scott and Sade and then . . . well, it *was* his birthday after all.

The guesthouse was filled with chintz-covered furniture and had a great bed looking out over the lake. That's where Brendan and I made love until "we couldn't keep our eyes open any longer." He was an incredible Prince Charming, in every way I could imagine. Even on his birthday.

I remember something else sweet. Just before we finally fell asleep, I sang, "Happy birthday, sweet Brendan. Happy birthday to you." I sang it with all my heart, and he joined in with all of his.

Forty-six

I AWOKE in the guesthouse with a mild headache from the wine I'd had, followed by a start of fear when I realized that I was alone. From the height of the sun, I estimated that a portion of the morning was gone as well. I gathered up my clothes and, to my relief, found a note lying on top of my sandals.

Dear Jen,

I was right, you are the best. I have a little business in Chicago. Nothing too important. See you tonight? I hope so. I can't wait to have you back in my arms. I miss you already. Hope you feel the same about moi.

XOXO,

Brendan

I clutched the note to my chest as I hurried across three back lawns in last night's black clothes. Euphoria and Sox greeted me at the top of Sam's porch stairs, weaving between my legs and complaining that their breakfast was late.

As I made my apologies, a red truck pulled into the parking area. Sam's gardener spilled out of the cab. I could see that Henry was in a state. Now what?

He called out, "Jennifer, everybody has been trying to find you."

At the same moment, I could hear the telephone ringing inside. *Not Sam,* I thought.

"One minute, Henry!" I called to him. "Telephone."

I threw open the back door and fumbled with the receiver before clapping it to my ear. I knew the caller's voice immediately — Dr. Max — but he sounded tenuous and strained. Not like himself.

"Sam is awake," he said. "Come right now."

Forty-seven

~

I GUNNED the Jag up Highway 50, tapped the brakes to take a right onto 67, and sped on. All of my thoughts were on Sam, so I didn't notice that Henry was following me. Not until his pickup truck pulled alongside me in the hospital parking lot and Henry cranked down his window. "She's been —"

"Sorry, what, Henry?" I yelled back to him. "I didn't hear you!"

"Sam's not in the ICU anymore. She's on the second floor. Twenty-one B."

"Thanks!" I shouted. Then I had a thought — *Could Henry be Doc?* He had brought up two children himself. He might even have a doctorate. I thought I remembered something about that.

Then I was too busy running and semipolitely elbowing my way through the milling crowd in the hospital lobby. I took the fire stairs two at a time. I found Sam's new room at the end of a gleaming linoleum hallway. I pushed open the swinging door. I even had a wisecrack ready: "It's about time you rejoined the living!" But I never got to say it.

My heart sank. Sam was lying absolutely still in the bed. Her eyes were closed tight. Dr. Max was bent over her, taking her vitals. *Oh God, I was too late.*

"What's happened?" I asked. "I got here as fast as I could."

Max turned and saw me. "Let's talk outside," he said. "C'mon with me."

"She's gone back into the coma, hasn't she?"

Max held up a hand to stop me from coming farther into the room. "No, Jennifer. She's out of the coma. But this is a good time for me to fill you in on some things."

We went to his office again, a beige square with prefab furnishings and interoffice memos tacked to the walls. As he'd done a couple of weeks before, Max led me to his swivel chair, then sat on the desk ledge, facing me.

"She's just sleeping," he finally said. "She was awake earlier. We tried to find you. Nobody answered the phone."

"But she's out of the coma?" I asked.

"Coma is not a restful state," Max continued, as if I hadn't asked him a question. "Even though they're unconscious, they still worry about stuff like who's feeding the dog, watering the houseplants, whether they've left the lights on. It's good for the patient to be reassured — that's why we stopped the hospital from shipping Sam off to St. Luke's in Milwaukee. We wanted her friends — especially you — to talk to her."

"Ship her off? This is the first I've heard."

"I know. Look" — Max waved a dismissive hand — "there was no need to get into it with you. A lot of people around here love Sam."

As I turned over that piece of news, Max explained that his father was on the hospital board. The two of them had pulled a few strings to keep Sam in Lake Geneva. Dr. Max went on to say that Lakeland Medical wasn't big enough to give patients long-term care. "Sam *is* out of her coma, but the trauma might have left her with physical or psychological difficulties."

"Did it?" I asked. "C'mon, Max, give me something here."

"She's talkative, but she doesn't always make perfect sense. She's weak. We'll keep her for a little while longer. Then she's going to need patience and a lot of care."

Max was staring at me, but why? In a flash of clarity, I realized what he was seeing. Smudged mascara under my eyes, sleep-smooshed hair — *and* I was wearing last night's rumpled clothes at 10:00 on a weekday morning.

Still, I maintained my dignity. "I want to see Sam," I told him. "Okay?"

"Absolutely. I just wanted to prepare you."

Max went with me back to Sam's room, then he left and I quietly approached her bed. I gently touched her arm. Suddenly Sam's eyelids flew open, and I jumped back. But her eyes twinkled as she looked me up and down.

"Jennifer," she said, and then smiled. "My girl is here."

Forty-eight

~

I BURST into tears and placed my arms around Sam's neck. It was so incredible, so unbelievable to feel her arms on me, to hear her voice again. I had almost given up hope that I would ever talk to her again.

She gently patted my back, just the way she'd done from the time I was two years old. I loved Sam so much that it was beyond scary to think of losing her. I'd wanted to see her again, to talk to her, and now it was happening.

I fluffed up Sam's pillow and sat on the edge of the bed. "Where have you been?" I whispered.

"I've been right here. Or so I've been told."

"Tell me," I said. It was one of our catchphrases. *Tell me* who you're seeing in Chicago. *Tell me* the scoop at the lake.

"Well, it was . . . strange," she said, pursing her lips. "I didn't know where I was . . . but I could *hear* things, Laura."

Oops. Laura was my mother's name.

Sam continued, unaware of her mistake. "The damned *elephant* over there almost drove me mad. But when the nurses came in, they barked about the daughters. I liked that!"

I translated as best I could. The "elephant" had to be the ventilator. *Barked about the daughters?* Who knew what that was?

"Did I say *daughters?* I meant . . ."

"Doctors?" I guessed.

"Right. I knew you'd understand. I tried to talk to you, Jennifer. I could hear you, but my voice —" She pointed repeatedly, *wordlessly,* at her mouth. "Nothing came out."

I nodded, because my voice felt trapped, too. Then both of us were hugging again. When in doubt, hug. I could count her ribs through her gown, her hands shook, and her words were jumbled — but it was okay. Sam was alive. She was talking to me again. This was what I had wished and prayed for.

Sam wanted me to talk for a while, so I did, and wound up telling her more than I had planned to about Brendan and me. Sam listened, but she didn't say very much. I wondered if she was following me at all.

Then Sam looked at me with her bright blue eyes and just about broke my heart. She said, "I want to go home before I die."

Forty-nine

MY RELIEF at seeing and talking to Sam faded some then, and even more as I drove back to Knollwood Road later in the afternoon. I needed to call her friends, but I had begun to worry about Brendan. What was he doing in Chicago? Was his tumor getting worse? Why would he leave Lake Geneva now? Plus I couldn't wait to tell him what had happened with Sam.

I didn't like being apart from Brendan, I realized that afternoon. I hated it, actually, and that was a bad sign.

I looped the Jag around at the end of the drive and parked under the oak tree out front. In the past few minutes, my fears had condensed into a headache. It was sitting right behind my left eye.

Once I was inside the house, I gulped down two Advils. Then I walked to Shep's house to see if

Brendan had returned. The house was dark, though. No one was there. *Brendan must still be in Chicago. Shoot. Where are you?* I really did miss him. And I was worried about him, too. Just general, neurotic, city-girl worry.

I trudged back to Sam's house, and I didn't know what to do with myself. Then I did. I took a packet of Sam's letters out to the porch. More than ever, I wanted to hear her stories.

What happened between her and Doc? Who was he? Would she ever tell me the whole truth? Was John Farley Doc? Was Henry? Or even Brendan's uncle Shep? Or was it someone I didn't even know?

I'd just settled into my favorite rocker when the sky darkened over the lake. The air was dense with ozone, and the imminent thunderstorm fueled a feeling of urgency about the letters. The pathetic fallacy strikes again, just like in a Brontë novel.

I *needed* to know how Sam and Doc's story turned out. I guess I wanted a happy ending. Who doesn't? But I had noticed lately that happy endings can be hard to come by.

I started to read anyway.

Fifty

Jennifer dear,

The longing I felt for Doc was unbearable at times. You can imagine. Sometimes it lasted for months. Here's what happened next. There were ten days every summer that were more torturous than all the rest. It was when Charles traipsed off to Ireland to play golf with his buddies and I don't know what else they did over there, though I'd heard rumors. While he was gone, all I thought about was Doc. I couldn't help it, and maybe I didn't really want to.

I remember one particular Saturday morning, in August of 1972. Charles was in Kilkenny and I was in downtown Lake Geneva.

All alone, as usual.

The back of my Jeepster was loaded with deer fencing when I stopped off for gas. Young Johnny Masterson was the gasoline jockey that summer, and he'd just filled up my tank when Doc's car pulled in on the other side of the pumps.

My heart started booming as soon as I saw him. This always happened, maybe partly because we had so many secrets but mostly because we were deeply in love. I gave Johnny a ten-dollar bill, and while he was getting the change, Doc stepped out of his car. He walked up to the Jeep. God, he was so handsome, Jen, with a smile that could warm anybody's heart. And those eyes of his.

"Do me a favor, Sammy," he said. "Don't fight me on this. Just follow me out of here when I leave."

I followed Doc for ten miles down Route 50, then he turned off onto the main highway. When we got to the Alpine Valley Resort, I parked my car next to his, then got into the passenger seat beside him. Was this what Doc wanted? Well, I did, too.

I went straight into his arms. "I've missed you. God, I don't know how much more of this I can stand," I confessed.

425

When Doc spoke, his voice made every cell in my body sing. "I know we've talked it to death, Samantha. Maybe it's wrong, but I just don't care anymore. I'm fifty years old. I love you more than I love anything in this world. I want to be alone with you. Please say you'll come away with me. *Now,* Samantha."

Jennifer, it was like exhaling after holding my breath for years. Suddenly the moment was there. All I had to do was grab it. What I'd dreamed about but hadn't dared believe could happen.

"Yes," I whispered against Doc's cheek. "I'll go away with you. Let's do it right now. Before I can even think about changing my mind."

Fifty-one

~

Jennifer,

No one else knows about this — only you.

Doc and I held each other for a long time in that parking lot. We were probably trying to keep up our nerve. I had no idea where we were going, but a few moments later we were on our way.

We held each other for the entire trip, and a hundred different, crazy thoughts were racing through my mind. What if we were caught? What would it mean to our lives? Could Doc and I make it through a whole weekend together?

We had been traveling for eight hours when a WELCOME TO COPPER HARBOR, MICHIGAN sign appeared in the headlights.

"This is it," Doc said. I squeezed his hand tightly, then scooched up and kissed him. *This was it, all right.* For the record, Copper Harbor is at the tip of Michigan's Keweenaw Peninsula, surrounded on three sides by Lake Superior. It's a staggeringly beautiful place. The air was cool in August, and I was wearing only shorts and a sleeveless shirt. Doc took off his jacket and draped it around my shoulders.

"It's called Raptor Lodge, and it's very small, very special," he told me. "I've wanted to bring you here for a long time."

I laughed. "And I've wanted to come with you, anywhere at all. But *this* is beautiful."

We walked into the main building and registered. I'm certain that we looked very much in love, and, Jennifer, we were. I generally don't like couples who are all over each other, but I couldn't help myself, and neither could Doc.

We walked to our room from the main lodge, and I couldn't let go of him. The night was alive with hoots and whistles and a light crackle as animals stepped through the underbrush. Nothing mattered to me but Doc and being close to him and what was going to happen next. In my whole life, I had been with only Charles, and look how that had worked out.

We finally saw our cabin in a moonlit clearing carpeted with pine needles. My mouth was suddenly dry as Doc fumbled with the key. My legs were shaking, too. Then he swung open the door and pulled me into his arms.

"Finally," Doc said, and smiled.

We kissed and started to pull at each other's clothes. Doc was kissing and touching me in ways I'd never experienced before. If this bothers you, go to the next letter, but it was so good for me. I was melting in his arms, and all my doubts about myself were dissolving, too. I felt sexy and wanted, beautiful, and even pretty good in bed. I had never known it could be like that, because it had never been even close to that good for me. I felt alive and free and *desirable*. I felt like a woman, and I loved every second of it.

Finally, Doc cupped my face in his hands and stared deeply into my eyes.

"You have *no* idea how beautiful you are, do you?" he asked, and seemed amazed at my naïveté.

"No," I told him, "no idea at all. Not until I met you."

Fifty-two

Jennifer,

I do have a few juicy details that I won't share with you, but that night with Doc was everything I had wanted it to be and so much more. I woke up in his arms and for the first time I could remember, I felt I was where I belonged. "Morning, Samantha," he whispered. "You're still as beautiful as I remember from last night."

I was *Samantha* to Doc — only to him.

We stayed in our cabin for most of the next two days. The truth is, we didn't want to be anywhere else. Everything was so new for us, and the exploration was, well, so much fun. On the second night, a ringing telephone jarred us awake.

I held on to Doc's arm and I started to

shake a little. No one knew we were there. Had Charles found us?

"Very good. Thanks," Doc spoke into the receiver. Now I was even more mystified. I didn't understand why he was smiling about being woken up from a sound sleep at quarter to two.

"Get dressed, Samantha," he said, grabbing for his clothes. "You're going to like this. It's part of the reason we're here."

Jennifer, imagine this. Just try to imagine what we did that night.

We took a short ride in the car, then walked, and ended up sitting on a huge boulder looking out over Lake Superior. I was hugging my knees. Doc had an arm around me, and the *only* thing between us and Canada was the vast glassy expanse of the lake. It was a little before three in the morning.

As we watched, as our eyes went wide, a glowing ribbon of green light stretched across the horizon and then drifted lazily upward, until it became a transparent curtain shimmering above the water. The hem of the curtain brightened with a reddish gleam, then veils of purple and blue flared, and the sky seemed to shiver and sway.

"Someone spiked the water," I managed to gasp. "Or I'm hallucinating."

Doc laughed. "This is the aurora borealis. Most people know the name, but they have no idea what it is. Now we do, Samantha. Isn't this amazing?"

It was an unforgettable moment. The entire sky was in motion, and as the undulating curtain passed right over us, bright points of light swirled like pinwheels. Doc said that the aurora was actually a stream of electrons powered by the solar wind, colliding with atoms of gas. "The impact causes the gas to emit light. The color of the light depends on the type of gas. The green and red lights are oxygen, blue and purple are hydrogen and helium. Sodium is yellow. It's like neon lighting without the tubes," Doc said. "It's neon in the wild."

I hugged him and whispered, "Thank you for this."

Doc shrugged. "I just arranged for us to be awake to see it."

"Don't let this end," I whispered against his cheek. And it didn't. Doc and I made love that night on a boulder under starry skies. Jennifer, it was an out-of-body, out-of-this-world experience, and I highly recommend "neon in the wild" to anybody with a little romance left in their souls.

Even if they're not quite sure if it's still there.

Fifty-three

Dear Jen,

Sunday morning came, and I woke up feeling sad and afraid. I wanted to leave Charles. Studying his face, I watched Doc sleep, his full head of blond hair, just lightly touched with silver. I memorized everything about how Doc looked, hating that it had to come to this. Time to collect my memories.

"I'm awake," he whispered. "I was just thinking with my eyes shut."

"About?"

"Oh, everything we did this weekend. You. You're even better than the aurora borealis."

I didn't complain — not a word, not a look. But Doc knew. "Don't be sad, Samantha," he said. "We just had the best weekend ever."

"I want to be with you," I told him. "I don't want us to be apart anymore. I don't think I can stand it."

"You read my mind," Doc said. "But I've been thinking about that for *years*. This divided life of ours, it can be, well, heartbreaking as hell. When Sara was sick, when we knew for sure that she was dying, I promised that I would raise our boys in a way she would always approve of. And you, you'd have to divorce Charles, and he'd fight it, wouldn't he?"

I put a finger to Doc's lips, not because I didn't want to hear what he had to say but because I could see the pain that it was causing him.

"When you're ready," I said, "I'll be waiting for you. There's one more thing that has to be said, so I'll say it. I love you so much. I feel like you saved my life."

"I love you, Samantha."

God, I loved hearing those words.

I was in a kind of daze as we said good-bye to the inn's owners, Mr. and Mrs. Lundstrom, and the hazy feeling continued for much of the drive back to Lake Geneva. I remember holding Doc's hand the whole way.

Then we were pulling into the parking lot of the Alpine Valley Resort. What an incredible letdown that was, what a heartbreaking moment. We held each other for a long time, just held on for dear life in Doc's car.

"I have to go, Samantha," he finally said.

"I miss you already, and you're not even gone," I whispered. "Please miss me, too."

"What a beautiful thing to say," Doc told me. "I love your humility." Then we kissed one last time, and I hoped it *wasn't* for the last time. It took all my willpower and strength not to bawl like a baby in his arms. But I *didn't* cry.

My Jeep was where I had left it. I got inside, and everything seemed unreal to my touch. We honked our farewells, and I pulled out onto the highway. I let him speed ahead.

As I made my way back to Lake Geneva alone, I thought about the aurora borealis, but also about losing Doc, and how I could possibly bear it. I cried all the way home.

Fifty-four

POOR SAM.

A wind-driven rain forced me off the porch and into the darkening house. Sam's loneliness, the unexpected sadness in her life, clung to me as I closed windows and mopped up raindrops from the windowsills. I thought about her good-bye to Doc, which sent my thoughts to Brendan. *Where is he? It's just awful outside. Teeming rain, and he's driving in it.*

I put Sam's remaining letters on the mantel next to the old marble clock — and that's when something else hit me. I had a deadline at 6:00 P.M. I'd completely forgotten about my column.

I settled into the blue velvet embrace of the sofa, booted up my laptop, and called up my file of rainy-day notions. Not one of them was worthy of

750 words, but after a couple of hours, a big idea did float up from the deep well of my brain.

It was so big, in fact, I wondered why it had taken me so long to come up with it.

I picked up the phone and punched in a number that I knew by heart.

"Debbie, there's no getting around this," I said. "I'm no good to the *Trib* right now, and I'm not being fair to my readers. It's hard to explain. So hard, I won't even try."

I told my editor how sorry I was, but I had to take a leave of absence. But I didn't tell her why. I didn't want Debbie's sympathy, and I didn't want to have to explain myself and what was going on with Sam and with Brendan.

When I clicked off the phone, I felt a rush of anxiety. It was like standing on the edge of a cliff and staring down into darkness and nothingness.

I still needed to visit Sam that night, but the rain was absolutely sheeting outside, obscuring the lake, even the trees beside the house. I almost made it out to the Jag when the single toot of a car horn got my attention. *Brendan!* He was driving his black Jeep down the puddle-soaked lane behind the houses.

He rolled down the side window and smiled, and all was forgiven. "Jenniferrrrr. I'm back. The rain was terrible all the way from Chicago."

I was soooo glad to see Brendan's smiling face. *There's your explanation, Debbie! That smile of his.* I tacked to the left and leaned a dripping, yellow-slickered elbow into the open window.

"Hey, buddy, mind if I hop in with you? I have news. Sam is out of her coma."

Fifty-five

~

"YOU'RE GOING to love her. Sam's much more interesting when she's conscious," I told Brendan as we rode to the hospital. "And she's going to like you, I guess. Or she'll pretend to, anyway."

Brendan started to laugh. "What's gotten into you?" he asked.

"Oh, I just heard a sad story, and then I saw your smiling face. Strange, interesting juxtaposition. I also took a leave of absence at work. Now I'm a beach bum, just like you." Brendan and I slapped high-fives over that one.

We arrived at Sam's room, and — what was this? — dozens of shiny Mylar balloons and streamers hung from the ceiling, with cellophane-wrapped baskets of fruit and gaudy flower arrangements competing for space on the counters and tables. Obviously, word had gotten around Lake Geneva, and maybe the rest of Wisconsin and Illinois, that Sam was conscious. I wondered if any of the flowers or balloons were from Doc.

She was wearing a blue-striped hospital gown and her complexion was still gray, but her hair was combed and she smiled when she saw me. She was alert and seemed almost herself.

"Hello. Hello, Jennifer. And who's the handsome one?" she asked.

"This is Brendan. I told you about him, but you probably don't remember. He is kind of handsome, isn't he?"

Brendan reached out and shook her hand. "Hiya, Samantha," he said, and my jaw dropped. I had no idea where that came from. *Samantha?* Like in the letters. That was what Doc always called her.

"Don't I know you?" Sam said. "You look like — oh, you know who."

"My uncle Shep?" asked Brendan. "Just a wild guess."

"That's the one," she said. "Of course you do."

Brendan cranked up Sam's bed a couple of notches; then we pulled a couple of chairs close. Sam started to give us a slightly fractured discourse on her day. But then she turned her eyes back to Brendan. She seemed just a little confused again. "I'm fine," she said, and winked at me.

Then she looked at Brendan again. "I hear you're a very good doctor, Brendan. So why have you given up hope?" Sam asked. "How can you leave somebody as special as Jennifer without a fight?"

I saw Brendan's head go back as if he'd taken a punch in the nose, but then he recovered nicely. "It's a good question, isn't it? It's the one I've been asking myself."

My eyes connected with Sam's. I don't know how, but she had gone right to the heart of the matter. *Wham, bam, thank you, Sam.*

"As you said, Samantha, I'm a doctor. We're a logical bunch, for the most part. Maybe too logical for our own good sometimes. I want to enjoy whatever time I have left, whatever time *we* have left, okay? I don't want to waste a second of it. Not one second. Does that make sense to you?"

Sam stared into his eyes and nodded. "Seems like a pretty reasonable philosophy," she said. "Hard to argue with."

"Thank you," Brendan said.

"So?" Sam said, her eyes going to me, then back to Brendan.

"So?" I said. Brave smile.

Sam's eyes stayed on Brendan now. "Fight it," she whispered. "I did."

Fifty-six

THE NEXT FEW DAYS were possibly the best, and most memorable, of my life. I was trying to live every day from sunup until I couldn't keep my eyes open. Suddenly it made all the sense in the world to me. I had a lot of time to make up with both Sam and Brendan.

Brendan was a reflective person who liked to think things through, but he also loved to top off his best thoughts by saying something funny, usually at his own expense, which fit with the way I saw the world. I was discovering that he had the most generous and giving nature. He wasn't overly protective, but he was there for me when I needed him.

Every time I looked into his eyes, or even saw him at a distance, I couldn't help thinking what a senseless, awful, messed-up waste it was that he was going to die. I wanted to argue with him about his decision, but I just couldn't fight. He was too smart, too nice; besides, it would have been a waste of our time together. The precious seconds of our summer.

We went swimming every day, even in the rain. We visited Sam, sometimes three times a day, and she and Brendan became friends. They were actually a lot alike. Brendan and I took long walks, and we had dinner together every night. We didn't eat much during the day, but dinner was always special.

Except for those blueberry pancakes, Brendan was *not* a good cook — though given more time to practice, he swore that he could be mediocre. So I cooked the meals; he did setup and cleanup. When he worked, he wore this Red Cross lifeguard T-shirt that I loved on him.

We really liked to dance to a favorite CD, or just the radio. I loved to be held by him, to be close, to listen to Brendan hum along to a song like "Something to Talk About." Or Jill Scott's "Do You Remember," or "Sweet Baby James," "The Logical Song," "Bad to the Bone," "Let's Spend the Night Together." Dozens of others, rockers and ballads — it didn't much matter.

They were our songs, the songs of our summer.

One Sunday night Brendan fell asleep before I did, so I took one of the last packets of Sam's letters

into the kitchen. I had counted the letters recently —
there were 170 of them. The longest was nearly
twenty pages; the shortest, just a paragraph. I'd
gone through at least three-quarters of them. Sam's
legacy to me. I'd be finished with her letters soon.

I sat at the kitchen table under the harsh glare of
an overhead light, and I read my grandmother's
next entry.

Dear Jennifer,

After Doc and I returned from Copper Harbor, our separation was even worse than I
had thought it would be. *Much worse.* Which
meant that we were deeply in love, terribly in
love. But this I already knew. During a late-
night phone call that fall, we arrived at the
inevitable conclusion: we had to be together
again.

But then we had to wait months, and when
Charles planned another golfing (or whatever)
trip in June, I made plans, too. I also picked
our destination: the town of Holland on the
eastern shore of Lake Michigan.

As we'd done before, Doc and I met in the
parking lot at Alpine Valley. We hugged and
kissed and grinned like teenagers watching
the submarine races. Then we took to the

road. It was a six-hour journey: a two-hour drive followed by four hours on the S.S. *Badger,* a car ferry that was a minivacation in itself.

I never wanted to leave Doc again. The two of us leaned over the railing and watched the ferry's engines distance us from our real lives with miles of churning wake. We had hot chocolate at the restaurant onboard and saw our first movie together (*The Pink Panther*) in the *Badger*'s tiny theater. By the time we reached shore, our skin was flushed and our hearts were singing. We were so much in love, and our weekend in Michigan was even better than the first. Neil Simon hadn't written *Same Time, Next Year* yet, but Doc and I were living it anyway.

Jennifer, I'm going to shorthand this just a little and stick to the high points, and the low ones.

The next summer Charles took his trip in July, and again Doc and I made our plans around his departure. We drove north, but then Doc surprised me. He had rented a house-boat in La Crosse, Wisconsin, a place where three rivers converge: the La Crosse, the Black, and the Mississippi. We set our course, and an

hour and a half later we docked in the small
town of Wabasha, Minnesota. Doc and I
celebrated with roast pheasant, baked raisin
beans, squash rolls, and apple brandy pie.
Possibly the best meal ever. Afterward, we
motored back down to the marina in La
Crosse and anchored for the night. We stayed
in a double berth under the sundeck. The next
morning we showered on the deck, squealing
under the spray. Then we joined a flotilla of
every kind of craft imaginable in the annual
Riverfest. There were late-night bands on the
water, fireworks, and happy children everywhere. Especially Doc and me. For four days
I was in heaven, and I didn't want to return
to earth. But, of course, I had to.

The plan for our fourth annual was a
glamorous trip to New York City, which I
looked forward to for a full nine months.
We booked a room at the Plaza overlooking
Central Park, had tickets for two Broadway
plays, box seats at Yankee Stadium, restaurant
reservations. This would be our best time
together yet.

As we waited in the flight lounge at O'Hare,
clients of Charles's who were booked on the
same flight to New York saw me and called

my name. I nearly fainted and turned the
brightest shade of red.

Doc was leafing through the *New York
Times* just a few yards away when he saw me
greet the Hennesseys and make up a story
about seeing a friend off on another flight.
Doc got the picture and slipped away. As
soon as we could, we met up again. We
decided against New York and headed to his
car. My heart was broken in little pieces.

"A fine kettle of fish you've gotten us into
this time, Stanley," Doc said. He switched on
the car's ignition.

"I just lied to the Hennesseys," I said.
"They're going to tell Charles. We should head
right home."

Doc nodded sadly, backed out of the parking space, then drove from the airport. It was
such a beautiful morning, so bright with promise. What a shame. My mind whirred with
heartbreaking disappointment as we eased
into the stream of traffic on the exit ramp.

"You know," I said, "I have another idea."

Doc smiled ear to ear. "I knew you would,
Samantha. No way I was going to take you
home, anyway."

Fifty-seven

~

Jennifer,

The Lundstroms were obviously surprised
when we arrived at the door of the lodge at
nightfall, but they were also glad to see us and
they had room. Once we had a key, Doc and I
headed up the familiar moonlit trail that was
alive with the sounds of the woods. I couldn't
wait to be in Doc's arms again. We'd already
wasted half a day.

I'll remember this for the rest of my life.
Just when we rounded a bend in the path, a
shadow crashed out of the underbrush and
into the pathway. I didn't know what it was,
but it was bigger than a horse and smelled
horribly. The thing brayed at us! I guess we
gave it a scare, too. Doc and I froze as the

beast clattered across the trail and down the hillside.

"That was a moose," Doc said, finally picking up our suitcases and the flashlight. We hurried to the cabin. Of course we couldn't sleep. And late on the Night of the Moose, we finally laughed about our close call at O'Hare. Then we made a plan to make sure it didn't happen again. From that day on, we spent our lost weekends on Michigan's Upper Peninsula. Mike and Marge Lundstrom became our good friends, and the cabin in Copper Harbor, with its fieldstone fireplace in the bedroom and view of Lake Superior, became our hideaway.

No one back home ever knew our secret, Jennifer. No one guessed about Doc and me, and our double life.

And don't you dare tell.

Don't put it in any of your columns, either. Or, God forbid, a book.

Fifty-eight

∽

Dear Jen,

This happened four years ago, but I couldn't tell you how I really felt about it. Not until now.

It was a chilly March night and snow was falling softly in Chicago, a great deal of snow. The wind was howling like a wounded animal, of course. Your grandfather and I were about to get ready for bed when he asked me to go out for a bottle of anisette. He had indigestion and thought the liquor would settle his stomach. It had worked before.

I had always taken care of Charles's needs and cared for him as much as I could, given how he had treated me. I had to go quickly because the package store would be closing soon. So out I went into the snow and wind. "Sam the dependable one" Charles called me sometimes, always thinking he was being endearing rather than condescending.

When I came back twenty minutes later, your grandfather was dead in his bed.

Jen, he looked just as when I had left him; wearing his favorite blue pj's from Henri Bendel, a Macanudo still burning in the ashtray, and the television tuned to the nightly news. It still shocks me when I think about how quickly he was gone. The heart attack must have come on him like a blown-out tire that slams a car into a telephone pole. Total devastation in an instant.

None of us even knew that his heart was bad. But Charles had never been careful about what he ate or drank or smoked, or especially how he carried on late at night. Jennifer, despite all the things I've told you in these letters, we had children and grandchildren and many, many shared experiences. When I looked at him in repose, I saw the face of the young man I had known many years before. A quick-witted boy who'd fought in a war, been unloved by his parents, and had struggled greatly to make his place in the world. I remembered the promise I'd felt for us in those early days, the love I'd wanted to give Charles, and certainly would have.

So sad. But some stories simply are.

Fifty-nine

THE NEXT MORNING I had a long, emotional talk with Sam about my grandfather, and about Doc. It was the best talk we'd had since she came out of the coma, and she was seeming more like herself every day.

"I read some more of the letters last night," I told her soon after I arrived. "I'm doing it the way you asked, a few at a time. I read about Grandpa Charles dying last night. It made me cry, Sam. Did you cry? You didn't say in the letter."

Sam took my hand. "Oh, of course I did. I could have had so much love in my heart for Charles, but he just wouldn't let me give it to him. He was a smart man in many ways, but so stubborn in others. I think he was so hurt by his father and his uncle that he never trusted anyone again. I really don't know, Jennifer. You see, Charles wouldn't tell me *his* story."

My eyes welled up with tears. All of this was so sad to hear. "He was always good to me, Sam."

"I know that, Jennifer. I know he was."

"He did have a temper, and there were always Grandpa Charles's rules of behavior in Chicago, and even here at the lake."

Sam finally smiled. "Oh, you don't have to tell me about Charles's rules of proper behavior. I know them by heart. And all about his temper, too."

I looked into her eyes, trying to understand everything. "So why didn't you leave him?"

Sam just smiled. "Finish the letters and we'll talk more. Just remember, they're not only about me — the letters are about you, too, sweetheart."

I had to laugh. "Sam's rules, huh?"

"Not rules, Jennifer. Just a different road I traveled. Just my side of things."

"And you're not going to tell me who Doc is, are you?"

"I'm not going to tell you, Jennifer. Read the letters. Maybe you'll be able to guess."

Sixty

BRENDAN AND I got a swim in just about every night at twilight. That evening I appeared in a blue Speedo racing suit with red piping, looking every inch the Big Ten swim champion that I wasn't. Brendan had on a pair of black boxers that weren't too boxy and fit him just right.

"You look really good," I told him. "Is that a sexist thing to say? Hey, who cares?"

"*You* look beautiful," Brendan said. Then his face turned unusually serious. "You're a gorgeous woman, Jennifer."

I hadn't heard compliments like those for a while, and I was starting to half believe them. I certainly liked hearing nice things about myself. Who doesn't? Maybe Cameron Diaz is sick of hearing compliments, but not me.

"Just stunning, Jen. You could have been in the movies," he continued.

"Don't blow it," I told him. "You should probably stop right there."

"Sorry, it's just the way I feel. One man's opinion. Others might look at you and see, oh, I don't know, Rosie —"

"You *are* going to blow it."

"But I see the most beautiful girl in the world."

I shook my head. "No, Brendan. Too over the top. Pull it back some. Not *too* far back."

"How about on the lake? Most beautiful on the lake?"

I shrugged, grinned. "*Maybe*. At this moment on the lake, which is mostly deserted."

"Well, that's settled — most beautiful girl on the lake!"

And then Brendan let go with maybe his loudest banshee scream yet. He almost sounded in pain. He took off for the water a step ahead of me.

But just a step.

"Last one to the buoy!" he turned and yelled.

"Last one to the buoy — what?"

"Is the biggest *loser* in the world!"

"Too much of an overstatement."

"Biggest loser on Lake Geneva! That we can see in our line of vision at this moment!"

"You're on!"

We hit the water and began to stroke furiously. I was feeling good and thought I wouldn't lose by as wide a margin as usual, which I, of course, would consider a huge victory. Moments later I reached out of the water for the buoy. To my surprise, Brendan grabbed the bobbing marker a couple of seconds behind me. I shook water off my face and hair.

"No fair! You *let* me win!" I yelped.

Brendan stared into my eyes. He was smiling, but there was something else in those eyes.

"No, Jennifer, I didn't."

Sixty-one

~

IT RAINED like the dickens the next day, and Brendan disappeared for several hours. He was starting to worry me, I'll admit. I was afraid that he might not come back one of these times, that he could get terribly sick or black out while driving, something bad. The rain had slowed to a light drizzle by the time he pulled into the driveway about four.

I couldn't wait to see him, so I ran outside into the rain and kissed him through the open window. I was so *happy* to see Brendan.

"Where'd you go?" I asked. "I woke up about seven and you were gone."

"Had a doctor's appointment in Chicago. You were snoring your pretty head off. I thought I'd let you sleep."

I made a face. "*I* don't snore."

"No, of course not." Then Brendan shot me one of his grins.

I didn't completely let him off the hook. "What did the doctor say?"

Brendan blinked, evidently composing what he was about to tell me. "The tumor is getting bigger," he said at last. "Not the greatest news, I'm afraid. Not too much of a surprise, though."

Then he covered the left side of his face with his hand. He drummed his fingers on his cheekbone. "I'm losing some mobility, Jennifer. Face is getting numb. I can't feel *this*."

I stroked his cheekbone myself.

"Sorry. I can't feel that, either. But I love your touch anyway. I love everything about you, Jennifer. Don't you forget that."

Brendan struggled with his footing when getting out of his Jeep. He almost fell. I was stunned, and suddenly realized how bad his day must have been. He smiled, though, and then touched my cheek. "I need a little nap. I think I'll go over to Shep's. I'll see you later, Jen."

"Are you okay?" I asked. I wanted to take Brendan's arm, to help him, but I was afraid he might not like it.

"Sure I am. Just tired. I'm fine. Just need a nap."

It was only four in the afternoon, but I lay down

with Brendan anyway. I wanted to be beside him, to feel his touch, to let him know that I was there for him. I was petrified inside, maybe realizing for the first time that I *was* going to lose Brendan and feeling what it would be like, and hating the feeling so much.

"Thanks," he whispered. "Tired."

Then he was gone.

Brendan slept in spurts. He clenched his fists several times. After about fifteen minutes, his eyes snapped open and he looked dazed. "Oh boy, Jennifer. Seems I dozed off, huh? More like I fell off a cliff."

I asked if he was in any pain and he answered by asking me to get a bottle of pills from his jacket. When I returned, his bed was empty and I heard him being sick in the bathroom. I was starting to get really scared now. I wasn't ready for this. Brendan had told me repeatedly that he could get worse in a hurry, but I'd chosen not to believe it.

"Jen, the Percocet is going to knock me out," he said when he appeared from the bathroom. "I'll sleep right through. Why don't you go home. Please. Do it for me. I love you dearly. And you are the most beautiful girl in the world, not just the lake. Go home for a while."

This was a little strange, but I couldn't — or

wouldn't — argue with him. I kissed Brendan on the forehead, on the cheek, then lightly on the lips.

"I felt that." He smiled.

So I kissed Brendan again.

And again.

The truth was, I didn't want to stop kissing him ever.

Sixty-two

I HAD a really bad feeling all through the night.
Shep was at his house back in Chicago, so I
checked on Brendan every couple of hours. Then I
finally fell asleep back at Sam's. He'd made it clear
he didn't want me with him that night. I felt I
needed to respect that.

When I woke up, it was morning and I was alone
in my old room. The sun burned through the gauzy
curtains, and my thoughts immediatcly went to Brendan. And what I thought was, *Brendan is going to
die soon*. And there was nothing I could do about it.

I listened for his yell — and then I remembered.
I'd left him at Shep's house, knocked out by painkillers. I pulled myself out of bed and dressed in
the first clean things I could find: washer-wrinkled
khakis and a white T-shirt. I jammed my sockless

feet into sneakers and went downstairs to the kitchen.

I looked out the window. No naked screaming men.

The Jeep was glistening in the driveway. Okay, Brendan was there. Maybe I could make him breakfast at least. I started over to Shep's.

I entered the house through the unlocked back door, called Brendan's name as I frisked the downstairs rooms with my eyes. When I didn't see any sign of him, I hurried up to his bedroom at the back of the house. The room was empty. The bed had been made with a nice white cotton spread.

It took me a moment to catch up. Brendan wasn't in the house. His things weren't there, either.

I threw open the screen door that led to the upper deck Brendan had so recently stained and water-proofed. From high up there, I scanned the yard and beyond. Brendan was nowhere to be seen.

Panic raced through me, and I tried to tamp it down. Maybe Shep would know where Brendan was. I raced back downstairs, my sneakers scuffing the polished hardwood, my eyes darting everywhere as I looked for the kitchen phone.

That's when I saw a pile of clues — obviously left for me. They were clustered on the white-laminate kitchen counter. Three items were clumped together;

a white no. 10 envelope, a set of car keys, a business card with a red bird on it.

The business card was from Cardinal Transport, a local taxi service.

The keys belonged to the Jeep.

The envelope was addressed to me. When I took the envelope in my hands, I felt something loose and jiggly inside. I ripped open one end, and Brendan's watch poured out into my palm. My heart was in my throat.

There was also a letter.

Sixty-three

Dear Jennifer,

It's just after five in the morning and I'm waiting for the taxi to take me to the airport. You know, it's lonelier than you could ever imagine. I know you're going to be hurt because I'm saying good-bye like this but, please, hear me out before you make a final judgment. I'm writing while I still can. There are things I want to tell you while I can say them. I want to minimize the hurt to you if I can. I believe this is the best way, the only way for me.

Do you remember when we were kids, how we lived for summer? I'd start to get a sense of expectation in early May that the days were getting longer and I would hope that this summer the sun would keep soaring in the sky and break through to the other side. That it would be like it is in the northern regions, daylight all summer long. Then June would come and the days really were longer. But after the Fourth of July, darkness reasserted itself and we had to accept the duality of light and dark.

In the same way, Jennifer, I'd hoped, and prayed, that we'd have more time to do all the things we wanted to do together. I wanted an endless summer with you. But then darkness always comes, doesn't it? Just a fact of life, I guess.

If I know anything, it's this: Our being together was the best possible thing that could have happened, and I want to leave that feeling of rightness intact and beautiful. I love you so much. I adore you, Jennifer. I mean it. You *inspire* me. I hope with all my heart that you'll forgive me for this and that you'll understand how unbearably hard it is for me to leave you this morning. Without our swim. Or some five-star blueberry pancakes. This is the hardest thing I've ever done in my life! But I believe in my heart it's the right thing to do.

I love you so much that it hurts me to even have the thought. Please believe that.

You are my light, you are my endless summer.

Brendan

PART THREE

~

*Leaving
Lake Geneva*

Sixty-four

BY THE TIME I'd finished reading Brendan's letter, I could barely breathe and the tears were just streaming down my face. I couldn't help thinking that somehow it was my fault he'd left. Just as it was my fault that Daniel was alone when he died in Hawaii. I slid his watch onto my wrist. Then I called Shep's law office in Chicago. I told his assistant that I had to speak with him. Finally I heard Shep's familiar, soothing voice over the phone.

"Shep, Brendan's gone," I managed to say.

"I know, Jen. I spoke with him this morning. It's for the best."

"No, it isn't," I said. "Please tell me what's going on. What is he doing?"

Shep hemmed and hawed, then told me some of the same things that Brendan had said in his letter. That he didn't want me to have to go through the final stage of his disease. That he loved me and was sick that he had to leave. And that Brendan was scared.

"I have to see him," I told Shep. "It can't end like this. I won't let it. Shep, I'll come to your office in Chicago if I have to."

I could hear Shep sigh deeply. "I think I know how you feel, but Brendan made me promise not to tell you. I gave him my word."

"Shep, I need to see him again. Don't I have anything to say about this? It's wrong to have Brendan make this decision without me."

There was a silence on the line and I was afraid Shep would hang up on me. Finally he spoke. "I promised him. You're putting me in an untenable position. Oh hell, Jennifer . . . He's on his way to the Mayo Clinic."

I couldn't believe what I'd heard. "What did you say? He's going to the hospital?"

"Mayo's the best place for this," Shep told me. "He's having experimental surgery in the morning."

Sixty-five

~

MY STOMACH was heaving, just as it had been a year and a half ago when I went to the hospital in Oahu to see Danny's body. Only now I was in my car, shifting gears literally and figuratively as I sped south on I-94 until the road split. Then I took I-294 toward O'Hare.

I called Sam on my cell, explaining what I could, and she told me I was the best fighter she knew and said she was proud of me. Then the two of us were crying over the phone, just like old times.

I'm sure people were staring at me as I boarded the American flight to Rochester, Minnesota. I was stiff-faced and distracted, and my eyes were swollen and very, very red.

A little over an hour and a half later, I drove a

rented car toward the Mayo Clinic. I was going to see Brendan, I hoped, and he was just where I wanted him: at one of the best cancer hospitals in the world.

Sixty-six

~

A REVOLVING glass door deposited me into the cool green lobby of the main building of St. Marys at the Mayo Clinic, a vast space with high marble walls and freestanding columns. This was where Brendan was to be operated on. I walked to the admissions desk, explained who I was, and asked how to find his room.

I was told that "Dr. Keller preregistered earlier today. He'll be checking into the Joseph Building at six o'clock tomorrow morning. He isn't here."

The crushing disappointment must have showed on my face because the twenty-something woman at reception opened a three-ring binder. She ran a finger down a list, then looked up at me.

"He said there was a possibility someone might come."

I didn't know what to say. "Well, I did. I'm here."

"Dr. Keller is staying at the Colonial Inn, one-fourteen Second Street, Southwest," she said.

I got directions, and soon the rented car and I were back on the road. The minutes whizzed by even as rush-hour traffic pinned me in place. Finally I broke through the logjam, which I wouldn't have expected in Rochester. A few minutes later I was at the Colonial Inn, and I was shaking like a leaf.

I found room 143 and knocked. There was no response from inside.

"Brendan, please," I said. "I came all this way. It's Jennifer . . . the prettiest girl at Lake Geneva?"

The door opened slowly and Brendan was standing there, all six foot one of him. His shoulders were still broad and he looked solid. His eyes were as blue as the northern sky on a day in July. He opened his arms and took me into them.

"Hey there, Scout," he whispered. "Prettiest girl in Rochester, Minnesota."

Sixty-seven

"I WAS MAD at you," I finally admitted as I held Brendan tightly.

"And now? What are you feeling now, Jennifer?"

"You're charming me out of it."

"I didn't realize I was being charming," he said.

"I know. It's just part of your personality. It's something in your blue eyes."

We swayed together in the doorway for a moment or two, then broke apart. It was only now that Brendan's eyelids drooped and his movements became noticeably slower and a little shaky — from pain medication or from the tumor? We sat down on the couch and I tousled the wave in his hair.

"Happy now?" he asked.

"Yep," I answered.

"God, I missed you," he said, and we kissed.

Then Brendan leaned back and stared at the ceiling. He seemed far away. "Want to hear the schedule?" he asked.

I nodded. I guess this meant that Brendan knew I wasn't going away.

He rested his hand on my knee. "Have to be at the hospital at six. Sharp. Adam Kolski is doing the surgery at seven. He's pretty good."

"Pretty good?"

"He's *really* good. Practically a godddddd," Brendan said. And suddenly there was that magnificent smile of his. "Of course I got the best."

"That's more like it," I said. And there, finally, was that smile of *mine.*

"I should warn you, after tomorrow I'm going to look like a cannon shot me headfirst into a brick wall. If things go well. I hope you really do love my charm, that certain something in my eyes."

"I love everything about you," I said. "I especially love that you're going to do this."

Brendan kissed me again, and I melted. Then he said, "Let's get out of here. Let me show you Rochester. And yes, this *is* a date."

Sixty-eight

A DATE. That was another cute line, and it reminded me of everything that was so good about
Brendan and me. We had the same energy, the same
passion about a lot of things, common interests; we
shared a goofy sense of humor; and it was so hard
to find someone who was right for you. God, sometimes it could seem impossible. For some people it
is impossible.

I drove and Brendan gave directions. About three
or four miles from the hotel, back near the hospital,
he told me to park anywhere I could find a spot.
Actually, the side street we were on was surprisingly crowded for a work night.

"What's here, anyway?" I asked.

"Stephen Dunbar's Pub," Brendan said. "This is
where we used to blow off steam when I was a resident. It's where I want to take you for our date."

"A bar?" I asked him. "Stephen Dunbar's Pub?"

He nodded. "I don't think I should drink tonight," Brendan said. "But I definitely think I should *dance*."

Inside, the bar was about half full, a nice, comfortable crowd, and there were couples dancing to a Red Hot Chili Peppers ballad I liked, "Under the Bridge."

Brendan immediately took me in his arms. "I like this song," he whispered against my cheek. And then we were dancing. "And I love dancing with you.

"Thank you for Jennifer," he continued to whisper. "She's the perfect one. All that I ever wanted out of life."

It sounded like a prayer to me. "I saw you praying once. In the kitchen," I confessed.

"Same exact prayer," Brendan said, and winked at me. "I've been saying it all summer."

We danced to all the slow songs that played on the juke, and we danced slow to some of the fast ones. I didn't ever want to let Brendan go, not even for a minute.

"What could be better than this?" he asked. "A date with my best girl, in my old school town, at one of the old haunts."

I felt so incredibly close to Brendan, so much in love with him, which made what was going to happen in the morning unthinkable. I didn't want it to happen, but tears welled up in my eyes. "Stop being so sweet," I told Brendan.

"No tears," he said, and wiped them away. "No tangles," he laughed, then winced a little at his own joke. Brendan could always laugh. At any time. About anything, even this.

We continued to dance, to an old Smokey Robinson and the Miracles song. "After this is all behind us," he said, "let's travel. I've never been to Florence, or Venice. China, Africa — there's so much to see out there, Jen."

I started to tear up again. "I can't help it. I'm not usually so sentimental," I said.

"Oh, it's kind of a sentimental time. Kiss me again. Keep kissing me. Right up until they operate."

So we kissed again. But finally we headed back to the Colonial Inn, where I thought Brendan would collapse into sleep. But he didn't.

"Every day from the crack of dawn," he said — and I completed the rest, "until we can't keep our eyes open one second longer."

About three, we finally did fall asleep in each other's arms, our fingers entwined, my head on his chest. I remember thinking, *This is the way it should be. Just like this. For many, many years.*

And then the alarm clock began to ring.

Sixty-nine

BRENDAN LEANED down close and gave me a kiss on the lips. He was already up and dressed. "Crack of dawn," he said. "Ready for a swim in the lake?"

"Don't make jokes now, not even good ones. Okay, Brendan?"

"My chances of surviving three years with GBM is less than —"

I cut him off. "All right, jokes are okay. Jokes are good." I came across the bed and kissed him. "I love you."

"I love you, too. Probably from the first time I ever saw you at the lake. You were, and still are, the most beautiful girl in the world. *In the world*. Got it?"

"I got it." I smiled. "Of course, it's only your opinion."

"Good point. But I happen to be right on this one."

I was pretty sure that I had my emotions under control for the moment. That's why I wasn't prepared for something so small to tear me apart. I noticed Brendan's hands shaking badly as he bent to secure a new pair of shoes that looked like his Nike cross-trainers but weren't. Instead of laces, the shoes had Velcro flaps. *Brendan couldn't tie his shoelaces anymore.*

He looked up, saw me watching him. "I *like* these shoes."

An image flashed into my mind: Brendan's swimming stroke as he powered across the lake on a summer morning. Now he couldn't tie his own shoes. I ached for him. Brendan knew what was in store for him: the pain, the sickening aftereffects, the very real possibility that he would die.

I put my arms around him. "This is going to work out," I said. It had to.

Less than twenty minutes later, Brendan and I stepped out of the hotel into hazy morning light. He stood quietly, resting an arm on the roof of the car, and he still *looked* healthy. He was taking in a coffee shop's blinking neon sign, then a fieldstone church across the street, as if he were memorizing each mundane detail.

"Pretty diner, pretty church, *very* pretty girl," he said. Then he climbed into the passenger seat. A little stiffly. I heard the seat belt click as Brendan strapped in for the ride of his life.

"Let's go, beautiful. We have an appointment in Samarra or someplace like that."

For one of the only times that summer, the two of us were mostly quiet. The early-morning drive took only a few minutes from the Colonial to the St. Marys underground garage. An elevator took us up to the first floor. From there, we headed along a stained-glass corridor to the Joseph Building, which was where Brendan would be admitted and prepped for surgery.

Brendan stopped and put his hands on top of my shoulders. He leaned in and held me and stared into my eyes.

"I think that I've run out of jokes, Jennifer. Do you mind if I tell you that I love you again?"

"No. Please." *Just keep talking. Don't leave me.*

"I love you so much, Jennifer. It's important to me that whatever happens, you know you did great, fabulous. You helped me be strong, more than you know. You did everything that anyone could do, and then some. . . . *Jennifer?*"

"I know," I finally said. "I got it." I held him even

tighter. My eyes squeezed shut, but tears were rolling down my cheeks anyway.

"You're letting me cry," I finally managed to say.

"Uh-huh. Yeah. That's because I am, too."

I looked into his eyes and saw that he was almost as big a mess as I was. Brendan leaned forward and kissed me on the cheeks, then my eyes, finally my lips. I loved the way he kissed, loved everything about him. I didn't want to let him go.

"There's never enough time, is there?" he said. "I think I have to go. I'm late, Jennifer."

Once we arrived on the fifth floor, the admissions nurse, a portly woman with strong freckled arms, sorted through a pile of papers. Then she called for an orderly, who appeared with a wheelchair. That's when the thought I really hadn't been able to face flooded my mind. *I might never see Brendan again. This could be it.*

"I love you," I said. "I'll be waiting right here. I'll be waiting where I'm standing now."

Brendan said, "I love you, Jennifer. Who wouldn't love the most beautiful girl in the world? One way or the other, I will see you."

He smiled that wonderful smile of his and gave me a double thumbs-up as the orderly wheeled him down the long hallway to surgery. Then Brendan let loose with one of his famous go-jump-in-the-lake screams.

I clapped my hands together and laughed. "Bye," I called. "Bye."

Brendan looked back, smiled again.

Just before he disappeared, he yelled, "Bye!"

Seventy

BYE?

Don't let it be bye.

I slid down into an upholstered chair in the corner of the hospital waiting room and began to imagine the operation going on six floors below me when Shep arrived with Brendan's mother and father, whom I had never met.

"He didn't want us to come," said Mrs. Keller. "He's trying to make it easier for us. Or so he thinks."

"He's always been that way," said Brendan's father. "He broke his hand once in high school and didn't tell us until it was nearly healed. I'm Andrew, by the way. This is Eileen."

We all hugged. Then Brendan's mother and father went straight to tears. I could see how much they loved their son, and it touched me.

The rest of the day crept by at an excruciatingly slow pace. I glanced down at Brendan's watch every few minutes, and the hands almost didn't seem to move. Brendan's father told jokes, which wasn't much of a surprise. My favorite was, "How do you recognize an extrovert computer geek? He looks at *your* shoes."

Other visitors drifted in and out of the waiting room, a few of them crying, most looking worried. The television flickered with never-ending images of the news, CNBC, ESPN.

As we waited I wondered if Shep might be Doc. But he hadn't raised his children alone. So he *wasn't* Doc — unless Sam had pulled a fast one.

At about four I left the waiting-around room for a while. I wandered down to the Peace Garden in the St. Marys compound, a square filled with bright flowers and a statue of Saint Francis. I heard a carillon concert, the bells ringing out a pretty rendition of "Amazing Grace." I got down on my knees and prayed for Brendan. Then I called Sam and told her about the day so far.

Finally I returned to the waiting room. My timing was excellent. Ten hours after I had kissed Brendan good-bye, a young doctor with dark hair and a cherubic face appeared. He announced that he was

Adam Kolski. He didn't look old enough to be a surgeon, let alone "practically a goddddd."

I tried to read his face, but my journalistic skills weren't working very well that day.

"Things went as well as could be expected," Dr. Kolski said. "Brendan survived the surgery."

Seventy-one

VISITORS were permitted to see patients in the ICU for just a few minutes. One person at a time. After the Kellers and Shep took their turn, I went in. Adam Kolski came along with me to check on his patient. "He's doing better than he looks," Kolski warned.

Brendan was unconscious. His head was swaddled in bandages, and his face was black and blue. Dr. Kolski explained that Brendan had been tubed and that machines could keep him alive, just in case.

There was a tube in Brendan's nose, another in his throat; a catheter led to a bag under the bed; and IV towers dripped saline and sedatives into his veins. Electrodes were stuck all over him, sending reports on his vital signs to several monitors; a blood pressure cuff on one arm inflated and de-flated automatically.

"He's alive," I whispered. "That's the only important thing."

"He is alive," Dr. Kolski said, and patted my shoulder. "He did this for you, Jennifer. He told me that you're worth it and more. Talk to him. You might be the medicine Brendan needs right now."

Then Kolski stepped out of the room and I was alone with Brendan. I took off the watch he'd given me and gently buckled it over his wrist, right next to the plastic bracelet with his name on it. I squeezed Brendan's fingers and leaned close to his face.

"I'm right here," I said, willing him to hear my voice. "You know, I've loved every minute I've spent with you this summer. *But especially this one.*"

Seventy-two

~

IT SEEMED as though my precious five minutes
with Brendan was over in about five seconds. I was
holding his hand, and then I was pulled away by a
polite but firm nurse who sent me reeling out to the
waiting room again.

Mr. and Mrs. Keller and Shep wanted to take me
to dinner, but I was emotionally and physically
wasted. I couldn't leave Brendan right then. When
they left, I sank into a chair and let the tears sheet
down my cheeks. I had restrained myself most of
the day, but now I had no reason to hold back. All
kinds of thoughts and voices were inside my head.
Brendan could die soon. Well-meaning people
would say, "Jennifer, you're still young. Grieve, but
you have to move on. Don't shut out love."

I wasn't — *I loved Brendan!* I hadn't shut out
love, but look where it had gotten me. I mopped

my face with tissues, then stared at the empty rows of chairs lit by harsh white light. Outside the window, the street whined with a thin stream of traffic whizzing past. I felt so alone at the hospital.

The minutes passed slowly. Eventually an hour went by. I would have called Sam again, but it was too late.

I finally dug into my handbag and lifted out the last packet of her letters. I untied the frayed red string and fanned out the envelopes. My name danced across the length of them in her clear and distinct hand.

I bought a cup of coffee from the machine, stirred in several packets of sugar. Then I pried open an envelope flap. "I need to hear your voice, Sam," I said.

In the endless white night of the hospital waiting room, I began to read the end of Sam's story.

Seventy-three

Dear Jen,

Here's what happened — everything changed in an instant.

Doc knocked on my kitchen door one pathetically hot day in August, and the moment I saw him, my heart started banging around in my chest. I was stunned and maybe even scared. Jennifer, he had never been to my house like that before.

"Is something the matter?" I asked. "Are you all right? What's happened?"

All he said was "Come take a ride with me."

"Right now? Like this?"

"Yep. You look just fine, Samantha. I've got a surprise for you."

"A good surprise?"

"The best I could come up with. I've been waiting a long time for this one."

Whatever he was up to, I was having none of it in my dirt-stained overalls and gardening clogs. So I let him inside the house and went upstairs to change. Fifteen minutes later I was wearing a pretty blue linen dress, my hair was neat, and I'd even put on some lipstick.

When he saw me, Doc smiled. "God, you're gorgeous," he said. Of course, he would think I was gorgeous if I were wearing a trash bag with a tuna casserole on my head. I told him so, and we both laughed, because it was true.

And then he grabbed both my hands. "Samantha, everything changes today."

"And you're not going to tell me *what* changes today?" I asked.

"No, I want to show you."

He wasn't just enthusiastic, he was very mysterious, Jen, which added to the fun. Of course, I was excited just to see him, to look into his face and see how happy he was.

And you know what? I really do like surprises!

Seventy-four

⁓

Jennifer, Jennifer, Jennifer,

That whole week the Venetian Festival had been going full blast in the village, and the streets were mobbed with tourists who'd come to the annual end-of-summer bash at the lake. Doc parked in a municipal lot a block north of Main Street and fed a pocket full of quarters into the meter. It seemed that we were going to the fair, and apparently we would be staying for a while.

"Is this your surprise?" I asked. "Because I kind of knew the festival was in town."

"This is just the venue," he said. "Don't be such a wisenheimer." Which was one of Doc's favorite words, if it even is a word.

Kids were screaming on the roller coaster, the air smelled of buttered popcorn and cotton candy, and it suddenly struck me that I was in a moment I thought would never come. There we were, Doc and I walking hand in hand together in downtown Lake Geneva. I looked up at him with a big question written across my face. "Is this your surprise? Because it's a great one, actually. Are we out of the closet?"

Doc told me that he had just dropped his youngest off at Vanderbilt University. "The nest is empty. No more Mr. Mom," he said. "I'm free."

Suddenly Doc pulled me into his arms and kissed me in front of God and everybody else in Lake Geneva. His kiss was so full of love that tears popped out of my eyes.

He looked into my eyes. "I wonder if anybody has ever had a love affair like ours, Samantha. You know, I doubt it."

"That's part of what makes it special, I guess."

The sun was warm on my face, the air was cool, and as I swayed in Doc's arms, I felt alive in a way I never had before. This was even better than our weekends to Copper Harbor because for the first time we were absolutely free. I was *flying*, Jennifer, but somehow my feet were still on the ground as we reached Library Park.

We found an empty bench next to the sea-wall. We watched the *Lady of the Lake* cast off from the Riviera Docks, and Doc bought hot dogs and beers from the Veterans' stand. We stayed way after the sun went down, watching the lit boat parade and the fireworks finale.

And here's the amazing thing. It would be insulting if it weren't so funny. During that whole day Doc and I spoke with people we knew, and not one of them noticed that we were glowing. I got it, of course. People just couldn't conceive of romance between the two of us. How strange and backwards the world can be sometimes. So many people just give up on love, even though love is the best thing that can happen to them.

I turned to Doc and told him how much I loved him and that I couldn't imagine a better surprise. He pulled me close. "Brace yourself, Samantha. Our day isn't over."

Seventy-five

Doc's car purred contentedly as we drove away from the festival, past the outskirts of town. I didn't have a clue what was going on. Not until we pulled into the lot of the Yerkes Observatory. It was quiet, and all I could hear were the chirping of crickets and maybe my own pulse beating in my ears.

Doc grabbed a plaid blanket from the backseat, and as we'd done years before, we ran on tiptoes across the lawn fronting the imposing building. A pal of Doc's had left a key for us in a crack between two bricks in the wall. We climbed the three flights of stairs to the largest dome and entered into darkness.

"Are you ready for this?" he asked.

I smiled and felt open to just about anything. "I've been ready for years."

He used a penlight to find a lever that actually lifted the floor until it sat still about five feet below the eyepiece of the telescope. Then he operated the cranks and winches that opened the dome revealing a wide swath of sky.

"Look at that, Samantha. Just look at it. It's heaven."

"Oh my God" was all I could manage to say at that moment, because I was spellbound.

Doc stood close behind me with his hands on my shoulders as we peered through the world's largest refracting lens. It did seem as if we were looking at heaven. The sky was bedazzling, to say the least. I didn't know what to gaze at first, but my eye was drawn to a dappled red globe the size of a silver dollar.

"That's Mars," said Doc.

Doc told me that Mars and Earth were in opposition that night, lined up in their orbits so that Earth was between Mars and the sun. He pointed out polar ice caps, dark smudges called limb haze, and what might have been a dust storm blowing across the face of the planet under its misty pink sky.

"The last time Mars was this close to Earth, cavemen were freezing their buns off in New

Guinea, hoping someone would discover fire," he said.

Next Doc spread the blanket on the hard-wood floor and led me to it. We sat down, shoulder to shoulder. I knew something good was coming, but I had no idea what it could be. "What?" I whispered.

"I've been waiting for just the right moment," he said. "You did say that you liked surprises, Samantha."

Seventy-six

"Samantha, I am such a lucky person," Doc said in the softest voice. "I found you a little late, but I love you more than anything else on this earth, and here you are in my arms. You are absolutely my best friend, my soul mate, my confidante, my sweet, sweet love. I don't like it at all when you're not around. I still can't believe that I found you, or you found me, at that awful Red Cross dinner dance. I really can't, Samantha — and now here we are."

I still didn't know where this was going, but my heart was starting to beat uncontrollably. Ever since I had known him, Doc had always told me, quite beautifully sometimes, how he felt about me, but that night was even more special, more passionate, more touching, and sweeter — which, in my opinion, is a good thing. He showed me a small box, and I shone the penlight onto it.

"Open it," he said.

I did, and my eyes widened immediately. Inside was a sapphire ring surrounded by small, gorgeous diamonds. It took my breath away, and not for the reason you think. Years before — *once* — I had pointed out this very piece in Tiffany's in Chicago. I had loved it then, but now it brought tears to my eyes. I couldn't believe Doc had remembered and was giving it to me.

He slid it onto my finger, then said, "I love you dearly, more than anything. . . . Will you marry me, Samantha?"

My eyes were so wide with wonder, Jennifer. Doc's face was framed by the sky and the stars above. I put my arms around him and held tight. I honestly had never expected this, never dared to think it could happen.

I could barely speak. "I love *you* more than anything, too. I'm so lucky I found you. Of course I'll marry you. I'd be a fool not to."

And then I said Doc's real name, over and over again, as the stars looked down on the two of us, and everything seemed pretty darn good with the universe.

Seventy-seven

~

I HAD FALLEN asleep after reading Sam's last amazing letter. But, boy, did I have questions to ask her when I got back to Lake Geneva. Or maybe even when I called her again from the hotel. Why hadn't she married Doc? What had happened to them?

I awoke to someone gently shaking my arm, calling my name. Morning light filtered through the plate-glass window of the waiting room. Adam Kolski hovered over me.

"Good morning, Jennifer. We could have gotten a more comfortable place for you to sleep," he said.

"Is everything all right with Brendan?" I asked immediately.

"He slept through the night, just like you. No promises, but he can move his toes," the doctor said. "He knows his name, and he knows yours. Actually, he's asking for you."

That perked me right up. "Can I see him?"

"Of course. That's why I came to get you. I want you to talk to Brendan. I need to find out if he really knows you. Come with me."

Kolski, the goddddd himself, opened the sliding doors to Brendan's small room in the ICU. "Just five minutes," he said.

I could see Brendan behind Dr. Kolski as I eased myself into the room. There was a rolled-up washcloth in his right hand. I took it away and slipped my hand inside his.

"It's Jennifer," I whispered. "Ready for our morning swim in the lake?"

There wasn't any response from Brendan, which didn't surprise me but also didn't make me feel reassured about his condition. I had no idea how much damage had been done during the operation.

"I'm here. I just wanted you to know. And *you're* here, too."

I was babbling a little but I didn't care, and I doubted that it would make much difference to Brendan. If he could even recognize my voice.

Then, as I stood by his bed, a miracle happened, or so it seemed to me. Brendan squeezed my hand, the slightest pressure, but it sent shivers through my body. I lowered my head. "I'm right here, Brendan. Don't try to talk. I'll talk for both of us. I'm here, sweetheart."

"Are you real?"

My head shot up and I looked at Brendan again. My God, *he had talked*.

"I'm here," I said, my voice cracking with unbelievable emotion. *Brendan had talked.* "Can you feel my hand? That's me squeezing."

"I can't see you," he said in a hoarse whisper.

"That's because your eyes are swollen shut."

He was silent for a long moment, and I thought maybe he'd fallen back asleep.

"I didn't think . . . I'd make it," Brendan said at last.

I could see he was trying hard not to cry, but then tears leaked out of his tightly closed eyes. "We're going to be okay," he said.

Suddenly I was seized with such an overpowering feeling of humility, but also love for this man. Brendan was reassuring *me.* He was there for me, even now, after his terrible operation. His voice was kind of faraway, but it was Brendan, definitely my boy. And he wanted to talk. "I was thinking . . . you sitting on the dock . . . shielding sun from your eyes . . . looking at me . . . I held that thought."

I looked at Brendan's face, loving him so much.

And then another miracle happened. His eyes opened to slits. And he struggled to make a cracked, semidrugged smile.

It was only the best smile I'd ever seen in my life.

"I love you so much," I whispered. "Oh my God, do l love you."

"Don't fight me on this . . . I love you more."

And at that moment I understood something that had seemed impossible — Brendan was going to live.

Seventy-eight

DURING THE NEXT few weeks everything in life seemed incredibly precious and had more meaning for me. Suddenly I was a regular at the Mayo Clinic and Lakeland Medical Center in Lake Geneva. All I was missing was a candy striper's outfit.

Brendan's recuperation was slow and excruciating, but he kept getting a little stronger every day, week after week. He was a favorite with his therapist, partly because he wore a different goofy hat every day, partly because he went three weeks without letting them know he was a high and mighty doctor, but mostly because he has such endearing ways.

And then one rainy morning in October, we were summoned to Adam Kolski's office in the St. Marys building. The godddd showed us some X-rays, then abruptly told Brendan that he could go home. He was in remission.

"You can go home, too, Jennifer," Kolski said, and offered a rare smile.

The next day Brendan and I set sail for Lake Geneva. On the way to Wisconsin, I was jumpy with excitement and maybe even a little case of the nerves. We were going to see Sam. She was back at her house, and there was something else. When I called and told her the news about Brendan, Sam said she wanted us to meet Doc.

Early October was a time of year I had never loved, because the sun drops below the horizon a little earlier every afternoon. But I was happy to see this particular October. I had so much to be thankful for. Brendan and Sam, and now I would get to meet Doc.

And then there was Sam's house — straight ahead. I could see Henry's old pickup parked by the garden. Hmmm.

Brendan climbed out of the Jaguar and took a deep breath of lake air. I called out in a loud voice, "Sam! We're here. You have company."

Then Brendan let loose with one of his whoops — not quite the usual volume but noisy enough to scare some bluebirds from overhanging tree branches.

"Race you to the lake?" he said, and grinned. I knew he was still a little weak, but he looked good and his famous smile was working just fine.

When Sam didn't answer, I slipped into the dark of the house to look for her. I called her name in every room I came to, my voice rising as my footsteps rang out on the hardwood floors. Fear came over me a little too quickly those days. Too many bad things had happened, or maybe it was that lately things had been going too well.

"Jen," I heard Brendan call from the porch. "She's out here. Sam's down by the lake."

Heart booming, with an almost girlish delight, I rattled down the stairs again, then burst out the back of the house. I saw that Sam had set up chairs under the shade tree — and she wasn't alone.

A man sat beside her in the shadows. He was wearing a golden ball cap with a V, probably Vanderbilt, which made all the sense in the world suddenly.

"Doc," I said under my breath. "I should have known."

Seventy-nine

I HURRIED down the sloping lawn as fast as I could go, right into Sam's outstretched arms. It felt so right to be there again. A moment later Sam moved over to Brendan and gave him a long hug. It was as if they'd been best friends for life.

Then she turned toward the man of her dreams. "I'd like you to meet Doc," she said to me. And to Brendan, "This is John Farley. He is a doctor, actually. In philosophy, from the Vanderbilt School of Divinity. Everything is coming together beautifully, Jennifer. Life does that sometimes."

My God, the Reverend John Farley was Doc, and he and Sam were such a handsome couple. I loved seeing them together like that. It just made my heart sing.

The four of us settled in under the shifting shade of an old maple tree. I said, "Wow," and my mouth

kept stretching into grins as I watched Sam and
Doc — John — exchange touches and glances.

I hugged Brendan, and he whispered in my ear,
"I agree — *wow*."

Everything *was* coming together pretty well, I
had to admit. A while later the four of us were clut-
tering up Sam's kitchen. Doc peeled potatoes in
maddeningly thin, unbroken curls. Brendan alter-
nated between shelling peas and eating them. I was
getting flour all over everything.

Until Sam finally said, "Everyone out of my
kitchen. Leave the cooking to the professionals!"
We laughed and moved the party out to the dining
room. Forty minutes later we helped Sam put the
meal on the table. Roast beef, sweet potatoes, onions
and peas, homemade biscuits.

Over dinner I asked John Farley a question that I
had been saving up. "You asked Samantha to marry
you. Sam, you said you'd be a fool not to." I looked
from Sam's face to his. "So what happened?"

Sam looked at Doc. "Well, I talked her into it;
then I talked her out of it," he said.

Sam laughed. "He just raised some good questions and issues. Like the fact of life that some busy-
bodies around town would have questions, and
opinions, and *judgments*. They'd make jokes about

the two of us being *The Thorn Birds*. I didn't think I'd like that so much. We were too used to our privacy. It also might be hurtful to John's congregation. Then he had a really good idea."

He tilted his head at Sam. "I said, what if we didn't tell anyone? What if we keep our love between the two of us? We talked about it, and that's what we decided to do. Everything about us had always been different anyway."

Sam reached over and took John's hand in hers. "Doc and I were married on a Sunday in August two years ago, in Copper Harbor, Michigan. No one knows that, except the two of you."

We clinked glasses around the table. "To Samantha and Doc!" Brendan and I said.

"To Brendan and Jennifer!" they said.

Sam gave me another big hug, and so did Doc. They both hugged Brendan. Then we sat around exchanging stories for the next couple of hours. We watched darkness come over the lake, and Doc told us about the stars, and I doubt that Stephen Hawking could have done a better job. I was so happy, and I remember every moment of that night in Lake Geneva. I always will.

Because less than three weeks later, something really terrible happened.

Eighty

IN SAM'S WORDS, *life works like that sometimes.*

Early in November I sat on the old blue velvet sofa in Sam's living room. Brendan held one of my hands, and Doc held the other. "It will be all right," Doc whispered, touching his chest with a shaking hand. "She's safe inside us. Sam is at peace."

Every minute or so, an umbrella would tip-tap the porch floorboards, then the front door would whine open and another of Sam's friends would blow in on a damp gust of wind. Soon the house was filled with people from Lake Geneva and Chicago and even Copper Harbor, all looking uncomfortable to find themselves there on that unthinkable occasion.

As I looked around, I could see intimations of Sam everywhere.

In my cousin Bobby's baby blue eyes, in the clusters of family photos on the walls, on my aunt Val's tear-streaked face as she stared out the picture window to the broken surface of a rain-swept lake. It was so sad, and almost unbelievable that the person who had drawn so many people together in life wasn't there with us.

Finally Doc leaned in close. "If you're ready, I think we should start. Samantha wouldn't want to keep everybody waiting. We shouldn't, either."

As Doc began to speak about his Samantha — though still not revealing their incredible secret — I pressed the side of my face into Brendan's shoulder. Doc was so brave up there, so eloquent, and more touching than anyone else in the room knew. Meanwhile, the deaths of other people I'd loved flashed through my mind: Grandpa Charles, my mother, Danny. Brendan gently held me, and I listened to Doc and then Sam's other friends, each telling a cherished story or remembrance.

Then there was a lull, and Brendan finally whispered, "Go ahead, Jen. It's your turn."

Eighty-one

I DON'T LIKE public speaking or being the center of attention, but I felt that I had to get up and talk. This was my grandmother, my Sam. I experienced the light-headedness that comes just before you faint as I walked to the front of the room.

I stood with my back to the lake, a favorite black-and-white photograph of Sam to my right. I looked out at all the sad yet expectant eyes of my grandmother's friends. Brendan smiled encouragement. Doc winked, and a calm finally came over me.

This is what I said:

"Please bear with me. I'm not good at this, but there are things I have to say. When I was growing up, I spent my precious summer vacations in this house with Grandma Sam."

I started to choke up the first time I said her

name. Then I didn't care if I was crying, and I surged forward.

"The two of us were best friends right from the start. We just clicked, had chemistry, shared a world-view, laughed and cried at the same things. I loved her more than anyone, and I admired her so much.

"I always told her my most private thoughts when we were in bed: Sam sitting beside me, her hand over mine in the dark. Some kids are afraid of the dark, but I loved it, at least when I was with Sam.

"It feels a little like that, now. I can't see Sam, but I know she's here.

"Not too long ago, I had retreated from life be-cause, well, I think I couldn't stand the pain of liv-ing fully. It was Sam who gently coaxed me out of my shell and removed my veil of sadness. It was Sam who showed me the way to find love again. Sam led me to Brendan, whom I love dearly.

"But there is a secret that I never got to share with Sam, so I'll tell her now. Sam, dear — Saman-tha — I have something wonderful to tell you. Brendan and I are going to have a baby. Your first great-grandchild."

Then I did start crying, but I knew I was smiling, too. I looked right at Doc, and he was beaming. So was Brendan.

"Can't you all just see Sam's face? The way it lights up, the way Sam *listens,* as if you're the most important person in the world?

"Right now, I almost can't believe that she will never see our baby, that she won't find a way somehow.

"But I also wonder if he or she will have Sam's beautiful curls. Or those sparkling blue eyes, or her amazing ability to love so many people, to have such great friends. But *this* is for sure. Our child will know all about his or her great-grandmother, what an incredible person she was. I have all of Sam's stories to tell. I know exactly who my grandmother was, and that's such a treasure.

"And boy or girl, no matter what, our baby's name will be *Sam.*"

Eighty-two

SAM'S FRIENDS and the family told stories about her for hours that afternoon; some close friends, and some not so close, stayed late into the night, and every story seemed a little better than the one before. Of course, I had more stories than anyone else. I had Sam's letters. I just couldn't tell anybody too much of what I knew. That was a secret among Doc, Brendan, and me.

Brendan's uncle came up to me before he left for the night. Shep leaned in and kissed me on the cheek. "I wanted to wait until it quieted down some," he said. "You did so great today, Jennifer. I loved what you said about your grandmother. Sam wanted you to have this. I've been keeping it for you at the law office."

I took a white linen envelope from Shep. Was it

one more of her letters? What did she have to tell me now? Another dark secret?

I slid my finger under the envelope flap. Then I took out a single page and began to read.

Dearest Jennifer,

I guess this is our last talk, and don't you dare be sad. That was never our style. When your grandfather and I bought the lake house fifty years ago, it was a fixer-upper on stony soil, but it had the most gorgeous views of the lake. I have so many glorious memories of this place, and so do you. I can still see you and your mother curled up on the couch in front of the fire while I cooked one of my dinners. Valerie gave birth to Bobby upstairs in the east bedroom, and both you and your cousin left permanent ice skate tracks on the kitchen floor. (Of course, I *knew* you did it.) I remember all the summers we spent on the front porch, but most of all, I remember the times I've had with you, Jennifer. You were always "my best."

I'm looking out across the lake now as I write. Winter will be here before long; the branches will glisten with ice, and snow will

blow across the lake like a fine lace curtain.
I can't wait for that to happen.

But I am also already looking forward to
spring. The freshly painted docks will go back
into the lake, the garden will shake off the
snow, and the perennials will reemerge. And
what I'm thinking is that the word *perennial*
is a misnomer. *Long-lived* might be more correct, because perennials don't live forever. Not
even sassy ones like me. This is why I'm
preparing for the future, today.

Of course, I'm taking care of everyone I
love, but I have a special gift for you. Actually,
it's *inside* the envelope with this letter. Use it
well — I know you will.

Jennifer, my heart is full, and my life has
been, too. That's a great thing. I have my Doc.
I have you, and you have Brendan. I couldn't
be any happier. What more could anyone
ask for?

All my love, and remember — *you are my
best friend, you are "my best."*

Sam

A small weight shifted inside the envelope, which
sent it floating from my hand. I bent to retrieve the

envelope, and a brass key tied to a round cardboard tag with a frayed red string slid out.

I picked up the key and looked at the tag.

On one side, Sam had written: *23 Knollwood Road, the house is yours now, Jennifer.*

On the other side was a short inscription. I looked at what Sam had written. Her last words to me, ever.

Love never dies.

EPILOGUE

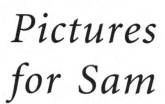

*Pictures
for Sam*

Eighty-three

~

BRENDAN AND I arrange ourselves on the couch in front of the handy-dandy, state-of-the-art Sony video camera, which is set up and ready for our very first home movie.

We're in our new Chicago apartment, with its view of Lake Michigan, and we're as excited as can be. This is an important moment in our lives, seminal stuff. At least, we seem to think so.

"You ready? Okay, I'll turn it on," Brendan says, then jumps up and switches on the video camera. He is full of life these days — in remission — like the rest of us, right? "You start, Jen," he says. "You're never at a loss for words."

"Hello, Samantha," I say, and grin like a fool and finger-wave to the camera. "It's Mommy, when she was thirty-five and not afraid to tell her age."

James Patterson

Brendan is leaning in beside me. "And I'm your proud, very happy dad, as of fourteen days and about eleven hours."

"We love you very, very much, sweetheart, and a couple of times a year —"

"Maybe more than a couple," Brendan says. "See, your mom and dad are frustrated actors. Obviously, we're windbags, too."

I say, "We're going to film ourselves and try to give you an idea of who we are, what we're like, what we're thinking about, and, of course, how much we love you."

I look at Brendan and he picks up the thread, which we have semirehearsed.

"So that when you get old and infirm like the two of us — or me, anyway — you'll be able to look at these tapes and know who we were. Is that cool?"

"And how *silly* we were. . . . But also how much we treasure having you as our daughter. Right now, you're sleeping, and you're a very, very good sleeper."

Brendan starts to clap, and also lets Sam see his movie-star smile. "Hooray! Good going, Samantha. Keep it up! You go, girl! Way to sleep!"

I say, "Samantha, you have the most beautiful blue eyes, a breathtaking smile, like your dad — and neither of us can get enough of you."

"You're also bald as a cue ball, but Mama dresses you in pink so we know you're a girly girl," Brendan teases, but sweetly, as is his way.

"Here's an interesting tidbit," I say. "When you were born, at the moment you appeared in the world, you looked around like a curious little bird peeking out for the first time from its nest. You looked right at me, checked me out — and then you looked at your dad, checked him out — and then you smiled gloriously at both of us. Now, supposedly, according to the doctor in the house, you couldn't possibly smile or see us yet, but we don't believe that."

"I'm the doctor, and I don't believe it," says Brendan. "Did I mention that you're bald as an egg?"

"You did," I say. "Now let us start at the very beginning of this wonderful story, the start of it all, Samantha. Let me tell you how you got your name. It's a beautiful name and an even more beautiful story. And you, Sam, are its happy ending."

And then I am silent for a moment, and I don't say this, but I am thinking, *Love never dies, Sam*.

About The Authors

JAMES PATTERSON has created more enduring fictional characters than any other novelist writing today. He is the author of the Alex Cross novels, the most popular detective series of the past twenty-five years, including *Kiss the Girls* and *Along Came a Spider*. James Patterson also writes the bestselling Women's Murder Club novels, set in San Francisco, and the top-selling New York detective series of all time, featuring Detective Michael Bennett. He has also had more *New York Times* bestsellers than any other writer, ever, according to *Guinness World Records*. Since his first novel won the Edgar Award in 1977, James Patterson's books have sold more than 300 million copies.

James Patterson has also written numerous #1 bestsellers for young readers, including the Maximum Ride, Witch & Wizard, and Middle School series. In total, these books have spent more than 220 weeks on national bestseller lists. In 2010, James Patterson was named Author of the Year at the Children's Choice Book Awards.

His lifelong passion for books and reading led James Patterson to create the innovative website ReadKiddoRead.com, giving adults an invaluable tool to find the books that get kids reading for life. He writes full-time and lives in Florida with his family.

EMILY RAYMOND is the ghostwriter of numerous young adult novels, including a #1 *New York Times* bestseller. She is the coauthor of *First Love*. She lives with her family in Portland, Oregon.

Books by James Patterson

FEATURING ALEX CROSS

Hope to Die

Cross My Heart

Alex Cross, Run

Merry Christmas, Alex Cross

Kill Alex Cross

Cross Fire

I, Alex Cross

Alex Cross's Trial (with Richard DiLallo)

Cross Country

Double Cross

Cross (also published as Alex Cross)

Mary, Mary

London Bridges

The Big Bad Wolf

Four Blind Mice

Violets Are Blue

Roses Are Red

Pop Goes the Weasel

Cat & Mouse

Jack & Jill

Kiss the Girls

Along Came a Spider

THE WOMEN'S MURDER CLUB

Unlucky 13 (with Maxine Paetro)

12th of Never (with Maxine Paetro)

11th Hour (with Maxine Paetro)

10th Anniversary (with Maxine Paetro)

The 9th Judgment (with Maxine Paetro)

The 8th Confession (with Maxine Paetro)

7th Heaven (with Maxine Paetro)

The 6th Target (with Maxine Paetro)

The 5th Horseman (with Maxine Paetro)

4th of July (with Maxine Paetro)

3rd Degree (with Andrew Gross)

2nd Chance (with Andrew Gross)

1st to Die

FOR ADULTS AND TEENS

Confessions: The Paris Mysteries (with Maxine Paetro)
Homeroom Diaries (with Lisa Papademetriou, illustrated by
    Keino)
First Love (with Emily Raymond)
Confessions: The Private School Murders (with Maxine Paetro)
Witch & Wizard: The Kiss (with Jill Dembowski)
Confessions of a Murder Suspect (with Maxine Paetro)
Nevermore: A Maximum Ride Novel
Witch & Wizard: The Fire (with Jill Dembowski)
Angel: A Maximum Ride Novel
Witch & Wizard: The Gift (with Ned Rust)
Med Head (with Hal Friedman)
FANG: A Maximum Ride Novel
Witch & Wizard (with Gabrielle Charbonnet)
MAX: A Maximum Ride Novel
The Final Warning: A Maximum Ride Novel
Saving the World and Other Extreme Sports: A Maximum Ride Novel
School's Out—Forever: A Maximum Ride Novel
Maximum Ride: The Angel Experiment

FOR YOUNGER READERS

House of Robots (with Chris Grabenstein, illustrated by Juliana
    Neufeld)
Treasure Hunters: Danger Down the Nile (with Chris
    Grabenstein, illustrated by Juliana Neufeld)
Middle School, Save Rafe! (with Chris Tebbetts, illustrated by
    Laura Park)
Middle School, Ultimate Showdown (with Julia Bergen,
    illustrated by Alec Longstreth)

For previews of upcoming books and more information about James Patterson, please visit JamesPatterson.com or find him on Facebook or at your app store.

Sᴘʀɪɴᴋʟᴇʀs sʜᴏᴛ ʙʀᴏᴋᴇɴ ᴊᴇᴛs ᴏꜰ ᴡᴀᴛᴇʀ over the lush gardens in back of the Beverly Hills Hotel. Night was coming on. I was armed, waiting behind a clump of shrubbery a hundred feet from Bungalow Six when footsteps came up the path. Captain Luke Warren of the LAPD came toward me, a gang of six cops right behind him.

For once, I was glad to see the LAPD.

I had information that Gozan Remari and Khezir Mazul, two heinous cruds who were suspected of multiple rapes, but hadn't been charged, were behind door number six. But unless there was evidence of a crime in progress, I had no authority to break in.

I called out to the captain, presented my badge, handed him my card that read, Jᴀᴄᴋ Mᴏʀɢᴀɴ, CEO, ᴘʀɪᴠᴀᴛᴇ ɪɴᴠᴇsᴛɪɢᴀᴛɪᴏɴs.

Warren looked up at me. "I know who you are, Morgan. Friend of the chief. The go-to guy for the one percent."

"I get around," I said.

Cops don't like private investigators. PIs don't play by the same rules as city employees, and our clients, in particular, hire Private because of our top-gun expertise and our discretion.

Captain Warren said, "Okay, since you called this in, what's the story?"

"A friend of mine in the hotel business called me to say that these two were bounced out of the Constellation for assaulting a chambermaid. They checked in here two hours ago. I've got a couple of spider cams on the windows, but the drapes are closed. I've made out two male voices and one female over the music and the TV, but no calls for help."

"And your interest in this?"

I said, "I'm a concerned citizen."

Warren said, "Okay. Thanks for the tip. Now, I've got to ask you to step back and let us do our job."

"Of course. No problem," I told him.

And it *was* no problem.

I wasn't on assignment and I didn't want the credit. I was glad to be there for the takedown.

Captain Warren sent two men around the bungalow to cover the back and garden exits. Then, he and I went up the steps and across the veranda to the front door with two detectives from the Beverly Hills PD. Warren knocked and announced.

We heard a shout through the front door, sounded like, "Go away."

I looked at Captain Warren. "He said, 'Come in,' right?"

The captain smiled to show me that he liked my way of thinking. Then, he swiped the lock with a card key, cocked his leg, and kicked in the door.

It blew open, and we all got a good view of what utter depravity looks like.

THE LIVING ROOM WAS DONE UP IN SILK
and satin in the colors of peaches and cream. Logs flickered
in the marble fireplace and atonal music oozed from the CD
player. Empty glasses, liquor bottles, and many articles of
clothing littered the floor. A room service cart had been
tipped over, spilling food and broken china across the Persian carpet.

I served for five years as a pilot in the U.S. Marine Corp.
I've been trained to spot a glint of metal or a puff of smoke on
the ground from ten thousand feet up. To be able to do that in
the dark.

But I didn't need pilot's training to recognize the filth right
in front of me.

The man called Gozan Remari sat in an armchair with the

hauteur of a prince. He looked to be about fifty, gray-haired with gold-colored, cat-like eyes. Remari wore an expensive handmade jacket, an open pin-striped shirt, a heavy gold watch, and nothing else—not even surprise or anger that cops were coming through the door.

A nude woman, bound with silk ties, lay at his feet. Her arms and legs were spread and she was anchored hand and foot to a chair, a footstool, and a table as if she were a Luna Moth pinned to a board. I saw bluish handprints on her skin, and food had been smeared on her body.

There was an arched entrance to my right that led to a bedroom. And there, in plain sight, was Khezir Mazul. He was naked, sitting up in bed, smoking a cigar. A young woman, also naked, was stretched face-up across his lap, her head thrown over the side of the bed. A thin line of blood arced across her throat, and I saw a steak knife on the cream-colored satin blanket.

From where I stood in the doorway, I couldn't tell if the women were unconscious or dead.

Captain Warren yanked Gozan Remari to his feet and cuffed him behind his back. He said, "You're under arrest for assault. You have the right to remain silent, you piece of crap."

The younger dirtbag stood up, let the woman on his lap roll away from him, off the bed, and onto the floor. Khezir Mazul was powerfully built, tattooed on most of his body with symbols I didn't recognize.

He entered the living room and said to Captain Warren in the most bored tone imaginable, "We've done nothing. Do you know the word *con-shen-sul*? This is not any kind of assault. These women came here willingly with us. Ask them. They came here to party. As you say here, 'We aim to please.'"

Then, he laughed. *Laughed.*

I stepped over the room service cart and went directly to the woman lying near me on the floor. Her breathing was shallow and her skin was cool. She was going into shock.

My hands shook as I untied her wrists and ankles.

I said, "Everything is going to be okay. What's your name? Can you tell me your name?"

Cops came through the back door, and one of them called for medical backup. Next, hotel management and two guests came in the front. Bungalow Six was becoming a circus.

I ripped a cashmere throw from the sofa and covered the woman's body. I helped her into a chair, put my jacket around her shoulders.

She opened her eyes and tears spilled down her cheeks. "My daughter," the woman said to me. "Where is she? Is she—?"

I heard the cop behind me say into the phone, "Two females; one in her forties, the other is late teens, maybe early twenties. She's bleeding from a knife wound to her neck. Both of them are breathing."

I said to the woman whose name I didn't know, "Your daughter is just over there, in the bedroom. She's going to be all right. Help is coming."

Clasping the blanket to her body, the woman turned to see her daughter being helped to her feet.

A siren wailed. The woman reached up and pressed her damp cheek to mine. She hugged me tight with her free arm.

"It's my fault. I screwed up," she said. "Thank you for helping us."

THE HOT SPRAY BEAT ON ME FROM SIX
shower heads. Justine lightly placed her palms on my chest,
tipped her hips against mine.

She said, "Someone needs a massage. I think that could be
you."

"Okay."

Okay to whatever she wanted to do. It wasn't just my car
that could go from zero to ninety in ten seconds. Justine had
the same effect on me.

As she rubbed shower gel between her hands, sending up
the scent of pine and ginseng, she looked me up and down. "I
don't know whether to go from top to bottom or the other way
around," she said.

"Dealer's choice," I said.

She was laughing, enjoying her power over me when my

cell phone rang. My fault for bringing it into the bathroom, but I was expecting a call from the head of our Budapest office, who said he'd try to call me between flights.

Justine said, "Here's a joke. Don't take the call."

I looked through the shower doors to where my phone sat at the edge of the sink. The caller ID read CAPT. L. WARREN. It could only be about the rapists the cops had just arrested at the Beverly Hills Hotel.

"The joke's on me," I said to Justine. "But I'll make it quick."

I caught the call on the third ring.

"Morgan. We've got problems with those pukes from Sumar," the captain said. "They have diplomatic immunity."

"You've *got* to be kidding."

He gave me the bad news in detail, that Gozan Remari and Khezir Mazul were both senior diplomats in Sumar's mission to the UN.

"They're on holiday in Hollywood," Warren told me. "I think we could ruin their good time, maybe get them recalled to the wasteland they came from, but the ladies won't cooperate. I'm at the hospital with them, now. They wouldn't let the docs test for sexual assault."

"That's not good," I said. I put up a finger up to let Justine know I would just be a minute.

"Mrs. Grove is very grateful to you, Morgan," the Captain was telling me. "I, uh, need a favor. I need you to talk to her."

"Sure. Put her on," I said.

Justine turned off the water. Pulled a towel off the rack.

"She's in a room with her daughter," Warren said. "Listen, if you step on the gas you could be here in fifteen minutes. Talk to them face-to-face."

I told Justine not to wait up for me.

By way of an answer, she screwed in her ear buds and took her iPod to the kitchen. She was intensely chopping onions when I left the house.

It was a twenty-minute drive to Ocean Memorial and it took me another ten to find the captain. He escorted me to a beige room furnished with two beds and a recliner.

Belinda Grove was sitting in the recliner, wearing the expensive clothes I'd last seen strewn around Bungalow Six: a black knit dress, fitted jacket, and black stiletto Jimmy Choos. She'd also brushed her hair and applied red lipstick. And although I'd never met her before today, now that she'd cleaned up, I recognized her from photos in the society pages.

This was Mrs. Alvin Grove, on the board of the Children's Museum, daughter of Palmer Tiptree of Tiptree Pharmaceuticals, and mother of two.

Now I understood. She would rather die than let anyone know what had happened to her and her daughter.

Dear Target Guest,

Don't put the tissues away just yet—because I have some never-before-seen photographs of the incredible journey you read about in FIRST LOVE.

In Fall 2014, Little, Brown Books for Young Readers is sharing FIRST LOVE with teen and tween book lovers across the country. Here are a few of the pictures they'll be adding to further illustrate Axi and Robinson's love story.

Sincerely,
James Patterson